PRAISE FOR *Look Back All the Green Valley*

"Fred Chappell's narrative voice is a wonder and a joy—a combination of elegant erudition, lyric brilliance, and the idiom of Appalachia. *Look Back All the Green Valley* is both a celebration of the southern Appalachian Mountains and a way of life and a lamentation for its loss....[Chappell is] a master storyteller...ranging from tall tales that provide out-loud laughter to poetic, lyric passages that produce a lump in the throat."

—*The Miami Herald*

"What a glorious time Fred Chappell must have had writing this fourth volume of his tetralogy...for it sparkles and amuses and rocks along in such an easy, happy voice....No one does a more impressive look back than Fred Chappell, our poet laureate."

—*Winston-Salem Journal*

"Chappell...narrates with his trademark voice, one both poetic and inclusive of the idioms of the Appalachian Mountain region....Intelligent and rewarding."

—*Publishers Weekly*

"There's something fearless about the fervid quality of this book that's strangely beguiling. You can enter the Kirkman family quartet at any given point, but perhaps it is Jess Kirkman's advanced age that has given this final installment a bittersweet tone lacking—because unnecessary—in the others. It makes *Look Back All the Green Valley* stick in your memory not like a fantastic tall tale, but like an urgent message from the author: Don't forget me."

—*The News & Record* (Greensboro, N.C.)

"Chappell draws upon the rich oral traditions, myths, and legends of southern Appalachia to take his readers deep into the heart of a world and time long past, with all of its magic, mystery, and wonder."

—*Bookwatch*

"Chappell's irrepressible humor and homespun wisdom depict a long-gone way of southern Appalachian life. A loving look back to a long-ago time and place."

—*Library Journal*

BOOKS BY FRED CHAPPELL

Novels

It Is Time, Lord
The Inkling
Dagon
The Gaudy Place
I Am One of You Forever
Brighten the Corner Where You Are
Farewell, I'm Bound to Leave You

Short Stories

Moments of Light
More Shapes Than One

Poetry

The World Between the Eyes
River
Bloodfire
Awakening to Music
Wind Mountain
Earthsleep
Midquest
Castle Tzingal
Source
First and Last Words
Spring Garden: New and Selected Poems

Anthologies

The Fred Chappell Reader

Essays

Plow Naked
A Way of Happening

Translations

Plautus: *Asses Galore*
Euripides: *Alcestis*

Fred Chappell

LOOK BACK

ALL THE

GREEN VALLEY

Picador USA   New York

Picador® is a U.S. registered trademark and is used by
St. Martin's Press under license from Pan Books Limited.

For information on Picador USA Reading Group Guides, as well as ordering, please contact the Trade Marketing department at St. Martin's Press.
Phone: 1-800-221-7945 extension 763
Fax: 212-677-7456
E-mail: trademarketing@stmartins.com

Library of Congress Cataloging-in-Publication Data

Chappell, Fred.
    Look back all the green valley : a novel / Fred Chappell.
        p.   cm.
    ISBN 0-312-24215-8 (hc)
    ISBN 0-312-24310-3 (pbk)
    I. Title.
PS3553.H298L66   1999
813'.54—dc21   99-27227
                                                               CIP

10 9 8 7 6 5 4 3 2

For Jim and Danielle Clark

Contents

THE MOON

BEHIND

THE CLOUDS

There was a moon, but it was buried behind toiling oceans of basaltic cloud, so that we labored in a darkness so powerful, we could smell it. The storm was nigh; mere minutes would bring it upon us, and we had no idea how far down we yet had to go.

We took turns digging, and when I leapt down for my second go-round, the hole was still no more than waist-deep. The pointed shovel went into the dirt easily enough; we hadn't had to use the mattock since we broke the turf, but there just seemed to be more earth in the ground than I'd imagined. The mound we built beside the hole kept spilling back in upon us because in such darkness we couldn't place the removals efficiently.

"Stop a minute," one of us said.

"No. Going to rain," said another.

"Hear somebody?" said the third.

"I thought maybe," said the first.

I paused and we listened, but the wind would whip up in gusts, then subside, sighing loudly, and we could hear only the groan and whimper, the keening and rumbling of a weather that was not our ally. Lightning flickered behind the clouds but gave only feeble and intermittent illumination. I could see my hands a little and now and then a gleam of shovel blade as it rose clean where I cut into the soil before spooning it up.

"Pity the man," said one of us, "who has to do this to make his living."

"He'd do it in the daylight," said another. "It's easier then."

"And with a big old backhoe," the third man said. "He don't care if he makes noise. He don't care if the whole world sees him."

I'd struck a vein of clay and had to push down with my foot on the blade. Then I had to chop at the bottom with short strokes and lever the clay up in bricklike chunks.

"What kind of youngun decides he'll grow up to be a grave digger? What would I say if one of my boys told me it was his aim in life?"

"Better throw out to the other side," said another. "Getting a little lopsided over here."

"Probably don't plan on it beforehand. We didn't plan on being grave robbers when we was younguns, but look at us now in the cemetery at midnight."

"I'll dig a little more here," I said, "and then dig on that side, and then you can get in the hole."

"Can't look at us," said one, "because I can't see us, it's so blasted dark."

"I don't like this business of grave robbing," another said. "It gives me the heeby-jeepers."

"Hear something?" one said.

I stopped chopping again and said, grunting, "I'm about ready to come out for this go-round. Whoever's next in the hole, be ready." I was breathing hard and sweating. My white dress shirt was soaked with sweat and painted with mud. Probably ruined, I thought, but after the week I'd spent in the hills, it was the only one not wadded up in the laundry bag.

"You say you don't like grave robbing," one of them said. "How would you feel if you was him?"

He meant me.

I thought for a moment I'd struck something solid and scratched around with the shovel point, but it must have been only a pebble.

"Gawd," he said, "I don't know if I could do it. Digging up my pa's bones in the dark of the midnight and the storm about to let loose. I'd feel mighty peculiar."

The lip of it was up to the middle of my chest now. "I'm coming out," I said, "to rest a little."

"Ain't midnight," one said. "You've been striking midnight for an hour now and it ain't nowhere near."

"I'd feel awful about it," another said. "I don't believe I could do it, no matter what."

I placed my elbows and forearms on the grass and began to strain. Then the big cloud overhead thinned a little and the lightning stroke shone through. "There's somebody else here," I said. "Give me a hand up."

"Who?"

"Where at?"

Two of them, I couldn't tell which, grasped me by the arms and under the armpits and dragged me out.

"Right over there, sitting on that tombstone," I said. "An old man with white hair."

"Shine the flashlight over that way."

"Somebody'll see."

"I feel like I know who he is," I said.

"Not at midnight, they won't. Shine it yonder."

Then there was another weak flare, and this time we all saw him. I felt certain we all saw him this time.

Chapter One

TRAPPED!

*Time has no secrets. You can watch a clock all day
and never learn a thing.*
—Fugio

My mother possessed a bristling armory of useful talents, but a gift for dying was not among them. I recalled the duties she had undertaken over the years, the offices she had fulfilled in regard to the jester's motley of business enterprises my father initiated. She had served as handmaid and general manager, as field laborer and nurse, as accountant and secretary, as critic and counselor, as gofer and governess, and their lives and happiness throve. Sometimes she had complained of her burdens, for they were weighty, but mostly she had performed those multifarious tasks cheerfully. My parents adored each other, even though the expression of that adoration was shadowed by a dark mordancy of temperament on her side and by a vigilant teasing playfulness on his.

He was Joe Robert Kirkman and she was his beloved Cora, his mainstay and counterpart but not his mirror image. Where his nature gleamed with streaks of fantasy and sparkled with uninhibited impulse, hers was rooted in the clinging clay of pragmatism and patched here and there with fatalistic gloomings. My mother was rather less gay than my father, maybe a little less generous, but she was equally brimful of life; it was only a quieter kind of life than his. Yet her fullness of life ebbed quickly from the brim when my father died, hammered to the floor of their living room by a massive heart attack. He had been watching the great spectacle on the television set he called, in one of his futuristic waggeries, his "visiscreen." It was an almost brand-new twenty-one-inch-screen Zenith. The date was July 20, 1969, only hours before one man ventured a small step and mankind made a giant leap. All during the 1950s, my father had predicted that Americans—men and women together—would rocket to the moon. His prediction was dismissed by our neighbors and even by his admiring cronies as being only another example of his plentiful eccentricities. But I believed him. When I was a teenager, I sometimes imagined that he might be the first man to fly to the moon.

Maybe he was.

My mother never recovered from the loss of her husband. Oh, she made it through the necessary rituals well enough; her usual valiant courage was equal to those ordeals. She managed to complete some of the most urgent of the business demands: tax forms, will probate, debt arrangements, deed searches, and so forth. But then her body began to weaken as her spirit crumbled and her strength of will deserted her little by little, like a cone of sand leaking away to the bottom of an hourglass. She claimed in these days that she could wish for nothing more ardently than to lie in the earth alongside Joe

Robert Kirkman, her Ariel, her Puck, and her Prospero all in one.

This wish is a common, an honorable, and an ancient desire. I remembered how Roman Ovid had given it warm incarnation in his *Metamorphoses* with the story of Baucis and Philemon. They were an elderly couple who had loved each other always, who had lived in peace and amity since their first hours together. When benevolent deities in human disguise made it possible for their secret hopes to be granted, the husband begged only that neither of them would have to experience the loss of the other. The wish was granted; Zeus changed Baucis, the woman, into a linden tree and her husband into an oak. Their branches intertwined and together they formed an everduring arch. When my mother voiced her wish to join my father, a few scraps of Ovid's verses murmured in my head.

And yet when death did approach, when my mother's heart fluttered and threatened to cease its pumping, she drew back by force of an undesired strength. The spirit was willing, but the flesh was yet too powerful. She suffered from congestive heart failure, a disease that filled her lungs with fluid and her mind with terror. Extinction drew nigh upon her, but then a glimpse into the unresonant abyss would send her soul scurrying, like a terrified lapdog, back to the warmth of the world, back to the treachery of living. After a while, she made a kind of peace, accepting the necessity of having to die in the good Lord's own good time and not according to a schedule of her own devising. But she bowed to it with an air of deep regret, as if she was disappointed in herself.

Then there came periods when she was bedridden. Now she would study her worldly affairs and think of duties undone, tasks that my sister, Mitzi, and I were to carry out. Some of these were merely trivial, but she would brook no argument, and we, ever mindful of her failing health, could offer none. When Mitzi and I conferred about some of these minor concerns, we would complain in good-humored mock-gloomy terms. "Trapped!" we would exclaim. "She's got us exactly where she wants us. We're caught like mice in a trap!"

Some of the things she wanted were of middling importance. The first of these was the burial arrangement. If she could not join my father immediately, as she so expressly prayed to do, she wanted to make certain that when she did die, she would be supine by his side. The second item of urgency was my father's last remaining hideaway workshop; it had been left untouched since his demise, and she wanted it cleaned out, sorted out, and set in order. There were other chores, too, but they were of less moment.

How could we deny her? There she lay in the bed she detested in the new-smelling infirmary she abhorred in the retirement community she was not reconciled to, and she issued Mitzi and me our orders in no uncertain terms. When she spoke to me, she tried to straighten herself, scooting back against two propped pillows at the headboard. She may have thought this taller posture lent her commands more authority.

It twisted my heart to look at her. Her face was gray and peeled-looking, her eyes watery. Painful arthritis had wrenched her hands into bony knots. Her hair had always been thin and was now so sparse that she had gathered it into a wispy topknot and secured it with a pink ribbon tied in a bow; this style resulted in a Kewpie-doll look that made her crushing sadness appear a little ridiculous. I couldn't help remembering how bright she used to look, her pert intelligence animating her features. That was the way she was *supposed* to look, I thought, and the way she looked now was like an ill-chosen frock; it simply was not *her*.

This room was too small for me to sit beside her. I had to heave a ponderous armchair, upholstered in squeaky lime green plastic, to the foot of the bed and lean forward toward the footboard bars as she laid out her plans. I expected to agree to her every demand, even to the ones that made no sense to me.

"You want to make sure Jeff Halsted finishes paying off his loan," she said, "and you need to send a gift for his daughter's high school graduation."

"All right," I said.

"What will you send?"

"I don't know. What do you suggest?"

She flapped a hand in listless impatience. "I'm all finished with those kinds of concerns now. You'll have to decide things like this from now on for yourself."

"I'll ask Mitzi. This is her specialty."

"You can't rely on your sister for everything, Jess. You've made a bad habit of that."

"That's true."

"And there's an awkward patch of ground by the corner of the Lindsay pasture that we never got resurveyed. You'll have to get that done if you want to sell or build there."

"All right."

"Have you heard any word about Aunt Bessie Scott? They say the doctors can't do a thing for her."

"I haven't heard."

She would think of more things to do or to inquire about, then stop. "Are you sure you'll remember all this?" she demanded. "Maybe you'd better get a pencil and write it down."

"We're all set," I told her. "Mitzi has a list all written out. Everything you've mentioned so far is on her list."

"Yes." She nodded sagely. "Yes, of course. Jess, I don't see why you can't be more like your sister. She knows how to get things organized so she doesn't waste time and energy. You—" Now she shook her head as if perplexed. "You're too much like your father, always trying to do a hundred things at once and never getting a one of them done."

"I wish I had Mitzi's skills," I said, but my contrite admission did not mollify her. She had already locked into her familiar routine of describing to me my character flaws and wouldn't be satisfied until she had tallied all she could think of. She began with the obvious—my excessive drinking and total lack of social grace—and went on to details of my slovenly appearance, then finished with a topic she knew would irk me sorely, the obscurity of my literary expression. I had the feeling that she was going to make me submit my shoe shine and the hinder surfaces of my ears for inspection.

Now she shifted back to the topics at hand. "But you understand how important it is to get the burial arrangements straight. And you know we've got to clean out Joe Robert's personal workshop."

"Well, I think Mitzi and I have about got the burial arrangements completed—and I came all the way up from Greensboro just to look into that workshop."

"That's the only reason you came?"

"And to have a cheerful visit or two with you, of course. We take that for granted."

Her expression was one of mildly sardonic amusement, but part of my sentence was true. I had come up to take care of the workshop, but the burial arrangements were far from complete. That matter weighed darkly upon me.

As soon as the spring semester had ended and I'd filled in the necessary paperwork and lugged it to the proper administrative pigeonholes, I'd left the neo-Georgian buildings of the campus and driven 250 miles west to the mountains of North Carolina to try to take care of family matters. Since I was likely to be gone at least a week, Susan stayed behind. Our garden would claim most of her attention, she said, but I pictured her grooming our cats, Chloe and Marty, reading the complete works of Margaret Maron, and eating nothing—repeat: *nothing*—but praline caramel ice cream. When I got back home, we would celebrate what I hoped would be my triumphant return. I would take her out to Valencia, a nifty Spanish restaurant on grubby Tate Street, where she would fall upon a mountainous green salad and a lamb chop like a ravenous animal, an unlikely hybrid of bison and tigress. But my return would hardly be triumphant unless Mitzi and I could get the business of my mother's burial straightened out. Unforeseen complications had arisen in that regard.

"You shouldn't rely so much on Mitzi," my mother said. "She has a busy schedule, an important career. You shouldn't go running to her about every little detail."

"Come now. I'm not entirely helpless," I said, feeling, as always, painfully vulnerable in the face of her criticism. "I manage to move about the world without continually falling on my face."

"Yes—because your wife props you up. Without her, you'd be facedown most hours of the day."

"I'm not such a hopeless case, am I?"

"You're a dreamer. Head in the clouds. Nose in a book. Pointless schemes. If Susan didn't look after you, I shudder to picture the condition your affairs would be in. Making footnotes. Writing poetry nobody can understand."

"Well, maybe I am a hopeless case. But you've had time enough to come to terms with it by now."

"What was the name of that book you wrote?"

"*River* was the first one." It was the hundredth weary time I'd said so. She knew the title and knew I knew she knew.

"And what was that strange name you signed to it?"

"My pen name is Fred Chappell. If I signed those books 'Jess Kirkman,' you'd have a conniption fit. Some dark family secrets are aired in those poems."

"I don't see how it could make any difference what name you put to it. I never heard of anybody who read your *River*."

"What—nobody? Not a single living soul?"

"Well . . . I did talk a couple of my friends into trying it, but they didn't understand it any better than I did."

"Maybe they're not used to reading poetry. Or maybe they just don't care for it."

"They're not dumbbells. . . . If you're going to write books, why don't you write what people want to read?"

"All right, next time I'll write a novel. It'll be a detective thriller. I'll put in a secret treasure and episodes of nail-chewing suspense and a flock of mysterious ladies. Plenty of women with possibly naughty ways about them. I'll sign it 'Jess Kirkman' in bright neon letters. How do you think you'll like that?"

"No, you won't," she stated firmly. "You won't ever write anything but more poetry. That's all you ever think about."

But my dear and cranky mother was mistaken. Just a year ago, I had actually begun a novel, a tale of intrigue, betrayal, sabotage, and lugubrious peril. My story took place in a university that resembled to a suspicious degree the University of North Carolina at Greensboro, where I taught gum-chewing sophomores and intensely political graduate students the arcanities of literature. My plotline involved a married chairman of a Romance languages department who was carrying on a weird affair with a junior colleague, a brash young woman who schemed to push him into divorce and snare him in remarriage by getting pregnant with his child. Her plans were complicated but not ruined by the fact that this à clef chairman (Professor L. J. Moreau in what we may guardedly term "real life") was the cautious but proud possessor of a vasectomy. Yet his paramour was not foiled. She got herself artificially inseminated at Duke University Medical Center, and then . . .

. . . And then my novel collapsed like a punctured soufflé. The observations of character transformed to smart-ass remarks, the "incisive wit" devolved into slapstick, and the satiric tone degenerated into spiteful gossip, and I found myself not describing telling incidents at all, but paying off ancient grudges and unforgiven slights. I had decided, ruefully but not reluctantly, that Jess Kirkman was not born to write novels. I was condemned to poetry. I was a dreamer: nose in a book, head in the clouds. Whoever it was who had brought these charges against me had told nothing but the flat-footed truth.

When I looked at her, my mother wore an expression that

convinced me she knew exactly what I was thinking at this moment. I hated that. "I have an idea how to make some money from my writing."

"Really?"

"Dante," I said, trying to sound confident and sensible.

"What about him?"

"I'm working on a translation of *The Divine Comedy*. It will sell pretty well, I think. People are always reading Dante."

She gave me a narrow look. "How's your Italian?"

"Not wonderful," I admitted. "But I've got learned friends I can go to when I run into trouble."

"Have you got a contract from a publisher?"

"Not yet. I thought I'd better try it out before I got in over my head."

"How's it going?"

"Not quickly."

She nodded. "Poetry again. That's all you ever think about."

"Unfair," I complained. "Not true at all. I think about lots of things. I think about you. How are they treating you in this place?"

This was my unsubtle ploy to steer the conversation away from my shortcomings into the broad fields of her displeasure with her situation. She was bedridden, emotionally fatigued, frightened, and heartsick, and her complaints reflected these qualities of her illness. She took the bait and began to expostulate, faulting every doorknob, coffee cup, thumbtack, toilet seat, television set, and mattress in the building. As I listened to this plenary bill of grievance, a freshet of relief welled up in me. Her querulous moods usually signaled that some measure of strength was returning. As her energy remounted, she became restless, and this exacerbated her bitterness.

I had heard these same complaints a number of times. My attention wandered and I looked out the window into trees glowing emerald in the steady June sunlight. Her room on the third floor gave my mother a view of the tops of the trees bordering the grounds, which were set against the darker

green background of Slater Mountain. The warren of streets
and houses that comprised the little village of Graceful Days
Retirement Community cozied up to the base of Slater, and
footpaths, neatly graded and pruned, led into the woods for
those seniors who enjoyed comfortable hikes.

She saw where I was looking, and her gaze, too, was drawn
to the window. The treetops swayed, flashing green and silver,
and then we watched a flock of goldfinches flutter down like
October beech leaves from the limbs of a red oak to the ground.
She fell silent, pursed her lips, and I could sense the sadness
of some fond recollection suffuse her mind. In a few minutes,
she said, "Whenever I see that flock of birds, I think of Joe
Robert, how much he liked to study nature and think about
birds and stars and things. If your father were here right now,
he would recall something interesting to tell us. I'm sure he
knew all about those birds, whatever they are."

"Goldfinches."

"Yes. He would know about them."

"And what he didn't know, he would make up," I said. "His
science always contained a fair amount of fable." Allegory, too,
I could have added. But that phrase might have brought her
attention back around to literature and to what she regarded
as the Cimmerian obscurity of my output. I planned to avoid
that thicket of accusation.

"Yes," she said, "he might well improvise his facts." She
launched into a story about a European tour they had enjoyed.
In the town of Roussillon in Provence, they were provided
with a bus driver, but the tour guide didn't show. My father
decided to serve as cicerone and devised colorful chronicles to
match points of interest in the landscape that rolled past the
bus windows. His conception of history rested on perfidious
princes, bloody revenges, daggers and crossbows and mutual
poisonings, and he was warmly partial to accounts of naked
ladies on horseback à la Godiva. The peaceful fields of
lavender, he made out to be corpse-strewn battlefields; the
gray castles surmounting the brushy hills still contained

dungeons, and the dungeons still contained the children of the children of figures like Duc Philippe of the Ugly Ankles and the unlucky queen, Matilde Who Had No Butt. These tales, my mother averred, had kept the tour bus teary-eyed with laughter.

I didn't believe her. Time after time, I had heard my father attempt to tell stories; time after time, he failed miserably, starting off as suddenly and loudly as an Atlas rocket and almost immediately plunging to piteous human ruin like Icarus, whose waxen wings were inadequate for the grand heights he strove to conquer. My father could shoe horses, build bridges, plumb toilets, and design futuristic aircraft, but whenever he tried to construct a story, he unfailingly banged his thumb with the punch line.

An attendant came in to ready her for lunch. I remembered that I was carefully enjoined not to call her "nurse." My mother was strong on that point: "They're not nurses. They only have one registered nurse on the whole staff, and she never comes around unless she's specifically called for. Can you believe that?" I made no reply, thinking that registered nurses probably were not needed here; an emergency ambulance would be the more necessary service.

"Good morning, Miz Kirkman. How are you this beautiful morning?"

"*Un*beautiful . . . Lorene, this is my son, Jess, who is not standing up when a lady enters the room. Pay no attention to his lack of manners. He's notoriously harmless."

In fact, I had been trying to rise to meet the thin young blonde with the startlingly white skin but had found my knees wedged against the footboard of the bed. I wrestled free, stood, and bowed. "Pleased to meet you."

"Well, it's good to see you," she declared brightly, "after all the things your mama has told me about you."

"Nothing good, I assume."

"Why, she does nothing but brag about you all the time.

You ought to hear the fine things she says about you."

"I'm pretty sure I never will," I replied. "Is she as mean to you as she is to me?"

"She's a perfect angel," Lorene avowed. "Couldn't be sweeter."

"It's only an act. When you get to know her better, you'll understand what I mean."

"What are you bringing me for lunch?" my mother asked her. "Not that gummy macaroni and cheese, I hope."

"Chicken croquettes today. And mashed potatoes. Apple pie for dessert. Do you want tea or coffee?"

Before she could answer, I began to take my leave, squeezing between Lorene and the bedside to give my mother an off-balance kiss on the forehead. I had to lean over so far, I feared I'd topple down on her. The kiss was dry and brief but still gave her time to whisper to me distinctly, "*I hate chicken croquettes.*"

"I'll see you soon," I said. "Is there anything I can bring you from town?"

Her reply was another wan flap of her hand, indicating that the town, along with the rest of the world, was at this moment of no interest to her whatsoever.

"Well—good-bye, then," I said. "Have a nice lunch." The remark was reflexive; I hadn't desired to rub it in about the croquettes.

Lorene pushed the tiered lunch cart to the door. I sidled around it on my way out and walked down the bland corridor, glancing, despite my wiser intentions, into the open doors I passed. Television sets flittered and muttered in the ceiling corners, flashing messages about detergents to women who would never again wash clothes. Alzheimer patients talked angrily to the walls; in other rooms were supine forms motionless under crisp bedclothes. Scoliotic women sat hunched in wheelchairs, poring over Bibles they could not read, could hardly see. On bedside tables sat weary potted plants, half-full water glasses with litters of pills beside them, sheaves of unopened mail.

I recoiled from these images in dismay, in dark fear. They

were too acutely prophetic. My mother hadn't yet advanced to the stages of disrepair I saw here, and I didn't want her to experience them. Yet I was at a loss to think what better state she *could* come to. The only alternative was death, because her health was not going to improve, except during brief periods that would be followed by fearful relapses. Congestive heart failure saps the system by little and little; so Dr. Amblin had told Mitzi and me. When the end came, it would be peaceful, he said, but the ordeal that faced Mrs. Kirkman was that of nerves. If you thought of it as war, congestive heart failure would be like a siege, he explained, readjusting his gold wire spectacles on his prominent nose. The body resisted until the very end, while the mind grew restless and the patient became irritable and moody. The end was assured, and it was a milder kind of death than many another.

The good doctor had hoped this information would be of some comfort, as much as would be consistent with the truth. He spoke quietly and meticulously, the fluorescent light of the hospital corridor making a silky silver mist of his fine, dry white hair. He was the image of a messenger angel at that moment, but his words brought no solace. Mitzi and I looked at each other sorrowfully, then looked away. I didn't know where to look, but I didn't want to see another human being.

His prognosis was accurate. The disease was carrying our mother away exactly in the way he had described.

I took the stairs down to the first floor and went out into the late-spring day. The smells of grass and trees and newly bulldozed clay and fresh asphalt in the parking lot assailed me and I realized that in the new infirmary building I had been smelling glue, the mastic of the tile floors and the sizing of carpet backing. That structure had been built so recently, it had no characteristic odor of its own. No one had died in it yet, and I wondered if Cora Kirkman would be its first victim.

I knew "victim" was unfair but couldn't help the way I felt.

I found the little dented yellow Toyota my wife had christened "Buttercup" and climbed in. But I didn't crank it. I only sat there in the half-full parking lot, clutching the steering wheel in damp hands. The day sang about me; two butterflies perched on a stalk of mullein near the curb. But I stared through the windshield at nothingness, at figments of dread I couldn't put a name to. This was my state of being after each visit with my mother, a familiar complex of emotion I couldn't get used to. I tried to collect myself but found me uncollectable.

Finally, I turned the ignition key and pulled away toward Asheville, toward the funky maze of hilly streets in the blue-green lap of the Land of the Sky. I was to meet my sister for lunch. We had scheduled a session of dark conspiracy.

Mitzi was a wizard at conspiracy, though she only called it "sensible planning." It was conspiracy nonetheless, because neither of us would dare tell our mother what we said during these meetings. It wasn't that we were selfish in trying to keep her ignorant, only that if she knew all the facts, she would complicate matters so thoroughly that we would never get un-tangled. So we fed her only enough information to keep her questions to a minimum.

I found the restaurant, the Whirligig Café, a cheery place with white tablecloths, a lace-curtained storefront window, and Matisse posters. I knew Mitzi would be late, so I took my faithful notebook with me. Her schedule was as busy as a stock-market telephone exchange, and I had learned to carry something to occupy myself until she showed.

I was ushered to a table by a young blond waitress whose plentiful freckles suggested yeoman ancestry and candid disposition. I ordered a glass of chardonnay; she delivered it efficiently and cheerfully, then left me to my doleful musings. In a few slow minutes, I could bear to think about my mother no longer and opened my notebook for respite.

Fat and battered, worn gray at every corner, its black leather scratched and scuffed, this notebook was my staunch comrade, my date book, workbook, and silent confidant. It held telephone numbers, titles of books and journal articles, partial

notes for lectures, names of those whose faces I could not recall, overheard scraps of conversation, fragments of poems in
progress or already abandoned. Unwieldy as it was, it had become a necessary appendage of my organism, and without it,
I felt like a quick-draw cowboy with an empty holster.

Some of the notes I could consider important. Here were
suggestions for my fourth book of poetry, to be called *Earthsleep*. This volume would be centered around the last of the
Pythagorean elements I was employing in my scheme. Earth
was my theme, and my connective tropes were gardens and
graves, intimate engagements with dirt. Two poems were to
be about ideal gardens, one that Susan dreamed of, and one I
would dream up myself as a utopian proposition for a poet
friend, George Garrett. For this latter effort, I had chosen as
epigraph a passage from Dante, the *Purgatorio*, Canto XXX,
where he describes the approach of Beatrice, likening it to the
first intimations of dawn overtaking the sky.

Then there were notes that concerned my projected translation: "*mondiglia* = alloy; *mi discarno* = I am withered; *greffo*
= cliff or bluff." Just now, I was struggling with a passage from
a canto of the *Purgatorio*. Here the poet looks at the steep climb
ahead and feels daunted. Conversing with an old friend, the
composer Casella, he asks for music to refresh his spirit before
he recommences his necessary journey. The composer obliges
by singing a setting he had made of a poem by Dante himself,
the canzone beginning, "*Amor che la mente mi ragione*." "Love
in my mind his sweet argument pursuing . . ." I looked with
despair upon my attempts to render the line into English meter
and rhyme.

Then there were other jottings, whose purposes I could neither recall nor deduce. Why had I written down terms like
courtlax, merle, nympholept, thrasicus, patera, zygia? Why had I
written "She moves like the reflection of a cloud on a running
stream"? How's that again? Who moves in such an unvisual-
izable manner?

I snapped the notebook shut. No time to speculate now—Mitzi had arrived.

She searched the room for me and I watched as she looked about, seeming to recognize everyone in the room, which by now had become fairly crowded. Probably she did know everyone, including the chefs and the dishwashers. When she spotted me, she smiled and waved and made her way through the tables as graceful as a hoopskirted waltzer. As always, I admired her social presence.

She was attractively but sensibly dressed in a female business suit, a sharp-shouldered dark jacket and medium-narrow skirt, both pinstriped. She had allowed a dollop of lace at the jacket pocket and a modest gold chain at the collar of the pleated white blouse. Small jet earrings peeked from under the curls of her dishwater blond hair. As she came to the table, she smiled and gave some sort of greeting to other tables. It was obvious that she was known and respected and well liked. I felt a flush of pride, family pride, I suppose, on seeing her cross the room.

My mother would delight to see me rise and pull out Mitzi's chair to seat her at the table, but it was only one of those reflex actions that are supposed to distinguish southern gentlemen from the lower animals. But since I am Appalachian by heritage, I don't consider myself a southern gentleman and don't particularly desire to be set apart from animals wild or domestic, which are never so low as to clothe themselves in bedsheets and burn crosses. Appalachia is a different world from the Deep South, though few will allow that it is a better one. We have our own supply of brutes, jerks, louts, thugs, and maniacs. They are only less well organized in our upper latitudes than in the more nearly tropical.

When I sat, Mitzi began talking immediately, as if feeling her time with me was already ticking away. "How is she?"

"Why, I'm doing fairly well, thank you," I answered. "Susan is well, too, and told me to give you all her love. The drive up from Greensboro wasn't bad at all. Traffic was light, and I got into the motel about ten-thirty last night. Slept like a top, though I can't imagine why tops have such a sterling reputation in the matter of slumber."

Mitzi giggled and laid her hand on my forearm. "I'm sorry, Jess. Forgive me. I'm so anxious about Mother that I completely forgot my manners."

"I understand. I'm the same way," I said. "You're forgiven utterly and completely."

"So how is she?"

"She looks pretty good and she may be doing a little better than last week, because she's getting cranky again. I take that as a good sign. When she's too peaceable, it means she's tired."

"So she wasn't peaceable?"

"Hardly."

"She probably gave you a rough time."

"I'm tougher than I look," I said. "I can take whatever she can dish out—just as long as she doesn't make me go and cut a hickory switch and bring it back for my own punishment. Do you remember that childhood ordeal?"

"That's one I was spared."

"The switching wasn't the hard part. It was the dread. I always brought back flimsy little switches. Then she'd send me out again for more durable material. So I had to endure my cowardice twice."

When our daisy-fresh waitress appeared, Mitzi ordered a sensible seafood salad and iced tea; I countered with a steak sandwich, feeling in my sister's cool presence that I was every inch the red-fanged predator. I added the auxiliary crimes of ranch fries and a glass of cabernet. The young lady replied with a gesture very close to a curtsy and departed smiling.

"What did she talk about?" Mitzi asked.

"Oh, you know. The burial arrangements, Daddy's workshop. About how we need to get things straightened out. About how no-account I am and how I should model myself after my smart sister. The usual."

She grinned. "Sorry about that."

"I'm used to it. . . . Well, almost. How are we coming along with the business of the burial, anyhow?"

"It's tricky," she replied. "There is just no space left in Mountain View Cemetery. When they made that mistake twelve years ago and got our family plot mixed up with the Ansons', we were sunk."

"I'm surprised Daddy and Mother didn't notice."

Mitzi nodded solemnly. "I am, too—not at Daddy so much. He just didn't care to think about graveyards and dying and all that. But Mother and Grandmother talked about it."

"Grandmother did, as I remember. But Mother would usually try to turn the talk in a different direction. It's only recently that it's become such a hot topic with her."

"Well, her space in the family plot got occupied. There lie Grandmother and Granddaddy and Daddy—and no room for our mother. The graveyard people have apologized, but it's not their fault. This happened under the old management, before the new people came. So there's just no room."

"Could we bury her standing up? Maybe there's room for that."

"Jess—"

"Just kidding," I said hastily. "But there is the possibility of cremation."

"All right. I'll let you be the one to tell Mother that she's going to be burnt to ashes and poured into a mason jar."

"Why do we have to tell her? She doesn't really need to know."

"You mean cremate her without telling her beforehand?"

"Well—"

"I can't believe you said that. You are surely not serious. That would be—be something. I don't know what."

"A betrayal," I suggested.

"Yes. It's like we'd be double-crossing her."

"So there's no solution to our little problem. But we're going to have to tell her something—and pretty soon."

"I know. And I've been thinking. There is one idea I've had, but I don't know if it could work out."

"What's that?"

"We don't have any close relatives left alive. But we do have some distant ones, and of course Mother and Daddy had friends, a lot of friends."

"True." I took a meditative sip of cabernet.

"And a number of them still live on their old homestead farms and keep up family graveyards on them."

"You think they might be willing to board our parents?"

"I don't know," Mitzi said. "It's just a thought I had."

I sipped and sipped again. "Might be worth a try."

"They've been well liked, you know that."

"Yes, but folks hereabouts are kind of touchous when it comes to their real estate. And now we're talking about the most personal sort."

"I know."

"These would be long-term leases, too. From here to eternity, as the fellow said."

"Yes. So what do you think?"

"I can't say. I've been absent from the mountains for twenty-one years and have lost touch with just about everybody. You know better about the possibilities than I could."

"It's worth a try," she said. "There just might be someone willing and able to take Mother and Daddy in."

"It would be a right neighborly thing to do."

She gave me a sharpish look. "That sounds condescending."

"No, no, excuse me. I wasn't making mock. It's only that when I return to my old haunts, my old way of talking comes back to me in spurts. I begin to sound like I almost belong here."

"Don't you?" she asked.

"I've been away for two decades." I felt slow-witted, desperate. "What would you say to Evercare?"

"That big new cemetery down by the interstate?" she asked.

"Where they use those flat metal things for headstones, those things that look like manhole covers?"

"Well . . ."

But we looked at each other and shook our heads in profound rejection and fell at last to our food. Mitzi nibbled in ladylike fashion, but caveman Jess took up his sandwich and gnawed like it was the thigh of a particularly juicy mastodon. A session with my mother always left me ravenous, even with a talk with Mitzi as a buffer. I signaled for another cabernet.

"Let me ask around," she said. "We might find some charitable souls. The location isn't too important, right? It wouldn't have to be in Harwood County, just as long as Mother and Daddy are together."

"Just as long as they're side by side, mingling their mortal remains under the cool green coverlid of Mother Gaia, we'll all be happy, you and I and our devoted parents."

"I can't promise anything," she said.

"I know you'll try your best," I said. "Now about this other matter—"

"Daddy's workshop."

"Yes," I said. "I don't see what makes it such a major concern. It's not the only private workshop he maintained. He always used to set up some little hideaway where he could go to take naps or repair tools or work out plans for construction projects or whatever. There was never anything in them but toolboxes and blueprints and busted furniture and old how-to manuals and so forth. He had six or seven places like that over the years, and they were always the same."

"This one is supposed to be different. He installed it a long long time ago, and nobody knew about it for years. Mother found it by accident one day when she spotted his parked truck. But he wouldn't allow her in. He said it was Dr. Electro's secret laboratory, no visitors admitted. He teased us with it. One day, he told Mother, a project he was working on would make a big hit."

"He was kidding."

"How do you know?"

"He loved to tease."

"Yes, but lots of times when you thought he was kidding, he was actually serious. Things I thought were teases turned out to be true. Stories I took for gospel turned out to be fairy tales he made up on the spot."

"He was your classic folklore trickster. I don't know why people put up with it. If I tried to get away with some of the pranks he played, it would be Judge Lynch for me and a mooring cable for a noose."

"They liked him. They trusted him to be mischievous but not mean. They knew him for who he was."

"Or thought they did," I replied, for I didn't believe that anyone had really known my father. They had recognized the goodness of his heart, the charm of his glance, his waggish temperament. They must have understood something of the trust he put in old-fashioned ideas of science, progress, the advancement of knowledge, the betterment of humankind through education and biological and cultural evolution. To my generation, these concepts seemed so quaint and outdated, they didn't deserve the title of "concepts"; to many of his generation and the one preceding, they were still dangerous irreligious modes of thought, snares Satan set for the vanity of fools. . . . I exaggerate now in order to show how he sometimes felt put-upon by certain members of the community, whom he termed "the benighted" or, in jollier moods, "our local medievals."

Yet even those whose notions he held in sorrowful scorn had respected him. They had wanted him to change his wicked modern ideas so that they could enjoy his company in the harp-plucking afterlife.

"Or they only thought they knew him," Mitzi agreed.

"Well," I asked, "what do you think Dr. Electro's great final secret revelation will be?"

She smiled. "Nothing amazing. It is probably just one more

big tease. But, what with one problem and another, we haven't got out there in ten long years to inspect the workshop. Mother wanted to make sure the job fell to you. She thinks there might be something there that only you would understand. . . . You know where it is, don't you?''

When I said I wasn't certain, she gave detailed directions about striking old Highway 23 and then described the building I was to look for. She pulled out a large ring of keys and handed it to me. It was this weight that had given her purse such an authoritative thump when she dropped it into the chair.

She rose and I rose with her. ''Which one of these opens the door?'' I asked.

''That's one of Professor Electro's secrets,'' she said. ''You'll have to puzzle that one out.''

She leaned to give me a farewell air kiss and, on her way out of the Whirligig, stopped to exchange brief wordage at no fewer than six tables.

I sat down to ponder, hefting the keys thoughtfully before laying them on the table. There were an even dozen—no, wait; one more made thirteen—and merely to look at them made me apprehensive. I signaled the waitress and ordered coffee and cognac. If the coffee didn't aid my deliberations, maybe the cognac would solace my spirit.

Chapter Two

THE TIPTON TORNADO

The hour strikes—but whom does it hit?
—Fugio

My sister was nonpareil in her line of work, and I wish I could better describe what that was. She labored in partnership with the chamber of commerce, chiefly in trying to attract new business enterprises to the Asheville area. This goal entailed cajoling and convincing fierce tribes of German and Japanese businessmen, some of them high-handed in manner or devious in strategy. Mitzi's open, sunny temperament, her cheerful democratic friendliness, might seem to have made her too tender-minded for the cause, but her humor and generous tolerance served to placate even the most obstreperous commercial war chiefs. She was also warmly esteemed by most members of the local business community. To her detractors, I imputed motives of jealousy.

A curious mixture of moral innocence and hardheaded business sense, she found it easy to be socially pliant, but such resilience is possible only to persons of stout character. Mitzi's character was undergirded with steel I beams. When she settled her mind upon a point, when she determined a course of action, avalanches and hurricanes could not swerve her from her track. This has been true since she was a small girl, as I now delight to recall.

One of the few enemies she ever collected was a first-grade classmate, Rollie Sikes. For an undisclosed reason, she and the gangly lad were at daggers drawn from the first day of school, from the first moment they spotted each other. But if the primal cause of this bitter enmity was obscure, its effects were real enough and were manifested in episodes of kicking and biting, hair pulling, and other gestures so ferocious that the behavior of the quarrelsome pair became an impediment to fledgling scholarship. The teacher, Miz Peters, came to our house to apprise my father of the situation. I was impressed by her neatness and plucky address. She knew that he had taught school himself on occasion and so would understand her concern. She was a pretty lady, and I felt some regret that she had not been my first-grade teacher, rather than dim and pudgy Mamie Letcher.

The news she brought baffled us. How could it be—our sweet Mitzi a tigerish bloodthirsty ruffian, the scourge of boys half again her size?

I still have a photograph of my sister at age six or seven, and a blonder, dearer, more angelic child's countenance even Donatello could not have drawn. Bright-eyed and dimpled, her knees just evolved from chubby to skinny where they hooked over the sateen cushion of the photographer's bench, she was not merely harmless but utterly winning. A cursory glance at the ancient photo assures us that this child is guileless; the camera confirms her innocence with disinterested authority.

Even so, when my father questioned her, she had to admit that she had been scrapping with Rollie Sikes and that her heart was set on beating him up. When he tried to light upon the reason for such dark passion, she closed her mouth as tight as a mason jar's seal and shook her head. She would not say.

"You must have a reason not to like Rollie."

Abashed, she stared at her feet, at the white snub-toed shoes with mother-of-pearl buttons.

He sighed. "All right. You don't have to tell me. All you have to do is promise you won't be fighting with Rollie anymore."

Her shoes hypnotized her; she stared at them as if memorizing every crease and scuff.

"You have to promise me, Mitzi," he ordered, but she wouldn't give her word. When she looked into his face so full of concern and pleading, her big blue eyes brimmed with tears. She was going to disobey him, and her refusal hurt like a live coal held in the hand.

He stroked her hair. "I simply don't know what to say, Mitzi. The best thing—the only thing—would be for you to keep away from him. Just don't go anywhere near him. Will you promise me that much at least?"

But she wouldn't promise, and he shook his head sadly and rose from his crouch and stalked away, defeated.

Trouble was, he couldn't bring his mind to bear upon Mitzi's problem. Once again my father was distracted and once again the cause was that one of our peregrine uncles had fluttered out of the empyrean to visit us, though the word *visit* was not my father's choice. His accustomed expression was *roost upon*. Some of these uncles—who were mostly honorary and not real kin by any stretch of the genealogical tables—he liked, some he abhorred, and some he was mystified by. Uncle Zeph Moseley exasperated him entirely.

Uncle Zeph was actual kin, though, a third or fourth cousin

to my grandmother. When I recall him now, I wonder if he might not have been slightly retarded, for her solicitude on his behalf was assiduous. Or maybe my father was correct and the old man was a slyboots strategist. He was a champion eater and no workhand whatsoever—but this description was standard for the majority of our intermittent uncles, and my father had ceased to remark upon these aspects of their personalities. And anyhow—as my grandmother carefully pointed out— Uncle Zeph did have one useful function: He offered up prayers. While he was in residence, she allowed no one else to say table grace or render parting benediction, not even Preacher Cobb himself if he had turned up for Sunday chicken.

Uncle Zeph was birdlike: skinny and long-shanked and stoop-shouldered, with bright eyes weak of sight, a pointy nose, and a habit of cocking his head awry, as if he were picking up sounds from underground. He reminded me of a green heron, being so angular and jerky of movement. My father christened him with a private name, "Robin Redbreast," a cognomen that made no sense at all to me until years later when I came upon the robin's scientific name in a handbook. *Turdus migratorius*, dixit the Latin.

The qualities that gave Uncle Zeph's prayers such distinction were two: epic length and enunciatory oddness. His voice was as high-pitched and insistent as a mosquito's nasal sostenuto; it alternated among a whine, a screech, and a mumble. This was true only when he prayed; his unsanctified voice was ordinary—and intelligible. His praying voice was unintelligible; it made a sound like a fat man trying to get comfortable in a new splint-bottom chair. His prayers began with the epistolary formula and ended with a radio commentator's sign-off. "Dear God," he would begin, and he finished by declaring, "That's all for now. We sure do thank You." The sounds that came in between had never been deciphered; it had not even been determined if they were actual words or only calls of a very rare bird trying to search out a mate that might not exist.

The other extraordinary quality was length. I am unable to

report the average time utilized by one of Uncle Zeph's prayers, for though there were many serious attempts to clock him, none was successful. For quite a while, the timekeeper would be attentive to his wristwatch, but as that voice hummed in the ear, a glaze came over the eyes. The minutes and maybe the hours snoozed away. By the time he reached his signature—"That's all for now"—the would-be observer had forgotten when he had cranked up, had forgotten his ambition to add the length of this blessing to the store of the world's scientific knowledge; it even had to be recalled to him that hearty cookery sat on the table awaiting the pleasures of appetite: corn on the cob, snowy cumuli of mashed potatoes, ham with redeye gravy, chicken fried in cornmeal and egg whites, green beans, cornpone—everything but biscuits. The baking women had learned to hold them out in the oven until Uncle Zeph concluded. Otherwise, they sat on the table growing as hard as roof tile and as stale as attics.

When Uncle Zeph finally departed our hospitality in order to blight the mealtimes of some other family of relatives or nonrelatives, my father exploded in an incandescent display of mingled relief and exasperation. "Damn it all to Hell, Hades, and Gehenna," he exclaimed, and went on from there for another sizzling two minutes.

"Now, Joe Robert," my grandmother said, "be careful about little pitchers with big ears."

He looked at Mitzi and me and shrugged. "What could these children possibly hear from me half as bad as what they've been hearing from Uncle Zeph? If you are going to criticize anybody's manner of speech, you ought to start with your own weird and precious cousin."

She considered the point. "I expect Uncle Zeph does the best he can," she said. "But you're not doing your best. You have the education and upbringing not to be using ugly bywords."

"I might be willing to dispute that with you—about Uncle Zeph, I mean. I believe I could defend the proposition that there is more heartfelt sincerity in ten seconds of my safety-valve profanity than in the whole first week of one of his table graces."

My mother chimed in. "That's not a gracious thing for you to say, Joe Robert."

He gave her a wolfish grin. "I had ambitions it wouldn't be."

"I can see the smoke rising from under your collar, but Mother is right," she said. "He does the best he knows how to do."

"What makes you think so? Just last Wednesday at suppertime, I had a revelation. I was sitting here at the table almost perishing of starvation, with a full plate in front of me, when it struck me that this man was not offering up serious prayer of any category. He was only mumbling incoherent nonsense, pulling our legs like they were made of warm licorice, making prize fools out of us and anybody else who'd let him bless so much as a single pinto bean."

"Now, Joe Robert," my grandmother cautioned.

"How am I wrong?" he demanded. "Did you understand his praying? Did you comprehend even one little microscopic syllable?"

"I believe he has a speech impediment," my mother said. "So that's not his fault."

"Speech impediment?" His feelings had been subsiding, but this suggestion goosed his temperature gauge again. "What speech impediment? We understood everything else but the praying, didn't we? Didn't we hear him say as plain as broad daylight, 'I reckon I might could do with a little more of them strawberry preserves'? Didn't we clearly understand that sentence every morning at breakfast seven days in a row? Those prayers are singsong phoniness."

"Don't say that," my mother pleaded.

He relented a little. "Well, if they're not phony, they're still abysmal. I submit to you, Cora, and to you, Annie Barbara, that any man who has a reputation for doing just the one thing for so many years ought to be better at it than the worst who ever tried the first time."

"Perhaps it's not so easy to offer up prayers," she countered.

"Sure it is."

"I don't hear you saying grace—or any other kind of prayer."

That was a telling blow. My father avoided saying prayers at table or in any other visible place, and I felt that I understood his feelings. Public prayers are embarrassing. Prayers are supposed to be utterly sincere, are they not? As full of intimate, untrammeled feeling as love letters. I, for one, would not care to have my purple-prose romantic missives read aloud to kin or strangers while the lettuce wilted and the soup grew chill. These are feelings too personal to share. Doth not Saint Matthew in his Gospel forbid us to pray in public, following the practice of hypocrites? Doth he not counsel us to enter into our closets, shutting tight the doors, there to pray to our Father which is in secret?

I knew, however, that it was not religious doctrine, but animal shyness, that caused Joe Robert Kirkman to avoid revealing himself in such manner. My mother was undoubtedly correct: He was clumsy at it because his instinct for privacy was too sorely tested by this particular ritual.

So with his next sentence, he sealed his doom. "Anybody in the world, anybody in this room, can make a better prayer than Uncle Zeph," he declared. "I'll tell you what we'll do. We'll have a prayer competition, among just the five of us. I'll be the sponsor and I'll offer an award. Whoever makes up the best prayer wins a prize."

"What kind of prize?" I asked.

"How about a pound of my renowned chocolate fudge with black walnuts?"

"Joe Robert," my mother said, "we are not going to allow Jess or Mitzi to eat a pound of fudge. And anyway, I don't have room in my calendar for the spare two days it takes to clean up the kitchen after one of your forays into cooking."

"All right. Then we'll say that whoever wins the contest gets to pick out his or her own prize. If I can't supply it to the letter,

I'll come as close to it as possible. How does that suit you?"

"Who is going to judge this contest?" my mother asked.

"Annie Barbara and I will be the judges, and I don't mind announcing that I expect to win hands down. Ten days from now, Wednesday week, the competition will take place right here at the supper table, and I already have my prize picked out."

"What is it?" my mother asked.

"I'll be telling you that in private," he replied.

"I know what my prize is," I said. I could picture it vividly in my head, the pungent-smelling sand-tan second baseman's glove I'd spotted in the sporting goods section of the Western Auto store. I'd tried it on, standing there in the narrow aisle next to the bicycles, and punched my right fist into the webbing. It was a perfect fit.

"How about it, Annie Barbara? Are you game?" he asked.

We waited with some anxiety for her answer. If my grandmother regarded the notion as sacrilegious or even just a half tone out of key with true piety, the contest would never take place. She was the arbiter of all religious proprieties, and none of us, not even my father, would dispute her decision.

She looked away from us for a space and we could see that she was cogitating deeply. At last she said, "Well, I don't see any harm in it. The way Joe Robert has set things up, there will be ten days coming when we'll all be thinking about prayer. That is a sight better than our present way of thinking."

"I know what I want if I win," Mitzi said.

"What's that, hon?" my father asked.

"A gun."

"My word. What kind of gun?"

"A big gun."

"What for?"

"To kill Rollie Sikes with," she said. "To shoot him dead."

The force of Mitzi's passion focused my father's attention upon her situation. He telephoned Miz Peters, her teacher, and made an appointment to talk with her again. Following that, he made a visit to the Sikes domicile and returned to report that Jim and Mary were just as mystified as we—as Rollie himself was. "Where is Mitzi now?" he asked.

"Sitting in the tire swing in the side yard," my mother said.

"Well, according to the Sikeses, it was Mitzi who initiated this monumental ruckus. They say that the first time ever she saw their boy, she ran over to him and started whaling away with her fists. For no reason whatsoever. He'd done nothing to aggravate her; he didn't even know her name. Of course, that's what Rollie told his parents. If we could get Mitzi to talk, I expect we'd hear a whole different story."

"What should we do about it?"

"I figure we might handle it the same way we would if I was still the principal at that school. I used to be, you know, and a pretty sound one, too, if I do say so myself."

"Well, you lasted eight months and they failed to assassinate you," she said. "So we might count your tenure a success. How are you going to handle this particular problem?"

"We'll let them fight it out. We'll have a full-fledged match with real boxing gloves and a referee and a stopwatch and a bell to ring—everything. The bout will take place at recess so the other kids who have recess then and the teachers and any-one else who wants to can witness the great reconciliation."

"Reconciliation?"

"Now, Cora, you've seen it happen a hundred times. When there's bad blood between a couple of younguns, they fight it out and become the best of friends."

"You're talking about big old high school boys. These are first graders, Joe Robert."

"It's the same principle," he insisted.

"But Rollie is twice the size of Mitzi! There's no way it can be a fair fight."

"We'll be right there overseeing. So will the Sikeses. So will all the teachers and everybody else. We'll get Bill Bannister to referee. Neither of the kids will get hurt."

"This doesn't seem right." She wagged her head repeatedly, whether in denial or in sheer disbelief, I couldn't tell.

"It's the tradition of school-yard feuds—a fair fight to the finish and shake hands afterward. You know all about that."

"But he's so big! He would make three of Mitzi."

I couldn't recall with exactitude what Rollie Sikes looked like, but if he kept growing at the rate of my mother's descriptions, he would soon be as tall as a sycamore rampant on a mossy plain.

"Now that might seem to be the case at first glance," my father said, "but Mitzi has a secret weapon. I'm going to teach her how to box."

"You're not going to teach our darling little girl to fight!"

"No sissies in this house—that's the rule. I will not encourage her to follow boxing as a profession."

She appealed to her mother. "Please, please tell Joe Robert not to go through with this craziness. Try to reason some sense into him."

My grandmother considered the point with grave deliberation. Then once again, she sided with my father. "It won't cause any harm for Mitzi to learn how to protect herself," she declared. "There's a lot of rough old boys in these parts. Mitzi will need to take care." She seemed to speak from country experiences of long ago, and my mother acquiesced to the proposal, but she was not happy about it.

And so, in the ensuing days, my father would take Mitzi's hand and they would toddle down the road to a little enclosed shed that sat on a hillside between the house and the barns. I believe this place was the first of my father's little hideaway workshops. In time past, it had been a harness room, but now the weathered little shack housed tools and a cider press and old math texts and different books and such other odds and ends as might fuel his fancies. These days, first thing after morning chores and before time to go to school, the two of them repaired to this outbuilding to undertake Mitzi's training. My father pulled a sweatshirt over his overalls; my sister was in blue jeans and boxing gloves. These were rust red pillowy appliances he had found God knows where. Attached to the limits of Mitzi's skinny arms, they presented the appearance of marshmallows pierced with toothpicks.

My father was on his knees before her, murmuring instructions without letup. "Come on now, come on. I am Rollie Sikes and you can lick me good because your daddy has taught you how to box. That means you can lick anybody in the world. Whoa now—keep your chin tucked in. That's the way. Keep your guard up, keep 'em up. Bring your elbows in to your sides. That's it." In a moment or two, her arms would tire and she'd drop her hands. Then he reached over and chucked her under the chin. "No now, keep your guard up. You can lick Rollie Sikes because you know how."

Mitzi came at him like a pinwheel on the handlebars of a speeding Schwinn. She was a whirlwind of overhand, underhand, and sideways lunges for whole seconds at a time. Then she gasped for breath; her arms sagged and she stepped back, red-faced and coughing. He would reiterate his strategic identity—"Here I am; I'm Rollie Sikes"—and she'd come charging again, flailing like the paddles of a window fan, a wild mêlée of elbows, knees, and blond curls for another twelve seconds or so.

Tuesday night, on the eve of the historic day that would include the highly anticipated bout of fisticuffs and the titanic prayer contest, we sat at the table, listening to my father pronounce his satisfaction. "Things are rolling my way," he proclaimed. "My prayer is all written out. It is a super jim-dandy, if I do say so myself. Intellectual substance—that's what's been lacking around here in the matter of the orison. I will remedy that. And we've got Mitzi looking as sharp as any pugilist who ever set foot in the rosin box. She has strength and endurance, and I took pains with her technique. All she needs now is a ring moniker."

"What's that?" I asked.

"Oh, you know," he said. "A catchy name to fight under. Joe Louis is the Brown Bomber; Jack Dempsey was the Manassas Mauler. What shall we call Mitzi? The Fearsome First Grader—how's that?"

I thought it was pretty dumb and said so and suggested Killer Kirkman or Murderin' Mitzi, but my mother quashed these sobriquets with swift and imperious authority. But when she was asked, she declined to offer a moniker, saying that the whole thing was ridiculous and, besides that, just awful. I figured she couldn't think of a good one.

"I've got it," my father declared. "Lay-deez and gennulmen . . . In this corner, wearing blue jeans and weighing in at sixty-two pounds, that maiden of mayhem, that princess of punch, Mitzi Kirkman—the Tipton Tornado!" He grinned, flashing that sliver of gold tooth cap at us. I judged it to be passable, but not a patch on Murderin' Mitzi. My grandmother and mother smothered their smiles with an expression of brusque disdain.

Nor did "the Tipton Tornado" meet a warm reception on Mitzi's part. She frowned blackly at her clump of potato salad and muttered, without raising her eyes, "I am the Baxter Buster."

"The what Buster?" my father inquired.

She blushed as pink as a summer tanager and said, no louder than before, "The Baxter Buster."

"What's that? I don't understand."

She wouldn't reply, setting her mouth in that thin line that signified a new Spanish Inquisition wouldn't wrest an explanation from her.

"Well, all right," he said, "if that's who you are, that's who you are. Lay-deez and gennulmen—I give you the Baxter Buster."

We could tell he was puzzled and disappointed, a little hurt that she had rejected the bold *nom de guerre* he had proposed.

My usual third period consisted of a geography class that featured age-cracked, out-of-date maps on a rickety stand, an ugly mustard-colored book, and prim little Miz Thatcher speaking crisply in front of a cloudy blackboard. But I skipped class on this momentous occasion, secure in my belief that my spiffy instructress would not punish a lad who wanted to observe his sister in a boxing match. Many had gathered, young and adult, the concerned and the merely curious. Siblings were in clots: here the four redheaded Holcombe boys, there the three shiny-blond Baxter girls. I stood in the school yard with a group that included my mother. She had allowed her fifth-grade English class a free cut for this event and would probably be reprimanded by the principal, Jake Silverside, for so criminal a dereliction.

I saw straight lines scratched out in the hard-packed clay. This was to be the boxing ring, and students and teachers alike had flocked to the edges. The Sikeses were there and with them the boy I took to be Rollie. His aspect surprised me. I had been expecting a gorilla-huge, beetle-browed, skulking villain, but he was only a first grader, tall for his age, but rather spindly, too. There was nothing about him to inspire fear or—as far as I could see—the kind of ferocious enmity Mitzi harbored. But I had to trust her instincts, receiving so little impression of his personality myself. He was dressed in everyday-type school clothes and the laces of his boxing gloves dangled untied.

Of his valiant opponent, there was no sign, and when I asked my mother, she told me that my sister and father were down in the furnace room going over some last-minute strategy. "Maybe you'd better run in and see about them," she said. "Tell your father that it is time to get this ordeal done with."

I hastened to obey and located them down there in that dusty, musty place with its recalcitrant furnace and webby ducts and pipes and the coal pile that loomed so threateningly out into the room. I knew that my father was familiar with this space. When he had taught school here—for a longer pe-

riod than he'd desired—he used to descend into these depths
to take a pipe of tobacco and hold colloquy with the gentle,
philosophical custodian who held sway over this demesne.

There was nothing remarkable here except for the bulging
hoard of lump coal straining against the front walls and shabby
chute gate of a makeshift wooden bin. The pile behind the
board lattice towered like a black avalanche over my father
and sister in their newly accustomed postures, she holding the
scuffed puff-ball gloves before her chin, he on his knees, softly
and carefully bracing her for the conflict. "All you need to
remember is that your daddy taught you how to fight so that
you could lick Rollie Sikes. You can do it because you know
how and you're not afraid of anything. Keep your guard up,
keep 'em up. I can lick Rollie Sikes; my daddy has taught me
how."

"Mother said it's time to come on up," I told him. "Everybody is waiting."

He gave Mitzi a last head pat, a final chin chuck, and told
her to go out to the playground and wait for us to arrive.
"Don't start the slaughter till we get there." He watched her
go up the stairs, swinging her bulky gloves at her sides. She
exited the door before he turned to me. "Jess, if you don't
mind, I'd like for you to give me a hand."

He walked over to the coal pile and inspected it with dubious
scrutiny. "This heap of coal looks awfully precarious to me. I
got to thinking about what might happen if some kids sneaked
down here to play around. It just looks dangerous."

"Yessir."

"Help me find some loose boards or a two-by. Maybe we can
prop this front bin wall and the gate so they'll hold for a while.
Then they can get a carpenter for a proper job."

We searched without success. Most basements and furnace
rooms have scraps of lumber lying around, but this one only
rendered up half-full paint cans and cardboard boxes of rags
and other jetsam useless to us.

Then he spotted a length of board and tried to pick it up. It was a long piece, lying flat on the gritty cement floor, with the farther end protruding under the chute gate into the coal pile. "This might be just the ticket," he said, and began tugging at it. It proved stubborn and he started wiggling it from side to side.

I could see the great heap tremble, separate chunks glinting in the dim light. Every tug on the board made it quiver more ominously. There was a low growling sound like a bear grunting at a woodchuck. "Watch out!" I cried.

"I think I've got it now," he said, and his last strained jerk brought the gate open and the whole mass rumbling out into the room. Startled, he raised his face, and a melon-sized chunk caught him on the cheekbone under the left eye. He dodged back pretty nimbly, but a couple of smaller pieces knocked him along the temple and on the hand he raised to protect his face. He yelped and swore and danced out of the way.

It came crashing out, most of it. I was lucky not to get hit with any tumbling lump, and my father suffered no further physical damage except for the scarring of his brown oxfords. A cloud of black dust rose around us and we both sneezed and looked at each other, relieved but still a little scared. We blinked and snuffled.

"Well," he said, "I guess it won't be falling on any younguns now." He essayed a laugh, but his voice was unsuited to the effort, and I could see he was feeling some notable effect of the anthracite.

"Are you okay?"

I must have been visibly frightened, for he tried to smile and said, "Oh, I'm all right. Just a little knock on the noggin. Might teach me some sense."

He didn't look all right, bleeding from his forehead and the knuckles of his right hand dripping. The yellowish tumescence below his eye prophesied a hen's-egg shiner of total-spectrum coloration.

"You'd better go see a doctor," I said.

"No call for that," he replied. "Where we'd better go is up

there to see how Mitzi is getting along. We don't want her to
start the fight without us."

"No sir."

He surveyed the furnace room, the gaped and broken bin
gate, the rubble of coal scattered over the floor even into the
dimmest corners, the furnace and near wall coated with coal
dust. "I guess we've done about all the damage we can do
down here," he said, but he didn't sound content.

We picked our way carefully through the rubble and climbed
the stairs and walked down the empty hall toward the door to
the school yard. For a little while, he strolled along steadily
enough, but then he began to weave and his steps became
uneven.

"Are you okay?" I asked. Then I resolved not to inquire
again, because he answered in such an irritated manner: "Just
fine, just fine."

But when we went out into the sunlight and the crowded
yard, he had to sit. He let himself gingerly down on the top
step and rubbed his face with his bleeding hand.

For a minute or so, no one spotted us. All eyes were upon
my sister as she marched back and forth in front of Rollie Sikes,
waggling those outsized boxing gloves vaguely toward his
chin. She was shouting as she marched, saying those slogans
she'd been instructed to say. "I can lick you, Rollie Sikes. My
daddy has been boxing with me in the basement and I have
learned the way to do it. I can lick you; I can lick anybody in
the world."

Awesome claims these, yet I doubted that they struck icy
fear into the heart of her antagonist. From where I sat, some
fifty yards away, her defiant challenges sounded remarkably
like a Carolina chickadee disputing a jay for possession of a
hawthorn perch. Master Sikes looked down upon her as if she
she were an overeager calf in his father's barnyard.

My father tried to rise but had to sit again. "I'll be all right
in a jiffy," he told me. "Just let me catch my breath for
a second."

Now the crowd had seen us and in one mass movement abandoned the spectacle of Mitzi to attend that of my father. They came scurrying pell-mell to look upon him as he sat there returning their gaze with bleary eyes, scarred, scratched, and bleeding. "What happened?" one cried, and then another and another. He tried to wave them away, but they swarmed him over, clucking in commiseration, making concerned and curious sounds. Some of them—quite a few, actually—were giggling.

It may have been this latter annoyance that restored my father's strength and brought him tottering to his feet. He swept his hand in a vague shooing motion and his undesired entourage fell back and were silent for a space. "Let a fellow have a little breathing room, if you please," he entreated. "We have an important sporting event on our hands here, and the trainer needs to be in her corner with his fighter." With that, he strode through the circle of gapers and made his way, wobbling only slightly, across the ground to where my mother and sister awaited him.

It was plain to see that Mitzi was in a highly excited state, angry and embarrassed. Her face was flushed and her eyes wild. My mother, however, looked wonderfully pleased and sweetly amused.

"Where is Master Sikes?" my father demanded. "There's not much recess time left, so we'd better get started in a hurry. Round one coming up. Where is our worthy opponent?"

"Gone," said Mitzi in a tone as forlorn as any funeral knell.

"Gone where?"

"Away," she said, the syllables as sad as those of the last keening mourner.

"I don't understand."

My mother explained: "Rollie decided that he was not feeling very well, Joe Robert. He asked his parents to take him home, and they hustled him straight into their car. Off they drove in a big hurry. It seems to me that this match has been canceled."

"What was wrong with him?"

"He just ran *away*," Mitzi complained.

"It might have been a sudden and unforeseen attack of pusillanimity," my mother said.

"Surely he wasn't scared," my father said. "Not a big old boy like Rollie."

"Well, you see, Mitzi had just been strutting about here and boasting what a world-class boxer she is. She repeatedly stressed the fact that she had been scrapping with you down in the furnace room. I have the feeling you may have coached her to say such things."

"Confidence," my father said. "It's the most important thing."

"Anyway," she continued, "when Rollie looked yonder and saw you coming out of the schoolhouse all bleeding and battered and black-eyed, I think he may have leapt to a hasty conclusion."

"You mean he thought—"

"I'm no mind reader," my mother said, "but the very moment he spotted you, he went white around the gills and began to describe the excruciating tummy ache he was suffering."

"He just ran off," Mitzi said. She seemed to consider this the deadliest of insults.

"His daddy tried to talk him out of it," my mother said, "but his stomach pain was too severe. The only solution was to take him home and put him to bed."

"Well, I'll be—"

"No, you won't," she said. "Not in front of all these children. In fact, I think the best thing for you would be to go home to bed. You don't even look as healthy as Rollie."

"I'm all right."

Then the bell rang and those who had been watching this conversation drifted slowly away. It was time for fourth period, but they were reluctant to leave a drama they seemed to expect to continue.

That wasn't the case. My father decided to heed sound

advice. He gave my mother hugs and pats and gave Mitzi a grave handshake and stalked off, still wobbly, increasingly purpling, to our disreputable old Pontiac station wagon at the edge of the field. He turned to give us an awkward wave, then drove away.

"All right, Jess and Mitzi," my mother said. "Time for you both to be where you're supposed to be." She knelt and helped Mitzi worry off the gloves, then patted her on the shoulder as we walked into the schoolhouse.

Mitzi was still steaming. "He just ran *away.*" She kicked the red clay dust, disconsolate as an eager bride deserted at the altar.

My grandmother prepared our evening meal, but my father set the table. This occasion was special—extraspecial—so he brought out silver candlesticks, a little tarnished, and placed linen napkins beside the good china with the silver-gilt rims. He had spruced himself up, all scrubbed and polished in his neat blue suit. He was not visibly bleeding and had managed to remove most of the coal smudge, but there was no hiding the landscape artist's palette of ochers, mauves, burnt siennas, and royal purples that his face presented. I had been ordered to bathe and don my Sunday togs, too, so that he was more cheerful than I, chipper as a house wren, whistling loudly and tunelessly all through the table preparation.

As we sat down to our mashed potatoes and stewed chicken, he pulled out their chairs for the womenfolk, even for Mitzi, and made an elaborate ceremony of lighting the tall yellow candles. Then he seated himself and told us there was a great deal to be thankful for on such a superlative occasion. "But there will be no table grace," he said, "because I am raring to get the prayer competition under way. Before we start on that, however, we must congratulate Mitzi on her stellar triumph of pugilistic skill and prowess." He lifted his glass of buttermilk in happy salute. "Ladies and gentlemen, I give you Mitzi, the

Tipton Tornado, winner and undisputed champion of the first grade."

"I didn't win," Mitzi said. "I was supposed to be the Baxter Buster, but we didn't have a fight."

"Nevertheless, you are the clear winner because your opponent forfeited the match. Do you know what that word means?"

"He didn't forget. He just ran away."

"Not *forget—forfeit*. If you run away from a fight, the other person wins. Those are the rules of boxing."

She didn't reply, and it was plain that she was still disappointed, still indignant.

"I'm going to ask you a question this one last time," my father said. "If you don't care to answer, you don't have to. But I can't help being extremely curious, and I expect we all feel the same way. Why was it you took such a dislike to Rollie Sikes? What did he do to make you so upset?"

Mitzi looked at him for a long moment, then hung her head, blushing again. She was making a regular habit of self-conscious reactions. "He said I was a baxter."

"A what?"

She breathed deeply and looked up into his lumpy face. "A baxter. The first day of school, he was standing in the hall with Sam Price and Sam said, 'Who is that girl?' and Rollie Sikes said, 'She looks like a Baxter to me.' "

My mother clucked her tongue and tapped the linen tablecloth. "You know," she said, "I never noticed it before, but Mitzi does sort of favor that youngest Baxter girl. What is her name?"

"Nelda," I said, "but I don't think Mitzi looks much like her."

My father didn't glance at us, intent upon my sister. "Tell me, Mitzi," he asked, "what do you think a baxter is, exactly?"

In a voice as shy as an eight-point buck stepping into a clearing, she answered: "A baxter is somebody that doesn't have a mother or daddy. Nobody likes them because they had to be born in the woods."

"I see," he said. "And you don't like to be called by that name."

"I'm not a baxter. Rollie Sikes is a baxter."

"But he has a mother and father."

"I don't care. He's a baxter anyway."

"We'll talk about this subject a little later," he promised. "It is just barely possible that you have mistaken the meaning of a word or two." He blinked his eyes and grinned. "Meanwhile, we have some pressing business on hand. It is time for our prayer contest. I've been looking forward to winning my secret prize." He winked at my mother.

"It may be that your confidence is misplaced," she said.

"Oh, I don't think so. I'm well prepared. But it's going to be a fair competition, and I'm going to ask Jess to start us off."

Three days ago, I had strung together the opening phrases of a sockdolager prayer. But with all the excitement, I'd forgotten to follow through to a middle, much less to a conclusion. Now I'd lost even my bravura beginning and had to improvise, mumbling and stumbling, while the vision of the baseball glove dwindled to the size of a Ritz cracker, then to the size of a sand grain, before vanishing entirely. There was nothing to do but mutter incoherently until I'd dribbled enough verbiage to pronounce an Amen. My eyes were closed, but I could feel my father's dead-level gaze upon my face like Buck Rogers's ray-gun beams.

Then he called upon my mother, and I judged her prayer to be no major improvement upon my own. She always assumed a hushed, sanctimonious tone that made my socks wet with embarrassment. She began conventionally enough, thanking the Deity for His gracious and merciful bounties, but after detailing a few of these, she waded into the mainstream of her discourse, a petition for Him to forgive us all for our faults. She discovered red-faced multitudes of these and did not decline to describe them in flamboyant detail. I may have been deluded, but it seemed she spent the best part of an eternity on my case and that she relished all too deliciously the displaying of my errors to God and family alike.

Next up was my grandmother, and it became obvious that she did not think this occasion called for an undue exhibition of piety. Her prayers were ever of the plainest sort, eschewing gorgeous rhetoric and exalted address. She prayed like an experienced carpenter constructing an oak cabinet, thoughtfully, deliberately, and without wasted motion. Every sentence was a board laid in place and her pauses the nails that clenched them in. Prayer was a familiar, almost an hourly, practice with my grandmother every day of her life and she built her devotions to be unassuming and durable.

My father had written out his prayer on loose-leaf notebook paper and he produced it with a flourish from his inside jacket pocket. It consisted of three closely inscribed pages that he unfolded gravely and began to read. It was no worse than one of Uncle Zeph Moseley's—I'll say that much for it—and it was obviously of a different stripe altogether. But in one important respect, it did resemble Uncle Zeph's offerings: It was incomprehensible, though not because we couldn't hear and distinguish the words. He enunciated every syllable with painstaking clarity. But the terms were so high-flown and abstruse and arcane that they sounded like gibberish. . . . Well, not gibberish, I suppose, for gibberish has no meaning. These words had meaning; they bore weighty planets of meaning. They creaked and groaned and finally disintegrated under the burden of so much significance. I can't now accurately recall many of the terms he employed, but I retain an impression of sounds like *ecphonesis, latitudinarian, eschatology, cenaculum,* and *Paraclete.* He even uttered fearlessly a dire term he had once interpreted from the boom of thunder during a hailstorm: *Tetragrammaton.*

He finished his reading at last and looked up, to find us staring at him in stunned silence. We all felt as if we'd been pounded by a blacksmith's hammer. He could deduce our verdict but remained unruffled, refolding the prayer carefully and restoring it to his pocket. "Seems to me that what we've needed around here is prayer with a little meat on it," he said coolly. "Intellectual substance has been lacking."

My mother reached over and patted his hand. "I think you have made up the deficiency," she said. "If we needed a little meat, you have brought in a whole roast ox."

"It was an incumbent duty," he replied. "Now let's hear what Mitzi has to say."

She bowed her head and pressed her palms together and squeezed her eyes so tightly shut that little wrinkles appeared at the corners. She took a breath and began to pray in a calm, earnest voice, and as she prayed, a luminance took shape above Mitzi's head, the kind of brightness you see in religious paintings. It was no earthly kind of light, all holy and pure and ethereal, full of mercy and loving-kindness, and it poured down upon that bowed head and golden hair. The candles on the table slowly diminished their flames and the room grew dim about us as she said, "O Lord Jesus God, please make me be good. Real, real good. And make everybody be good. And make everybody be happy. Real, real happy."

My grandmother would be placidly content with her own prayer, but I think the rest of us were suddenly abashed. The way Mitzi prayed was the proper way to do it—with perfect candor, confident receptiveness, and unmistakable clarity of language. As I watched her sitting there, bathed in that mild celestial glow, I was ashamed of myself and began to make my usual private vows to improve the condition of my mind and spirit.

But before I could formulate so much as a whisper of resolution, the supernal glow disappeared and the room was plunged into a fathomless blackness that extinguished even the dimly burning candles when Mitzi uttered her perfervid, unfeigned, and apostate addendum:

"But don't make that baxter Rollie Sikes be happy. Make him fall down on his nose."

There was silence for a long space—and of course my father

couldn't bear that. "Lay-deez and gennulmen," he began, "I give you the undisputed champeen of the reverential petition, that Belle of the Boxing Ring, that Prepotent Princess of Prayer, Mitzi . . ." But then his voice crumbled, whether from pride or sadness or joy, I couldn't know, and he fell as silent as the candles smoking in darkness on the table before us.

Chapter Three

DR. ELECTRO'S SECRET

LABORATORY

Manhood is but an hour in the life of a Boy.
—Fugio

I found the building that housed my father's hideaway workshop just where Mitzi had located it for me during our lunch meeting. This nondescript edifice stood halfway between Tipton and Asheville on old Highway 19 and 23, a three-lane road that seemed a little shabby now that it ran parallel to busy Interstate 40. On I-40, the big rigs huffed and growled up the mountain slopes toward Tennessee while passenger cars zipped past them like shoals of minnows disporting around lazy brown trout. The old highway I traveled transported farm pickups mainly and battered old cars stuffed to the dashboards with noisy families. The few business establishments posted along the roadway were faded, looked seedy and down-hearted.

But this was not true of the enterprise at hand; it was hardly overflocked with customers, but its quietness seemed to come from an innate modesty rather than from disuse. The name of the business was announced diffidently on a neatly painted blue-and-white sign stationed in the grass demilune of a gravel driveway: TIMES PAST ANTIQUE CLOCKS. This building belonged to the Kirkman family and we rented out the upper floor. My father's workshop was below, tucked away in the long base-ment area not visible from the highway.

I wriggled out of Buttercup, the Toyota, and locked it out of habit. When I stepped onto the porch, the tin roof over me clicked loudly with the day's warmth coming on, and I looked up and saw a mud dauber busy at his adobe construction. I breathed in the free June air and the gray homely smell of weathered wood before opening the shop door and slipping inside.

In here, it was a different world, an alternative dimension of existence. The light seemed hazy after the broad bright sun-shine, and I actually heard the room before I could form a picture of it: a staccato cantata of ticking, ticking, tocking. Some sounds were insectile, as of grasshoppers, crickets, and locusts clucking and chirping. Others resonated more deeply, like water drops falling on overturned washtubs or woodpeck-ers tapping on empty rain barrels. Now and then there was a cicadalike rasp as a clock gathered itself to perform some mys-terious inner function. This panoply of sound disoriented my senses, immersing me in its pool of particulate stutter. I felt dislocated from the world, from my ordinary self.

''Hello? Hello?''

I had called out before noticing that a smallish older woman stood slightly behind me, almost at my elbow. She was dressed in a white blouse and gray skirt and the discreet clock de-sign on her open gray sweater suggested that she was the proprietress. Her hair was a stiff blond gone almost completely to silver. Because I hadn't seen her, her soft voice surprised me, and my expression must have been a startled one, for she smiled to reassure me. "What help can I be to you?" she asked in a voice gentle and, I thought, a little worn, a little resigned.

I informed her that I was Jess Kirkman, come to inspect the basement area at my mother's request.

"Oh," she said. "You're Mitzi's brother—Joe Robert's boy." She gave me a keener and more thorough look-over, and I already felt her measuring me against my father, for she must have known him.

"That's right." I did not shy at her calling me "boy." Everyone who had known my father called me that. When I got to be a graybeard loon of ninety-five, when my voice trembled like a plucked mandolin string and my memory lay in dusty ruin among the smoky decades, there would still be someone who saluted me only as "Joe Robert's boy." Truth to tell, I didn't mind.

When she had given me her mild but longish appraisal, she nodded agreement. "Your daddy meant a lot to me," she said. "It was hard when he died."

"I think he was important to a number of folks," I said.

"My husband and I ran this place together. Then Royal passed away, and I was ready to give up. I didn't see how I could stay in business, what with the debts and all the new expenses. And then the insurance company went back on their word. Joe Robert helped me out some—well, a lot. He helped a lot."

"When was this?"

"We opened the shop in 1948. Then Royal died in 1960, and for the first year after that your daddy leased me this building for a dollar a month. He called it his 'souvenir dollar,' and he wanted me to pay precisely on the dot. It was important for a clock shop to be punctual, he said. I think he meant that as a joke."

"I'm surprised I didn't meet you and your husband when I was a youngun."

"But you know, it seems like you did. It seems to me I can almost remember you as a child, all dressed up in a cute little black costume."

"What sort of costume?"

She closed her eyes for a moment. "I don't know. It's like a memory and not like a memory. Like something I might have imagined."

"Perhaps my mother had something to do with the monthly dollar," I said. "Do you know her?"

"That would be 'the sly Cora' he spoke of. I never got to meet her. He said he didn't want to bring her here because she'd find out about his workshop downstairs, and he was whipping up a surprise for the whole family. She'd spoil it all if she saw, he claimed."

"I never heard her called 'the sly Cora.' "

"Well, he said he named her that because she was so full of mischief, always up to something."

"My mother? Are you sure?"

"He told me a story about when they taught school together up at Tipton. She taught Spanish and English and he taught science and geography and math. He had in mind to show his science class about Benjamin Franklin's kite, how it discovered electricity. He didn't have any cloth to make a kite with, so she offered to make one for him out of an old petticoat that had gone to rags. But she sewed firecrackers into the sides of it and braided a long fuse into the tail. Then when she was holding the kite for him to get a running start to make it fly, she lit that tail fuse, and when the kite was in the air, it blew all to ruin. Four or five times he told Royal and me that story and laughed himself red in the face every time. He said he wished he could dream up a sweet prank like that and he thought maybe he would make that his life's ambition. . . . Those were his very words, 'sweet prank.' "

"I seem to remember hearing that story."

"Do you think it's true?"

The kite story had passed from the realm of family reminiscence into folklore and looked now as if it were on its way to epic status. I'd heard it from my mother and father and grandmother, from aunts and uncles, from friends, acquaintances, and rank strangers. There were many versions of the tale, sometimes similar, sometimes exotically different. Any one of them had proved an adequate hour-killer down at the old community gossip post, Virgil Campbell's Bound for Hell Gro. and Dry Goods. Now Mr. Campbell had passed away and his establishment had turned into a consignment clothing shop, but the story of the kite still lived on and bade fair to survive us all.

When I tried to answer the question, it was no longer a simple one; she was requiring me to measure the amount of historical truth in a myth. So I ducked the issue. "I think it's true enough for its purpose," I said.

She turned to the matter at hand. "Your sister told me that you were going to sort out your daddy's workshop downstairs and clean it up. That might take a bit of doing. I've only been inside a couple of times, but there's a lot of clutter."

"I'll just sort things out a little. We'll hire someone to come in and finish cleaning up. I won't be around here long enough for that."

She nodded. "I understand that you teach at the Woman's College down in Greensboro."

"Yes—only they don't call it that anymore. I suppose Mitzi told you about me."

"Oh my," she said, "where are my manners? I didn't introduce myself. I'm Dilly Elden."

I took her proferred hand and bowed. "J. Edgar Hoover, at your service, ma'am."

She smiled. "I can see you've got some of your daddy in you. I'm glad of that. He was an awful good friend to us."

"Sounds like you miss him."

"I miss him being downstairs. He'd almost always stop by for a chat before he went down to do whatever he was working on. We've never been too busy in here. He and Royal used to talk about clocks by the hour. He knew all about them. Must have been quite a collector."

"I don't think he collected them, but I'm not surprised at his interest. He loved mechanisms. Did he ever repair any of these clocks for you?"

"Oh, no." She spoke in a solemn tone. "He had other business in hand. After we talked for a while, he'd go downstairs and be as quiet as a mouse. Except for that one time."

"How's that?"

"There was one space of time we heard explosions. This is going back about twelve years now."

"Explosions?"

"Well . . . not really. More like noisy firecrackers."

"How long did it last?"

"Not long. Maybe a week. When I asked him what in the world he was up to, he laughed and said he was conducting experiments."

"Did he say what kind?"

She hesitated. "Something about the . . . propulsion of projectiles and . . . Something else. I can't put tongue to it right this minute."

"Sounds scary."

"No. Joe Robert wouldn't do anything so risky it would endanger our business. It was something about projectiles and—"

"Rockets?" I asked. "He was a real fan of Robert Goddard."

"Dessert tarts," she said. "The propulsion of projectiles and the ballistics of dessert tarts."

"The pro—"

She nodded emphatically and with a trace of pride. "I remember it now. I made him say it five or six times. The propulsion of projectiles and the ballistics of dessert tarts."

"Very mysterious."

"Well, your daddy had his secrets, but I wouldn't call him a mysterious person. Anybody could read him like a book."

"I couldn't."

She gave me another keen glance. I could tell that my confession surprised and puzzled her, but she was too well mannered to pursue the topic. Instead, she offered to show me around Times Past. "If you like clocks, there might be some things to interest you."

"I'd love to see, but I'd better get started with the workshop. I don't know what might be waiting on me down there. I'll come back up after a while."

"Maybe I'll brew a pot of tea. Do you like tea?"

"You're very kind," I said. "I look forward to that."

She reminded me how to find the outside steps to the basement at the west end of the porch. "Do you have a key? I hope so, because I couldn't help you if you didn't. Your daddy never gave me one."

I produced the big ring with its array of hardware and shook it to make it clatter.

"Oh my," she said. "I saw you carrying that but didn't know what it was for. Do you know which is the right one?"

"It'll have to be trial and error, I'm afraid."

"He must have had a lot of doors to open."

"Nobody knows how many," I said.

The wooden stairs leading down were sagging but sturdy. It was the peeled-pole railing that needed replacement, the tenons sprained and the nail holes splitting. A lush meadow stretched from the lower wall of the building out toward a gravel road a half mile distant, the expanse creased darkly in the middle by a small stream. Bee balm and tall daisies and nodding Queen Anne's lace spotted the greenery and the sunlight gleamed in it and all the meadow folded and unfolded in the gentle breeze.

There were a couple of somber windows milky with cobweb in the concrete-block wall, but I could see nothing when I shaded my eyes and tried to peer through. The door lock was no special gadget, just an ordinary Yale with its U-bar through a hasp secured with wood screws. But my clattery ring of keys held at least a dozen Yales, and I tried nine before coming upon the one that clicked the reluctant lock open.

I pushed the door slowly and the musty smell of desertion washed over me instantly. When I stepped inside, I was met by an impression expectable, almost comforting, and I regretted that my feet on the gritty concrete floor made an intrusive grinding noise. It was all dust and dull disuse, but I imagined for a moment that I could smell traces of Prince Albert smoke and JFG coffee grounds and denim trousers and wet wool and corduroy. This room was his kingdom and those were the characteristic smells of my father wherever he traveled, night or day.

The switch by the door cut on two of the three naked bulbs overhead, shedding a dim yellow glow upon the clutter. The prospect was, at first glance, pretty much what I'd expected. There was a long workbench against the far wall, with shelves under the countertop; a rickety doorless kitchen cabinet stood on the other side. Boards laid across three sawhorses made a bench against the left-hand wall and this makeshift structure supported maybe two dozen terra-cotta pots holding pitiable remains of flowers. On flimsy cane-pole racks overhead, stalks of weeds and herbs lay shriveled almost to dust. To the right was a beat-up rolltop writing desk and four card tables standing nearby; on them sat old radios, coffeepots, ashtrays, ceramic coffee cups, notebooks, fanned-out or precariously stacked sheaves of scribbled pages, and books, books, books. Before the desk sat a sturdy rectangular steamer trunk, its edges lined with steel molding. The two iron support posts in the center of the room were accoutred with pencil sharpeners.

Idly, without a thought in my mind, I opened a cardboard folder that lay on one of the card tables. Dust flew into my nose from the breezelet and I snuffled. Inside were a few badly typed pages clipped together. "Last Will and Testament" was printed in faint pencil at the top of the first page, but it was not actually a legal document, as I realized when I read a little way into it. This was another sort of writing altogether; the true legal will had been made out in lawyer Schulman's office and had been probated and had endured all the clerical indignities that are visited upon such papers. The sheaf in my hands was of a much more personal nature.

I stood gazing at it for a long time before putting it back in its folder and setting it aside to be taken, along with his notebooks and other material, back to my motel room for closer inspection. Then a hurt surged up in me and broke over my thoughts in a cresting of unshed tears. I had to sit down in an unsteady metal folding chair and I dropped my chin to my chest, as if I sat in prayer. But I was not praying. How is it possible for us to miss our loved ones so continually that we get used to the ache of loss? That is what had happened to me, but now and again there were particular sudden moments of sorrow that hurt like saw teeth across a careless thumb. This was such a moment, here with all these things that had been my father's and that now gave my drab feelings images to cling to.

The intensity of these feelings surprised me. It had been ten years since he died, but at times it seemed but a brief few months. There was a period, four years ago, when my sense of loss had diminished and the vividness of his memory had dimmed. But lately, both had returned with fresh force and I felt sometimes that he had zoomed off the planet for only a short while and was expected back at any moment. Mrs. Elden spoke of him that way, too, and so did some others I talked with. For my mother, no time had passed; her sadness was as keen as if he had been buried only last week.

I walked it off. At first, I only paced from wall to wall, wandering without purpose, loitering before tables, benches, and cabinets without seeing what was there. Then the room overpowered me and for relief I went to the open door and gazed out into the sunlit meadow.

The hour was mirror-bright; from weed to weed drifted butterflies yellow and white, and birds throbbed and warbled. All
quick and present life was out there, vibrant and urgent. The
life inside the dark room behind was imbued with a graver
tone, but it *was* life, unmistakably. The past is never obliter-
ated; it has a patient, enduring existence where it collects like
groundwater in holes and crevices and hidden lodgments—in
attics and basements, in sealed trunks and stubborn drawers,
in closets and pockets and in cardboard folders. In these places,
its visible colors are bland, but its secret strength gathers like
thunderheads.

I turned away from the daylight and began to look about
the room. The objects that met my eye were mere lumps of
matter because at first my sorrow prevented my seeing them.
After a time, they began to shape to identities, some familiar,
some new to me. Ashtrays were scattered around, heaped with
pipe dottle, and red cans of Prince Albert stood sentinel beside
them, along with fragile booklets of cigarette papers. Cracked
teacups were mounded with small bolts and screws; jars were
filled with sorted nails. Balls of string and twine, tape mea-
sures, a Mickey Mouse alarm clock, a tangle of fish hooks, a
Boker pocketknife and a hawksbill, a belt of rattlesnake hide:
the ordinary gimcrackery of a restless masculine imagination.

Other items were more telling. A spacious corner of the saw-
horse bench was crowded with Cherokee artifacts, pots and
shards and birds carved from walnut and cherry wood, a heap
of quartz arrowheads, rose and yellow. My father admired the
Cherokee Nation immensely; in fact, he was a little daft on the
subject of Indians. I recalled how on our long Sunday drives
through Jackson or Cherokee County he would spot a fellow
taking the air out on his cabin porch. Nothing could stop him
from bouncing our clumsy station wagon through the ruts and
mud holes, splashing to a stop before the house. He would
dismount and hold long converse with some ancient Cherokee
paterfamilias. Often blind, these old gentlemen were always
imperturbably polite; they remained calm and grave in the face

of his excited questions and did their level best to assuage his curiosity. But this was difficult, given the nature of his most earnest queries. My father believed that the people of the nation held the keys to the secrets of life, that they were immersed in a wisdom taken directly from nature, imbibed through the pores, as it were. He would set them cosmic conundrums while my mother and sister and I sat in the station wagon, squirming with impatience and red embarrassment.

I recalled that on one occasion he returned to the wagon looking dolefully let down. "You know," he said, "I don't believe that fellow is full-blood Cherokee. I asked him where dreams come from and what they mean and he said he didn't know." He was disconsolate as he wrestled the car around and headed back toward the highway, muttering. "Probably he just didn't want to tell me—and the way we whites have treated them, I don't blame him."

So I could have predicted this cache of Indian artifacts as well as the photographs of rockets fixed to the concrete-block walls with masking tape and the books about space travel by Willy Ley and Arthur C. Clarke. The rocket photos were glossy glamour jobs, dramatic shots of mankind's last noble aspiration—that was my father's phrase for the enterprise of space exploration. Here were the primeval *Hermes A-2*, the stubby *Atlas* that followed soon after; here were the hapless *Vanguard*, the ugly *Vostok*, the powerful *Saturn*, the classy *Voyager*s, the heroic *Apollo* 7. Amid these supermodern images was a dearly old-fashioned one, a crinkled magazine engraving of Benjamin Franklin sailing his silken kite, touching his finger to an enormous door key while deadly lightning jagged the heavens. I had seen this picture before; it had occupied a place of honor in each of his workshops. Beside the engraving of Franklin was stuck a French postcard that showed the funerary monument of Jules Verne in Amiens, the famous image of the science fiction writer conquering death, as he struggled to ascend once more toward the skies.

Then there were the notebooks, more than a score of ordinary spiral-bound copybooks with yellow, red, and blue covers. I opened three of them to what I thought at first were pages and pages of secret code, though more thoughtful examination revealed them as genetic charts. He must have been trying, on the evidence at hand, to breed a new hybrid of geranium. Now the stalks were black and withered in the pots, the soil dried and cracked.

Another fattish notebook intrigued me with the letter *F* marked on the blue cover with black crayon. It carried a title page written in his firm businesslike hand: "The Thoughts of Fugio." Here was a collection of maxims, epigrams, mottoes, and proverbs, and as I turned the pages, I wondered what sources he had plundered to discover them. Some of them were couched in language almost Augustan in tone, while others had to be of recent origin, since they used modern topical terms. I decided, with astonished excitement, that these sentences were original with my father; I was looking at genuine specimens of his creative impulse. Nothing could have delighted me more. *Fugio*—in Latin, "I flee." I took the word to refer to this workshop, to this notebook and the others, to the hours he had spent here over a period of twenty-one years, in retreat from his daily tasks and humdrum responsibilities.

These aphoristic lines must be fair copy taken from foul manuscript, I thought, because there were no cancellations, no crossed-out words or phrases, no misspellings, no errors in sentence construction. Every word was set down neatly, sharply. "Life is an elegant sufficiency; eternity a wishful superfluity." "Well Begun, Half-Done; Halfhearted Never Started." "Befriend the End." "Make the passing shadow serve thy will." "I tell time, but it does not reply." "Dies Light, Die all; No man knows when."

There were thirty pages of this stuff, and he had set himself stern limits. Few sayings took up more than one line and none more than three. Curious about the final sentence he had penned, I flipped to the last page. The thought was unfinished: "Thought is to time as . . ." Was this not evidence that I held in my hands the original and no copy at all? He had not transcribed his sentences, but composed them as he went, choosing one word at a time, as pensive and deliberate as a stonemason selecting the next smooth river rock to set in his wall.

I laid the notebook down reverently. I could never have expected to find so rich a trove of my father's thinking. I'd never known him to put anything on paper but the most necessary business documentation. Here were laid out his private ideas and feelings. I felt a lovely gratitude—not toward him, because he wouldn't have known I'd ever see these pages, but toward the circumstances that brought me to find them, toward, I suppose, the Fates.

On the card table lay a thick packet of letters bound with a red ribbon faded to pink. They were all in his hand and addressed to my mother at an address in San Francisco. The postmarks dated from a single period of about six weeks, a time I recognized as one when my mother had visited her brother, my uncle Luden, to try to help him through one of his rougher passages. That was a month of some importance in my memory.

My father and I had been left lonesome in the white house down the hill from my grandmother's house. We made out the best we could, inexpert as bachelors and missing my mother sorely. My father looked forward to her return so eagerly that he had planned a splendid celebration; he would construct a bridge, handsome and elaborate, to span the small creek that ran between our lawn and the vegetable garden. It was the genuine article, an arched bridge with rose trellis entrances, to be whitewashed till it shone like a table knife. We had labored with painstaking pride and had looked upon the finished work as a statement of enduring love.

But time is no friend to love. The bridge had been swept ruinously away when person or persons unknown opened the floodgates of a reservoir on the hill above our little holler. The overspill from the Challenger Paper and Fiber Company destroyed our visionary gift in a single violent moment. "Bas-

tards!'' my father cried out. ''Those bastards!'' He never for-
gave the dark satanic paper mill and told me many times, not
long before his death, that he was still intent on a juicy revenge, still planning and scheming.

From the bundle of San Francisco letters, I extracted a single
example, opened the brittle envelope carefully, and slid the
missive out. I read a couple of lines then put it back. However
original, even eccentric, my father may have been in some
respects, in his protestations of devotion to his young wife, he
was humbly conventional. This fact pleased me but caused me
to feel that reading further would be unseemly.

Included in the packet of letters was a loose newspaper clipping, which, because it was so innocuous, was utterly baffling
in this context. It was merely a head shot of a bespectacled,
placid-looking man with a brief caption beneath. The clipping
evidently was taken from the Tipton newspaper, *The Mountain
Voice*, because the caption informed me that T. J. Wesson, an
engineer in the Water Control Division, was retiring after
twenty-eight years' service with the Challenger Paper and Fiber Company. But someone—it must have been my father—
had drawn a black ballpoint circle around Mr. Wesson's head
and disfigured his face with crosshairs. My father had got this
gentleman centered in his rifle sights and I wondered why. Had
he been a rival for my mother's affections? Why else would
his picture have been included among the love letters? I
scratched my head in puzzlement.

More predictable were the books tumbled about: old math
and chemistry and physics texts for high school and college, a
1948 issue of *Life*, which must have dated from about the time
he opened this workshop, an array of rose manuals, a *Boy Scout
Handbook* and a *Bluejacket's Manual*, some engineering text-
books, mechanical and electrical.

But then there was a musty Arden edition of *Twelfth Night*,
forest green but splotched with mildew. I recognized it as one
of my mother's teaching texts, but it must have come into his
possession, for when I opened it, the annotations were in my

father's hand. I flipped through them with only gentle interest until I touched one that struck me dumbfounded. In the margin beside the happy scene where Sir Andrew Aguecheek and Sir Toby Belch tope and confabulate, he had scribbled, "Pythagoras. See *Fred Chappell's* scheme!"

I looked about for copies of my books, *River, Bloodfire,* and *Wind Mountain,* but they were not here. Nevertheless, my father had read them; his notes in the Shakespeare proved as much. And he had not glanced through them casually, but had grasped my plan of organizing each volume around one of the four Pythagorean elements—water, fire, earth, and air. These days, I was at work on the concluding volume, *Earthsleep,* and finding it a difficult way to trace. Would I now feel his glance over my shoulder when I sat down in my lonely motel room to compose?

Yes.

But didn't I always feel that intimidating gaze upon me whenever I wrote, the invisible presences in the room of my father and mother, my aunts and uncles, my grandmother and all the community of our common mountaineer history?

Yes.

Other books: a large, badly illustrated Bible with a concordance in the back, histories of gardening, well-thumbed biographies of Charles Darwin and Isambard Kingdom Brunel, a dilapidated copy of *Origin of Species,* a history of rose culture, and three volumes of Rick Brant's Electronic Adventures by John Blaine: *The Rocket's Shadow, Sea Gold,* and *100 Fathoms Under.* These latter books had belonged to me when I was a wide-eyed youngun; I wondered if my father had preserved them out of nostalgia or whether he found intrinsic interest in them. He was never beyond reading books favored by the young. A tatterdemalion copy of *Robinson Crusoe* testified to that interest.

There was a leatherette photograph album with thick black pages. Rubbing the dust off, I opened it and found but two pictures. The first was a darkening Brownie shot of a handsome young man in military uniform. He stood stiff, with a shy arm around my mother's shoulder; she looked pleased by the gesture. Before this pair, Mitzi and I were ranked, small, fidgety, squinting into uncomfortable sunlight.

I remembered the soldier. Johnson Gibbs had been rescued from abusive parents to come and live with us on the farm, to become one of us forever. My father must have taken this picture of the tall, blondish, red-faced young man so obviously proud before the camera. He lived with us until he was eighteen years old and then marched away to the army.

His photo also appeared on the next album page, but it was only a standard military head shot above a newspaper column. The story below it gave some sparse details of his death in a training accident at Fort Bragg. A mortar round had fallen short and taken his life, while wounding six other soldiers only slightly. After this page with its pasted-in clipping, the rest were empty, as black as interstellar void.

Other tables, other memories:

Here lay a pair of child's boxing gloves, the reddish leather moldy and wrinkled; there was a scatter of farm tools—hames, strap buckles, clevises, ring bolts, and such; here was one of Mitzi's blue plastic barrettes, there a cup and saucer from her toy tea set. A baseball scarred and chipped and brown from rough usage and clay smudge recalled Johnson Gibbs's legendary misadventures on the mound, but a half-naked tennis ball that looked as if it had been scorched over a campfire evoked no memories at all. It was a puzzling object, almost as puzzling as the contraption it lay beside.

This was an ungainly mechanism constructed of blue-black stovepipe metal, the joints tightly crimped together. It looked something like a miniature cannon except that its mouth pointed straight up toward the ceiling. The base had been wrapped around a Y-joint of terra-cotta pipe and this had been carefully chipped away so that the tail of the inverted Y protruded into the cannon barrel. The front part of this section was broken open for access, like the opening of a kiln or furnace, and in fact the terra-cotta and the wood of the table beneath showed signs of some slight charring.

Beside this contraption, a notebook lay open to a baffling diagram. Was it an explanation of the machine? There was a plethora of drawn arrows and dotted lines and it seemed that some round object, maybe a basketball, was supposed to roll along a chute. From the end of the chute, it was to drop for some distance onto a lever, causing the other end to fly up and bring down a brick weight that would set off a series of triggers. Rube Goldberg would have been proud of the design. The purpose of all these interacting gizmos was to cause a rounded disk to leap into the air, turn over three times, and propel itself full-face forward toward what looked like a chess piece, a knight in armor astride a prancing horse. It didn't make sense to me, and the fact that my father had drawn a big black question mark beside the diagram indicated that he was doubtful of its efficacy. But the final reason for the gadget, I couldn't figure.

I found a photograph of my mother. She wore a tam-o'-shanter aslant and a plaid jacket with large checks. Her face was the same pert little oval it was now, only unravaged by time and illness. The picture must have been taken in the late 1920s. There was always something mischievous in her expression. Had she enjoyed, even then, making mild trouble for others? The picture was framed in heavy silver, so I had to wonder why it was stuck away in a drawer. Why had my father not displayed it proudly in full sight?

Then I considered that this workshop had been my father's serious retreat from business responsibilities, his Merlin's cave, where as boy wizard he had played hooky from the dire dull duties that my mother represented. She had stood as symbol of adult business for Johnson Gibbs and my father in the old times and nowadays for me and even for Mitzi. Her own mother, my grandmother, had recognized this officiousness in her and would smile gravely. My father had loved my mother, of course he had loved her, but why should he have let her photograph spoil the fun of his hideaway?

In another drawer were melancholy, gaudy postcards from distant strands. I thumbed through them carelessly, recognizing only a few of the correspondents. Uncle Luden had sent one from Reno; he proved luckless at poker but hoped for better fortune from the slots. Here in crooked tall printed letters was my own brief message from summer camp; I reported that I was having a good time. Now I wondered if that bulletin had been true. My father's old crony, Virgil Campbell, had posted one of Sally Rand holding an oversized bubble; he complained that Chicago was not all it was cracked up to be in the matter of good drinking whiskey.

Mr. Campbell's postcard lay on top of a faded red sheet of paper covered with blotchy mimeography. It looked to be an amateurish advertisement or prospectus of some sort, for across the top was lettered the legend SATANIC ENTERPRISES AMALGAMATED and below this was a crude little sketch of a devil's head enclosed in a wobbly cartouche. I read the text that followed:

Fight it though they may, SIN is the HOT investment property for the worldly-wise investor who desires to gather investment income from a SURE THING.

Many people have invested for many years in scattered and separate aspects of Sin, but there has never before been opportunity to invest in all the Sins at one time under a single corporate plan.

The efficiency of this approach is self-evident, but until now no one has thought of trying it.

SATANIC ENTERPRISES AMALGAMATED fills the gap. Your success as an investor is assured, for SIN NEVER GOES OUT OF STYLE. Worldwide depressions, revolutions, wars, famines, plagues—nothing slows down the public demand for SIN. As an investor in SEA, return on your capital is GUARANTEED. You cannot lose money! And you stand an excellent chance of MAKING A KILLING!

SEA has offices in Paris, France; Tijuana, Mexico; Las Vegas, Nevada; New Orleans, Louisiana; and Tipton, North Carolina. Naturally, its actual address and the names of its officers and employees have to remain *secret,* but THIS IS THE REAL McCOY.

SEA guarantees that a single modest investment will help to finance ventures in the following Sins and MANY, MANY MORE!

- adultery
- buggery
- cannibalism
- demonolatry
- embezzlement
- fanny pinching
- heroin
- idol worship
- Jansenism
- kept women
- lottery rigging
- murder
- nepotism
- oneiromancy
- pickpocketry
- quackery
- racketeering
- stealing
- tax fraud
- usury
- vice
- wife beating
- xenophobia
- yellow journalism
- Zoroastrianism

For obvious reasons, checks cannot be accepted. Send cash in the amount you wish to invest to:

> SEA Corporation
> Box 182
> Tipton, North Carolina

Remember! Your investment is GUARANTEED!!!

This prospectus must have been one of my father's sillier jokes, I decided. Surely no one could take the thing halfway seriously without being sunk in depthless ignorance and overwhelming greed. What possible monetary gain could be gotten from Jansenism, oneiromancy, wife beating, and Zoroastrianism? My surmise as to its authorship was confirmed by a marginal note in my father's handwriting. In parentheses next to the term *xenophobia*, he had scribbled "(especially *Uncle* Zeno-phobia!)."

I slid the red sheet back into the drawer and moved on.

Leaning into a far corner was a cardboard tube about three feet long. I'd taken it to be a fishing-rod case, but it didn't look sturdy enough now that I saw it more closely. Inside was a rolled square of oilcloth, clean and pliant. Upon it was drawn a map in an amateur hand, a schema in India ink but with various symbols in colored inks.

It, too, was the work of my father. He had traced in the shapes of the mountains and areas of forest with a solemn naïveté. Through this rural landscape meandered a double line with multitudinous twists and turns, hairpin curves and switchbacks and tributary divagations. Here, I decided, was a river with a road that ran beside it. I knew the area depicted. The river flowed through the tangled mountains of western North Carolina into Tennessee, and the names of the three large areas gave me to know I was looking at a map of the western part of Hardison County with its local informal divisions: Downhill, Vestibule, and Upward.

Inside each of these three large areas were designated four points of interest, each given two names, a place name and the proper name of a person. I recognized such place names as Glutton Field, Sassiefat, Honey Cove, and Truelove, but none of the personal names was familiar to me. Schematized, the series of names presented this array:

DOWNHILL	VESTIBULE	UPWARD
Mrs. Sinkins	Frances Shaylor	Susan Louise
(Bailey Ridge)	(Sassiefat)	(Dinnerbell)

Annie Laurie (Lazybones)	Martha Flandry (Irongant)	Mrs. Mawley (Stoutman)
Bess Lovett (Glutton Field)	Julia Mannering (Featherbed)	Helen Wilson (Easy)
Betty Uprichard (Proudvale)	Marie A. (Honey Cove)	Jane Smith (Peace)
	Gold Mine (Truelove)	

The larger topography of Hardison County was familiar to me. Here was Forgetful River with the gravel road that ran beside it. Below the point farthest east, Truelove, was a place near the top of the mountain called Peace, and not far from it was Truelove and there the last proper name, Gold Mine, was marked with a red *X*. Other places had dots of different-colored inks as markers—peach, pink, cerise, white, yellow. The color for Gold Mine was a splotch of shiny gold paint hardened to a button.

I looked at what I held in my hands and my mind leapt immediately to a conclusion so silly, I had to giggle. Was not this childish map my father's little black book, his dating agenda? What could it be but a geography of the frolicsome ladies of Hardison, females ready and willing to slip on the grass green frock? I tried to shove this far-fetched notion away, but it wouldn't budge. I racked my stunned brain for another hypothesis, but it was too late—my first hypothesis had already taken strong root. I read the map again, from one side to the other, top to bottom, but except for the name Gold Mine, it could be nothing but a list of women and their residences.

Maybe even Gold Mine was a private nickname or endearment, signifying the apex of the amorous experiences Hardison had to offer, the sexual jackpot, so to speak.

All right, Jess, settle down, I thought. Pinch yourself awake. This idiotic theory your horny little mind has spawned does not square at any point with what you know about your father. Joe Robert Kirkman was as shy about sexual matters as any ten-year-old tomboy. At least in public he was. Could I actually convince myself that my father had been unfaithful to my mother in such an outsized, Paul Bunyanesque fashion? And if he had been a backwoods Lothario of such (ahem) enviable proportions, how was I to feel about that? Proud? Ashamed? Or merely amazed?

It was easy to decide not to tell my mother I had found this map. An investigation was needed to determine its true nature. Maybe I never would tell her.

Once again, my father was too many for me, the elusive fox I had pursued all my life with no real hope of bringing to earth.

I rolled up the map—slowly, carefully—and slid it back into the tube. Looking around the room, I decided what I would take away with me—the map first of all, and then as many of the notebooks as seemed helpful, including especially "The Thoughts of Fugio," and a sheaf of the loose-leaf diagrams and drawings. I needed a container for these and spotted a rectangular box of heavy cardboard crammed into an undershelf of a workbench. It was empty and clean enough on the inside, though coated thickly with dust on the outside. I brushed it off and saw that the box was space black, with silver edging along the corners and with a small insignia embossed into the top. This latter was a golden streaking comet set against a square of silver. It must have held a child's costume, a play space uniform. Elegantly printed by the comet symbol were the words *Galactic Patrol*. Again, I was mystified, being pretty certain that I'd never possessed such an outfit. And yet I almost remembered it. It was as if I'd dreamed of it or seen it in a catalog when I was eight or nine years old. Or perhaps I'd seen it in a shop window. I felt like I was trying to recall something that had happened in the future instead of the past. Maybe it had belonged to Mitzi, though it was hardly the sort of fantasy she'd preferred, all tea parties with her dolls and Nurse Cherry

Ames, with an occasional foray into the illogical universe of Nancy Drew.

All the rest of the stuff could be boxed and stored and I would later make a more leisurely and formal inventory. But I would report my present findings—most of them, anyhow— to my mother and sister. Then we could discuss what to do with them piece by piece.

Mitzi, for all her canny business sense, was sentimental at heart and would probably wish to conserve everything, all the precious memories. But my mother might well decide to discard almost all of it. Lately, she, who had always been proud of her possessions, had taken to decrying *things,* pronouncing the word as if it carried some stigma of the sacrilegious. She thought she wanted to meet eternity unencumbered.

As for me—well, I had changed my mind. At first, I'd thought it would be a grand thing to leave this workshop just as my father had left it, as a sort of museum. It had already stood here for three decades, a place where one could read with these objects an autobiography of my father's spirit. His was a soul that could imbue such insignificant paraphernalia with personality. But now I knew his soul had different qualities than I'd been aware of, and there might be parts of his life better left secret for a while.

Even so, there was a lot of mere detritus here: empty cartons, broken tools, dead flowers and dessicated herbs, cracked flowerpots, scraps of lumber, and so forth. I began to work in earnest and shifted this refuse into a heap beside the doorway, snuffling and sneezing and dirtying my clothes thoroughly. I tried to organize some of the other stuff, stacking the garden manuals in one place, the rose books in another, the juvenile fiction in a third. I let the stovepipe-ceramic Engine of Unguessable Purpose stand where it was, a visible reminder of all the puzzles I had plunged into down here.

This donkey labor took the better part of two hours and morning had leaked past noon. I gathered the notebooks into a carton and shouldered it. With one last studious estimate of the room, I sighed, and my emotions grew so intense and yet remained so scattered, I could not name them all. Perhaps longing was the most powerful. But I took a long, dusty breath of resolve and removed from these shadows into the bright June day and its vivid murmurings. I set the box down so I could lock the door behind me.

The carton I deposited in Buttercup before I kept my promise and returned for a tour of Times Past. Even though I was pre-pared for the sound of the shop, it still surprised me with its totality. To enter here from the swarming daylight was to travel from an organic world to a mechanical universe in which the smells were dry and indefinable, where sound was delivered only in small packets, where time slowed and be-came palpable.

Mrs. Elden came to meet me, smiling softly. "Well," she said, "I can see you've started on your task."

"I made a little progress."

"There's a washroom over in that corner, if you'd care to clean up. I'll put the water on to boil for our tea."

After I had washed my hands and face and tidied my clothes, she gave me the tour, guiding me along the solemn aisles and counters. It was clear that she took a solid pride in her shop, though it could not have been among the most profitable of businesses.

"These are reproductions," she explained, "almost all of them. We do have four originals I'd like for you to see. But all of them are interesting if you like clocks. Do you?"

"I've never thought much about them."

"I never gave them a moment's consideration till my hus-band got interested. He was ready to retire from being the head mechanic in an automotive shop; he'd gotten sick of all the banging and grinding. It had affected his hearing. 'Dilly,' he told me, 'I'm going to get into some line that is peaceful and quiet. So drive carefully. If you dent a fender, it'll have to stay dented. I'll never lift a hand to it.' Clocks he thought of as peace and quiet. So we got some books—a lot of books—and read all about them and opened up Times Past together.''

"These are handsome machines."

"Thank you." When she pointed out an English tall clock after a design by Daniel Quare, I had to ask how to spell his name. "He was a famous clock maker," she said. "One of the best. The original would date to about 1700." Then she showed me a small French fusee clock with its innards behind glass, all exposed to my ignorant gaze. Then came all sorts: tall clocks, shelf clocks, grandfathers, grandmothers, swords and light-houses, clocks of every heritage—Flemish, Spanish, German, Shaker, Japanese. The great makers were represented in re-production: Ezekiel Jones, Simon Willard, David Rittenhouse, John Schmidt, and that mysterious fabricator, Preserved Jones of Providence, Rhode Island. I made what I hoped were ap-propriate noises of admiration.

But she noticed my bewilderment. "Oh, I don't mean to bore you. Your daddy took such a keen fancy, I thought you might be interested, too. He used a ten-dollar name. 'Horologes,' he called them."

"I'm interested—but just too unlearned. I don't know how to appreciate what I'm seeing."

She nodded gravely. "I was that way myself at first. But when I studied up, it was different. . . . Oh, I hear the kettle singing. Let me go pour up."

I followed her into her little office with its hot plate and telephone and filing cabinet and enviably orderly desk. The only timepiece in here was an electric wall clock, and she caught me looking at it in surprise.

"That's what I set the others by," she explained. "You prob-ably noticed that I set them all for the same time. No other clock shop does that."

"I had noticed, but—"

"Let me show you one more, the pride of the shop." She poured up the tea and we went out to a farther aisle near the front of the store. "Royal never would tell me how he managed to get hold of it. Probably he didn't want me to know how much he had to pay." She pointed out the features of a long mahogany wall clock I could recognize as being exceptionally handsome. "It's called a banjo clock and we're pretty sure that it was made by Eli Terry in Connecticut, probably around 1810. He was very painstaking and usually built tall clocks. A Terry banjo is very unusual." She described what I was inspecting, the wood, the chasing, the spandrels, and the delicate painted enamel cartouche with its peaceful shepherd and comely shepherdess.

"What a fine piece!" I said. "How much is it worth?"

Her smile was wryly melancholy. "Only what I can get for it. I'd love to find a buyer for this item. I don't want to keep originals, since I can't trust anybody local to repair them. It's better for me to stick with reproductions. There don't seem to be many serious collectors in these parts."

She led me back to the office and handed me a cup of tea. I'd expected it to be mild herbal stuff, but it was a brew as black as a shoe sole and it gave off a powerful aroma.

"Couldn't you advertise for a buyer?"

"Yes. But I don't know how much to ask for it. The antiques business is a trickier one than you might think. I don't want somebody taking advantage of me."

"I hadn't imagined. It seems such a classy trade."

"Reproductions are all that folks in these parts really want. Just pieces they can show off and talk about—but not like Royal and your daddy. That pair could spend hours discussing escapements and slave pendulums and crown wheels and so on. I'd get a little dizzy listening to them."

"My father liked most things mechanical."

"Well now, I might disagree with you just a little bit. He said that a clock was not his ideal horologe. He was very deliberate on that point."

"What did he call it? 'Ideal—' "

"Not his 'ideal horologe,' he said. He told us that a proper way of keeping time had to be more than mechanical. It ought to be a living thing, connected with the cosmos."

"Sounds pretty wild."

"Every time Joe Robert started talking about his 'sympathetic horologe' with its 'sidereal correspondences and principles of vitalism,' Royal and I would look at each other and wink. We didn't understand what he was going on about. Still, your daddy was a smart man. I think he had a deep, secret plan. He believed in different times at once."

"How's that?"

"I don't know what I mean," she said, and drew her shoulders inward and looked wistfully into my face. "That is, I don't know what your father meant. He said that people, all of us, lived more than one life at a time. We lived on many different time tracks at the same time but only knew one at a time. But each life affected all the others a little bit. He said it was like plucking one guitar string. The others would vibrate slightly if you did that."

"Sympathetic resonance," I ventured.

She nodded. "Yes—like his 'sympathetic horologe.' When that was complete, it would enable us to live two or more lives at the same time. One day when I was so blue after Royal died, he told me not to be too sad, that we'd all meet again in 1949. When I reminded him it was already 1961, he said, 'Yes, and we'll meet both times eight years from now.' From 1961, he meant."

I confessed to being utterly and completely baffled.

"I'm sure I didn't explain it correctly. Royal and I would tease him, but what he said almost made good sense while he was talking. Later on, when you tried to figure it out, you couldn't. I think it all depended on his 'ideal horologe.' You can be sure he had something in mind."

"I expect you're right about that. He was an inveterate schemer and an incurable dreamer." I thought of the objects in the workshop below and of the objects piled in my car; I thought of the awkward map with its roll call of females.

Then there was the sound of a striker on a bell. After a suspenseful pause, it was answered by other clock tones of every pitch and timbre, chesty grandfathers, tenor banjos, tinkling shelf clocks. *One. One. One one one one.* It seemed to take a long time, and after the last one had sounded, the air hummed with overtones. I could feel the echoes on my skin.

She smiled at my expression. "It's quite a noise, isn't it? You ought to hear them boom out at twelve. I keep them set for the same time, just to remind me."

"I see," I said, and went on to make my manners, preparing to depart.

"Because the hours are so slow, I want to mark them off. At my age, they're supposed to just fly past, but they don't. They get longer and longer every day. When Royal was alive, they were shorter."

I nodded and said good-bye. "Thank you for the tea. Thanks for everything. You've been very hospitable."

"I hope you'll come back to see me when you return to the basement. It's been good to remember Joe Robert and the old times. I'm not as busy here as I'd like to be."

"I'll stop in again. Good-bye."

"Good-bye," she said.

I went out and stood in the sunlight, blinking my eyes at the brightness. I thought how we all have our rituals of remembrance, probably many we're not even aware of. Dilly Elden set all her clocks to strike at once; it brought her lost Royal to her mind. I was collecting my father's leavings, reading his words, tracing his routes. I was pursuing the image of his spirit, a diminishing image, through a wilderness of time-tangled shadows.

Chapter Four

AT THE GRAVE

OF VIRGIL CAMPBELL

Every hour is another syllable in your epitaph.
—Fugio

I woke at 8:30 and spent a dull hour bathing, shaving, and groaning before heading into the dime-bright day to break my fast. My Holiday Inn was on the southern outskirts of Asheville, gaudily embedded in an ordinary strip of gas stations, burger joints, and convenience stores, so that the food in my immediate vicinity did not entice me and I decided to motor into the city. I drove up Biltmore Avenue, taking note of an environment that was in some ways familiar but in other ways strange to me. This side of town illustrated clearly what most of Asheville had become—a mixture of old and new, of the seemingly permanent and the obviously impermanent. Here was a mélange of small business firms, some of them looking down-at-heel and clinging to musty hopes, while next door might be a spiffy architectural firm with gold lettering on its frosted-glass door. Chlorinated beer joints, antique clothing shops, upscale art galleries—Artsy-Fartsy nudging cozy shoulders with Drunk Funk. The same principle seemed to hold in the Blue Luna Coffee Shop, where I had decided to take breakfast: Sober businessmen, chattery gallery habitués, and smiling tourists took decaf cappuccinos at wobbly little café tables.

I fortified my breakfast—fruit, croissant, and espresso—with the local newspaper, noting on one page and another the progress of projects Mitzi had spoken of over the past months. She was submerged in Asheville civic affairs and I could only guess at the amount of time she gave over to them. The hour wore on, the day grew even brighter, and still I sat dawdling. Last night's wordage overdose left me feeling still unmoored; I had toiled and toiled at a passage of *Earthsleep* that wouldn't come clean, an elegy for one of my father's faithful cronies, Virgil Campbell.

Mr. Campbell had been a shaggy, large figure in my mind since childhood. He was a ruddy-faced, paunchy man of middle height with a fringe of silky white hair growing around a bald spot as precisely round as a tonsure. But he was in no sense a monk. A prodigious toper, a golden codger given to good humor and practical jokes, a foe to bluenose and hypocrite, he had explored the tall tale and the whiskey jug with intrepid thoroughness. In his time, he had taken speckled trout, black bear, and lickerish women in easy sport, and he knew the creeks and hollers of our mountains the way a tobacco auctioneer knows a prime leaf. He knew the inhabitants, too, the old women and the young, the lunkhead boy and the wise porch whittler. I had not laid eyes on him since I was sixteen, the last time I had visited his dim and redolent grocery store perched next to his house on the east bank of the polluted Pigeon River. But he was with me always when I wrote my poems; he had come to represent for me one whole indigenous strain of Appalachian custom. He had appeared in *River, Bloodfire,* and *Wind Mountain* as one important archetypal figure for our mountains, and now that I had come to *Earthsleep,* it was time to finish him off, signaling the end of an era. I had heard that he died after I moved to Greensboro but had not been able to gather details of his passing. For my purposes, though, those would not be necessary; it was his absence that counted in the poems, and not the circumstances that caused it.

The greater part of *Earthsleep* would concern itself with those who had passed away, taking an old world with them. Here I sat in the new world, under a poster of a Parisian restaurant and next to a cheerful placard announcing the new Blue Luna Catering Service, and pondered the Appalachian past. It seemed a thousand years gone, ten thousand miles away, and I had struck flinty difficulties in trying to revivify it in my lines.

Finally, there was no putting off my interview with my mother. I left money on the fashionably rickety table, retrieved Buttercup from the gravel parking lot, and headed south again, the ten miles to Graceful Days Retirement Community.

The day had kept its early promise, rendering up a blue blue sky—"Carolina blue," some natives name it—embellished with a fleecy cloud or two and an unimpeachable concert of birdsong. I had rolled down every window to welcome June into the car. I wished the Toyota were a box kite so that when I skimmed over the top of the next gentle hill, I would simply rise and rise and float about the air, looping and veering like a lazy crow in an updraft.

These fancies brought me to the open-gated entrance of Graceful Days and I waved gaily to the elderly gatekeeper as I pulled through. When I parked the car and entered the infirmary, my frame of mind was a mellower one than yesterday's. I had a premonition my mother would be feeling better now.

My intuition was correct. No sooner had I entered her room and saluted her with a kiss on the forehead than she began griping about everything she could see or recall. The windows were dirty—if these people had to lie in bed with nothing to do but look outside, the glass would be clean enough, you could bet on that. After meals, it took forever to get the dishes cleared away; the soiled plates sat on her roller tray for hours, making the room all smelly. The ear frames of her reading glasses had got bent and the glasses slipped down her nose so she couldn't read. She even complained about the carpet in the hall; she said it was too "tacky" and that it snatched at her slipper soles like Velcro when she plodded along with her walker, and one of these days it would bring her tumbling down.

"Does that mean you're thinking about getting out of bed and taking a little exercise?"

"Why not?"

"That's good news. It's what the doctor advised."

"Oh, *him*." She shooed the thought away with both hands. "My semiannual visitor."

I knew for a fact that Dr. Amblin was a faithful weekly ministrant, but I forbore to contradict her. She was feeling so much better today that her temper was as edgy as a newly sharpened bush hook and she would welcome any opportunity to pounce upon a subject and worry it at tiresome length.

"Well," I said, "let me bring you up-to-date. I found Daddy's workshop all right and got into it, and I've piled up all the indisputable junk so we can cart it away. But there was a lot of other stuff, too. Maybe I'd better tell you about it." I went on to give what I designed as an amusing account of my discoveries. I spoke of the dead flowers, the hybridization charts, the rocket photos, the Indian artifacts.

When I described the baffling terra-cotta–stovepipe thingumajig, she wagged her head in puzzlement. "I doubt if you'll ever figure that one out. Your father was always playing with some little device like that. It was probably a model for an invention."

"Maybe so. But I can't understand what it is supposed to do."

"You might find something about it in one of those notebooks."

"I'm going to go through them," I said. "In fact, I've already started. But they're just as weird as that machine. A lot of the pages I can't make heads or tails of."

"Science. When Joe Robert got to talking about science, I never comprehended a word he said."

"Well, it's not modern science. Not all of it, anyhow. It looks more like magic. Arcane symbols, mumbo jumbo, strange diagrams."

"Oh no," she protested. "He didn't believe in superstitious things. 'I am the mortal enemy of trumpery,' he used to say. 'I am the champion of reason.' That attitude got him in hot water more than once."

"I don't know what it is. I'll keep trying to find out. I'd meant to read more of the notebooks but haven't got to them yet."

"Why not?"

"I needed to do some of my own writing."

"More poetry, is it?"

I confessed.

"Another Fred Chappell book?"

"Guilty as charged, Your Honor."

"I'll never figure out what you think you're up to. Never. You're just like your daddy that way. Look at us now, trying to figure *him* out. What else did you find?"

"That's about the size of it," I said. "The rest is only odds and ends. Flowerpots, old radios, and stuff."

"No," she declared. "There's something you're not telling me about."

"And what might that be?"

"I don't know." She gave me a look of stern disfavor. "But I know you're hiding something."

"I didn't find anything that should give you the least little bit of concern."

"Well, if you won't tell me, you won't. I just hope it's not something that has any legal bearing. Joe Robert's affairs were complicated, and after he died, there was a mountain of paperwork."

"I know. I wish I could have helped."

"So do I. If you hadn't moved down to Greensboro—"

"I wouldn't have a job. I'd be running bootleg whiskey; I'd be a black disgrace to the family name."

"No, you wouldn't. You don't have the gumption or the expertise. You'd be holed up in a corner somewhere, writing poetry and pretending you were somebody else. *Fred Chappell.* Lord, what a silly name."

"Yes, a silly name . . . Look, how long are we going to quarrel with each other this morning?"

"How long have you got?" she asked, and this remark broke the combative mood. We both giggled and spoke of other topics, and by the time I departed, we were able to feel that our interview had been a pleasant one.

There was little of the morning left, but I did want to get some work done. Returning to my motel room, I left a message for Mitzi at her workplace. Then I opened up Dante again.

I had been toying with the fifth canto of the *Inferno*, the part that describes the punishment of the spirits of the lustful. This canto tells the famous story of the murdered lovers, Paolo and Francesca, and the poet has imagined this compartment of Hell as a great tormenting whirlwind that constantly drives and buffets its victims with violent, ever-changing currents:

> There here, here there, yon-hither, lover and lover,
>> Hopeless of the comfort of coming together,
>> Of satisfaction. In torn air they hover.
>
> As starlings at the onset of cold weather
>> Flocking take wing upon the winter sky,
>> So here, the human birds all of a feather.

And like the cranes who always make their way
  Flying a single long unbroken line,
  And crying stridently their broken cry,

Shadows were carried toward me on this wind,
  Wailing wailing wailing without surcease.
  "Master, who are these souls so harried, so blind?"

And Virgil, the "master" who guides Dante through the ed-
ifying spectacles of Hell and Purgatory, replies, "The first of
those whose stories you are curious about was the empress of
many nations." He identifies Semiramis, queen of Assyria, but
he doesn't actually say "many nations." He says *"molte favelle,"*
"many languages." I was pondering the possibility that Dante
meant to imply condemnation of the Babel of Eastern tongues.
Was he also hinting that the curse of Babel was connected to
Semiramis's spectacularly lurid sexual career? Did multiplicity
of languages echo promiscuity?

My version of the *Comedy* would not think to crawl along
the lowly literal earth, but to ascend the heavens on the view-
less wings of poesy. Even so, this was a subtle mass of elegant
Italian matter for me to try to cram into my grubby American
duffel bag. So, after fretting and fiddling for twenty minutes or
so, I gave up and took one of my father's spiral-bound notebooks from the stack on the desk beside me.

That passage from the fifth canto had reminded me of him.
One of his best, and most elaborate, tall tales was about a hur-
ricane that tore through Hardison County in the 1930s. This
storm had been given the name Bad Egg by the local jokesters,
and my father had described it at great length, recounting the
awe-inspiring incidents that had happened to him and detailing meticulously the embarrassments of several well-known
citizens of Hardison. That tall tale, that "windy," was the Kirkman fifth canto, for he had alluded to Paolo and Francesca in
his story, tucking in a little jest that Mitzi and I were too young
to understand. Whether my mother had noticed it, I couldn't
know.

But his notebook was even more frustrating than Dante's Italian. What were these scraps of sentences, these words and phrases, in English, debased Latin, and impenetrable code? What were these symbols and tiny sketches? Sun and moon conjoined in a single countenance, an androgynous figure holding an orb, zodiac signs . . . There was a crude sketch of a tree trunk entwined with flowers and at the bottom of these ill-favored scratches the letters *G M*.

G M = Gold Mine? A reference to his map of Hardison County?

But a tree trunk made no sense. Flowers made no sense in this context. And for all I knew, *G M* = General Motors.

I sat frowning at the page until the telephone rang and Mitzi wished me a cheerful good day.

"Hello," I said. "How are things at your end? Have you found anybody willing to share their family graveyard with Daddy and Mother?"

"I'm working on it. You know, the response may be favorable. I've only got four calls out, but the two I've heard from are people I didn't call. So word is getting around. If you'll telephone me tomorrow, I might have some solid information."

"Who did you hear from?"

"No close relatives. They call themselves 'distant.' "

"Distant will do, if they're willing and have the footage to spare. But I won't be able to call you tomorrow. I'm driving over to Hardison County."

"What for?"

"This will take some explaining," I said. "Are you ready?"

"Shoot."

I proceeded to give Mitzi pretty much the same account of my discoveries in the workshop that I'd given our mother, except that I included a detailed description of the scandalous map.

She laughed. "What do you think that's all about?"

"I'm not sure."

"I can't make heads or tails of it. But isn't it just like Daddy? A secret map. You wouldn't have thought of a better way to characterize him if you were writing a poem."

"What about these names? You know Hardison County, and all this part of the world, pretty well. Have you ever heard of Bess Lovett down in Glutton Field? Or Frances Shaylor in Sassiefat? Martha Flandry over in Irongant?"

"I'm unacquainted with those names."

"I hesitate to tell you what's crossed my mind."

"Spare me nothing. I'm a big girl now."

"Did you ever hear rumors about our daddy having love affairs? A secret romantic life?"

Her long silence signified astonishment. I pictured her expression as she tried to decide if I was joking. At last, she replied, "Did you say that something crossed your mind or that you'd finally lost your mind? You can't be serious."

"Well—"

"Are you talking about girlfriends? Mistresses in slinky lace nighties? I can't believe you would imagine such a thing."

"But I have the map here with all these names on it. Betty Uprichard, Julia Mannering, Marie A. It's not like it says Joe Blow and Daniel Boone and Teddy Roosevelt."

"This is not even silly. It is just plain dumb. How did you come up with this nonsense?"

"Annie Laurie. Susan Louise. Mrs. Mawley."

"The important name is Gold Mine. What you found, Jess, is a secret treasure map."

"But—"

"Don't go butting at me. It's like our daddy all the way down to the ground. He was twelve years old till the day he died. Doing amateur science experiments, building model rockets, flying Ben Franklin's kite. This treasure map is something out of the Hardy Boys."

"Or maybe Rick Brant."

"Who is that?"

I told her about the boys books in the workshop: *Sea Gold*, *The Rocket's Shadow.*

"So there you are," she said, chuckling. "Just as I told you. It's only one of those kid things he'd fool around with. Junior G-man saves the world."

"Well, suppose it is a childish game, a secret treasure map. Why does it carry the names of all these women?"

"I don't know. It's play-pretend. They were all glamorous Nazi spies. Or eighteenth-century bluestockings. Or those are code names for weapons of superscience. All I know is, they're not the names of any Hardison County sweeties."

"You're probably right, but I think I'll investigate."

"How?"

"Tomorrow, I'll go over to Hardison and see if I can track down any of these names. I'll follow the map he's drawn. If they're real people, somebody will know about them. Sassiefat and Irongant and the rest are all tiny communities."

"Jess, if you try to trace down what's drawn on that map, you'll be the very same kind of little boy our daddy was. Hunting out fatal women, searching for lost treasure. Blackbeard. Captain Kidd. Yo-ho-ho and a bottle of rum."

"But what if it's true? What if there really is a gold mine?"

"Of course there is. Guarded by the ghost of Long John Silver and his merry band of Jolly Rogers."

"I'm serious. I'm going to go over there. It's been a long time since I traveled that way. West Hardison County was one of Daddy's favorite places. That's where you find the real mountain culture, almost unspoiled, he used to say. Do you remember how we all used to go on picnics on Betsey's Gap or over in Vestibule? I went fishing with him lots of weekends in Downhill. Those were the best times."

"Yes. But that was years ago."

"I'll never have peace of mind till I check this map out."

"In that case, you should go," Mitzi said. "But if you figure on prospecting for gold, you'd better take a shovel and a jackass—or would the latter be redundant?"

"I'm more interested in the women. Maybe I can work up a date with one of these gals. Helen Wilson in Easy—I like the sound of that."

"If it were me, I'd think about the gold mine."

"I need your help," I said. "You keep in touch with some of the good old Hardison County folks. Whom should I contact to show me around?"

"You're serious, aren't you? You are actually going to follow up on that fairy-tale map, even though it's a complete and utter waste of time."

"I'm sure you're right. Whom should I get in touch with?"

The note of long-suffering in her sigh indicated what a hopeless case she thought me, lost to the light of sanity, just as our father had been. "If you're dead set, then I suppose the person to see would be Aunt Penny Hillis. She was younger than Daddy, but they were good friends. She must be in her early seventies now."

"I vaguely remember her name. How would I go about finding her?"

She gave me clear and simple directions and I scrawled them down in my black notebook. I thanked her and promised to split our gold mine proceeds fifty-fifty.

"I can see the mother lode pouring in," she said. "I won't know what to do with all my riches. And won't your wife be surprised?"

"Just think Lamborghini cars and Dom Pérignon bubbly. Myself, I'm going to see if I can get lucky with one of the toothsome girls listed on this map."

"Yes, why don't you? They'd only be in their seventies and eighties by now. I'm beginning to think that's about your speed."

"Don't let Susan hear you say that. She's expecting big things of me when I get home."

"I imagine she has a better chance at a gold mine," she said.

"How about Aunt Penny Hillis? Should I give her a phone call to tell her I'm coming?"

"I'm not sure she has a telephone. When you find her, tell

her you're Joe Robert's offspring, and she'll be glad to talk to you. And tell her I send my best wishes and hope that she's well."

"I'll do that. Thanks, Mitzi."

"Don't thank me. I feel like I'm aiding and abetting a total lunatic."

"Your pockets will jingle," I said, and we chatted awhile longer before ringing off.

Mitzi's skepticism was well founded. No one had ever fancied our father a ladies' man; he certainly wouldn't have harbored that ambition. He belonged to the breed that used to be called "a man's man," a fellow interested in "manly" pursuits like hunting, fishing, trapping, playing football, wrestling crocodiles, skinning mules, and fighting cannibal tribes bare-handed. He believed in all the bromides about how science equals progress, sports build character, and that courage in the face of danger is the noblest quality of the soul. The great outdoors, fairness in competition, cleanliness of mind and body—these were the qualities that sterling young lads must instill in themselves so they could become leaders of tomorrow. When he thought of some acquaintance of his who might be termed a "ladies' man," a tinge of jovial contempt colored his expression.

But then, I knew him only as a boy would. My father had a sexual life, of course. Mitzi and I were living proof of that. He was a healthy adult male; he must have had a normal amount of appetite and all his sexual fantasies could not have centered upon my mother, however desirable he found her. His call to adventure must have influenced his love life to some degree.

And it was becoming clear from the other evidence of his workshop—the geranium breeding, "The Thoughts of Fugio," the woozy stovepipe invention—that I hadn't known my father nearly so well as I thought.

The difficulty of the enterprise would have intrigued him—those thirteen place names on the map were no more than forty miles apart at their farthest points, and I had to remember how artful a dodger my father had been. If he set his sights on enjoying a dozen ladies of Hardison, he would not stint his efforts. I could picture him devising stratagems and working out schedules, tooling into Easy and slipping out of Sassiefat, checking off the names of the complaisant one by one. What I couldn't picture was his doing the actual doing, tumbling the downy women in feather beds, haylofts, and mossy bowers, kissing and squeezing and then brushing away their tears when he left them wistful but contented and sped away in our crumbling Pontiac station wagon, trailing a cavalier plume of dust all down Froglevel Road.

No, Jess Kirkman, I told myself. Restore your mind to sanity.

One fact, however, was incontrovertible. Here was his amateur's map; here were the names of women posted in the crannies of hollers and the elbows of creeks, all color-coded. They were not mere compass points; they had stories attached to them, and the ones my imagination constructed were spicy narratives indeed. Romance and intrigue were written into this map, and I was making it my job to bring all to light.

Idly musing, without deliberation or thought of any kind, I picked up the notebook containing "The Thoughts of Fugio" and opened it at purest random. This was the sentence I lit upon:

Seven Sisters strike the hour together.

What Seven Sisters? Who were they? Bell ringers? Union organizers? A set of matched clocks? More romantic conquests whose names I'd find listed on another, as yet undiscovered, map of trophy females?

I could not begin to guess, and so when a glance at the bedside digital clock informed me that the hour was ten minutes past one, I decided to leave these fruitless speculations and travel out to the graveyard in Tipton where my father lay buried. I needed to recall to myself how he was situated there and I hoped that a graveside visit would inspire some helpful cog-

itations. I was becoming entangled in so many puzzles, I began
to feel physically constrained.

I took the freeway out of Asheville and got on Interstate 40,
but then at the first junction, I got off and joined old Highway
19 into West Asheville. This stretch of highway was familiar,
even though I had not driven it in decades. It had transformed
into the usual urban strip, crowded and noisy, and gaudy with
chain eateries like Bojangles', Hardee's, Kentucky Fried, Long
John Silver's, and so forth. I was hungry, although reluctant
to decide between Red Lobster and Golden Dragon.

One dyspepsia was as good as another, I figured, and when
the tallest and most lurid neon caught my eye, I pulled into
the parking lot of a place that looked a little newer than its
neighbors. The sign was a green-and-pink-and-blue miscrea-
tion, a towering caricature of a mountaineer. The figure was
the cliché we all recognize, with its big floppy hat, its goofy
facial expression, the balloon-toed bare feet, and the corked
jug marked XXX. Hillbilly Heaven was the name of this establishment, and I will admit that part of my motive for my choice
was a perverse mild curiosity. Who were the saints who inhabited this Heaven?

I was ushered from the foyer to a booth upholstered in vile
blue plastic by a girl in an outlandish "hillbilly" outfit. Before
long, another young lady approached, bearing a glass of water
on a tray. Her costume was odder than that of the hostess: a
stiff white blouse with leg-of-lamb sleeves and a long, plain
white apron over a longer gray skirt, from under whose hem
peeped the tips of Nikes. She also wore a largish calico sunbonnet, which must have made peripheral vision a chancy
proposition. "We're mighty proud to have you amongst us today," she intoned. She handed me an awkward oblong plastic
menu and asked if I'd like something from the bar.

"Better give me a moment to think," I said.

"Just set back and take your ease," she said. "The potions
list is on the back of the menu. I'll be here to take your order
in two shakes of the spotted pup dog's tail."

Off she went, and I glanced at the list with some apprehension, then began to study it with growing horror:

> *We've got the whistle-wetters you've been a-cravin' fer,*
> *neighbor. Jest don't tell the revenoors what we're up to!*
> *Only rock back and sip on one of our tasty specials!*
>   *White Litenin'! This un's a double-vodka white chocklit*
> *remedy with a sprig of cool-down mint. Mm-mm it'll hush*
> *up yer mug—'ceptin' when you-uns holler fer more!*
>   *B&B—that's right, folks, good ole bourbon and branch!*
> *But with a special secret spicin we throw in fer free! Don't*
> *ask your server what it is 'cause she won't tell till the ole*
> *gray mare has kittens!*

I rubbed my eyes and blinked them repeatedly, but the words still didn't go away. I peeked at the remainder of the offerings—Grammaw's Simple, Granpaw's Log Splitter, Phoebe Redd's Love Spell, Tennessee Deelite, Rocky Top Rumbustious, Mountain Dooley, and so forth—and settled upon black coffee as my beverage of choice. I felt the wisdom of my choice confirmed by the defiant declaration at the end of the list:

> *We gyarantee our toddies untouched by Yankee hands!*

The foodstuffs were described in the same unearthly jargon. Meats and vegetables, breads and desserts were set out in terms that some well-paid assassin of language had slung together while nibbling bagels in a Madison Avenue deli and thumbing through precious antique issues of L'il Abner comics. I felt vaguely guilty about even reading this menu and looked about me to see if anyone else had noticed me going through it.

But the other diners looked contented, local customers and tourists alike. They munched with complacent studiousness such items as Downhome Corneypones and Ticklish Tater Toes. Cultural pollution had not damaged appetites.

My server returned with her shiny prefab smile. For the first time, I noted her name tag: L'IL LIZA JANE. The role she was playing made it difficult to tell, but she seemed genuinely friendly beneath all the commercial effrontery.

"Now what might we be a-helpin' you with?" she inquired.

"I don't mean to be impertinent," I said, "but how can you see where you're going with that coal hod wrapped around your face?"

"You mean my sunbonnet?" She grinned and teasingly lifted the left edge of the brim, peeping out from under like a kitten looking around a doorjamb. "Oh, you get used to it."

"I'm betting that your name is not really L'il Liza Jane."

"No, sir. My name's Janet."

"Where do you come from, Janet?"

"Canton, Ohio."

"And what are you doing down here, so far from home?"

She had already jettisoned her Hillbilly Heaven accent and now her personality began to gleam through the façade. She was an earnest but cheerful young lady, a junior at Western Carolina University. She had taken this summer job to be near a boyfriend who lived in Waynesville and worked for his daddy in the construction business. She hadn't quite decided on her major area of concentration, torn between anthropology and folklore studies.

"Folklore?" I asked. "Don't you get enough of that in this restaurant?"

"Oh, it's definitely phony," she said. "But I don't mind. This place pays better than the others and all this hillbilly stuff gives the customers something to chat with me about."

"How about the homegrown natives? Don't people born in these parts resent it?"

"They don't complain to me. In fact, they seem to like it. Of course, I don't always know who's local and who's a tourist."

"To tell the truth," I said, "I don't quite know which I am myself."

When she asked for my order, I said, "I'd like coffee and a hamburger. Do I have to call it a Nowhars Burger?"

You'll smack yore lips and say thar hain't nary a better burger nowhars.

She giggled. "No, sir. Call it anything you like."

"Apple pie for dessert, then."

"Thank you, sir." She went away, performing an act of mercy by taking the menu with her. I sat in a darkened mood, my mind buzzing with language. I wondered if somewhere in the tall-fir reaches of upper Minnesota there was a soul-food restaurant called Rastus's. It would offer a dish called Greasy Greens: *Wrap yo' honky ass roun' dese yere collards and learn to do de funky chicken.*

Probably not, yet even my supersensitive politically correct grad students were not roused to indignation by Jed Clampett and Elly Mae and Jethro and the see-mint pond. Hillbillies were not a fashionable minority group.

But my thoughts were running out of control. All this silly façade was no more than harmless hokum, bait for a quaintified tourist trap. I tried to think how my acerbic Florentine comrade, il signore Alighieri, would react to Hillbilly Heaven and decided he would be violently inflamed by the menu. Just how low in the regions of the Inferno would he place the originator of Ticklish Tater Toes?

Pretty far down, I thought. Circle Eight, the Second Bolgia, where the Flatterers had to endure in the afterlife an output similar to their own in mortal years. They who perverted language would be dipped in excrement forever. *"Lo fondo e cupo . . ."*?

So deep this crater was that we could see
    Down to the bottom only if we stood
    On the tallest cliff, on the arch's topmost key.

We climbed; from there we saw down to the bed
    Of the foul lake where people were plunged in shit
    Of human flavor, as if by privies fed.

Ah, Dante, how beautiful the justice of thy *Comedy*, how fitting for black misdeeds like White Litenin' and Nowhars Burgers. I thank thee reverently and hope that you will look forbearingly upon my errors of translation.

From Hillbilly Heaven to my destination graveyard was only a short distance, but I wanted to make the most of it. This rare June day, already cleansing me of the plastic vexations of the restaurant, invited any leisure I could afford, so I continued toward Tipton on Highway 23, shunning the efficient I-40, which bordered my right-hand side most of the way. I wanted to see the old sights, the funky concrete-block beer joints, now darkened and weedy, the high, rickety railroad trestle where we youths had dared too many foolhardy japes, the svelte grassy hills on the left-hand side, all crowned with oak and beech and hickory. Shining Creek accompanied the road first on one side and then the other, and the sun lit the stones in its shallow depths till they shone like big glass buttons. The hill into Tipton proper was a steep one, and as soon as I crested it, I plunged down into a grid of narrow, mostly deserted streets, decrepit office buildings, and dingy storefronts.

For a moment, I missed the old times, which I was mostly glad were gone. Tipton was a small mill town, economically almost a subsidiary of the Challenger Paper and Fiber Company. The factory itself was modest in size by the standards of Detroit or Gary, but in the close-set green hills, it seemed monstrously huge. The gray buildings were tall and hangarlike, surrounded by wood yards stacked with piles of logs, hardwood and pine, and the rail tracks squirmed through them, gleaming in the sunlight like rivulets of snowmelt. Over this busy but lonely scene towered the smokestacks, gushing oceans of chemical smokes white and gray. This smoke was laden with particles of deadly, smelly grit, which it deposited upon trees, houses, cars, livestock, and human lung tissue.

The dark satanic mill was still in place on my right-hand side, poisoning the sky with smoke and the Pigeon River with ebony acids. I recalled how thoroughly my father had detested the Challenger outfit. His list of complaints had been a lengthy one: It despoiled all nature; it transformed the formerly free-hearted small farmers into factory robots; it made a whole beautiful geography dependent upon its own economic welfare; it dulled the minds of workers and stifled the ambitions of their children. When I had remonstrated, saying that Challenger provided livelihoods for thousands, helped to build schools and medical centers, and was generally a fairly benevolent enterprise, he fell glumly silent. His own business enterprises, especially those involving retail sales, were heavily dependent upon the factory payroll, and when he complained, he was only biting the tentacle that fed us.

But his grievance was more than philosophical. This was the factory whose irresponsible reservoir overspill (*"Bastards! Those bastards!"*) had swept into stinking oblivion one of his proudest dreams, that little white garden bridge intended as a love offering to my mother. Nothing but revenge would ever reconcile his feelings.

"I have a little retribution in mind for this Challenger gang," he said one time. "You know, when I went to them to discuss that handsome bridge you and I built being washed away, they wouldn't even see me. They told me to get a lawyer and take them to court—as if I had money to contribute to the fat wallets of lawyers, as if any judge or jury in this county would find against Challenger. 'Get a lawyer': They actually sniggered when they said the words."

"What sort of retribution are you planning?"

"I don't quite have all the details worked out. It has to be something that won't hurt anybody physically or financially and will make Challenger look dumb. Something they wouldn't expect in a million years. And it has to be perfect justice."

"Do they know you're planning to get revenge?"

"Not unless you tell them," he said.

I gave that remark the cool silence it deserved and we continued our game of checkers.

This fleeting recollection disquieted me. I was going out to visit my father's grave. What memories might assail me now? My mental state had been slightly wobbly ever since his death ten years ago and my examination of his workshop had dispirited and irritated me.

During most of my years, he had been an enormous presence in my life. Now he was gone, but his presence seemed as large as ever. Or maybe it was his absence that was so large, larger even than his living presence had been. When my father departed, he took a whole era of thought, a whole manner of living, with him. I recalled how it had been the same for him when his mother-in-law, my grandmother Annie Barbara, had died. He had loved her dearly and thought her the genuine avatar of the soul of our mountains, admiring her ceaseless industriousness, her restrained humor, her oak-solid religious conviction, her clever resilience, her abiding faith in the family. We had sat together in a separate room when my grandmother died and we could feel her demise at a distance, through the hall doors, and through the very walls that kept us apart but could not keep us apart. During that fearful hour, he had said to me, "Jess, if we lose your grandmother, if Annie Barbara Sorrells dies, a world dies with her, and you and I and your mother and sister will have to begin all over. Our time will be new and hard to keep track of. The time your grandmother knew was a steady time that people could trust. But we will lose that; we're already losing it."

That's how it had been for him then and how it was for me now as I staggered on after his loss, feeling the winds of time against my face, thrashing and buffeting me as I lurched blindly forward into the light of day and the dark of night.

I shook my head to clear it. I was pulling out of Tipton now, leaving behind the great coal heaps and woodpiles that fed the Challenger maw and turning onto a weed-bordered two-lane highway that led west into the country. I passed a sturdy but abandoned river-rock schoolhouse on the right and glided down by hilly pastures and meadows undulant with breezy tall daisies. I breathed the refreshing warm air and could hear birds and insects singing in the greenery. The sun was pleasant on the arm I dangled out the car window.

Mountain View Cemetery was about ten miles from Tipton, set atop a rounded hill surrounded on three sides by cool wooded mountains. This graveyard had been here since the turn of the century, established by a local Methodist church, but the cemetery had outlived the fire-razed church and now housed moldering bodies of every denomination.

A grassy car path led through the leaning brick entrance walls around toward the crown of the hill, and I maneuvered Buttercup quietly along, picking out names on the stones, families I remembered from my youth: Smathers, Burns, Shaver, Bascom, Early, Willis, Burnet, Caldwell, Raper. At the top, I stopped and climbed out, and the day fell silent about me—no birdsong or sawing of insects or distant motors. I felt an incipience in the moment.

Yet when I climbed down the hill to my father's grave, I was afforded no grand revelation. Here was the gray stone, still new-looking, the front face polished glassy. Here was his name, Joseph Robert Kirkman, with the implacable dates beneath. Below them, nothing. There was no inscription on the stone. My mother and sister were waiting for me to devise one to be cut there, but I had shirked the obligation. An epitaph seemed a finality all too final.

There was, though, one candidate for the inscription, a suggestion my father had made himself. That was when Uncle Runkin came to visit our family. All our pass-through uncles had seemed exotic to me when I was a lad, but none was odder than this gaunt, hollow-eyed old man with his husky whisper and dire superstitions. He was not half in love with easeful death; he was totally infatuated with that dark condition. Of death and all its pomps, he thought continually; his whole life had been but an impatient training session for that ultimate moment. We had once tried to frighten him with a skeleton in his bed, but he had only detached the skull and startled my mother with it. I had inventoried that skull in the workshop.

My father suggested to this odd bird several sharply ironic epitaphs for his tombstone; in private to me, he mumbled some brightly obscene ones. But Uncle R. did not take the bait, considering my father a light-minded, flighty fellow who was unworthy of serious study, since it was obvious he spent little time pondering death. Yet my father had thought about the topic in some measure. When I asked him what message he wanted carved on his own tombstone, he hesitated not an instant before replying, "Make it say: *Let me out of here, there's been a terrible mistake.*"

So here I stood at my father's grave, gazing stupidly at a chunk of blue-gray rock and thinking not a single blessed thought. I could feel it as a certainty that no revelation, searing or comforting, would come to me. This delicious warm spring day was the revelation; its blue eminence flooded life and death equally. I looked at the graves, the sky, the green dogwoods, the neighbor stones.

Suddenly, I felt empty, vaguely weary, my errand here a fool's. The dead are not silent, not even shy; they are speaking to us continually, as voluble as the October wind among the falling leaves. There was nothing I could hear at the gravesite that I did not hear always and everywhere, nightlong, daylong. A grave plot and a truculent stone would not make those voices more intelligible.

I turned to go but then caught sight of a figure on the hill above. It was only a brief glimpse of an old man, nondescript except for his silver hair, who was slowly making his way among the graves before rounding the hill crown out of sight. I couldn't name the figure but knew I knew him—someone from a time long past, from my boyhood. I hadn't seen his face, but the general aspect was unmistakably familiar. He left a trace in the daylight, like an unplaceable perfume or a half-recalled snatch of music.

I trudged up and around for a closer view, perhaps to accost and speak to him, but when I got there, he had disappeared. I scouted through the greenery but found no sign of him. I sat down on a small headstone, a child's marker, and tried to collect my thoughts. Who was he?

Well, he was my accidental guide to revelation, for my eyes fell now upon the stone opposite me and the name lettered there produced an electric thrill. I had not known Virgil Campbell was buried in Mountain View Cemetery—yet there was his name, weathered and lichenous, directly across from me.

He had to be buried somewhere, of course, but I could never have imagined him settled here. If I'd thought, I would have called this place much too stodgily conventional; Virgil Campbell wouldn't be caught dead here among the certifiably respectable. On all sides lay doctors, lawyers, deacons, grandmothers, patriarchs, insurance salesmen, Sunday school teachers. When I'd imagined where he might be interred, I located him on a misty mountaintop somewhere in Jackson County. There at the edge of an oak grove, with a tipsy stone canted above him, Virgil Campbell lay sleeping off this lifetime, the fumes from his long carousal absorbing into the black earth and silver rootlets, until his head cleared enough for him to rise again, splash his face with icy brook water, and take his habitual morning dram, that first drink of the day, which he referred to as his "heart-starter." This modest tomb in the wildwood would be reverently visited by bear hunters, bootleggers, and randy widow women. In the moony midnight, they would make lantern-light pilgrimage to Virgil's grave, there to lay wreaths on the ground, drink dutiful toasts, and perform sex rites of lusty homage.

But no—that was all idle fantasizing. Here he lay among the straitlaced, those whom all his years he had held in jolly contempt; the butts for his barbs, the fodder for his foolery—they now ringed round him here like a smugly satisfied crowd at the river baptizing of an avowed reprobate.

My heart was bitter. Is there no justice in this life? I wondered. Nor in the life to come? Here was an imbalance demanding remedy. I went back to the car and got my trusty black leather notebook and an extra ballpoint pen and returned to Virgil's grave. If I could not write my father's epitaph, at least I could attempt a fitting one for Mr. Campbell.

He had once procured a job for my father when he sorely needed a position, because he liked my father for what he considered his eccentricities, and his admiration was returned for much the same reason. Both gentlemen sought out the company not only of high-minded community leaders and stolid farmers but also of seamy politicians, rambling gamblers, sly poachers of national park deer, bounders and rounders, humorous, patient fishermen, banjo pluckers, and well-tested connoisseurs of corn whiskey.

Now they shared another similarity: Neither of them could boast an epitaph for his headstone. I bent my heart and mind to the effort and wrote:

In this universe bizarre
Virgil Campbell shone a star.
When Saint Peter asked Him why,
God would shake His head and sigh.

This first effort wasn't exactly a world-beater, but I had hopes to do better. The poetry biz is a chastening one because the scribbler spends so much time denigrating his own efforts. The most telling critiques of a poet's work are the canceled pages crumpled miserably in the wastebasket.

Underneath this grassy sod,
Virgil Campbell's gone to God.
He'll look upon the man and say,
"We'll share a jug come Judgment Day."

No use telling the swarm of the cozily churched that Virgil would find favor in the eyes of the Deity; they considered him not merely ungodly but also antigodly. My father, however, never believed that his friend was against religion. "It is not irreligious to detest the sanctimonious," he said, "nor to belittle the pretensions of the hypocrites."

Ranting preachers, desist and cease:
Virgil Campbell deserves his peace.

My father never participated in Mr. Campbell's vendetta against the pulpit-thumpers, but I have good reason to think he approved of it. In the Stalwart Faith Covenant Church, Preacher Hobart had clicked on the reading lamp at his podium and the attentions of his flock had been enlivened by a rowdy phonograph blasting out "Freight Train Boogie." Virgil & Co. had been at the wiring. In the Ancient Truth Pentecostal, Virgil's friend Lettie Hunter had joined the crowd of members who were speaking in tongues, but it became noticeable that her glossolalia was interspersed with phrases of intelligible English, and that these, when pieced together, provided a startlingly vivid portrait of the sexual proclivities of the Reverend Clem McAfee, peculiarities that Lettie must have observed at close range. As for the black demon with yellow flames shooting from its mouth and shaggy ears that so alarmed the brush-arbor meeting down at Little Fields—well, friends and neighbors, who can fault the good that resulted? Two drunken errant souls were brought back into the folds of the religionists. They had seen the terrors of hell firsthand and found them stoutly convincing.

Preacher, you and Virgil must
Be weighed by God as equal dust.
In His justice you may find
You had no reason to be unkind.

No need to detail the other pranks, such as the plagues of mice, bats, and garter snakes that periodically annoyed the concrete-block and plywood edifices of the Master's Voice Gospel Meeting House, the Mount of Olives Hard-Shell Baptist, the Drovers Branch Faithful One True Church, and the Born-Again Servants of the Lord on Clanton Hill. Nothing was ever proved on Virgil, and if he boasted about such things over a dram of peach brandy in a hound-dog midnight, word never reached the repentant dawn. He knew when to hold his tongue.

> Virgil Campbell in the clover
> Is lying dead—but not dead sober.

He was no Voltaire—and neither was my father, who always claimed to adhere to the religion that any sensible person follows. When pressed to name the brand of this faith, he would reply, "No sensible person talks about his religion." We never puzzled out what sort of creed it might be, though perhaps my grandmother gained some idea through their frequent dinner-table debates over points of doctrine. As *avocatus diaboli*, my father tempted my grandmother with arguments taken from the traditional ancient heresies, from Albigensianism to Zealotry, with perilous sorties into Catharism, Manichaeism, and Pelagianism. Though innocent of the names of these doctrines and of the libraries of tedious palaver they had generated, she was able to confute them one by one with simple quotations from the Gospels.

On one point, however, he did confound her. When he asked if she judged their mutual friend Mr. Campbell to be a just and godly man or an unspeakable double-dyed villain, as so many of the starched-collar righteous made him out to be, she hesitated, colored a little, and murmured something about judging not lest that ye be judged. It was apparent that she liked him as a person but disapproved his unhousebroken

ways, and I speculated that if she had outlived him, she would
have sorrowed at his passing.

> Virgil Campbell's come to terms.
> With the angels—and the worms.

She was as straitly religious as any divine in past history or
contemporary life and she was not fearful to mark the degrees
of piety she detected in the souls of others, especially in the
young members of her family, but she shied away from weighing the final merits or demerits of the man she would call only
a ''rapscallion'' and nothing more condemnatory.

> Underneath this verdant grass
> Virgil Campbell rests his case.
> If you think him a disgrace
> He welcomes you to take his place.

But now the thought came to me that in trying to phrase an
epitaph for this man, I was seeing through the smoky focus of
a literary lens, fashioning him into a symbol of mountaineer
independence of spirit and rebellion against convention. I, too,
was judging him. My verdict was admiring and not censorious,
but it also was narrow and self-serving. I had been too young
to know Mr. Campbell as a man; he had been a legendary
figure to me when I was a child and I had but perpetuated a
child's vision in the poetry I wrote as an adult. Perhaps it was
time for me, too, to take a more balanced view and give this
earthy hero some right-of-way.

> Earth, receive
> Your playful lover
> To his one sleep
> With no hangover.

Chapter Five

BACKWARD IN TIME!

Time is Place.
—Fugio

Another beautiful day, and here I was in beat-up Buttercup, rolling right merrily along on my way to the nineteenth
century—which was how I'd always characterized Hardison
County. Isolated from the mainstream current of North Carolina time by tall mountains, Hardison presented a different
world, one more homely, more rural, more rough-hewn than
Asheville or even the industrial but countrified Tipton. I always
felt myself a stranger there, though our family had blood ties
with a number of Hardison families and both my parents
counted many of the natives fast friends.

My father had a particular fondness for the area; to him it represented, he said, the genuine old-time mountain ways and the true Appalachian temper of life that he thought were being crowded out and watered down by the exigencies of these latter decades. "Pretty soon, people won't know anything about mountain folk but Snuffy Smith in the funny papers," he once told Virgil Campbell. Mr. Campbell had replied that all the reliable old-time skills were not extinct and, eager to show the justice of his assertion, offered my father a friendly sup of Rudy Ledbetter's corn squeezings. My father assented to the quality of these *good herbs* but insisted that the old ways were passing and the new ones were shoddy. Virgil's response was predictable: "Tell you what, Joe Robert—you drink to the old days and I'll drink to the old *and* the new. We'll see which one of us gets the better deal."

But my father was right. In Hardison County, people dressed differently, ate differently, spoke differently, though they seemed largely unaware that they did so. They were so thoroughly "country" in outlook that they could hardly imagine any other way of life, and when it was necessary for them to do so, when in order to make a living the young men had to move away to factory cities like Detroit and Pontiac and Gary, they took their mountain cultures with them, and it required more than one generation to erase it from their manners. Even then, it was never entirely gone.

I had been fiddling with the Toyota's tinny little radio, tired of the self-pitying whine of Nashville country and the boiler-factory fury of heavy metal, and was just about to turn it off for good when I heard a voice that seemed distantly familiar, as if it were carrying mournfully through the veils of gray years. It was a woman's voice, a contralto as rich as aged port, resonant but nearly opaque, as swept with lonesome expression as the wind in pine tops under a winter full moon. I couldn't place it for one whole chorus—and then I could.

Like the sunset's fading rays
The happy times are gone all away.

Look back look back the Maytime days
Look back all the green valley.

Oh don't you recall, Jess Kirkman, from the days of your
early youth the enrapturing presence of Aunt Samantha Barefoot? She brought the troubadour glamour of music to our
happy household. Don't you remember how her cream-
colored cowgirl hat sat slanted over the post of a chair back?
We thought it so picturesque that my father scrambled to get
our dusty Brownie box camera to take a shot of it—though of
course the light wasn't right. It was never right to suit him,
and so no photos ever recorded Aunt Sam's visitations among
us. They were real, sure enough, but as legendary and un-
provable to my friends as the miracles of saints.

 She had rich red hair, a broad freckled face, and a nature as
open as a field of red clover. To my grandmother, her presence
in our midst was a towering joy and a secret sorrow—for Aunt
Sam reminded her how her straitlaced, stern father, my great-
grandfather Harker Purgason, had not allowed her to pursue
the music that she and Aunt Sam made so sweetly together.
Long and often, she must have thought how she never got to
share the limelight with her dearest cousin, who traveled to
the bright-lit cities and friendly hamlets. But her sadness—
with which no envy seemed to be mixed—never showed.
When Aunt Sam appeared, my grandmother greeted her with
warm hugs and kisses, to which her famous cousin responded
with copious tears. She wiped them away with handfuls of
Kleenex, as businesslike in the gesture as if she were white-
washing a gatepost, and sent me to her yacht-sized emerald
green Cadillac for a fresh box of tissues.

My father had finally prevailed upon the two ladies, after
hours of teasing, bribery, threats of blackmail, and abject beg-
ging, to perform together. My grandmother sang and Aunt
Sam played the ruined piano. "Down in the Valley," they sang,
and "Bright Star of a Summer Evening," and "Down by the
Flowing River, and "Look Back":

The time is gone that was so sweet
And never another shall we meet.
Look back look back the Maytime days
Look back all the green valley.

The memory was so vivid that I drove without thinking and
didn't waken from my trance until down past the little community of Saw Neck in west Harwood County. That song by
Aunt Sam appeared in a new CD of old-time mountain music
from way back in the forties; it was an anthology album that
included songs by George Smathers, Bascom Lamar Lunsford,
and two other tunes by Aunt Sam. This intelligence the radio
announcer confided to me before he dribbled out to insignificant sibilant whispers and snorts of static, then faded altogether.

I turned off the radio, wanting to hold warm these memories
as long as possible. I had been trying to remember the old days,
thinking I might stumble upon clues that would help unravel
the knotted puzzles of the present dilemmas that faced Mitzi
and me. Aunt Sam's music had opened another sluice gate and
I needed to examine this fresh flow.

The newest puzzle that confronted us was in large part of
our own making. We had hoped that when we put word out,
old friends and distant relatives might volunteer to lodge in
their private family plots the graves of our parents together.
I'd thought it a slim hope; it was an extraordinary favor to ask,
for mountain folk hold their ancestors in tender reverence,
sometimes more devotedly than the character and behavior of
the departed might warrant. We might count ourselves lucky
to receive two or three offers of afterlife hospitality.

But at 8:30 this morning, Mitzi had telephoned my motel
room to inform me that we had received no fewer than a dozen
invitations and that more could be expected, perhaps four or
five more.

"This is a handsome development," I replied. "Shows you
how well they have been respected over the years."

"Yes, that's true. But—"

"But what? Aren't you pleased they have so many friends?"

"Don't you think it gives us a whole different problem?"

"Oh, I see. You think we have too many offers."

"Someone is going to be disappointed if it doesn't turn out for them. From the way they talk on the phone, quite a few will be. I think there may be some hard feelings to come out of it."

"Toward us? Toward you and me, I mean?"

"Toward us, yes. And they might be a little mad at whoever we decide should be . . . the hosts, I guess we might call them."

"Hard to imagine anyone getting jealous over such a matter."

"I think they might. I could name two or three who are already on uneasy terms with one another."

"Well, if that's the case, what do we do about it?"

She paused, and from the amused tone of her voice, I could tell she enjoyed saying, "Now that's a problem I'll leave for you to solve. You've been claiming that you want to do more to help me with managing our family affairs. If you can figure a way out of this dilemma, it will help immensely, believe me."

"Ouch. I was hoping you wouldn't take me seriously. In fact, I was counting on it."

"This is your golden opportunity."

"All right," I said, "I will gather my unruly little gray cells into a bold platoon and march upon the problem. No conundrum is too complex for Hercule Kirkman."

"That's the spirit," my sister said. "When you come to think, it's a happy kind of problem, to be overstocked with goodwill the way Mother and Daddy are."

"Let's hope I can find a happy solution."

"Are you still bound and determined to go to Hardison County today?"

"Your telephone call delayed my departure," I said. "I was actually on my way out the door."

"I figured a good night's sleep might bring you to your senses."

"But Mitzi, I've been sleeping all my life, and Susan tells me I'm not sane yet."

"She's right."

"I'll call you when I get back," I said.

"Good. Maybe you'll come up with an answer while you're driving aimlessly around."

"I'll try," I promised.

But I was convinced my journey wasn't aimless. There were things to be learned in Hardison. It wasn't only the map of erotic possibilities that motivated me. I thought that a reacquaintance with the place might cause me to recall details and events to help reconstruct my father's frame of mind in his later years. That part of his life—like much of his youth—was hidden from me.

We had not fallen out with each other. He always showed generous tolerance and forgiveness of my opulent store of foibles and idiocies. But a distance of two hundred miles, though it cannot weaken the bonds of affection, will diminish closeness of contact, and I had not been able to keep up with any of my father's new enthusiasms. These affected his nature more than happened with any other person I knew of. In acquiring a new hobbyhorse, my father became, to appreciable degree, a new man, another facet being cut into the bright jewel of his character. If he had taken a fancy to the byways of Eros, he would not stop until he had discovered adventure in them; it would be the same if he had taken up glider piloting.

I turned off to the right from I-40 at Arness Store, a cavernous two-story white structure with a veranda. The downstairs store was still in business, selling groceries and notions, but the upper living quarters, where old Drew Arness had housed his wife and three sportive daughters, was obviously deserted. I expected that tobacco-spitting, crotchety old Drew had long ago arrived in heaven, if that was the outpost he had set his compass toward; his three blond daughters would have married local boys who worked for Challenger or had emigrated to Cincinnati or Pontiac. If I stopped here now, I would find mere strangers. Only the initials carved into porch bench and support posts would recall how the twig-whittlers and snuff-dippers had exhausted the sunny afternoons of their leisurely decades. Wistfully, I watched the building dwindle in my rear-view mirror.

Here the asphalt left off and dust sprayed up behind me and gravel clanged the undercarriage. I had to slow to thirty, the large rocks and the ruts bouncing me in my seat like a Christmas-toy limberjack. The forty-six miles into the heart of Hardison County would take a little more than two hours, I figured, and it wasn't only because of the roughness of the road. I was traveling backward in time, headed back to the turn of the century, and Buttercup had to plow against the time stream into a period when Toyotas didn't exist, when August was the month of rabies, when farmers shucked corn on Saturday mornings to take to the gristmill. There would be changes in Hardison; the county wasn't a time capsule. It would be different; the appearance of Arness Store alerted me to that. But it would still be Hardison.

Over the washboard stretches, the car jolted so violently that my teeth clicked together and once I bit my tongue. The road had narrowed to what was actually but one lane, and though there was room for an oncoming car to get by, the margin was close. I hoped I wouldn't meet one of the big farm ten-wheelers in a blind curve, the behemoth looming upon me under the guidance of a moonshine-sipping tobacco farmer. Those encounters were a trifle too exciting for an absent-minded Dante-pondering poet in his vulnerable Buttercup.

In some of the curves, I could glance off to the left between bushes and see down into the valley, where curly Antler Creek glinted in sunlight. Mostly, though, the vista was hidden by the crowns of black oak and locust and hickory. The air had become cooler and I breathed deeply the smells of forest moistness and road dust.

At the top of Painters Mountain, I pulled into a wideout,

squirmed out of the car, and tramped over to the saddle of Betsey's Gap for a look-see. There lay the central narrow valley of Hardison, stretching northward. A road, this same road, ran through the valley, following Forgetful River in and out of the shaded crannies. Forest and dappled pastureland, cloud shadow and river gleam, a house or two with plumes of smoke rising above sheeted tin roofs, and mysterious blue smokes wafting out of wayward hollers: These were the general sights for which memory supplied the closer details.

The stretch of road leading from the foot of Painters was hidden, but farther into the valley I could make out the three major divisions. On the right-hand side lay the hills and folds and creeks of dark Downhill, where there were the hamlets, or the scrawny settlements, of Proudvale and Lazybones, Glutton Field and Bailey Ridge. Downhill had a sad reputation as a breeding ground for bootleggers, poachers, cow thieves, and worse. I recalled it mostly as a place of bush-cluttered trout streams, creeks where a fellow could take a hefty brown, but not without losing a fly or two and, as my father said, "his religion—if a trout fisher has got any religion except trout."

On the other side, the west side of Forgetful, was the area called Vestibule, in which were situated the settlements of Featherbed, Honey Cove, Irongant, and Sassiefat. Vestibule had neither the darksome character of Downhill nor the happy one of Upward. It seemed, for all the earnestness of its inhabitants, a tentative sort of place, as if it wished to be something else. Where Downhill was umbrageous and secretive, Vestibule was a close-minded spot, indeterminate in temperament.

To both these places, Upward contrasted brightly. It was sited upon higher ground, so that both dawn and tawny sunset bathed its slopes with light. Stoutman, Dinnerbell, Easy, and Truelove were its major points—well-groomed, leisurely hamlets that boasted fertile farms and generous orchards. The winters were milder there and mountaintop breezes gentled the summer heat. The family who worked a homestead in Upward was an object of admiration and not a little envy.

Those were the traditional descriptions of the three areas, accounts I heard passed among my elders numerous times when I was growing up. Now I stood listening again—and looking and smelling, for here on the upper threshold of the valley, the world was a more vivid place. The odors were stronger: Tree leaves and weeds smelled greener, the earth smelled rootier and more animal, and even the rocks looked and smelled stonier, seemed to throb with a pulse of primal existence. The grasses here, seedy and shaggy, made the tame grass I saw every day look secondhand. Birdsong sounded different here than in Greensboro or even in Tipton—not louder, but vivider. It was also more various, for the summer birds of Piedmont, North Carolina, are mostly a predictable lot—jays, robins, cardinals, catbirds, and so forth—while in the mountains, buntings, purple and painted, are not uncommon, nor scarlet tanagers, and the twilights are often made melancholy by the distinct but ever-distant call of a whippoorwill.

I rested my foot on a strand of rusty barbwire and gazed down the slope before me. Here, in an orchard of scraggly apple trees, our family used to spread picnics on occasional Sunday afternoons. My grandmother would usually elect to stay home and keep long company with her Bible. My father and mother and I would unfold a worn blanket over the tough, springy grass and take down the chicken sandwiches and the potato salad and the tomatoes ripe for slicing and the sweaty jug of lemonade. Then we would tote Mitzi from her little seat in the station wagon and set her on the blanket like a stuffed toy animal. She would sprawl facedown and begin to coo, her eyes unfocused and googly. There was a time when Johnson Gibbs accompanied us, proud to be part of a family. After his death, we picnicked seldom, and then, after a while, never again on Painters Mountain.

The orchard was sparser now. Some trees were left, stunted by wind and twisted into spooky shapes that used to remind me of the Arthur Rackham illustrations in my fairy-tale books. If those trees bore fruit, it would be the hard, small yellow-green apples boys used to battle with, stinging noggins but never breaking skin.

Turning away, I crossed the road back to the car. There in front of it, I found the kind of arrangement I'd almost forgotten about. A small stream of water was jetting into a roadside ditch. Someone had improvised a sluice from a half round of birch bark to make a fountain of the mountainside spring. It was a hospitality gift to travelers, an example of what one might learn to expect from the people in Hardison, shy but well disposed, willing to be friendly but never intimate.

I gathered a palmful of water and splashed my face and open mouth. I could taste Painters Mountain, the humus and leaf mold and mineral rootlets of turkey oaks. Strange that so pure a taste should contain so many varied elements, known and unknown. This flavor brought back not memories exactly, but echoes of sensations of long-ago time, savors of many past things that a few drops of water could revive in the mind.

After drinking another mouthful, I watched the jet arc down upon a leaf of sapling that had rooted in the ditch. There it broke into large drops that fell in turn onto a broad leaf of dock weed. These shattered into droplets that gladdened the yellow-green patch of moss below. This tiny cascade recalled an image it took me almost a full minute to place: It was that diagram I'd found among my father's papers of a falling object that set off multiple triggers to cause a disk to bound from a lever. Was his drawing a schematization of a waterfall? Had he been trying to figure out a problem in elementary hydraulics?

I shook my head. Maybe that could be the case, though his diagram was much too neat for such a system. Perhaps I'd never discover what he'd been thinking about.

After stretching my arms and my shoulder muscles, I got back into the car and rolled down the mountain, being particularly careful on this stretch of road, which contained a sampling of the latter end of the alphabet—*S, U,* and *W*—in the form of hairpin curves and switchbacks. When I reached the valley floor, I felt some relief but did not pick up much speed.

This road was still a bumpy proposition and I recalled how easy it was to fishtail on the gravel of the curves, even on the modest ones. Anyhow, there was no necessity for hurry; I knew where I was going and whom I needed to see.

Four miles brought me to where Bitter Branch poured into Forgetful River, just on the edge of Downhill. Across the road, a weather-darkened house sat comfortably on a hillside and a set of rock steps led to the unrailed wooden steps that gave access to the porch. This was partly screened by a trellis made of stretched cotton twine. Morning glories had begun to curl up the strands toward the eaves, but I could see through them an elderly woman in a large wooden rocking chair. If I had followed my sister's directions correctly, this should be Aunt Penny Hillis taking her ease in the cheerful morning.

I cut the motor, rolled down the window, and called, "Howdy." It wouldn't do to get out and begin ascending without permission.

"Howdy," she replied.

"Can I come up and talk to you a minute or two? You'll know who I am when I tell you."

"Well, yes, I expect I will," she said, and her little jest found me so unprepared, I didn't catch her meaning till I was halfway up the hill.

I climbed to the foot of her steps and halted. "I'm Jess Kirkman," I told her. "My father was Joe Robert."

"Come on up," she said. "I ain't set eyes on you since you were a shirttail youngun. Come on up and let me see if I can tell any difference."

I obeyed her friendly behest and stood before her, feeling the pressure of her gaze as she measured me head to toe and back again. Her hair was iron streaked with silver and her shrewd eyes were as green as bottle glass. She wore a flower-print cotton dress and a white apron and her smooth hands lay idle on a hoop of embroidery.

"I was saddened to hear of your daddy passing," she said. "I counted him a good friend to me, as he was to one and all. I miss the visits he used to make, for he never failed to come by once a month, and sometimes more."

"When was this?"

"Oh, the past ten years or so of his life. He called on lots of folks over this way. It always heartened people to see him coming with his flower bushes."

"Flower bushes?"

"That wasn't all. He'd bring notions from Tipton or Asheville, things we don't so often have in these parts. Picture Bibles, you know, and scarce colors of thread, lemon-drop candy for the younguns, fancy ribbons for the girls. And he would do what favors he could. Wrote I could never say how many letters for folks, sent off orders from catalogs, called up politicians to get boys into the army and navy, wrote to colleges to get some of our honor students enrolled."

"Sounds like you managed to keep him busy."

"No, that was the thing. He never was too busy to pull up a chair and set a spell, talking and joking. That contents an old woman like me a great deal."

"Well, if that's true," I said, "I wish you'd offer me a chair."

"Oh my gracious," she exclaimed. "You try this cane-bottom over here next to me. It wasn't so much I forgot my manners. You just looked to me to be in a hurry to get elsewhere."

"I'm not," I said, "but I think I've picked up the habit of looking that way. I've lived a number of years now in a fairly big town." I lifted the sturdy straight chair over and eased into it. The leg knobs by the seat were so polished by sitters, they shone like brass.

"So you're Jess," she said, "and your sister is Mitzi. I've heard that Cora has been feeling poorly. I hope she is doing better now."

"She has good days and bad."

She nodded sagely. "That's the heaviest burden—losing loved ones."

"We haven't lost her yet. She was pretty feisty yesterday morning."

"But you lost your daddy."

"Yes."

A deep silence passed between us until she said, "I expect you'd find it an uneasy job, trying to live up to what your father was."

"No, ma'am," I said. "I've been too scared to try. I just hobble along the way I am the best I can."

She nodded again. "One of the flower bushes he brought me was a white rose. Planted it right there by the corner of the porch. Had plenty of sun, but it didn't thrive. Withered black and died in just a few weeks. I believe it was more of a disappointment to him than to me. Part of his big plan that didn't work out."

"What plan was that?"

"He had a lot of mighty big plans—so many, I couldn't begin to tell. But this one project—that's the name he called it, 'a project'—was to make Hardison County bloom. He was going around planting flower bushes, finding out the best soil and water for every different flower. 'We'll try to make it one big garden,' he said, 'the whole county.' "

"Was he being serious?"

When she smiled at me, her face and even her body seemed to change. I'd been thinking that she was friendly and cheerful, only subdued and a little diffident, but perhaps I was mistaken. Her smile shone so warmly that it revealed the steady contentment, the happy patience that nourished her nature. She toyed with the hoop of cloth in her lap and I noticed that her hands were unchanged by her years, as smooth and pliant and delicately modeled as a young woman's.

She followed my gaze. "I brought my embroidery out here to work on, but I forgot to fetch my spectacles. So I've just been settin' and rockin' and takin' the glory of the morning."

"That's a fit occupation for any sensible person."

"I've got pretty good sense," she admitted. "Always did have. But it ain't near as useful as I thought it would be."

"How's that?"

"It's kept me from doing some things I might have liked to do." But when she smiled again, there was such happiness in her face, I could not imagine that any joy had ever evaded her reach.

"They tell me my father didn't always act sensibly. And that's the way I remember him, as a man with a streak of wildness."

"I've heard 'em talk that way about Joe Robert, saying he would do some awful foolish things at times. But I don't put a lot of stock in what the idlers say. Always seemed to me he knew what he was doing, only he wasn't telling all his mind to all the world."

"What do you mean?"

"He had plans, those 'projects' I mentioned. Like getting this county planted with flowers. I think that just about everything he did that people couldn't understand was part of some thought-out plan he'd made."

I nodded. "I believe you're right. I'm just beginning to find out about some things. But I don't much understand them, I have to tell you that."

She kept silent and I understood that she didn't wish to pry but was willing to hear what concerned me, so I plunged into my queries. "I'm trying to run down the names of a number of friends he had over in these parts."

"How is that?"

"I was going through some of the things he left behind and found a list of names. They sounded like the names of folks Mitzi said you might know about, so I thought I'd do a little detective work."

"What would be your reason to find them out?"

"Might be he owed some money," I said. "Mitzi and I would want to settle up any debts he might have left behind."

Now she gave me a serious look, though her voice sounded amused. "Or it might be that they owed him a little money and you wouldn't mind collecting it."

"I wouldn't say no."

"What would some of these names be?"

I mentioned Martha Flandry and Helen Wilson and Frances Shaylor, but she denied any knowledge of them. "There was an Annie Laurie listed down, but no last name."

"Well, let me see. It's a proud name for a girl baby. . . . There was an Annie Laurie Hannah that married Little Jack Little, but that's going back too far. Your daddy wouldn't ever have met her. There's Annie Laurie MacDonald down at Crooktree, and her mother was named the same, I believe. There was Annie Laurie Hunnicutt that wounded her brother for an injury he did her, but she moved away from Bailey Ridge to who knows where. There was Annie Laurie Branley, but she died from blood poisoning when she was twelve or thirteen. That's all I can think of."

"None of those sounds right," I said.

"Do you know whereabouts she is supposed to live?"

I pulled out the little copy I'd made of the map, though I didn't need to. Those names were already indelible in my mind. "At a place in Downhill called Lazybones."

She shook her head; she seemed quite put out that she was of no help. "I can't say I know her. Of course, I won't claim to know everybody. Maybe there'd be somebody over in Lazybones to help you out."

"I thought I might try that possibility."

"I wouldn't think you've got hold of a list of debtors, if money's what you're after."

"How come?"

"All the names you've mentioned so far are women's names. If it was money, it would be almost all men."

"That's true. What do you think this list is all about?"

"I couldn't say, but I'd give a pretty to know. I never heard that your daddy was so awful handy with the ladies, if that's what you're supposing. Had too many other things on his mind."

"Mightn't there be some things about him none of us knew?"

She didn't answer for a space, but an unreadable smile crossed her lips; it caused me to imagine what a beautiful young woman she must have been. She was beautiful still in her kitcheny, wholesome way. Time had transformed her looks but had not ruined them. "You'll stay and eat dinner with us," she declared. "It ain't fancy, but there's plenty of it and not but two of us here to do it justice. That's my nephew Cary Owen that comes over every day at dinnertime to see about me."

I protested weakly, knowing already that she would have her hospitable way with me.

"Cary will be along in about an hour, I reckon. If you didn't mind to, you might go out to the garden and pull us some green onions and new lettuce. I'll make some fresh corn bread."

"I wish you wouldn't trouble yourself about me."

"It wouldn't be no trouble even if you wasn't Joe Robert's boy. Cary's coming over anyhow and we've got to eat. . . . You'll find a little egg basket back there at the end of a beet row. Just gather a mess of whatever looks good and bring it back to the kitchen."

She rose from her rocking chair with elastic spryness, almost bounding from it, and made her way toward the screen door. I'd been thinking of her as a small woman, but she stood five feet ten or so, and her movements showed strength as well as agility.

Aunt Penny's garden was like the woman, cheerful, friendly, and well disposed. I was not surprised at its cleanliness and orderliness, but I was taken aback by its size. It must have been a good acre and a half, the greater part taken up with rows of corn, calf-high green flourishes of blade. Here were lines of beets, carrots, onions, and potatoes, the furrows between as weedless as hotel carpet; here were bush beans and pole beans with climbing strands of twine between the locust posts. Tomatoes were staked and would bear ripe fruit in a few weeks and okra was beginning to stand spindly and awkward above the rows of savoy cabbage.

I thought of salad with oil and vinegar and set to picking three kinds of lettuce—Boston, oak leaf, and butter. To go with these tendernesses, I pulled a dozen scallions, figuring Aunt Penny might fry them up in a little bacon grease. That salad and a hunk of corn bread and a glass of Côte du Rhone would make a splendid lunch. But of course there would be no wine; sweet iced tea, maybe, or cold buttermilk.

Beside her small screened back porch was an old-fashioned water pump, and I jacked it till cold water splashed the lettuces and onions shiny. Then I shook them fairly dry and took them into the kitchen, where she was setting out of an old oaken food safe a platter of fried pork chops, a yellow bowl of stewed chicken, half a round of the corn bread she already had made (the new batch was in the oven). It was dark and crusty and white-mealed and flat. It was not the custom in Hardison County to add eggs to corn bread to make it tall and light. Folks here liked it hard enough to break off in chunks into glasses of buttermilk so they could eat the resultant sludge with spoons. This dish, they called "crumble."

She was humming as she placed the dishes on her worktable but stopped long enough to make the formulaic apology. "We don't eat fancy here and I don't have much to set before you today, but you're welcome to what we've got."

"Looks like plenty to me," I said. "Looks plenty good, too."

She handed me a blue spatterware kettle. "If you'd step out and pump some water, I'll make fresh coffee. This other has been on the stove so long, it would just about burn a hole in your stomach."

I obeyed with a grin and, when I brought the kettle back,

ventured to ask about her nephew, Cary Owen, whom she was expecting for the meal that she called "dinner."

"He's my cousin Amy Owen's boy," she said. "He kindly looks after me, chopping kindling and all, plowing my garden and hoeing in it. Been real helpful around the house. Mostly, though, I like to see him because he brings the news."

"What kind of news?"

"Gossip," she said. "I don't get out and around much anymore, can't even make it to church on Sunday. And I never did have a telephone put in, so about everything I know that goes on in the world, I get from Cary Owen."

"Why didn't you install a telephone? Looks like that would be handy in case you got sick or had an accident."

"My brother Ben and his wife, Julie, had the first telephone I ever saw. Stuck it on the wall of their kitchen, right by the cookstove. One time I was working there by myself, fixing dinner for when they got back from a sickroom visit they were making, and it begun to ring. I'd never talked into one, though I'd seen Julie do it just as natural as daylight. But I couldn't make myself answer it, had to leave the earpiece hanging on the hook. I thought, What if it is something awful? What if somebody has died or their house is on fire? I had a hundred thoughts like that, and all of them were bad ones that scared me. So I figured if I got a telephone, I would just spend my days being afraid it would ring and me too nervous to talk to it."

"I see."

She chuckled. "What you see is a way-backward foolish old woman. You're used to the newfangled."

"I think you might have a point," I said. "If I had to guess, I'd say that I've probably received more bad news than good by answering a telephone."

"I expect bad news will reach me soon enough," she said, rubbing the tip of her nose with a buttery forefinger. "It always outfoots the other kind."

She added a joint of oak to the firebox and pretty soon the kettle was boiling and she made coffee of the sort I remembered. It would be as black as bitumen, as bitter as raw mustard greens, and almost as thick as the cane syrup used for sweetener. When I poured a dose into a blue-speckled chipped tin cup, I felt I was pouring the mornings of my youth, winter mornings with the windows steamed and the kitchen as cozy as a wool blanket, or hot August mornings with all the doors and windows open to birdsong. The smell more than the taste brought back sounds and images that seemed a hundred years past. These memories so submerged my senses, I didn't hear the door open.

"Good morning, Cary," Aunt Penny said. "I hope you're feeling sound today."

"Howdy," he said, and gave me a sharp once-over, head to toe two slow times, just as Aunt Penny had done.

"Cary, this here is Joe Robert Kirkman's boy, Jess. You'll remember Joe Robert and Cora."

He nodded and, having received this intelligence, took it as a reason to examine me up and down again, inspecting more closely than before what sort of figure I presented. I don't know why I had been expecting a tall, fair-complected youth with a talent for banter. Perhaps Aunt Penny's remark about Cary Owen's office of carrying gossip had conjured that image, but it was far from being the case.

He was a shortish, thick-chested, square sort with swarthy skin and dark eyes that smoldered with almost feral intensity. He looked at me as if he desired to weigh my worth—not in comparison with my father, as so many of the locals did, but as a man in my own right. His stare seemed to probe beyond my present physical appearance into my past, uncovering things I had forgotten, bringing to light what I would have preferred to keep dark.

"All right," he said, "I'm glad to meet you."

But he didn't sound glad in the least, brusque and grumbly. His appearance was really rather fearsome, startling because his dark eyes and dark skin were in violent contrast to his white hair. He was older than I'd expected him to be, but I could not assign an age to him, the details of his appearance being so anomalous. There was a line in Dante that would fit him pretty well except for the detail of his years: *"un vecchio bianco per antico pelo"*—"an old fellow with age-whitened hair."

"Jess has come over this way to look for some people his daddy used to know," Aunt Penny told him. "I was sort of thinking that if you didn't have anything real urgent to do this afternoon, you might take him around to the likely places."

"Oh, I couldn't ask you to do that. If you'll just give me a few directions, I'll make out fine," I said.

He nodded to Aunt Penny. "Be glad to," he said, though again he didn't sound glad, only willing to obey. I had the impression that he expected to be given this particular duty and had performed it many times before, though I couldn't locate a basis for my thought. There surely wouldn't be mobs of people come looking through Hardison County for the ghosts of past time.

"No, really," I said. "I couldn't put you out."

He turned his attention, that scrupulous weighty gaze, back to me. "We'll be going along after we eat dinner," he said. "You just tell me where you want to go."

When I said all right, he nodded again as curtly as before, and this gesture seemed to give permission for the three of us to move into the dim little dining room and seat ourselves at the table.

As I ate my salad and corn bread and the thigh of a stewed chicken, Cary Owen talked in a low, guttural mutter to Aunt Penny, bringing her up-to-date on the doings of people I'd never know. He poured forth a steady stream of information about births, courtships, marriages, crops, and especially deaths, and Aunt Penny took it all in, smiling pleasantly and nodding, now and then interposing a question to help her get straight the lineage and family situation of the subjects under discussion.

I drank two cups of the asphalt coffee, the memories it roused so forcibly assailing my mind that I felt more than a little dizzy and closed my eyes for a moment.

ON THE

FOGGY

MOUNTAINTOP

It seemed I was standing on a foggy mountaintop and the mist was so thick, I couldn't see who was speaking. It was a familiar voice as it sounded close by my ear, just behind me on my left side. Dry, flat, almost without inflection, it seemed to have been going on for a long time.

"So there she was, standing before the Pearly Gates, with no idy what would happen next, when all of a sudden they opened up, just as swift as the wings of a grouse taking flight when some hunter has scared it up in an open field, and there was a great light all around her, so much light, it blinded her for a minute.

"She wasn't scared; nothing to be scared about, she was sure of that. But her mind was all confused—well, overcome, I reckon, by a splendor she had always counted on but couldn't really imagine, no more than you can imagine what it would be like to be a water droplet inside a rainbow and able to see all the brightness and color around you.

"But her mind cleared in a short space and she could recognize who it was standing before her, shining like a cloud in the light, but still a real person, too, tall and strong. It was his heavy key ring that gave him away, Saint Peter standing there as plain as a pear tree in blossom.

" 'What are ye a-waitin' for, Annie Barbara Sorrells? You step right in our House of Many Mansions this very instant. You know *they's a place set for you at the table with the Lord. Been set for you a long time past. What are ye dawdlin' along out here for?'*

" 'Well, I didn't know,' she said. 'I wouldn't want to presume.'

" 'Now you know better than that. You just come along this way, and if there's any little favor you'd like to ask, I'll see if we can't take care of it.'

"So she hung back a little at that, but when he urged her along again, she said, 'Well, there is one thing I've been concerned about, and maybe you could set my mind at ease.'

" 'And what might it be?' Saint Peter asked her.

" 'There's not but one person I'm worried about,' she told him, 'and that's my handsome son-in-law, Joe Robert Kirkman. I'd like to tell you he's a good man at heart but maybe not so clever as he thinks he is. He read this book by Charles Darwin and some other books, too, about how monkeys turned into human beings. They plumb addled his poor brain, I think. I wish you'd take notice when he comes along and maybe show a little mercy. . . .'

" 'Don't you fret about a thing,' Saint Peter told her. 'We've got a plan up here that takes care of fellers in Joe Robert's situation. He is an earnest seeker after truth and will be rewarded for his efforts. Up this way, we don't put a lot of stock in a person's scientific notions. Why, we've got people here in the highest places of honor who believe the sun travels around the earth. We never tell them any different— they've got more important things to think about now. . . . But Joe Robert's rowdy friend Virgil Campbell has presented something of a problem.'

"Annie Barbara heaved a big sigh. 'I didn't expect he'd have much of a chance,' she said.

" 'Oh, he'll do well enough when the time comes,' the saint said to her. 'But first we'll need to put him to labor for a while, let him kind of work off his demerits, so to speak.'

" 'That could do him a mite of good,' she said. 'A little hard work never harmed anybody.'

" 'We have got endless acres of the finest vineyards you could picture,' he said. 'And an ace distillery that runs a whiskey beyond

mankind's neediest hankering. It seems in good order for Virgil to be our wine and liquor sampler and do all the tasting for us. We set a handsome table up here and we don't allow any slouch vintages. . . . So you don't need to worry a hair of your head about Joe Robert or Virgil. You just step this way and—' ''

Now the soft, flat, opaque voice faded away for a moment. I looked all about me but could glimpse nothing in that dense white fog. Then the voice started up again, as if it had not left off:

''That puts me in mind of a woman that used to live over near Drovers Holler—''

''I know who you are!'' I cried. ''You are my eerie and mysterious uncle Zeno, who will never stop telling stories. I remember you from long ago, from when I was only a youngun.''

But when I said that, speaking aloud, the mist disappeared from around me and I stood alone in the early-morning sunlight, looking out over the valleys and pastures and shady groves of Hardison County, at a world nearer and farther away than any I'd known before.

Chapter Six

CLUES OF

THE

SECRET MAP

Time does not pass.
It stands still and we pass through it.
—Fugio

All the rest of the day, during our grand tour of west Hardison County, I kept thinking how much fun it would be to tell Susan about it, about the places we visited and about this strange figure Cary Owen, he of the snowy hair and umber complexion and deeply searching eyes. He fulfilled Aunt Penny's promise of him as one who knew the highways, byways, and pathways of the county, held its motley history in his head, remembered its citizens and their stories, and could give account of each and every one. Dubious though he admitted to be about the purpose and object of our journey, he was the most knowledgeable of guides, a man willing, even anxious, to share his expertise with me.

I had made a copy of the map on a sheet of typing paper, only leaving out the name Gold Mine on the off chance that it might designate something of pecuniary value prudent to keep secret. He glanced at it briefly, remarked that the distance proportions were wrong, and handed it back. "I can take you where you've got to go," he said glumly, "because there's not all that many ways to get there 'less'n we'd care to take the back trails."

"No reason to," I said. "This map follows the roads."

"That's right," he said. "So just go along this one tracing the river and turn off at the bridge into Downhill and we'll head on up to Bailey Ridge."

Forgetful River divided the valley; Vestibule and Upward were contiguous on the left-hand side, spread out on the lower slopes of the Blue Ridge range of mountains. Downhill was in a deep holler on the right-hand side and the dirt road plunged steeply, numerous tight hairpins making the progress slow. Farther on, the grade leveled out, but Cary Owen informed me we would be turning off onto an even smaller road that would take us a little way up again. There we would find Bailey Ridge, where the map located Mrs. Sinkins, who, my companion told me, was not an inhabitant of the place now or in the recollectable past.

I recalled Bailey Ridge as a place name in a story my mother had told me about that superlatively feisty woman Ginger Summerell, she who had courted her truelove successfully by cracking him repeatedly on the head with stones, pistol barrels, and hammers. So this place was legendary to me, though Cary Owen threw a new light on things when he said it was first called Horney Ridge after the patriarch Barton Horney arrived there just before the Civil War. But there was bad blood between the Horneys and the Baileys, and finally the latter prevailed by violence, taking the name as well as the land from their blood foes.

"But it might ought to still be called by the old name," Cary Owen said, "because this is the place where the horniest people in the world live."

"I've heard that said about Greensboro, Asheville, and Paris, France," I said. "What makes you sure Bailey Ridge has dibs on the bedspring prize?"

"Because," he began, and launched into episode after salty episode of the trouserless doings of Suggses, Barlows, Watsons, Flemings, and others, a catalog of people whose loins never allowed them repose, it seemed. These escapades ranged from plain old open-air country-style coupling (and tripling and quadrupling) to multiple adultery, simultaneous multiple adultery, barn-dance orgy, Sunday school–picnic orgy, incest, bestiality, incest combined with bestiality, and everything else beyond, below, behind, and between. The Bailey Ridge folk enacted fantasies that had been dreamed nowhere else in the solar system, and so ingenious and complex were the arrangements, physical and social, that Cary Owen's vocabulary was inadequate to describe them and he took to making vague but highly suggestive motions with his hands.

"They ought to change the name again," I said. "Instead of Bailey Ridge, call it Happy Hilltop."

He gave me that dark, intense, unnerving stare. "They ain't happy," he declared. "You better believe they ain't happy, none of them."

I tried to counter with a story of my own, a tale about my sexually gluttonous friend, the celebrated poet Jim Dickey. His erotic ambitions had earned him a place in that part of Dante's Inferno reserved for the Lustful. Dante's guide, Virgil, speaks of him in Canto V:

> "The other of those you see in this loud hell
> You'll know for certain," he said. "Without dispute
> The horniest creature alive since Satan fell.

"James Dickey's his name, the poet in the cowboy hat,
  Whose greatest fame is propositioning
  Every woman from here to Ararat.

"No one will deny the man can sing;
  But also no one will deny that ever
  And ever he pursues but that one thing."

Yet Cary Owen topped my story about Jim and the Black
Leather Stewardess Coven with a story about a jackleg Hardison County preacher named Gaddon, one of whose adventures included a mother, daughter, grandmother, holstein
cow, Nubian goat, and—though I may misremember the exact
details—three Chinese sailors and a duck.

That tale set me silent for a while and I observed the farm-
steads we passed. Scrawny and ill-kempt, most of them were,
with sagging barbwire between the leaning fence posts and the
weedy ditches, brambly banksides, and slatternly kitchen gardens. I noted that there were mighty few flower gardens, a
peculiarity, because mountain women love their flowers and
cherish their blooms.

He nodded wisely. "That's right. Not many flowers in Downhill."

"Why's that?"

"Don't nobody know, exactly. They just don't seem to take.
Your daddy tried setting out flower bushes in lots of different
places around here, but not much ever come of it."

"I never heard of a whole big area where flowers wouldn't
grow."

"There's a whole lot of things about Downhill people don't
understand," Cary Owen said, and then proceeded to enu-
merate a host of anomalies of nature that surely deserved mention in scientific study. Sometimes fires flamed without
consuming corporeal fuel, he told me, and there were certain
places where rainbows visible elsewhere could not be seen by
Downhill observers, and even the broad noon daylight had a

kind of darkness in it. Other oddities he mentioned, too, so many that I lost track of what he was saying until he told me we had come off Bailey Ridge and were rolling into Glutton Field.

In Glutton Field, too, no flowers throve, though the farms here seemed a little more fertile than those in Bailey Ridge. The people appeared healthier, too, not gaunt and suspicious, but plump and self-contained. We saw them at work in their fields and gardens and Cary Owen pointed them out by name, each and all, from leathery grannies to freckle-faced younguns, and told me stories of drunkards and spendthrifts, reprobates and wastrels, the arrogant and the penurious. He told me the tale of Lane Gentry, who let himself grow so mountainously fat that he broke the back of his favorite horse. I told him of Big Mama Stamey, the moonshining woman who became so wide in girth that she was made a prisoner in her own house, the doors no longer accommodating such a breadth of avoirdupois. I'd got the story of Big Mama from my father, who passed it to me from Virgil Campbell; it was the sequel to a tale about a Founder's Day parade out in Hayesville, in which Big Mama was a proud exhibit, being at that earlier time not yet housebound.

In Proudvale, he regaled me with the chronicle of Broadus Waner, who was so vain and boastful of his prowess as a catch-as-catch-can wrestler that, having bested all the competition he could find in Hardison or out of it, undertook to wrestle a standing barn and succeeded so thoroughly that he pulled the structure down upon himself and was crushed nigh to death. I swapped one with Cary Owen on this subject of false pride, but my little offering was no match for the epic of Broadus Waner.

We had been asking all along the way of any knowledge of a Mrs. Sinkins or a Bess Lovett or a Betty Uprichard and received but curt and sullen answers for our pains. The denizens of Downhill were obviously not concerned to win friends and influence people in their favor. They were a glum and guttural bunch, men and women alike. I noted this fact aloud and Cary

Owen only said, "If you had to live in Downhill, you'd find them worse than you think." The way he put it struck me—as if one did not choose to live in these shadowy parts but *had to.*

Lazybones was the last quarter of Downhill left to visit, and my dark-eyed guide told me it was named after a feller from old time back name of Darl Simpson, who was the laziest devil that ever occupied shoe leather. "You hear that expression of speaking about lazy people being too trifling to strike a lick at a snake. Well, it was the true fact about Darl Simpson. Had him a little old flimsy shack up in the holler yonder and it was all growed up about with weeds and brush and, sure enough, he was too lazy to keep them out and the copperhead snakes moved in on him, must've been dozens. Bob Jackson told him, 'Darl,' he says, 'you better take care of them copperheads or they'll likely take care of you.' And Darl, he says, 'Well, Bob, these here copperheads will make many a good meal for the blacksnakes that will show up as soon as word gets to 'em.' He didn't worry about no copperheads biting on him; Darl Simpson never moved fast enough to alarm a snake."

I left Lazybones as ignorant as I had come concerning my father's map. We asked about Annie Laurie five times and only a tight-lipped negative shake of the head gave signal that the three men and two women we questioned were not deaf.

I understood how unlikely it was that I was going to learn in my journey the secrets of my father's treasure map. I was lacking the key, the important bit of information that would decode its central riddle. But the more of Hardison County I saw, the more stories I learned from Cary Owen, the more I knew, or felt I knew, about my father and the interests of his last years.

His ambition to turn the county into a showplace for flowers—what an odd scheme, yet how characteristic . . . There is nothing weird or crazy about the desire to grow flowers, but to grow them in places where you hadn't been asked and

that you visited only on regular but rather infrequent occa-
sions—well, that was something only Joe Robert Kirkman
might dream up. I was beginning to understand part of his
rationale: He was testing different locations, the different
amounts of sunlight, drainage, soil composition, and nutrient
content for each species or strain of flower. He was experi-
menting with the different varieties, probably in order to determine the sort of plantings that would grow best in our own
properties back in Harwood County. Hardison was his exper-
imental greenhouse, so to speak.

We regained the river road without retracing our route and
headed toward Vestibule. I was mighty glad to be leaving
Downhill; its dull oppressiveness and sulky countenances had
flattened my spirits. Cary Owen showed no change in face or
demeanor, but I had the impression he, too, was cheered to
depart that unenlightened space.

Vestibule seemed at first not much better. It lay higher on
the mountain slope, yet it was not so lightsome or cleanly as
it might have been. Our destinations were the settlements of
Honey Cove and Irongant, Sassiefat and Featherbed. The first
two were tucked into the folds of blue-shadowed hollers; the
third and fourth lay open to the midafternoon hour.

Featherbed was our first stop, for no better reason than that
the name my father had coupled with it, Julia Mannering,
seemed a handsome one, had an air of class about it, I thought.
When I voiced my supposition to my companion, he only gave
me that deep-searching stare. "It's a name that don't belong
to Featherbed, then," he said.

I could see what he meant, for though Featherbed was
somewhat neater, a little livelier than the places we had visited
already, there was a whiff of Downhill in its aura. But where
Lazybones had seemed so indolent as to be immobile, Featherbed was not completely somnolent. There was a feeling of
expectancy, as if this place were still hoping and waiting for
something to happen, for a decision to be made. In Downhill,

I'd felt that all hope had been given over, that nothing would ever change. What decision, what action might transform Vestibule, I couldn't imagine, but there seemed at least a possibility of possibility.

I stopped the car in the middle of the road—no fear of blocking traffic—and strolled over to a woman busy in her garden. She was a tall, rangy female with fading copperish hair and a guarded expression in her eyes. She watched my approach with sharp suspicion and did not halt the steady action of her hoe among the potato plants until I hailed her.

"Excuse me, ma'am," I said. "We're looking for somebody named Julia Mannering and we were hoping you could help us out."

She looked at me with alert curiosity. "Now, who might you be?" she demanded.

Cary Owen leaned out of the car window to admonish her. "Lorna Mae Tyler, that ain't no fair way to talk to strangers. Why don't you just tell the man what he wants to know?"

"Why don't you, Cary Owen?" she replied. "You know ever last body they is to know in these parts. You could tell him your own self."

"But he didn't ask me," he answered, and his tone was gruff.

"I'm glad to introduce myself, Miz Tyler," I said. "I'm Jess Kirkman. You might've known my daddy and mother, Joe Robert and Cora."

"Can't say so," she retorted, "and don't know that other 'un, either."

"You never heard of Julia Mannering?"

A head shake was all her answer.

"Well, I thank you anyhow," I said, and turned to go.

"Would she be an English person, you reckon?" she asked.

"I'm not sure," I said. When I faced about, I saw that she had a wistful expression on her face, an expression full of sad yearning.

"I've heard tell an English lady used to live around here somewhere. When I was a little girl, the old folks would mention her. But now there don't nobody remember nothing about her."

"Was she called Julia Mannering?"

"I don't know what she was called, but that name sounds like it might belong to an English person."

"You know, it sort of does," I said, smiling.

My smile was met with a sudden fierce query. "Do you know any English persons? Have you met them yourself?"

"I know a few," I said. "I met lots when I was in London, but I don't really know them."

Her face freshened with amazement. "Have you been across the seas to England?"

"Yes."

"On a journey, or were you in the war?"

"I'm a little too young for the Second World War. I went there to do a little work, but mostly for pleasure. My wife went with me."

"Did she now? I bet she like to died of delight."

"Well, that's putting it a little strong, but she mostly enjoyed the country a great deal."

"I wish you'd set down with me and tell me all about it, every little thing."

"I'm afraid I've got to hurry on. I have only a few hours to try to trace down some people. I wonder if you might have heard of Martha Flandry or Frances Shaylor."

"No, but I've always dreamed of going to England. To see Big Ben and the London Bridge and the changing of the guard."

"Maybe you'll go sometime."

"And maybe I'll see the queen. Wouldn't that be something?"

"Then you must make up your mind to go and do so."

Her mouth turned down and a weary frown creased her forehead. "Won't never happen. I'm too a-scairt. Anyhow, nobody ever leaves Featherbed."

"Nobody?"

"Nobody I ever heard tell of."

"Why not?"

Her look was so full of despair, it was daunting. "Just because it's Featherbed. That's all the reason there is."

"Well, I thank you for talking to me," I said.

"I hope you find who you're looking for, but if they've got good sense, they wouldn't be from around here." She turned and trudged away. I watched her go back to her station in the potato patch and begin digging dispiritedly.

"Good-bye," I said, but she didn't answer.

When I got into the car, Cary Owen said, "She's wrong about that."

"About what?"

"I heard her telling you nobody ever leaves Featherbed, but lots of them do. It just takes some of 'em an awful long time. And they all want to be somewhere else."

"Why don't they just pick up and go?"

"They can't. That's the way it is. I've known Lorna Mae since she was a pigtail sprout. She's been talking about the country of England ever since she heard of it. But so far, she ain't took hardly a step in that direction."

"Well, you and I can leave Featherbed," I told him. "Let's head over to Sassiefat."

"Straight ahead," he said. "Then turn off at Acorn Branch."

Sassiefat was renowned for its vintners and topers—that is, for its moonshiners and drunkards. The phrase "comes from Sassiefat" is still used to assure doubting Thomases that the shine they are thinking about purchasing is prime quality, not cut with wood alcohol or poisoned with lead salts from car radiators employed as filters. I confided to Cary Owen that I had indulged in a sip or two of Sassiefat back in the old days, when Virgil Campbell, just for fun, sneaked Johnson Gibbs and me a tumbler or two from the jug he kept in his back room under burlap camouflage. "I wasn't much of a judge, you understand, only eleven years old, but I do seem to recall it was smooth sailing all the way down."

He nodded with that unearthly gravity that shadowed his every word and gesture, then told me the story of Foley Hooper, a bootlegger long renowned for the quality of his product. The tale was that Hooper had found a way to get around the government agents who so unmercifully harry the innocent, hardworking whiskey makers of Hardison. Instead of spending all his time trying to hide his still where they'd probably find it anyhow, Foley Hooper decided to take pains with the whiskey, to make it the very best that money could buy. He ran a handsome operation, keeping the vats, the pipes, the worm, and the jars clean and sparkling, buying Harb Riley's fine Silver Queen corn to process, and using nothing but pure Dixie cane sugar to start the ferment.

When he was satisfied he had formulated the finest moon he was capable of, he finagled the two revenuers, whom everyone knew by sight, into trying just a sip or two—and then a sample quart. That's all it took. Wasn't long before those two agents developed a yearning taste for the stuff so powerful, they preferred it to the finest bonded whiskey legality could offer, scotch, bourbon, or Irish. One of the government men, a New Englander by birth, went so far one excited evening as to declare that the Bureau of Alcohol, Tobacco, and Firearms ought to subsidize Foley Hooper's potion and thus run his low-down, poison-brewing, hog-filthy competition out of business. "We'd be doing more for the health of this nation than the FDA," he said between hiccups.

There came a time, though, when Foley began to experiment with his good herbs. He was a restless perfectionist by nature and kept changing his recipe, trying to refine it to ambrosial status. His first trials were tentative; he dropped dried apricots into the jugs to fix a comely amber color and confer a fruity flavor. Then he tried one runoff with dried mint, and the succeeding one he cut with hard cider, thinking to add sparkle. But then come springtime, he took a notion to infuse his whiskey with blossoms, searching for nuance; he tried pear blossoms, apple, red clover, locust tree and sourwood and sarvis. He even tried the bashful wild violet.

It came to him on a day in June that liquor as good as Foley Hooper's deserved no flower less royal than the rose. Now roses won't grow in Downhill, and though they will bloom in Vestibule, they don't truly flourish there. Only in Upward do the most fragrant and colorful rosebushes display their pride. He began making many a trip into Upward and returning to Sassiefat with his car trunk stuffed with rose petals. This was too expensive a proposition, however, because the folks in Upward were not champion whiskey bibbers; he couldn't trade product for flowers and had to buy the puffy, sweet-smelling toe sacks of bloom for cash money. For a while, he was willing to shell out because he was so fond of the results. He would tell his customers, "Boys, this batch is as soft as goose down and as pleasing as a fresh-bathed woman." He would smell the bouquet (though smelling is just exactly what one strives to avoid in the case of corn whiskey) and raise his eyes to the heavens and smile (yes) beatifically.

Alas.

He had become too much the *raffiné* connoisseur and his makings lost popular appeal. He had so successfully defeated the oily raw taste of the native stuff that his customers plumb forgot they were drinking a juice that might run as high as 120 proof; they found themselves getting sozzled when they'd set out for no more than a cozy glow. Then there was the other problem: A few hearty pulls at a jug of Hooper would leave a man smelling like a rose garden—or like the plushest of Asheville brothels, an odor that gave rise to ferocious wifely suspicions. Since Hardison wives are not the sort to keep their suspicions silent, many an argument occurred that was settled with rolling pin and iron skillet. A quart of Flowery Foley, as it came to be called, might be well worth the fifteen-dollar price tag, but it wasn't worth a cracked pate and a deserted bed.

Turned out it didn't matter. Hooper had lost interest in the whiskey side of his product anyhow. The blossoms had taken all his heart. He moved out of Sassiefat into Upward, smack-dab in the settlement of Truelove, and there he grew flowers of every sort and distilled perfume from them and sold his attars to the big outfits like Lanvin and Revlon, who denatured them into mass commercial commodities with names like In the Mood and Come Hither, Big Boy.

And that is the tale of Foley Hooper, just as Cary Owen told it to me. If I found it improbable when I thought it through again in order to recount it to Susan, that was mere congealed hind-sight. When he told it to me as we rumbled through Sassiefat, stopping here and there to inquire about Frances Shaylor and receiving negative replies or none at all, I did not doubt a word he spoke. His hollow voice, his searching stare demolished my skepticism the way a final brief equation in a topological the-orem nails the case shut.

The name Irongant was a mistake, my guide informed me as we entered the area at a slightly slower clip, allowing for the bumpier road we now traveled. Back around 1915, the U.S. Postal Service was trying to establish names for all these scat-tered mosquito-bite hamlets. The postal man took one look at the muddy road before him and lost all enthusiasm for follow-ing it farther. He accosted a bearded mountain man with a rifle held in the crook of his arm and said, "Scuse me, feller, but what's up that way?" He wrote down what he heard, but the laconic hunter had said, "Aaron Gant," referring to an indus-trious but luckless farmer who lived near the head of the holler. So Irongant it became. I'd thought of it as a rare com-pound of Saxon (*iren*) and Norman (*gant*, meaning "glove") terms, which is the kind of folk etymology that can come about only as the result of too much store-bought education.

But here we struck upon the closest thing to a clue so far. There was a ramshackle one-room grocery store, without a sign to announce its purpose, and we stepped in to inquire. Mr. Blenley, the old fellow who owned this establishment that seemed to sell only lard and snuff, considered our query long and hard as he sat beside a cold wood heater and sucked at a cold briar pipe. "Martha Flandry," he said once and said again, as if the saying of her name would call her out of dusty disuse. Then he shook his head. "I can almost put my tongue to it but just can't quite. If you'll wait a spell and watch my store for me, I'll step acrost the road and ask my wife, Effie."

We waited there among the snuffboxes and blue-and-white lard buckets for a long five minutes till Mr. Blenley returned, his expression as abstracted as before. "She's in the very same case I am," he said. "She can almost place the name of Martha Flandry and then she can't. It seems like something we ought to know easy." He gave us a resigned smile.

As we stepped out the door, taking our mannerly leave, I asked about the spindly rosebush that stood so naked and forlorn at the edge of his packed clay driveway.

"Well now, a feller give that thing to me," he said. "I knowed it wouldn't take here, but nothing would do Joe Robert but to set it in the ground. That was a man with some convincing ways. I told him, 'Joe Robert, it ain't never going to amount to nothing.' And he said, 'Well, Bill Blenley, that's what they said about the air-o-plane, but one of these days we're going to fly to the moon.' I told him, 'They'll be flying to the moon before that there rosebush blossoms,' and he only grinned at me. He was a wonderful man for grinning."

I asked if he knew the name of his rose that was so peaked-looking.

"That's one more thing I've lost beyond recall. He told me the name of it and I knew it as good as my own. But seems like these days I'm not even lighting on my own every time."

"Thank you, anyhow," I said. "You've been a lot of help."

"I don't see how," he said, and shook his head regretfully.

"Well, you have been and I thank you."

I made my departing manners, which he interrupted with a

mournful query: "You don't take snuff, do you?"

"No, sir, I never have."

"Don't suppose I could interest you in some lard."

"Not this time. Maybe next time I'll be needful."

"Come again anyhow," he said. "I won't hold you to that last promise."

Cary Owen and I decided to leave Honey Cove out of our itinerary. The day was drawing on and we had only an initial to go by. To search for Marie A. would entail a lot of standing about while a lady scratched her head and said, "Now that might be Marie Andrews that used to live up the holler that way, or maybe it might be old Aunt Marie August that used to midwife over in Featherbed." Then she would go into the house and bring out her mother to look at the strangers who'd come querying, because, as is well known, folks can't answer a question correctly until they see who's doing the asking. A question hanging in the air without a face and body attached to it deserves no reply because it has no character. Might as well be a form on a piece of paper left in the mailbox, and nobody in Vestibule is going to answer one of those whether it comes from the Yew Ess guvvamint or Sears and Roebuck their own selves.

So off we lumbered to Upward, enjoying the gently graded clay and gravel road across the ridge. As we topped the hogback, we could look down into the coves and see the creeks and trailways to Stoutman, Dinnerbell, and Easy. Truelove we couldn't glimpse; it lay behind a stretch of forest that crowded to the tiptop of Brightening Hill. But all below lay a green and pleasant land as peaceful-looking as a swan gliding over an unruffled lake.

The road down into Dinnerbell was covered with a fine gravel that crunched reassuringly under the wheels, and the banksides were resplendent with wild flowers of every color. The settlement was surrounded by broad cultivated fields and the fifteen houses were clustered within rock throws of one another. The place was loud with birds and bees and there was an air of unostentatious prosperity that promised contentment of mind and soul. Each time we stopped to ask about Susan Louise, we were entreated to step down from the car to have a bite of this and take a little sup of that.

But nary a hint of Susan Louise could we come by, so on to Stoutman we scurried, there to inquire about Mrs. Mawley. I admired the easy confidence of the Stoutman citizens, their self-assurance and level comportment. Here, too, invitations to food and drink showered upon us, as well as invitations to stop and rest and enjoy a tour of the grounds and livestock, the fat barns and gentle pastures. Those ignorant outlanders who call southern Appalachia a poverty pocket with an eternal hole in it ought to come take a gander at Stoutman; they'd trade their whole Chicago and their whole Miami for a forty-acre plot of it in a New York nanosecond.

This tiny hamlet was well regarded for the bravery of its men, Cary Owen told me; it had furnished America with no fewer than six famous war heroes, two for the First World War, four for the Second. One of them, William Sondergard, had managed to survive Verdun and had returned to Stoutman with a slakeless thirst for peace. Thus he welcomed the hardships that a circuit-riding ministry imposed and brought the Word of Light (as he termed the Gospel) into holes and corners of the mountains so remote that in some places the dwellers had forgotten their religion and lapsed to heathenism, worshiping no deities but a few dark unnamed elemental powers. These superstitions Preacher Sondergard had to uproot and some of those deluded folk so disturbed by his ministry did not take to him in friendly fashion. But he quelled his foes without force of violence and brought them into the paths of righteousness. The loss of his left arm at Verdun seemed to affect him as a minor though perpetual botheration.

Cary Owen told me other stories of this sort, chronicles of martial prowess and spiritual triumph, till my head rang with the thunder of arms. The valor of our mountain men did not surprise me; they are renowned for their courage in battle. But I was surprised to learn that so many notables came from this one small place.

Stoutman might supply our country with warriors bold and brave, but it yielded up not a single Mrs. Mawley of any description—just as Cary Owen had predicted.

In Easy, we heard music. On a green hillock sat a neat little bungalow with a front porch all surrounded with geraniums and blue petunias, and on the porch a trio of nimble pluckers backed up an easy-working sawyer—that is to say, a pulsing rhythm guitar, a lilting mandolin, and a cascading banjo accompanied the sightless silver-haired fiddler who was making slick business of "Billy in the Lowlands."

We eased out of the car and stood at the roadside, listening our fill. When the tune finished out right on the dot, the guitar player hailed us. "Come on up and take a seat. We're only limbering up right now, but we're fixing to rip into 'Sourwood Mountain' in just a jiffy. So come on up and share a sip of this sweet cider with us."

We declined with real regret and I asked if any of them knew a Helen Wilson and got the expectable reply: "Not really, but if you'll whistle a note or two, we'll try to fake it." That ancient cornball wheeze pleased the quartet so thoroughly that they repeated it a few times to one another. The blind fiddler reveled in it most heartily. I laughed for politeness' sake, but Cary Owen didn't crack a smile.

The mandolin player spoke up. "If you do happen to find this here Helen Wilson and she ain't married, I wish you'd come back and tell Junior about her. He's been a-courtin' the girls since he was knee-high to orchard grass and ain't had a bit of luck."

The guitar player grinned and blushed. "What do you know about it, Harley? If I was to have any luck, you'd be the last in the world I'd tell."

"If you was to have any luck, you'd come crowing like all the roosters in Hardison on the morning of Judgment Day."

Countered Junior: "Well, I don't see how you're doing so hot. Ain't no wedding band on your finger."

Says Harley: "And none through my nose, neither, and won't be."

"Boys," I said, "it is plain to see you-all have scouted out the females in Easy. If there was a Helen Wilson here, you'd know her. Question is, Would you tell me or would you keep it to yourself?"

"Depends," replied the whole quartet at once.

"In that case, I'll try to be satisfied that you don't know. But I thank you for your honest answers and for that mighty fine music. I think you boys could go professional if you wanted to."

"We are professional," Junior said, "but that don't stop us from liking to play. Show him our bona fides, Harley."

Harley reached into the back pocket of his blue jeans and wiggled out a worn black leather billfold. From it he produced a card and offered it to me, half-proudly half-shyly. "That's us," he said.

I read it aloud. " 'The New Briar Rose Ramblers. Traditional and bluegrass. Weddings, dances, private parties. With that old-time spirit.' "

Junior backed up Harley's claim. "That's us for sure."

"The original Briar Rose Ramblers was a group way back when," I said. "They played for Aunt Samantha Barefoot."

"We named ourselves after them," Harley said. "Dobber there claims some kin with Aunt Samantha." He nodded toward the banjo player, who colored and smiled—unwillingly, it seemed.

"What manner of kin?" I asked. "She was my grandmother's cousin."

"Had an uncle who was second cousin," he said in a voice as low and musical as a dove's coo.

"Now you've met everybody but John," Harley said. "He's

a world-beater on the fiddle. He can't see, but he can talk."

"How do you know?" asked Junior. "He don't never say anything."

"Say something to the man, John," Harley commanded.

"Howdy," he whispered. Then aloud: "How'd I do?"

"Okay, except you were pointing in the wrong direction," Junior said. "If you'd said something good, he'd've missed it."

"How would the Ramblers like to play for a picnic I'm planning?" I asked. "This would be Sunday afternoon over in Asheville."

"Picnic?" Junior asked. "With food to eat and all?"

"We plan on offering food at our picnic. Drink, too. There'll be eulogies and speechifying, just about everything a picnic needs."

"Fireworks?"

"Not on a Sunday in town."

"How about girls?" Harley asked. "I'm inquiring for the sake of Junior, who is too bashful to ask."

"Can't promise girls," I said, "but you never know who might show up. Of course, we can't offer much in the way of money."

"Money!" exclaimed Junior. "You mean actual cash dollars?"

"Hush, Junior," Harley instructed. "The man said money, but he didn't go as high as a dollar."

"I was thinking two hundred for the four of you," I said. "How you split it is up to you. That's if you take the offer, of course."

"We took that offer as soon as you showed up in your yellow car," Harley said. "You didn't even need to say. Last few times we've been paid with the promise of a chicken."

"And ain't seen even a feather yet," Junior assented.

"All right. I'll call you with the details." I glanced at the card. "Will this number reach you all right? I'll need to tell you how to get there."

"It's Harley's number," Junior said. "As soon as you get back in your car, he's going to go inside and set by the telephone till he hears you talking over it. Don't worry about us finding our way. If there's money involved, John will guide us right to it. He has developed a keen sense of smell.''

The fiddler nodded. "I can smell the difference between a twenty and a fifty," he said.

"How do you know?" Harley asked. "You ain't never been near a fifty.''

"But I been thinking it'll be unmistakable.''

"Good enough," I said, then had an afterthought. "Oh, do you-all know that tune by Aunt Sam, 'Look Back—' ''

" 'Look Back All the Green Valley.' '' Harley finished my sentence. "That's one of our best numbers. We'll do you a proud job on that one.''

"I look forward to it," I said.

We decided to bypass Peace. The name Jane Smith had never interested me, and Peace, I was informed, was hardly a wide spot by the road. We'd see all there was to see as we drove through.

On the way into Truelove, Cary Owen told me the story he declared was the best he knew about the place, the tale of Aunt Sophie Medlin and her double wedding band commemoration quilt. If I'd listened only to the timbre of his voice and not to the words, I would have thought it a sorrowful story, full of gloom and depression. But though it was sad enough, it wasn't gloomy, and I understood that he himself took some pride in its incidents and maybe some solace from its telling. Even so, his voice retained its sepulchral quality, as solemn as a funeral knell on a dark and cloudy day.

The event that Aunt Sophie's quilt was to commemorate was the twenty-fifth anniversary of the day she wed Booker Medlin. "I know you must have seen a double wedding band quilt," Cary Owen said. "Has the circles inside and outside of each other, locked together like that. It is a complicated pattern to make and especially hard for Aunt Sophie to do because she was sewing it all by herself, without the aid of quilting bee or doting friend. It was to be a secret surprise for Booker, and if any of her friends helped her, word would get out. They were fine upstanding ladies, but given to tattle. So she was doing it all alone, hiding in the attic sometimes and sometimes in the barn and without the benefit of a quilting frame, and you can recognize how cumbersome that was, plying her needle best as she could and then bundling it all up to hide whenever she was called to do her daily chores. How she could keep a straight seam, I'll never know.

"And the double wedding band was not the only design she was stitching in. There were all kinds of other little figures and pictures that would remind them of the things that had happened in their twenty-five years together—the two babies they lost and their parents and other kinfolk that were gone and some special times they'd had. This patchwork of calico and linen and feed-sack print was telling the story of their marriage, and the quilt would have pictures on it that would mean something to Booker and Sophie and maybe not much to folks like you and me.

"It got to be a taking piece of goods, as busy as a beehive with all its little birds and butterflies and flowers and fruits and love hearts. Bible verses, too, stitched in gold-colored thread. There might be some people that would fault it for having too many different things, but there's some people that will blame honey for being sweet. I don't pay that sort any mind; I know the nature of them.

"Aunt Sophie had labored five years on that quilt, stealing the minutes from her chores and giving up any resting time she could have used. She had it all planned out, everything that was going to be pictured on it and the time when it was to be finished, down to the very day and hour. She had got it laid out just exactly correct.

"Right after dinner of that anniversary day, Booker told her he was going to ride the bay mare over to Sassiefat to inspect a whiteface heifer he was thinking of making an offer on. She knew that was a fib; he was probably headed out to see Nyla Barnes, who had a china soup tureen she didn't want any longer and which would look good setting on Aunt Sophie's table when the preacher came to call. Booker was trying to surprise her with a present just like she was trying to surprise him with the quilt, but Aunt Sophie could see right through her husband every time.

"As soon as he was out of sight, Aunt Sophie climbed up to the attic and brought her quilt down and spread it on the settee to have a long look. She couldn't help being pleased with what she'd done. Here was the big double band that circled border to border on all four sides and the smaller double band that occupied the middle. And all around the small one she'd put stars and roses not as big as your thumbnail and their initials, hers and Booker's, in script letters so fancy, you'd find it a little hard to read them. Daisies and maple leaves, candy canes and yellow birds. Even a weather-vane rooster like the one Booker had mounted on top of the barn.

"She looked it over again and again, and she was as proud as could be, but thinking about the amount of work that had gone into it seemed to make her tired all of a sudden. All the whole energy of mind and body just drained out of her like creek water through a toe-sack seine that boys catch minnows with. There was just one thing she wanted to add, the date of their anniversary today, and so she put that in and laid up her needle and thimble and the old bent wire-rim spectacles she used for sewing and sat down in the armchair across from the settee and gazed her fill at her handiwork till she went sound asleep. She slept for a good long time, maybe an hour or better.

"She woke up just about the time it was growing dark outside, and what had brought her awake was her niece, Prissie Hopper, shaking her real gentle by the shoulder. She opened her eyes, to see not only Prissie but three of her neighbor ladies, Maude Taylor and Hassie Burnside and Jenny Caldwell, all gathered to watch her. She could read from the fraught expressions on their faces how scared they were to talk to her, how they dreaded what they had to say and she had to hear.

"It was Prissie that dared to speak up. 'Aunt Sophie, I've got something to tell you that's a mighty bad thing.'

"Aunt Sophie smiled at her niece a gray little smile and patted her hand to comfort her. 'Hush now, Prissie, and help me stand up for a minute, if you please.' When she was steady on her feet, she walked over and examined her quilt like she had never looked at it before. She looked it all over, edge to edge, like it was something new to her and not something she'd worked on every spare minute for five long years.

"Then she looked at her friends, each of them in the face, and said, 'You see this here quilt I'm a-making? Well, it ain't a quilt no more. It has been turned into a bright and shining robe that clothes my man Booker in the halls of the Lord. I know he died; don't nobody have to tell me that. While I was sleeping there in that armchair, it came into my sleep a picture of him in a place as bright as a rainbow. He was wearing my quilt, only now it was his robe for always and it just fit him perfect. Oh yes, he's gone to a better place, Booker has, and I'm going there, too. I only don't know when and will have to be content to wait.'

"She looked at them, smiling with tears in her eyes, and they came forward to give her hugs of comfort, but she didn't need that. The comfort was in the vision she had seen, and it lasted her all the rest of her life—seven weary years, that was. She lived content and died happy, doing kind deeds to others and saying kind words. She set an example to one and all. She was so satisfied that all would be revealed to her at last that she never even asked how Booker had died. That happened when his bay mare Sugar throwed him at Coleman Mill Ford and he hit his head on a big rock."

His story carried us all the way into Truelove, where it stood peaceful atop Brightening Hill—so named, Cary Owen told me, because of the mica in the soil that glittered in the hillsides and pastureland. There even used to be a small mine on the north side where they dug it out to fashion those isinglass windows for woodstoves, but folks up here in Truelove didn't much cotton to mining. They preferred planting orchards and raising sheep to rooting around in the dirt and took not the slightest interest in minerals.

Truelove was prosperous enough anyhow. The dozen houses—rock bungalows, neat white frame houses, and sturdy log cabins—that comprised the settlement were trim and clean. Folks waved to us from their yards and porches as we passed. Early suppertime smokes were rising from chimneys, silver-gray wreaths curling through the late afternoon.

We didn't stop to inquire, for our clue in Truelove was that mysterious name Gold Mine, and I didn't need Cary Owen's assurance to comprehend that no such enterprise was to be discovered in this place. But the drive was so pleasant and the hour so inviting that I drove on to where the road ended, at the very top of Brightening Hill.

Here was a wide grassy spot that had once been the grand domicile of the Treloft family, the original settlers. Truelove was a corruption of Treloft, a nickname given out of fondness. This family had throve well in here, my guide told me, till one Sunday when they were at church and their house caught fire in a way nobody ever figured out and was consumed entirely. Nothing remained but the tall, lonesome river-rock chimney and a broken hollow oak tree that now stood in the spacious yard with a rose growing all about it. The family had moved away, first to California and then beyond the ken of anybody, and this place was all that was left of them in Truelove.

Now Cary fell silent for perhaps the first time in our journey together. We looked upon that rosebush for a long time. It was the most splendid specimen I had ever seen. It seemed wrought upon its host tree, almost as if someone had fashioned its trailings and twinings by hand, and it was a cloud of golden light in which the blossoms were eminent but not isolated points of effect. It was light and mist of light at once; it was both crown and aureole of Brightening Hill, holding the last sunshine in the sum of its bloom like pale wine in a cup of gold; at the same time, it spilled the light out upon the hour like a visible perfume. If my journey to Hardison County had lacked sufficient motive and steady purpose, this revelation of yellow roses, gold and fire of gold, would now serve for aim and end, a satisfaction of desires I had not been able to put a name to or even to locate in my heart.

I was no rose expert, but I could recognize a few different strains. When I asked Cary Owen the name of the flower, he shook his head doubtfully and said he thought it might be a Glory John but that he wasn't sure. I took that name to be a local version of Gloire de Dijon and knew he was mistaken. When I asked if my father might have planted this bush, he replied, "Well now, that might could be the case. The Trelofts had gone before your father took to bringing his flowers around, so he'd had to've planted it after the house was burned down. I've heard tell that roses always take well where there's been a house fire." Then he added with particular emphasis, "Yes, I expect it was Joe Robert Kirkman that set that rose there."

We looked at it until the light began to fade and then I turned Buttercup around in the narrow space and headed back toward Aunt Penny Hillis's house. In my rearview mirror shone the spectacular glow of the yellow roses climbing into the red-streaked sunset and the image was so wholly powerful, I almost thought I could feel the pressure of its light on the back of my neck.

Aunt Penny kept after me to have supper with her and stay overnight and I kept refusing as politely as any Oriental ambassador regretting some mishap at a dinner party. "You don't want to be driving over the mountain in the dark, what with them crazy, reckless bootleggers making their hauls," she said. "No telling what might happen to you."

I added another spoonful of sweetening to my cup of her titanium-strength coffee. "I have to be stirring too early in the morning to stay with you, so I think I'd better start out for Asheville before the moonshiners begin rolling. They won't be driving this early in the evening."

"Maybe not," she said, "but you can at least have a little bite of supper. It ain't nothing fancy, but there's plenty of it and we'd be proud to have you."

"You've already treated me so well, I feel dreadfully beholden. And I'm telling the truth when I say I've got to get back. I sure do appreciate everything you've done."

"It's a pleasure to see you all grown up," she said. "In a certain light, you look pretty much like your daddy, and that brings back a happy time to me."

"I'm glad to hear you say so."

She gave me one of her sharpest glances when she asked, "Did you find any of them womenfolk you were looking for?"

"Not exactly, but I think I picked up a useful clue or two."

"Wasn't nothing about anybody owing anybody money, was it?"

"No, nothing like that," I said, and turned to Cary Owen, who was sitting at the end of the table, sipping his coffee and watching me intently. "And that reminds me to ask, Mr. Owen—how much do I owe you for taking me around the hills like you did?"

"Nothing."

"I'm awfully obliged. I'd be glad to pay whatever you think it's worth."

"Well," he said hesitantly, "not no real money. But if you was to happen to have a shiny dime, I might take it off of you."

Aunt Penny laughed softly as I was going through my pocket change. "Cary Owen collects dimes," she said. "The shinier the better."

I took my brightest ten-cent piece and laid it in his palm. "Are you going to do something special with all your dimes?"

"No," he said, and his dark stare bore into me like an iron rod. "I only keep them to remember folks by."

———

Then there were more entreaties for me to stay and more excuses on my part, until finally I was able to take my leave, trailing apologies behind like a newlyweds' car trailing the mischievous greetings, toilet paper and string of tin cans, of devoted well-wishers. I drove over the mountain tired and happy and almost unbearably wistful.

Now my hair has gone to gray
And all the sweet times departed away.
Look back look back the Maytime days
Look back all the green valley.

Chapter Seven

ON THE TRACK

OF THE FOX

The question is not what, *but* which, *time it is.*
—Fugio

I sat with my first cup of coffee in Waffle Stop, a chain breakfast bar that offered cat-piss coffee and a soupy haze of cigarette smoke, musing upon the ruins of the morning and penning a few dislocated sentences into my notebook. Ten o'clock already, and I was still tired from yesterday's journey through west Hardison.

The shock of being catapulted back into present time was unnerving. In Hardison County, there were no Waffle Stops, no Taco Bells, no Burly Burgers, no Hillbilly Heavens, but only a few local cafés—and these were to be found only in the

towns of Marshall and Hot Springs. Everything else was
quartz-hard country living without our accustomed contemporary amenities—if a Waffle Stop may be fairly called an
amenity.

Yet I wouldn't have been sitting there silently grousing if I'd
had a more successful quest into time past. I had learned a few
things—well, actually, I'd learned a great many things, but my
hard-won discoveries wouldn't add up to make a whole picture. I'd learned, for example, that the Annie Laurie listed on
my father's map had no last name; that Julia Mannering was
not an Englishwoman, as the lady in Featherbed had so ardently desired; and that Marie A., she of the intriguing scarlet
initial, was the unlucky Marie Antoinette of revolutionary re-
nown. I had learned that all these names, including the entic-
ing Gold Mine, were but the intimate yet official names of
different breeds of rose.

Why had I ever imagined they might be sexual conquests?
The notion was even sillier—stupider, actually—than Mitzi
had allowed. Was there some deeply hidden part of me that
wanted to find out my father as the carefree philanderer, the
circuit-riding Lothario? A lot of parents hope that their children will grow up to fulfill those daydreams they could not
achieve for themselves. Was it my secret desire to be a garland-
laden conquistador of hayseed females, so that I projected this
fantasy on my dead father?

O perish the thought.

Truth was, I'd simply been grasping at straws, as mystified
by my father's map as by the strange diagrams and notations
and equations scattered throughout his notebooks. I had not
possessed the proper key, the knowledge that all these names
were the names of roses and that the different dots spotted
beneath them on the map made up a simple color chart, indicating the hue of each flower. He had set out the bushes in
different locales, trying to see which areas would be congenial
and which would be unfriendly. Gold Mine was marked so
prominently because it was the most successful of his plant-

ings. And it *was* spectacularly successful; that image of the sunset oak tree enrobed in a golden splendor of petals still shone
in my mind as if I were seeing it through this window before
me instead of eyeing dourly the impatient nosings of cars
through the dull intersection.

Still, some questions remained unanswered. Why had he
experimented with thirteen plantings? I was beginning to understand that nothing he did was arbitrary. As Aunt Penny
Hillis had said, he was a man with a plan—with multitudinous
plans, in fact, and each of them complex beyond any simple
appearance. The number thirteen was significant in some arcane way.

And why, except for Gold Mine, had he chosen flowers with
feminine names? Why had he chosen those exact locations?
Was it only for reasons of nurture—sunlight, soil composition,
and so forth—or were there other matters at stake?

The answers were hidden in time, but I had made some progress toward comprehension. I could quell my restless imagin-
ings about my father's love life and put away my avaricious
dreams of gold ore. I could begin to interpret some of the jottings in my father's pages in a new way. He had described a
woodcut he found in a book about an ancient alchemist, Nicholas Flamel; it depicted a rosebush hugging a hollow oak tree
in the center of a beautiful garden. From the wall at its side
gushed out water, which at some distance away cascaded into
an abyss. Up and down the water's course knelt a crowd of
people, feverishly digging into the earth with their hands,
seeking the wellspring. They would never be able to find it;
they were all blind. They were waiting for the one seer to appear who would uncover the source of purity and health and
serenity and make it available to all.

It now seemed to me that Joe Robert Kirkman, he who fancied himself the representative of science and reason and human progress, had begun to think in mystical terms and to
occupy his days with symbolic gestures. He had not been able
to achieve his ambitions in the way of science and futuristic

thought. He had been ousted from the public education system of North Carolina for discussing in a public forum the tenets of Darwin. This occurrence he always considered an abject personal defeat as well as a cataclysmic setback for the forces of reason. He had gone into private business, becoming an ingenious and profit-making entrepreneur, but such success looked small in his eyes. Was William Cavendish a shopkeeper, was Isambard Kingdom Brunel a furniture retailer, did Michael Faraday make money by leasing mobile homes to shaggy-haired newlywed youngbloods barely weaned from their motorcycles?

No. But all these things, and others more embarrassing, had happened to Joseph Robert Kirkman, and his failure had blocked the advance of progress in Harwood County to untellable degree. When he stood, head bowed, hat in hand, before the Gates of Pearl and the saint with the massy key ring said, "Good morning, Mr. Kirkman, and how do you give account of your life—for good or ill?" my father must mumble his sad reply: "Well, sir, I failed in my main goal, though I had the good intentions which pave that unfortunate infernal road you are bound to set me to travel."

Now, whether the scales of heaven will be overbalanced toward darkness by a schoolteacher's disappointed effort to plant his Darwinian rosebush in an indifferent soil, I cannot say, but I can aver that my father would expect no mercy on this score and that all his triumphs, his thousand kindnesses and acts of charity, his wit and daring and easy humor and abundant generosity, would not add up to a moiety in his eyes. The main thing in life, he thought, was to discover the secrets of nature, to bring them to light and make them pliable to the hand of mankind, so that disease, poverty, ignorance, and—yes—*evil* could be eradicated from the planet. This was a philosophy he shared with President Lyndon Johnson and Captain Marvel.

Perhaps you have seen the cover illustrations for the old pulp science fiction magazines. The muscular, intrepid spaceman, having arrived on a distant planet, steps out of his rocket, ray gun in hand, to save the horrified blond damsel from the clutches of some ill-tempered ambulatory fungus with too many tentacles.

That is my father, rescuing the Princess of Rational Thought from the Superstition Monster—only his space suit is such a one as Charlie Chaplin might wear: ill-fitting and spotted with leaky Band-Aids, surmounted with a fishbowl helmet direly in need of Windex. Upon close inspection, his superscience ray gun turns out to be a water pistol. The damsel in distress, bearded and balding, bears an unfortunate resemblance to Charles Darwin.

But bravery is everything in the hero business and if our champion's armament is outdated and fanciful, maybe he can win the day by force of personality. When he could not by main strength bend the world to his will, my father often had the power to charm it.

Anyhow, this was my working theory for the present moment: that, unable to make manifest his visions in practical terms, he had retreated to visionary ones; instead of performing miraculous deeds, he had turned to symbolic rituals. Lord help us! Here in his notes he was describing the ideas of Nicholas Flamel, and there were lengthy quotations from the pages of Raymond Lully, Cornelius Agrippa, Paracelsus, Albertus Magnus, and Arnold of Villanova. The presence of this latter thinker was not surprising; he was an early rationalist, an iconoclast ahead of his time. But there were also lines here from the dream of Bernard Trevisan:

Break for me but one seal that is unbroken.
Speak for me but one word that is unspoken.

The thought struck me that my father probably had not become enamored of alchemy; it was more likely that he had been investigating the history of science in order to turn it to some practical purpose. It would be entirely within the compass of his nature to conceive the idea that science needed reforming in order to make itself more attractive both to young students and to the general populace and that he was the man to reshape its concepts from stern mathematical inexorabilities into smiling blandishments.

But whether this really was his plan, one of his "projects," as he had named his dream castles to his friends, I could only guess. The problem in tracking down my father was not that he had failed to leave a trail but that he had left too many of them. He was a fox of many stratagems; I believe, in fact, that he might have closely identified himself with that swift and canny animal.

Having sipped enough bad coffee and crunched enough arid toast, I retreated to my motel room and called my sister. Her secretary informed me that she was in a meeting at the moment but would be free soon and was eager to talk to me.

I plunked open my Dante almost at random and began making notes. "*Cupe* = desires, or wishes; *sereno* = clarity, or brightness; *temo* = ???" I found myself ascended to that double circle of light in Canto XIII of the *Paradiso*, where Saint Thomas Aquinas attempts to explain to the puzzled and questing poet why our world, even though fashioned by God, is cumbered with imperfections. The fault, says the saint, is not in the Maker but in the materials He has chosen to use; they have their own various characters, which become impressed upon His concept the way wax remains imperfect wax even when it is shaped into a seal: "*La cera di custora . . .*": "Now if the wax were perfect in itself, changeless as the unchanging spheres of heaven, the Ideal would shine completely through . . ."

No, no. That wasn't right. I was tired; I wasn't even getting the argument straight. When the phone rang, I took it as a mercy.

"Well," said Mitzi, "you're back from your journey. Did you hunt up your trove of sexy women in Hardison County?"

"Only Aunt Penny," I said.

"She's a lot more attractive than some of the girls you used to date. Did you find out anything at all on your wild-goose chase?"

"Mitzi, don't give me a hard time. I came up smelling roses." I delivered my floral bulletin and added a few of my less audacious surmises.

"Roses!" she exclaimed. "Well, that sounds like Daddy all right, but I wouldn't have guessed the answer in a thousand years. How did you figure it out?"

"I was talking to a storekeeper, a Mr. Blenley, over in Irongant—"

"I know Bill. What did he tell you?"

"Nothing. But it was the way he didn't tell me. I asked about a scrawny little rosebush on his property and we chatted for a minute or two. I inquired after Martha Flandry and he said the name sounded familiar to him but he couldn't place it. He asked his wife and she said the same. Then it came to me that Daddy must have mentioned that name when he planted the flower and Mr. Blenley had forgotten, but not entirely."

"Good work. You sound like that Aunt Sherlie Howes Grandmother used to tell us about. What did they call her?"

"The Figuring Woman," I said.

"That's right. Did Bill Blenley manage to sell you any lard? I hear he has some for sale."

"I told him you were anxious to obtain a hogshead of his very finest."

"Thank you very much. Now what is your next brilliant move, Dick Tracy?"

"That depends on what you have for me. Your secretary implied that you are rarin' to speak."

"Only that our plan has been a raging success. In fact, we've been too successful by far."

"Lots of folks want to shelter the graves of Mother and Daddy?"

"Lots and lots. I finally set an arbitrary cutoff point at fifteen offers. But we may have got upward of twice that number. I stopped counting."

"And now the problem is how to accept one of them without slighting people and causing hard feelings?"

"That's right. Have you got a solution?"

"I've been thinking about it and have made a few moves. Do you know personally all those who have made an offer?"

"Almost. There are a few I never met, but I've heard of them and have a pretty good idea who they are."

"But the others you know personally?"

"Yes."

"I wonder if I might know them."

She sighed. "I can't tell you that. You must know a few at least, no matter how long you've been away from the mountains."

"Are there any of them you particularly favor? Secretly, I mean."

"Maybe—but I don't think we can just pick favorites."

"Who are they?"

"Well, there are the Hillyers, who live down toward Saw Neck. In the old days before they moved to Tipton, Daddy and Mother used to play cards with them every Saturday night. Mother was especially fond of Aunt Jenny."

"Do they have a nice place?"

"They used to have about two hundred acres, but since Jenny died, her husband has sold off a lot of it."

"Who else strikes your fancy?"

"The Irelands are grand folks, Uncle Gray and Aunt Ora. They're getting on, though. Uncle Gray must be ninety, or pretty near."

"What kind of place do they have?"

"Nearly three hundred acres all told. They raise some cows and goats and sheep."

"Sheep are nice."

"You hear different things from different shepherds."

"No, I mean . . . pastoral. Pastoral like in the Bible. Do they have any children?"

"Yes. Three males, all in their thirties. This was Uncle Gray's second wife. He was a vigorous sixty. They've all got families, except for the youngest boy. I wish I could remember his name. But they're an athletic crew; two of them play for the Challenger semipro softball team. All three work for the paper mill."

"How about the Hillyers?"

"They've got a daughter married to a dentist in Maine and a boy—well, he's a man now, of course—working at the Ford plant in Sharonville, Ohio."

"Do you think either of them might move back here to the mountains?"

"I don't know. Why do you ask?"

"If they decide to sell the property, we'd be back where we started, only having to move *both* Mother and Daddy again."

"That's true—and it brings up another problem."

"Uh-oh."

"I started wondering about what it takes to exhume a body and bury it someplace else, so I called up David Evans at Peace in the Valley. You remember him; he directs the funeral home that laid Daddy away."

"I remember." How could I forget the interment of my father?

"Well, when I spoke to him about the idea, he told me we should be careful about what we're getting into. To begin with, we have to get a disinterment permit from the Department of Health. That will take awhile. And we have to use the services of a funeral home. The director has to be in attendance at the disinterment. And we have to use the correct equipment and make sure we place the vault and casket inside a concrete liner."

"I hadn't thought."

"Well, who would? But there you are."

"Must take a long time to get all of it done up proper."

"Believe you me."

"That is bad news. I need to be in Greensboro as soon as I can, sweating out my translation. Summer is the only time I have to work. Really work, I mean."

"Oh yes, your Dante. How's it going?"

"Don't ask."

"As bad as that?"

"*Nel mezzo del cammin di nostra vita Mi ritrovai per una selva oscura.* That is to say, I'm having a midlife crisis and have got lost in the murky briar thicket."

"Maybe it'll get easier as you go along."

"I hope so. That's why I want to get back home and begin work in earnest. So give me those addresses, if you please."

"Whose addresses?"

"The Irelands' and the—Hillyers', is it? I'm just curious to see what kind of farms they have. We want our parents to have the prettiest spot, don't we?"

"I suppose, but it's going to be a sticky proposition if we just choose somebody we like. It will seem unfair to the others."

"We can explain to them. Do you think you can get them to come out for a picnic Sunday afternoon? All fifteen of the people who offered, along with their families? There must be a local park with a shelter and a big barbecue pit for cookouts. We'll have a family gathering–style picnic."

"There's one down off Montrose Street. But that's a big undertaking."

"Well, if you could reserve the space for us and invite everyone over, that would be helpful. They might enjoy a picnic."

"I don't know if all fifteen groups can come," Mitzi said. "Some of them are pretty old and there are some who'd be coming a fairly long way."

"That's all right. We'll gather those that are possible and explain our position to them and they can carry the word to the others."

"I'll do what I can."

"Thank you, sister. And now if you'll give me those addresses . . ." I wrote them down on a fresh page of my notebook.

"You make it sound like you've got this all figured out," Mitzi said.

"Maybe I have."

"Uh-oh," she said. "Now I'm really worried. But I'm going to leave it in your hands. Just don't drop the ball."

"Oops!" I said, and we rang off.

Okay, let's see: I needed to organize the picnic for Sunday afternoon, to telephone the New Briar Rose Ramblers, to have a look at the home places of the Irelands and the Hillyers, to establish a strategy for choosing the gravesite, to figure out how to comply in short order with the reburial regulations, and to lay the groundwork for the whole scheme.

In order to get the groundwork laid, I'd have to interview my mother again, and I decided to do it immediately. Time was short and all the gears had to mesh or I would be driving back and forth from Greensboro to Asheville for months to come. I could live with that necessity, but the uncertainties and anxieties would do my mother no good. For her peace of mind, we had to get things settled.

This time, the visit was a pleasant one. She had enjoyed a peaceful night's sleep, her appetite had returned in some measure, and she knew I had gone over to Hardison County to poke about and so would have a story to tell.

She sat up in bed, pulled a blue chenille bathrobe around her shoulders, and clasped her hands on her stomach in an attitude of long-suffering patience.

I reminded her of Aunt Penny Hillis and delivered that lady's fond greetings, and she was pleased to listen, nodding and smiling quietly. "She was ever a dear one," my mother said, "so cheerful and forward-looking. You'd never know she lost so many children. Her husband deserted her, you know. Just went off one day and never came back. Of course, there was a lot of speculation about that. He'd been cruel to Aunt Penny, word was, and she had two big, strong, silent, protective brothers. They're gone now, too. I'm sure she's terribly lonely."

"She seemed happy enough," I said. "She made me stay to lunch and eat out of her garden."

"Well, she would, wouldn't she? That's the way she always was. Joe Robert was awfully fond of her. Aunt Penny was one of his true favorites."

"He got along well with most folks, didn't he? I never heard of him having an enemy."

"He did, though. There were some who couldn't stand to see him coming. They thought he was reckless and ungodly. He stuck in the craw of some who thought they were the finer examples of morality in this sinful world."

"Would that include the Hillyers? I heard they might be sort of down on him."

"Good Lord, no. David and Jenny were our best friends when we lived down in Saw Neck. That was before you were born. Every Saturday night, we'd go over to their house and play setback. David was as religious about his Saturday-night card game as he was about church on Sunday morning. Jenny would set out cake and pie: I would always take something, but it was never as good as what I ate there."

"So you always got on well with them."

"I wish I could see both of them right this minute. But Jenny's gone now, like so many of my old friends."

"How about the Irelands? Still friendly with them?"

"Oh yes. But it's been a long time since we've been in touch, ten years at least, maybe longer."

"Anyhow, you're not on the outs with them."

She made her mouth prim and shook her head. "Never. But what's this all about? Why are you so interested in our friends from years ago?"

"No special reason. I just picked up a lot of gossip when I was in Hardison."

"Not from Aunt Penny."

"No," I admitted. "She tells stories about folks, but they're not gossip, exactly. I heard a lot of things from Cary Owen."

"Good Lord," she said, "is that strange man still around? Seems like I've been knowing him since I was in pigtails."

I pointed out that he was younger than Aunt Penny.

"Yes, but he doesn't seem so, does he? Isn't he one of the oddest characters you ever met? When I was a little girl, I was so frightened of him, I'd run to Mother and press my face against her hip and pull her apron over my head."

"He does look kind of ominous, but I found him harmless enough. He was an endless source of information about the people in Downhill and Upward and Vestibule. I never asked a question he couldn't answer, and he volunteered a lot I didn't ask about."

"Cary Owen knows everything about everybody," she said, and then gave me a careful straight look. "What were you plundering around in Hardison County for? What made you go over there?"

She'd caught me unprepared and I had to fumble. "Nothing . . . I mean, not anything that makes sense. We used to go over there a lot, our family, when I was a kid. You remember. I just wanted to scout around and see if anything came back to me from the old days."

"Like what?"

"I don't know. . . . Anything."

"Jess, you're keeping things from me and I don't much care for it. It's bad enough I have to lie here in this place like I'm in the state penitentiary without worrying my head off about what you and Mitzi are up to."

"What in the world can you imagine we'd be doing?"

"The only thing I know is that I don't know. There was something you found in Joe Robert's workshop that you won't tell me about. It really is very annoying."

I decided to reveal to her the secret of the Rose and unfolded some of the facts of the case, the map I'd come across and the trail it led me on and some of the adventures that had befallen me. I made the escapade sound as amusing as I could and recalled the greetings of all the old-time Hardison folks who knew her. I reported, with seemly embarrassment, how dumb Mitzi regarded my quest.

"She has a point," my mother said, "and a sharp one, too. Why did you want to drive all that way just to look at some rosebushes?"

"I didn't know they were rosebushes when I found the map."

"What did you think they were?"

"Well . . . I simply couldn't guess. One of them was called Gold Mine. That was worth checking out."

"Gold Mine used to be a well-known flower. What were the other names?"

I mentioned a few, careful to include Annie Laurie and Marie Antoinette, but she was not to be deceived. "Martha Flandry, Helen Wilson," she said, tasting the syllables. Then her expression cleared and her tone became sardonic. "You thought those would be names of girlfriends he had. Tell me the truth, Jess. Isn't that what you thought, that your father had a map full of women instead of a little black book like other men have?"

"I have a little black book, too," I said, "but there's nothing much in it but lines of Dante I can't figure out."

Her tone was firm. "You don't count; there's nothing in your books but poetry. Nothing else in your head. Come on now, isn't that what you thought, that Joe Robert was diddling the women of Hardison County?"

"Not exactly."

"Oh yes, it was." She nodded, emphatically agreeing with herself. "Let me tell you the trouble with that little notion. Your father was interested in so many different odd things, he was likely to forget all about sex. I kept having to remind him. When I could get him to remember, he was quite enthusiastic and we used to—"

"Hey," I said, "I'm real sure I don't want to hear about this."

"Why not? How do you think you came into this world, you and Mitzi?"

"I hope to God you found us under cabbage leaves."

"Sometimes I wonder if I didn't find *you* there," she replied. "I don't understand why you're so embarrassed."

"I don't want to hear about my parents' sex life. It's more than embarrassing; it's mortifying."

"And yet you went a long distance and spent a whole day investigating your father's sex life, or what you thought it had been or might have been."

"No. That is, I was pretty sure it wasn't a dozen flesh-and-blood women, but I couldn't figure out what else it could be."

She shook her head slowly, sagely. "No, that's what it was. For years now you have been trying to figure out Joe Robert's mind, what sort of person he was. Don't you feel you know your own father?"

"Yes. Well . . . no. I know him in the ways he relates to me, but I don't know how other people saw him or how he saw them or what kinds of things he thought about."

"He thought about everything. He thought about you a lot. How would you describe your relationship?"

"I think he found me dull. I think he found me constrained by books and ideas instead of being inspired by them, sparked, as he was."

"He loved you very much."

"I expect so, because he didn't strangle me. He was full of wild romantic longings that could only find expression in business schemes and charitable deeds and in those crazy ideas and activities he called his 'projects.' I was full of those longings, too, but mine came out as destructiveness, of myself and others, too. He must have found me thoughtless and even cruel at times."

"Well, yes, you puzzled him, but he loved you and tried to understand."

"That's what I'm trying to do, too. I want to understand."

"He wanted to understand because he loved you. You want to understand because you want to try to make things up with him when it's too late."

" 'Make things up'?"

Now she looked away from me, out the window into the gray day, and her voice sounded distant, abstracted. "You felt unworthy of him. You still feel the same way. You want to figure him out like a puzzle so he'll be solved in your mind and you can make your peace."

"Are you sure about all this?" I asked, but I knew she was right. She had my number. My cheeks felt hot with shame and my throat was tight and had I not been careful, I would have leaked angry tears. That would be the second time in three days—and I am not known as a copious weeper.

"Oh yes, I'm sure," she said. "But the point is, Jess, that you can't. You can't make it up to him, because he's dead. He's gone where you can't make him sad or ashamed, or proud, either. I don't think you'll be able to figure him out. I couldn't; all those years we lived together, I never knew from one minute to the next what he was going to do or think."

"Didn't he tell you what was on his mind?"

"Some things he told me. But he thought so many things, there was no way I'd ever know them all. I didn't understand most of the things he did tell me—so what he didn't tell, I expected I'd never comprehend."

"Aren't you even interested? If you'd been looking through his things out at the workshop and came across the map and the weird gizmo and the other stuff, wouldn't you try to find out what it was all about?"

"No," she said quietly, "not unless I was sure it had something to do with you or Mitzi or me. Otherwise, I'd leave well enough alone."

"Well, I can't do that. You may be right that I'm trying to make up with him when it's too late. I think you are right, because your saying that makes me feel bad, terrible. If it wasn't true, I wouldn't feel so hurt. I probably have other motives, too, that I don't know about. But one of them is the sheer interest of the matter. You said it was like a puzzle—well, finding out these things is like being in a detective story. I keep learning something new."

"What do you learn?"

"For one thing, I found out that he read my poems. There was a note in a volume of Shakespeare that proved at least that much."

"Did you actually think he wouldn't read your books?"

"He never mentioned them, not a word."

"And had you actually thought he'd talk to you about them?"

"I thought maybe."

"Poetry," she said, and with that word she canceled the topic. The term *poetry* now had for her the force of malediction. *Poetry* explained my wayward and drifting existence to her; it was the vice that had brought me low and made me crazy. How could she take seriously the ravings of a prodigal son who wrote poetry? No wonder I wanted to be Fred Chappell instead of Jess Kirkman; no wonder I chose a phony name, the silliest in the telephone book. Fred Chappell showed that in my heart I, too, was ashamed.

And yet she herself used to harbor secret urges toward poetry. Maybe it was the fact she had denied them that made her bitter about the subject.

At the Blue Luna, I picked up a scant and tardy lunch, settling for a slice of rosemary-Parmesan focaccia and a cup of Kilimanjaro. At 2:15, there was only one other diner, and the midafternoon coffee-breakers had not yet appeared. That gave me an opportunity to chat with the jovial but dark and slender young lady behind the cash register. I asked her about the café's catering service I saw advertised in red and yellow chalks on the slate behind the big cutting board. Would they deliver to the large rain shelter out at Montrose Park? I saw they didn't serve wine in the coffee shop, but could they arrange to have a few bottles, along with a dozen or so beers, included in the package? I also ordered a case of soft drinks. Could they set up linen, dishes, and so forth?

Receiving warmly affirmative answers to all these queries, I unsheathed the difficult question: "What kinds of food can you offer for a picnic? Your cuisine here is a modified Californian, isn't it? But the people I want to invite are mostly older people, country folk. I'm not sure how they would take to an Alligator au Pair." I was referring to a featured sandwich, avocado with prosciutto and Brie on a sourdough baguette.

She smiled and patted me on the hand. "Shug," she said, "where do you think I was born? Laguna Beach? Sausalito? My dad and mama live in a little old cabin up toward the head of Morgan's Branch. If you've got good old country people coming to your picnic, some of my aunts and uncles might be amongst 'em."

I evinced surprise at this intelligence. Her beaded headband, the sleeveless denim tunic that displayed her sun and moon tattoos, and her array of turquoise rings had led me to expect that she hailed from some New Age colony that had set up housekeeping on one of the bushier fringes of Pisgah Forest.

"Shirl," she hollered, "take the register for a minute while I talk to a catering customer." When a pretty blond girl appeared from the kitchen, my newfound friend patted my hand again and said, "Let's go sit at the table over there and figure the menu out. Would you like another coffee while we talk? On the house."

I refused the coffee but followed her to the table and we began discussing such things as organic salads with sunflower seeds and other Santa Barbara delicacies. Her name was Debbye ("not *i, ye*") Crabtree, and when I introduced myself, she was pleased to tell me that she knew my sister and that her parents had known my father and regarded him well.

For all her tattoos and Mexican sandals and mysteriously symbolic headband, she talked slowly. And when she patted my hand or touched my arm, her manner was not flirtatious, but maternal for all her young years, and her speech was a languorous drawl. There are some who would describe it as a country drawl, but I must forbear, since it is the same one I possess—flavored with the rural, slightly refined by contact with urban talkers, always tinged with a faint ironic undertone. My university crowd had shed a slight academic tint on my sentences; Debbye's California sojourn had brightened hers a little.

So, did she think that offerings from Blue Luna would be palatable to my crew of plowman granddaddies and apple-pie grandmothers?

"Aw, hon," she said, tweaking my elbow with those long fingers that flaunted a mauvish green polish on the nails, "when I first came to work in a restaurant and tried to read the menu, I didn't say *focaccia*. I pronounced it *foke-a-see-ya*. Now I'm a food freak like you wouldn't believe. If I can pick up on this kind of spread, anybody can. I've got so I can cook just about everything on the menu, including the baked breads. Once people from around here try it, they generally like it."

"Don't they make fun of it?"

"We encourage that. It's part of the joke."

We chatted and finally settled on their free-range chicken salad, Asian coleslaw, breads and cheeses and fresh vegetables and fruits, and a lot of other heroic stuff, all bursting with vitamins and unsullied by any taint of the laboratory. For potables, lemonade and sun-brewed tea, and she would arrange for the wine house across the street to supply a few bottles of wine and beer, though we agreed that this was not going to be a crowd of chardonnay cherishers and pinot partisans.

I took a happy leave of the Blue Luna, feeling I'd got a few things out of the way. The picnic didn't have to be a great social success; it was more in the line of a business meeting, after all. The disposition of our parents' graves was our principal concern, though it would be nice for us, especially for Mitzi, to establish or reestablish contact with some of those who knew our family. All the people from the old times were drifting apart; it was almost as if we could see them leaving us as we stood here in present time, watching them board buses and trains and airplanes to travel onward, with only a longing backward glance as gesture of farewell.

These reveries had made me melancholy, homesick for times I could never reclaim, for hours that I had seemed to lose even when I lived through them. Perhaps I had missed a great deal, reading so continually and seeing the world through the windowpanes of books. But then, maybe not. If books had made up a large part of the experience of my youth, it only meant that what I'd missed in immediacy of experience, I'd gained in variety, looking so widely into the thoughts and dreams of others, of travelers and sages, of soldiers and scholars and all the mighty dead.

Whether that was the case or not, these musings caused me to decide to drive by our old domicile on the farm north of Tipton. I was headed that way to see if I could find the Irelands and Hillyers, so when I left Asheville, I headed west again, taking the superslab this time, and hurrying along at the upper zone of the speed limit.

When I'd gone off to study at the university, my parents and grandparents had left the farm. My father's business enterprises made living closer to Asheville a matter of such obvious convenience, it bordered on necessity. They had built a nice large placid-looking house in one of the new developments, following my mother's design. She had never cared much for farm life and sometimes spoke bitterly against it, though on this subject, as on many others, she would vacillate. Sometimes she would extol the bucolic virtues, telling me that the old-time religious values were the only true ones and that this modern world was going to hell in a wicker egg basket. She managed to imply that I belonged to the modern world while she steadfastly did not, so that all the immorality, corruption, and deceit that furnished such plentiful material for newspaper stories must somehow be partly my fault.

Mostly, though, she would rail against the old days, informing me how difficult life had been, especially for females, especially for her. *"Hard,"* she would say. "You've got to understand how it was hard." That aria would go on for numerous choruses and *hard* was a part of its every refrain.

I made good time and skirted the back way around Tipton and followed one of the outlying streets until it changed into the dirt road that led by our farm. The gravel road had washed away and the bed needed to be scraped; Buttercup lurched from side to side over the rock-ribbed depressions and thumping ruts.

We had leased our old farmhouse to the Hanson family, a blue-eyed, milk-faced crew of healthy individuals. They farmed only enough to keep the acres from turning into wilderness; both the parents were chemists, working in the Challenger laboratories, trying to figure out some way to stop the mill discharge from coloring the river onyx. The boys were twelve and fourteen, and this afternoon I found them playing a seemingly improvised intricate ball game under the great walnut tree and the towering black oaks in the front yard.

The house looked different. It was not only that the Hansons had added a deck to the right side of the sturdy two-story brick structure. Mitzi and I had known that would produce an odd appearance when we allowed them to build it. But there were other subtler changes, too, unnoticeable except to someone who could remember it vividly as it used to be, when the windows wore glass curtains instead of shiny nylon drapes, when the upstairs windows had pull-down shades instead of venetian blinds, when there was a lightning rod with a blue glass ball by the chimney instead of a television antenna strapped to it. These details, and others equally insignificant, affected me more strongly than the structural addition; it was no longer "our house."

My attention was drawn to the tall, flushed boys intent on their game. I tried to figure out how it worked. The boys were throwing a dilapidated baseball up on the roof and trying to catch it when it came down. I remembered playing that sort of game with myself for hours on end, bouncing a tennis ball along the ridges of the barn's galvanized tin roof. But the Hanson boys had developed a more interesting activity. Most of the time, they missed the mark they were aiming at and the dull-colored baseball simply rolled down the slope, picking up speed till it overleapt the guttering and dropped into their hands. If they could place it just right, however, throwing it so it would glance lightly off the chimney of gray brick, it would roll gently along the side of the single dormer in the middle of the roof, then coast down the front part of the roof and drop into the gutter. When that happened, I could hear it traveling in the trench of the gutter, making a hollow metallic sound until it reached the corner of the house. But it did not drop into the drainpipe; there must have been a square of mesh screen over it. Instead, it slammed with some little force against the corner butt of the gutter, which was more sharply canted than most eave guttering. The butt end was not solid; it was a spring-hinged flap that would pop open to eject the baseball, and the trick was for one of the boys to be there when it fell. This was no easy maneuver, there being so many bushes and flowering plants in the way; they had to be nimble to accomplish their goal.

I'd never seen any guttering arrangement like this one before and recognized it immediately as my father's handiwork. Who else would imagine such an innovation? Its purpose I could not discern merely by looking, but it surely had not been devised merely to play this game the Hanson boys had improvised. Then it came to me that I had examined the model of this weird mechanism when I'd gone through the things in his workshop. That inverted terra-cotta Y stuffed into the length of stovepipe: A sort of cannon it must have been, and it was supposed to throw up a projectile that would perform for him just as it did for the boys. It wouldn't be a baseball, though; maybe a lead ball like the one shot-putters throw, or— I recalled—that nine-pound Civil War cannonball that had sat on the long bench among the rocketry books.

What had he planned to use for a cannon? Why, the chimney itself, of course. He would find a way to load a charge at the top of the fireplace, and when it was set off, the cannonball would scoot up the flue with just the right amount of force to emerge from the chimney top, roll along the side of the dormer, drop into the guttering and trundle down to the end, burst open the hinged flap, and drop onto the lever that set off the action of the other levers, resulting in the propelling forward of a disk of some sort that would flip over in the air three times before hitting its target. When I looked at the porch, I could see in my mind's eye where each of the four lever arms would be stationed and how they would act together. What I could not figure out was the nature of the disk nor why he would want it to behave in that way. Again, I was lacking the key. Some piece of essential information was escaping my attention or perhaps my memory.

There was another question, too, one that pointed up the difference between my father's ebullient confidence and my own cautious skepticism. He had believed the gizmo would actually work, that all the actions and interactions would mesh and that his Unidentified Object would take flight. I didn't think it was possible. In the first place, the charge needed to throw the cannonball to a height of twenty-five feet would also damage the fireplace, cracking the mortar and knocking down bricks. My mother would have put the kibosh on that in short order. Then there would be no way to regulate the charge exactly enough that the cannonball would loop gently out of the chimney mouth and take the desired route instead of leaping high into the air and falling with a destructive crash onto the roof. He would have had to place a deflector up there, and even then it would be extremely chancy.

So he had begun his strange project and never finished it.

He must have finally decided that it was impractical. But had he ever realized how outlandish the whole idea was? I wondered if my father had ever had any apprehensions—not about his soundness of mind, but about how he might be perceived by others. What if some concerned and kindly neighbors came to think their funny friend would be better off in the charge of the boys with the butterfly nets? How would he defend himself when examined by some gray institutional psychiatrist?

He would not fare well. I recalled what he had once said about psychoanalysis: "It is the disease for which it pretends to be the cure." This is not the kind of sentiment that endears Freudians, Jungians, Reichians, or Maslovians to oneself.

If he had been fooling around with the fireplace, making adjustments to my mother's nice house, he would have had some colossal explanations to erect. I was more curious about the nature of that flying disk than about anything else connected with this mechanism.

Suddenly, I was tired of trying to figure it out, tired of watching the Hanson boys at play, red-faced, shouting, calling each other fond obscene names.

I turned around in the driveway and headed back toward Asheville. *Tomorrow* I would visit the Hillyers and the Irelands and get everything in order for the picnic that I hoped would wind up all these affairs neatly. I imagined myself standing before this assembly of my parents' friends and saying, in the manner of William Powell as the martini-inspired Thin Man, "Perhaps you are wondering why I called you all here together."

Chapter Eight

OLD TIMES

THERE ARE NOT

FORGOTTEN

When *is everywhere.*
—Fugio

Mr. Hillyer was what folks call "a well-spoken man," meaning that he showed a fine intelligence, commanded a supple vocabulary, organized his thoughts in ready fashion, and was a patient listener. That's what most people mean by "well spoken," though not many could put it in those terms. Sometimes the phrase is one of mild opprobrium, implying that to be well spoken is not in the tradition of the Appalachian mountaineer, whose sometimes inscrutable taciturnity is locally regarded as a virtue having something to do with valor and manliness.

Don't ask me why. It's one of the great folkish mysteries.

We sat on an old oaken bench beneath a couple of refreshing sycamores in the sparsely grassed front yard of his farmhouse. The morning was already too warm and beginning to cloud; the delectable June weather was soon going to turn rainy. Mr. Hillyer told me so in his quiet voice, speaking his prognostication so matter-of-factly, I had no room to doubt that it was going to pour buckets. I only hoped it would hold off until Monday, when, if all my jerry-built plans stayed glued together, I should have finished my mission.

When I told him how much Mitzi and I appreciated his kind offer to accommodate the graves of our parents in his own family graveyard, he nodded slowly and said he was proud to have the opportunity, that he and his wife, Jenny, and Joe Robert and Cora went back a long way together. He expected he owed us Kirkmans a few favors, he said, but that wouldn't be the reason he made his offer. He just enjoyed thinking about the old times, when life showed a more favorable countenance, and he hoped having Joe Robert's grave nearby would help bring these times to mind.

"Are things pretty hard for you now?" I asked.

All his motions were deliberate, even when he shook his head no. "Not any harder than they are for most old folks. Not nearly as bad as for some, I know that much. But every time I look in the mirror, I expect to see a twenty-six-year-old man with a strong arm and a willing heart. What I see instead is an eighty-two-year-old dried-up, creaky-kneed codger with his mind gone upstream and downstream all at once."

I was startled, having put his age in the late sixties or early seventies.

He caught my expression and nodded. "Confusing, isn't it? I see an old, old fellow and you see somebody that looks younger than you expected."

"Well, I'm getting on up there myself," I said. "I anticipate finding out all about it."

"Probably so," he said, "and no way to tell if it's good luck or bad. I lost my Jenny last year to the cancer, and that's about as tough as it can get, having to watch your nearest and dearest suffer like that. My boy came in from the Ford plant in Ohio to stay with me and my daughter came down from Maine for a few days, but I was mostly alone. Now I'm alone just about all the time, and I reckon that's why I dote on the past years so much and try to wish them back."

"And my daddy and mother were part of the past?"

"For a good many years." He looked across the yard at an abelia bush so alive with honeybees, it seemed to throb with its own sunlight. "For a good many years, yes. Your folks would come over to our house every Saturday night without fail and we'd have us a round or two of setback. That was the game we liked in those days and wouldn't hear of anything else."

"It's not a game I know. Was my daddy a pretty good player?"

"I have heard tell it's a form of whist," he replied, pronouncing it *whusht*. Then he turned his long, ruddy face toward me and gazed steadily into my eyes with brown eyes so dark, they seemed sunken beneath his bushy gray eyebrows. He hadn't shaved today and there was a light frosting of white beard along his cheeks. "No, your daddy was a spotty player, if you don't mind my saying so. But Cora was very good—sharp as a whip, never forgot her cards. When we paired off together, Cora and me, there was no stopping us. . . . Except once in a while one of Joe Robert's harebrained plays would work out for him and we'd all sit there dumbfounded while he had a big laugh."

"What kind of harebrained plays?"

"I wish I could describe them to you, but I can't, because I never caught on even at the time. All I know is that they were plays nobody else would ever think of."

"Sounds typical for my father."

"Well, it won't seem like much to you, but a Saturday-night card game was some of the best entertainment we had in those days. You understand, there wasn't much variety—no television, and not everyone cared to have a radio until the war broke out in Europe. Then we all tuned in. Square dances about once a month, a barn raising once a year. Of course, the ladies had their socials and their sewing circles. Church was a big thing. I'd go to church faithfully, even though I'd sit in the pew, going over in my mind the hands of the card game the night before. I guess I'm just not cut in the religious mold. Never go to church anymore, never think about it."

"I'm not much for organized religion, either," I offered.

He raised those wire-brush eyebrows. "Might take after your daddy in that respect. There was a time he and I went to lots of churches, one after the other. . . . Would you like to take a little walk and see what we've got to offer in the way of a resting place for your folks?"

"Sure," I said. "I'm much obliged. What did you mean when you said 'we'? 'What we've got to offer'?"

He rose slowly but with a single steady motion. His gaze slid off my face and found the round pasture hills out beyond his house and barn. It seemed as if he took walking strength by resting his eyes on them. "I meant Jenny and me," he admitted. "I still think *we*. I reckon I always will." He gestured eastward toward the hills. "Let's head out that way and I'll show you the family gravesite."

He was a tall man, spare not because of age but in his natural build, and he set off with a slow but long-legged pace that covered ground with clean efficiency. I had to match him a little better than stride for stride to keep up.

"You say you and my father visited a number of churches?"

"That's right. We took in about fifty all told in the space of a little over a year, every last one we could find in Harwood County. We had to be able to get there early enough on a Sunday morning, so there were a few we omitted."

"What was your purpose in doing that?"

"I didn't have a purpose. I only got talked into going by your daddy. This idea was all Joe Robert's."

"What was the idea?"

"He said he was collecting religious points of view. His mother-in-law kept pestering him to go to church and he told her he'd go to church all right when he figured out what the very best one was. Religion was too important, he told her, for a man to make his church choice without shopping around to see what was being offered. I think the real reason was that he was gathering notions to confound her with when they argued religion. That was a big thing they had together, Annie Barbara being so pious and your dad so full of mischief. He wanted to try out on her some of the messages the wild and woolly preachers delivered from their pulpits."

"How did that work out?"

"We heard some strange things back in the hollers and up along the creeks. Heard some mighty fine music and heard some preaching that made us pinch ourselves to keep from laughing. We found out, too, that there were some fundamental disagreements among the various ministries and no way to reconcile them that we could see."

"Like what?"

He paused his uphill march and turned to survey the ground we'd covered. We hadn't come far, but I could tell he liked to look back at his house a quarter mile down the slope. It was a tall two-story structure and I had to surmise that he'd sealed off a number of the rooms, with only himself there to keep the place up. It had been some time since it last had been painted and most of the paint had weathered away, leaving the house gray and plaintive beside the shadowy sycamores.

He sighed a brief sigh before turning to travel on. Then he smiled quietly. "Well, there seemed to be a lot of confusion amongst 'em about when the world would end. One would say one date and another would say another and the others would set out a whole different mess of them. That caught Joe Robert's attention and he decided to make a little fuss about it.''

"How's that?"

"He sent out the same letter to six of them, saying he had an important announcement concerning their church and if they would agree to meet with him on a certain Saturday afternoon down at Virgil Campbell's Bound for Hell Gro. and Dry Goods, they might find the discussion a profitable one. Now when he included that word *profitable*, he ensured that they would show up, maybe smelling a donation of some sort. But of course they didn't know your daddy's turn of mind.

"Anyhow, there were the preachers gathered around that cold woodstove in the month of April, I think it was, and they had dressed up in the best they had because they wanted to impress this stranger person who had taken an interest in their good works.

"Of course, your daddy showed up late so that those six hard-shell preachers had to stand around eyeing each other with dark suspicion, each wondering how to get the jump on the others if there were any church donations involved.

"After a while, Joe Robert appears, not dressed up in the least, just wearing the overalls and brogans he wore every Saturday when he took his corn into the Tipton Farmers Federation for milling. But that was all right, you see, because those preachers took it as an eternal truth that a truly rich man doesn't dress up and put on airs. It's an old saying from long ago: Poor in the mouth, money in the bank.

"So there they stood waiting, all expectant, and there was your daddy taking his time, chatting with Virgil Campbell and buying a few notions and a little poke of peppermint drops for his mother-in-law, till he finally comes over to where the posse of them is standing around the stove, and he says, 'Gentlemen, I thank you for coming. I know you have important things to do and I count your presence here a real favor. Now me, I'm just a dirt farmer and my wife is a poorly paid schoolteacher, so we don't have a lot of money and we need to be careful with what we've got. Nevertheless, I've managed to set a little bit aside and I've been thinking about making a few investments, and that's where you come in.'

"And with that, your daddy took out a little notepad from his back pocket and a pencil stub from his bib. 'I've been attending your Sunday services,' he says, 'and I must say I've heard some sterling ministry. I doubt if there's a county in any state in the whole United States that can offer up the brand of preaching that ours does. I sure do admire the way you gentlemen put the Good News out. But I've run into a little difficulty here. . . .'

"Then he opened up his notepad and commenced to go down the line on them. 'Reverend Hangnut,' he says, 'seems to me you prophesied that the world was going to come to an end in the year 2000. Is that right? Looks like I've recorded you saying that last July the twentieth.' When Preacher Hangnut nodded his head, Joe Robert turned to the next one. 'Reverend Pferddars, I have it down here you prophesied the year 2010 would be the last of us. Is that correct?' Yes, said this preacher and the next and all of them together. Your daddy had gathered dates of 2000, 2010, 1985, 1999, and 1988. Then he came to Preacher Butloe and said, 'Now, Reverend Butloe, you didn't exactly prophecy a date, but said that in certain verses of Leviticus, Numbers, and Revelations we would find the ciphers that added up to reveal the date when our sinful world would pass away and Jesus would return in all His glory. I have run those figures through my accounting department, Reverend, and I find that by your prediction, the world already ended in 1883. So I surmise I have made an error of interpretation somewhere along the line and I'll need your help in seeking out where I took the wrong path. But we can do that a little later, after I make known to you what is on my mind.'

"And then Joe Robert leaned back against the barrel of dog biscuit that was sitting in front of the meat counter and folded his arms against his chest and scanned the six preachers one after another with as steady a look as a marksman sighting down his rifle barrel.

" 'The problem I have as a businessman with a little money to invest is that I am all confused. I need to make a long-term investment or two to take care of my children and grandchildren and to make sure we don't lose our farm out of the family to taxes or bad times. So I need to know exactly when the world is going to end. If it is the year 2000, well then, those new ciphering gadgets made by International Business Machines look like strong investments. If it is 1999, then I might go with Corning Glassware, which is developing a glass cable that can look anywhere into the human body. If it is the year 2010, I believe there will be a mining enterprise on the moon, sending back silver and other valuable minerals to the planet we will still be living on come Judgment Day—that is, the Day of Judgment by your calculation.

" 'I'm not a deep Bible scholar myself, but I put a lot of faith in that holy book. I reckon that's why we have preachers in the world, to help explain the words of God to old boys like me that are not often privy to the mind of the Lord. So here's what I want you to do: I want you gentlemen to get down on your knees and pray together; I want you to read your Bibles down to the last verse on the last page; I want you to consult the soundest authorities—and then arrive at an agreed-upon date among you when the world will end. For my purposes, I need the year, the month, the day, and, if possible, the very hour, because in the investment business, we can't afford to be imprecise. I have twelve hundred dollars to divide amongst you if all six of you can agree when that awful day of doom will befall. Two hundred dollars is not any grand fortune, I admit, but it ought to buy a few hymnals at least.'

"Then there was a silence in that grocery store you could break up with a plowshare. The preachers looked at Joe Robert and then they looked away. They looked at one another, kind of peeking to see what each was thinking. Then they looked at that old oiled-down pine floor and cleared their throats one at a time. Finally, one of them spoke up—Preacher Pferddars, I think it was—and he says, 'Well, Mr. Kirkman, that's as fair and handsome an offer as I've had lately, and I'm going to ask my reverend colleagues here if we can't meet in council and take the matter under advisement.' They all nodded their heads and said that's what they'd do, they'd take it under advisement, and your daddy said he looked forward to hearing from them.

"As they were filing out one by one, Joe Robert asked Preacher Butloe if he didn't want to stop for a minute and help him with his figures to show him where he'd gone astray with the year 1883, but the preacher refused, saying he would meet with the others in solemn council and come back with the revised official and final figure. It might be just an elementary mistake in arithmetic; that was the kind of thing that could happen when a mere mortal man, even a preacher of the Gospel, got all excited by a revelation from the Most High.

" 'Very good, Reverend,' your daddy said. 'I can understand how that might happen. You go on and hold your council with the others and you-all get word back to me through Virgil Campbell as quick as you can. I'll take it as a favor, though, gentlemen, if you will keep this information confidential from everybody but me. You can see how valuable it is and how it will lose its value if others find out and jump on the same investment bandwagon I'm on. That would send the stock price shooting up like a skyrocket. Now I do understand that there are some unprincipled people in the world that go around to the brokerage houses and peddle their prophecies to the highest bidders. There are some big-money boys that would pay a whole lot more than I am able to pay to find out when the last great battle with Satan will take place on the fields of Armageddon. But you gentlemen are the ministers of the Gospel and the keepers of the keys of sanctity, so I know my information is in safe hands.'

"They went out then, and for a minute it looked like they

might get together right there in the parking lot. But they didn't. They sidled off from one another, kind of sneaking, like each one of them thought he had a bad smell on him the others could notice. Then they drove off home."

We had reached the top of the highest hill now and stopped to survey the layout. When I looked back toward his house, it was harder to distinguish than before, not because of distance—we hadn't come all that far—but because its grayness and the air of times past around it faded it into the landscape. The sky was high and gray, without the black underclouds that promise immediate rain, and it shadowed the pastureland so that it didn't glow green as on a sunny day, but took on a deeper and more peaceful hue.

Mr. Hillyer pointed eastward to the next hilltop, a little lower than the one we had mounted. It was crowned with a grove of oaks and made a pretty picture. "The graveyard is just around on the other side," he said. "I hope you'll find it fitting."

"Is there a road back around, or is this the only way in?"

"It was put there when we used horse-drawn wagons for most purposes. I've got a little Ferguson tractor in the barn that would do right well if it still runs. I haven't cranked it up for I guess two years now. I'm afraid I can't claim that I'm still farming. I mostly live on Social Security and a little retirement policy Jenny took out for us."

"Looks like there's a lot of farm here for just one man."

"For one old Methuselah, there is. I still kept a milk cow till just about a year ago. But the last time Marigold stepped on my foot, I told her, 'Girl, you just bought a ticket to the stockyard.' Now the Pet Dairy man pulls up at my mailbox every day with milk or butter or eggs, whatever I want. I don't even have to leave him a forkful of hay."

"So then what happened with my daddy and the preachers?" I asked.

He paused to recollect where he'd left off, then nodded his characteristic slow nod. "Nothing happened for a long time—or nothing we could know of, because we didn't hear the first word from any of them. Your daddy and I figured they were hashing it out, pounding their Bibles till the red ink ran like blood and arguing which day of the week the good Lord had planned to throw the switch on the world of mankind.

"So Joe Robert sent another letter. He wrote that he was disappointed in not hearing from them, as it was important in investing in stocks to get in on the ground floor before prices start to rise out of the reach of the modest means he could command. So he had taken, he said, to tuning in a certain evangelist who spoke on the radio and had such a persuasive manner and cited so many smart biblical texts that he had been convinced by the Reverend Alvin Allen and his Golden Ministry of the Airwaves that the world was going to end in 1975. It just so happened that date coincided with a special investment he had in mind that would mature in the late 1960s and give Joe Robert and his family a handsome-enough income that they could live prosperously until the twenty-third of December, 1975, at which time Gabriel would sound his trump and the walls of all creation would come tumbling down.

"Unless his preacher friends here in Harwood County could offer good and sufficient evidence that the date the radio evangelist prophesied was incorrect, he would accept 1975. It was too bad, he wrote in his letter, that the fine Harwood preachers had to forfeit the two hundred dollars apiece, but he could well comprehend how the settling of the date of Judgment Day would be in no manner an easy undertaking and he thanked them sweetly for their time and concern. But he would go into the First National Bank of Tipton come Thursday and tell Bob Brendan that he was moving all his investment capital. The men of God would understand that this particular investment strategy would have to be a secret between Joe Robert and banker Brendan, because if rumor got out, the investment would be a lot less desirable."

We were crossing the depression between the two hills and I noted that the pasture hadn't been limed or grubbed for some years. There were scattered patches of bare soil, and browning grass and thistles were numerous, a strong sign of neglect. We began the easy climb toward the small grove at the top.

"Come Wednesday evening after supper, he got a phone call from Brendan. What was Joe Robert up to now? he wanted to know. He had been getting calls and visits, bribes and other sundry offers, from a bunch of Holy Roller preachers. They wanted to know what stock Joe Robert was investing his money in on Thursday and they didn't want the banker to tell the other preachers, only the one calling at the time. And they wanted him to advise your daddy that the world wasn't going to end in 1975, but in 2010 or 1988 or 1999 or whenever, depending on which one of the six called. What kind of prank was under way? If Joe Robert was going to pull one of his rusties that involved Brendan and the First National, he at least ought to have told his friend about it first.

" 'Well,' your daddy said, 'the reason I didn't tell you was that I didn't really expect them to fall for it.' Then he explained what he had done and Brendan said that the joke had worked out fine, but what was he supposed to do now?

"Then your daddy started to laugh. Had they really offered bribes? Had there really been a half-dozen preachers trying to bribe a Republican banker with offers of money? How much had they offered? 'The best promise I got was for twenty dollars,' Brendan said, 'and I've got to tell you, Joe Robert, I felt insulted. Seems to me I ought to command a higher price than that. A banker is only as good as his reputation, and a measly twenty bucks means that mine is abiding poorly.' Your daddy said, 'Down-and-out preachers in hard times. Getting so the collection plate is skimpy.'

"Then he told Brendan to tell them that he, Joe Robert Kirkman, who was just a backwoods dirt farmer, had come across a surefire investment that would pay out millions in the year 1968. It was an investment the big-shot Wall Streeters knew nothing about as of yet. Brendan was to let them one by one worm the name of it out of him and swear each of them to secrecy. Then he was to give them the number of a local post office box where they could write for sealed information about this amazing investment. Brendan started chuckling, so your daddy knew he'd go along with it. 'What's the number of that post office box?' he asked, and your daddy told him. 'All right, I've written that down,' he said. 'Now what's the name of the company they're investing in?' 'I'll send you the brochure,' Joe Robert told him, except he had to say it wouldn't be a real brochure on fancy slick paper with photographs; it would only be a mimeographed description of the company on a sheet of bright red paper. He wanted Brendan to understand, however, that if he himself wanted to invest in the brand spanking new enterprise, Joe Robert could undoubtedly get him all the shares he desired at a whopping big discount. No questions to answer, no papers to sign—just send the naked cash money to a phony name—Burnette or something—Box One eighty-two, Tipton, North Carolina. But banker Brendan allowed as how he'd forgo the pleasure just now and would wait till he saw the stock listed in the *Standard & Poor Index*, and Joe Robert said, 'Well, Bob, I think you might see the heat death of the universe before that happens.' Brendan said the heat death of the universe sounded dangerous, and Joe Robert said it wasn't due for a while yet.''

Mr. Hillyer smiled at his fond reminiscence of the total joke. ''So banker Brendan knew better than to invest, but those preachers didn't. Every last one of them sent for the flyer about the stock and every last one of them sent what money he could to the post office address as an investment. Plain cash money, I mean, in a plain brown envelope, like they were buying smutty pictures. Do you know the name of the so-called company they were investing in?''

Of course I knew, but signaled no. I wouldn't have spoiled Mr. Hillyer's story for a handful of General Motors stock.

He was as gleeful as a schoolkid with a frog in both pockets.

"Satanic Enterprises Amalgamated," he said. "That was the company name, and the description told all about the sinfulest kinds of things this company derived its income from. I can't remember them all, and there were some I'd never heard of and probably couldn't pronounce to this very day. Maybe those preachers had never heard of some of those devilish doings, but they must have grasped the general idea—and they sent their money in anyhow. It might be they thought they could make money off of Satan and turn it to pious use, beating Old Scratch at his own game, so to speak. Or it might be they only wanted to line their own holy pockets. Whatever their motive, your daddy wound up with about fifteen hundred dollars all told."

We had reached the grove now and Mr. Hillyer found a leafy path, somewhat overgrown, that led into it, and I walked along beside him, shuffling through leaves and scraping by sapling limbs. It was dark and cool in here under the clouded sky.

"What did he do with the money?"

"The first thing your daddy did was to cancel the post office box he'd rented under that phony name. I can't quite remember what it was—I. K. Burnette, maybe? I. K. something, anyway."

"I. K. Brunel," I told him.

"Yes," he said, surprised. "That's it. How do you know?"

"It was a name he liked."

"Well, he canceled the post office box and after that did nothing at all for quite a while, three or four weeks. Then he wrote a letter and got it mimeographed and sent it to all of the investors. It was brief and reported that Satanic Enterprises Amalgamated was unhappily announcing bankruptcy and that the company was disbanding. It had turned out that while there was indeed a large and steady demand for sin, it was still a drug on the market. It seemed that the scarlet opportunities Satanic Enterprises was offering for money, all the interested prospective clientele already knew how to get for free. And that was the end of it."

"You mean he kept the fifteen hundred dollars?"

"I mean that was the end of Satanic Amalgamated. No, Joe Robert sent the money back to each and all. He got cashier's checks made out and added a donation of ten dollars to the amount. But you know what he did? He bought six sympathy cards at the drugstore, the kind of card you send to somebody when they've lost a dear one, and he put the check inside of that. On each card, he wrote the message, 'The wages of sin is death'."

"I'm glad to hear that story," I said. "It kind of explains some details that had mystified me." I told him about finding the Satanic flyer among my father's effects in the workshop.

He nodded. "That was Joe Robert all right. That was him all over. He was always pulling practical jokes like that one. Most of them weren't so complicated, though. That has to be the most complicated one he ever dreamed up."

"I don't know," I replied. "Maybe not."

"Well, here we are," Mr. Hillyer said. "It won't look like much to you, but it means a lot to me, and you'll be able to keep it up better than I could."

In truth, the Hillyer graveyard did look sadly abandoned. The surroundings were pleasant: The grove at our back was mostly free of undergrowth and the tall white oaks might fairly be described as stately. On the slope before us ridged cow paths were cut into the side of the hill and at the bottom a sluggish small stream oozed through a reedy patch of marsh. Opposite us was a taller hill, patched with rangy thistles and sporting a couple of shaggy crab apple trees.

The graveyard itself was a small oblong with six plots tucked in amid the dock and plantain in the scruffy grass. Two of them were children's graves, and Mr. Hillyer nodded his slow nod when he caught my surprise. "That's right, Mr. Kirkman," he said. "We lost two babies to diphtheria, Jenny and I did. Maybe that's a reason I have let this spot run slovenly. When I come up here, I remember our sorrow over our children, so I don't visit much. There's plenty of room, though. Right over there at the top edge might be a good place for Cora and Joe Robert."

It looked suitable, but I thought the situation with Mr. Hill-yer and his family was too disheartening. Graveyards are not supposed to be dance halls, I understand, but suppose that on some wild and windy moonless night that threatened rain in floods, with lightning scarring the darkness livid, my father did triumph over death. His favorite gravesite was pictured on a postcard from France; in Amiens lie the remains of Jules Verne, with a statuary showing him flinging back the lid of his coffin, his cerements all disheveled, and rising toward the glorioled future. He once brought the card out of the jumbled depths of a desk drawer to show me. This was when our death-intoxicated uncle Runkin was visiting and we had all become depressed by his untiring devotion to the Grim Reaper. "Here," my father said, tapping the postcard with a blunt forefinger, "this is what a proper tombstone ought to look like. Uncle Runkin doesn't have a clue."

I took it from him and peered at it closely. "Does it have an epitaph?" I asked. "The picture is too small to see if it has."

"I forget the French," he replied, "but I think it says something like 'You can't keep a good man down.' "

Suppose, then, that on that tumultuous night I had been imagining, my father, like the industrious author of those fab-ulous romances, tore back the lid of his coffin, plunged up through the rooty sod, and breathed the free night air again. Wouldn't he want a dancing ground upon which to leap and cavort, rattling his bones like castanets and singing a gay habanera as he zigzagged away to find where Virgil Campbell lay and rouse his dormant friend for a night of rattle-bone jollity?

If so, the Hillyer earth was the wrong place to inter him; it was too somber even for a graveyard; too much sadness made the atmosphere heavy with an insupportable history of suffering.

I noted with something like alarm that Mr. Hillyer's spouse was missing, and when I mentioned the fact, he nodded once again his deliberate nod. "Yes. I couldn't bear to be that close to her when she was dead. All I'd remember would be the pain and agony of her final days. She's laid away over in Grace Hill cemetery. That's where I'm going, too, when it's my turn. So there will be plenty of room here for good and all. I don't expect my son or daughter will care to be buried here."

I made a murmur to signify comprehension, but it seemed that one thing Mr. Hillyer had not thought of was the disposition of his farm. His children would sell it off soon after his death; it was plain to see they were not returning to Harwood County.

"It would be a pleasure to think of Cora and Joe Robert being here," he said. "It would be almost a comfort."

I thanked him genuinely and profusely for his kindness and we began our leisurely journey back toward his house.

The front door was open at the Ireland house, but the screen door was closed and I could see nothing beyond it but a cool darkness. The house stood still and silent, but when I rapped on the jamb, finding it hard to make an audible sound against the solid wood, three people answered. I could make out their figures, veiled by the screen mesh, but not much else.

"Yes, sir," asked a strongly masculine voice, "what can we do for you?"

"My name is Jess Kirkman," I said. "Joe Robert was my father and Cora is my mother. I believe my sister has been in touch with Mr. Ireland."

It was a voice older than the first that replied. "That's right, except that it was your aunt Ora she spoke to, not me."

The door swung open and out stepped an old gentleman in a red plaid shirt and denim trousers supported by a pair of braided leather suspenders. His sandy hair was growing sparse and he was a little less than medium height, with an agile, wiry build. He offered a handshake. "I'm Gray Ireland and these are two of my boys, Tod and Bud. I won't say either of them is the best one."

I shook his hand and smiled. "I'm sure they're as good as the best boys there are."

But when they shouldered through, I felt I'd chosen an inaccurate noun. Both men were in their mid to late thirties and they almost dwarfed their father. They had his sandy hair plentifully and his sandy, freckled complexion, but each stood more than a head taller than he and both were as brawny as dockworkers. They seemed friendly enough, and I was glad of that.

"He'd've said the same thing if Ned was here," one of them said, and gripped my hand with his monstrous one; he could have crushed my knuckles like Rice Krispies. "But he's working three till eleven over at Challenger and went in early for some reason or other. I think he's been sparking one of the secretaries in the bursar's office." Then he added, as if it were an unimportant footnote, "I'm Tod."

"And I'm Bud," said his brother. "Pleased to meet you."

Bud's handshake made little impression on me, since my hand was still numb from his brother's grip. Tod's greeting hand had felt a little like I'd slammed my poor paw in a car door.

"Bud," said his daddy, "run around to the back of the house and fetch your mother. Tell her some important company has showed up."

Without a reply, Bud went back into the house. I could feel the structure tremble, even out here on the porch, as he marched down the hall.

"Sit you down over there in that stout rocking chair," Uncle Gray said. "Aunt Ora will be here in a minute. She's in the backyard gathering clothes off the line. I told her it probably wouldn't rain till late Sunday evening, but she said she didn't trust my weather wisdom." Then he added, as if without thinking, "She's not really your aunt. It's only that your family called us Aunt Ora and Uncle Gray for as long as I can remember."

Deducing that the non sequitur was an Ireland family trait, I agreed with his observation. "That's what I remember Daddy and Mother calling you," I said, "though they would have been about the same age you are. That's kind of odd."

"She sure was a pert and pretty little thing, your mother was." He seated himself in a straight chair directly across from me while Tod eased into the blue-and-red porch swing. The chains squeaked their protest and I was fearful the eye hooks would pull out of the tongue-and-groove pine ceiling and send Tod crashing down. "And it's been so long since I seen you, you weren't no bigger than a possum baby, hardly. I could just about hold you in the palm of my hand."

"Of course, Ned might be sparking more than one secretary. It would take more than one to drag me into that dadblasted old mill before I had to go on shift," Tod said.

"You're just jealous because he's such a ladies' man," Uncle Gray declared. "You're restless because you went and got married before you were out of knee britches, hardly."

"You married?" Tod asked.

I didn't mind his frank curiosity because he was so obviously good-natured. He and Bud both had florid complexions and eyes so pale, I couldn't assign a color to them, but I figured Tod to be the younger, his features very similar to Bud's, only not so pronounced. "For a long time," I answered.

"How long would that be?"

"Since the Pleistocene age," I replied, then, seeing that this little sally made no more impression than a honeybee bouncing off armor plate, added, "For about twelve years now."

"How many children?"

"None."

"Gaw," he said, thunderstruck. "Not any in twelve years? I ain't been married but six and I've already got four."

"Hush your bragging, Tod," his father commanded. "It ain't like you done it all yourself without any help from Mary Ann."

Tod grinned and rubbed his hands together. "She sure is a looker, though. I got to admit that."

"Your wife?" I asked.

"No. Nancy Merkle that ole Ned has been sparking."

"Oh."

"Her, too, though."

"Who?"

"My wife, Mary Ann. She's a handsome woman. You'd enjoy to see her."

I could discern that strong concentration was required to follow the Ireland manner of discourse. They treated conversation as if it were hopscotch played without benefit of markers for the squares. I was a little relieved when Bud returned with his mother, opening the screen door for her with a hint of ceremoniousness and ushering her toward me.

"This here's my mom," he explained proudly.

"How do you do, Mrs. Ireland?"

Ash-blond and taller than her husband, she presented a neat and secretly humorous aspect. She was not willowy; her slenderness had within it a sinewy strength. She didn't offer her hand but bowed instead; it was a slight but graceful mock curtsy and it underlined the quiet humor in her eyes and in the set of her mouth. Her age had to be pretty much the same as Uncle Gray's, but she looked almost as young as her two sons. "You ought to call me Aunt Ora," she said. "I imagine you've been doing that all your life anyhow."

"Yessum," I said, "because that's what my mother and daddy called you."

"I hear Cora's been ailing," she said. "I hope it's nothing serious."

I told her congestive heart failure was a drawn-out, complicated, and uncomfortable process but that my mother, after the initial overwhelming panic, was handling it as well as could be expected.

"Please tell her I send my love and for her to get well soon."

"Yessum."

"And sit down. All you boys sit down."

I hadn't noticed till then that Tod and Uncle Gray had both stood when she entered out onto the porch, showing their manners to the woman of the house. Bud brought up another straight chair from the far end of the porch; it was padded, seat and back, with flat cushions in a flower pattern. Aunt Ora sat gracefully, smoothing her apron and dress over her knees.

"Scuse me, if you don't mind," Bud said. He went back into the house, easing the screen door shut quietly.

His departure gave me an obscure but genuine moment of relief. The brothers looked so much alike, even with the difference in age, and dressed so similarly—blue jeans and starched white shirts with the cuffs rolled to the middle of the forearm—that I had been feeling a little confused. It wasn't that I mixed them up, only that one of them seemed a sufficiency. When both were present, there was an impression of clutter.

"Your sister tells me you're looking to the disposition of your daddy's remains," Aunt Ora said.

"Yes ma'am." *Disposition* surprised me; it was a word I was sure I wouldn't hear from the other Irelands. "And my mother's, too, when it comes time."

"We all hope that won't be for many years." Aunt Ora smiled gaily when she said that, as if she was strongly confident the wish would come true.

"Yessum. But—"

"I know, but we have to hope for the best." She waved her hand as if to shoo away inevitability. "Well, your daddy and mother are so dear to us, and we feel like we owe them so much, we were almost gleeful to hear of Mitzi's request."

"We're real proud of her. Read about her in the newspaper ever week or so, what good things she's doing for this part of the country." Uncle Gray nodded vigorously, applauding his own fine estimate.

"My mother?" I asked.

"Uncle Gray is talking about your sister," Aunt Ora explained, and I thought that she was used to bringing the family conversations back on track, interpreting the leaps for visitors like myself whose wits were less than adequately nimble.

"Oh, yes, Mitzi is very civic-minded," I said. "She finds it easy to keep busy."

"Joe Robert was a good old soul," Uncle Gray said. "There

ain't hardly a day goes by I don't think of some fool thing he did that wasn't so fool once you figured out what he had in mind."

"That raffle," Tod said.

"Well, it wasn't a raffle; it was just a contest."

Aunt Ora came to my rescue. "Your daddy held a contest one time for Challenger employees. It was a guessing game. He had a big box of canned goods, all homemade. They had been put up by your grandmother Sorrells over the years and she had neglected to label them and it was impossible to tell what might be in those mason jars. So your daddy set out six of them on the counter down at Virgil Campbell's grocery store and said that any Challenger employee who could guess what any three of the six contained would get a whole case of what he called 'mystery jars' for free. All they had to do was sign their names on a list and write down their guesses. He guaranteed the food was good; none better—he staked his word on it. He just didn't know what kind of food would be revealed when the jars were opened."

"First shift," Tod said.

"Oh, that's right; I'd forgotten. The entrants were limited to employees who were working first shift on such and such a day. I can't remember what date it was."

"And department," said Tod again.

"Yes. They had to put down what department of Challenger they worked in. Then a drawing was held of the guesses that had been written down, and I forget who it was won that case of canned goods, but Joe Robert wished him the best of luck in figuring out the contents of the jars. 'Don't make up your mind till you open them whether you'll be eating breakfast, dinner, or supper,' he said. . . . Oh, it was Miller Jameson who won, that's who it was. I just recalled."

"T. J. Wesson," Uncle Gray intoned.

"That's right," Tod said. He nodded in wise confirmation.

"So Mr. Wesson won the contest?" I asked.

"No, that was Miller Jameson," Aunt Ora explained. "T. J. Wesson was the name he was trying to find out."

I confessed to being utterly confused.

"Goes back to when you were nothing but a weed of a boy," Uncle Gray said. "Your daddy had set out a big neat kitchen garden across a little creeklet down at that white house where you used to live."

"That was before your granddaddy Sorrells passed," Aunt Ora said. "Then when he was gone, your family moved in with Annie Barbara to help her with the farm and all."

"Flooded the whole blessed thing," Tod said. He sounded as if he'd just heard the facts for the first time.

"That's right," said Uncle Gray. "There wasn't nothing left of the garden, hardly."

Aunt Ora interposed. "You see, Jess, your daddy had set out that garden and built the cunningest bridge across the little creek as a present to your mother. He put a lot of store by that bridge. He told me once that he built it partly to make up for some shenanigans he and his friend Johnson Gibbs had performed that displeased his spouse sorely. I remember he said exactly that: 'We displeased my spouse sorely.' But the Challenger factory had a reservoir up on one of the hills that surrounded your house and somebody opened the floodgates at the wrong time and it drowned most of your daddy's garden and carried his proud bridge away."

Bud backed through the screen door, protecting the tray he held at chest level. On it sat a beaded pitcher of lemonade, glasses, and a plate of cookies. He offered the tray to his mother, but she refused the refreshments with a gesture almost unnoticeable. Then he came round to the rest of us. "I might should've made coffee instead," he said. "It's such an overcast day."

"I don't know," I said. "This is mighty good." Though I'd taken a glass and a cookie for mere politeness' sake, I enjoyed the light tang of the lemonade and the oatmeal cookies studded with what I took to be raisins and flavored with something I couldn't recognize.

"Bud made them cookies," Tod said.

His brother colored as if the observation was an insult of high degree, and the effect upon his ruddy complexion was a hue of spectacular scarlet. "Naw I didn't, not exactly."

"His wife showed him how a little bit," Tod informed me gravely, "but he went and made them himself."

"They're really good. These raisins are unusual."

Bud spoke in a low and shamefaced tone, as if he were confessing to homicide. "Them's currants."

"Ah," I said. "And there's another taste I can't quite—"

This time he whispered as if the fact clenched his doom forever: "Cardamom." His face was as red as the stripes on Old Glory.

"So that's how he found out," Uncle Gray said. "They wouldn't nobody else ever have thought of it, hardly."

"Found out what?" I asked. "Who found out?"

Aunt Ora smiled. "It was with that guessing game and the drawing that Joe Robert found out who was personally responsible for washing away his bridge. The supervisor in control of the reservoir that day was a gentleman named T. J. Wesson. He was the one who gave the order to open the floodgates all at once. It caused a lot more damage than just your daddy's bridge and garden. There were plenty of people mad about it, but most of them worked for Challenger, so they couldn't complain too loudly. They might suffer consequences, you see."

"Wasn't a gentleman. Bastard." Uncle Gray was vehement.

Aunt Ora smiled shyly. "Yes, that's what Joe Robert always said when he thought about that flood. He couldn't help himself. *'Bastards bastards bastards,'* he would say, till he finally vowed to break himself of the habit."

"How was that?"

"Because that's what he was," Bud offered. "He didn't give out the least little apology to any of the people he flooded with that damn fool order. He just laughed at 'em. 'So sue me,' he said."

"No, I mean why did Daddy vow to break himself of the habit of cussing T. J. Wesson?"

"Because of your little sister," Aunt Ora said. "Mitzi got into the habit, too, of calling anything she thought bad 'bastard.' You can imagine how unhappy that made your grandmother. So your daddy had to stop."

"Well, he couldn't stop, hardly," said Uncle Gray. "It was too late."

Aunt Ora managed the difficult feat of uttering a delicate, ladylike snorting giggle. "I'm afraid so. There was a time when *bastard* was your little sister's favorite word."

I finished my lemonade and set the empty glass beside me on the porch floor. I refused with a motion when Bud gestured for me to drink a refill and eat another cookie. "Seems like you-all know this story pretty well."

"We heard it more than one time," Aunt Ora said. "It got to be one of Joe Robert's favorites."

"I remember the bridge and how upset he and I were when it was destroyed," I said, "but I didn't know all the other parts to the story. It is more complicated than I suspected. I'm finding out that everything about my father is more complicated than I'd thought."

"I'm not surprised at that," said Aunt Ora. "Joe Robert had a clever mind and he didn't like to do things only one way or think about them only one way. He liked to make several plans at once and to follow them all. That's why we never saw him defeated."

Uncle Gray demurred. "Uncle Zeno," he said, and shook his head as if at a deeply sorrowful memory.

"Oh, yes," agreed Aunt Ora, "I'd forgotten. Uncle Zeno must have been one of Joe Robert's rare defeats. He could never get the better of that old fellow."

"Uncle Zeno!" I cried. "I remember him. And, you know, I saw him just the other day."

The four of them looked at me in a very odd manner.

"Must've been better'n a hundred," Tod said.

"Hundred at least," Bud said.

"Hundred and ten anyhow," Uncle Gray said. "I don't see how he could still be alive, hardly."

I decided to hold my peace, needing to sort out my thoughts. "I must have been mistaken. You'd have heard if he was still alive and in these parts."

"Oh yeah," Tod said. "If he was a hundred and twenty years old. We'd've heard."

Aunt Ora said, "He would be legendary. Well, in a way, I suppose he *is* legendary. He was a storyteller, you know. I don't mean a liar kind of storyteller. He just told stories about people, mostly true, as I've heard."

"That's what I remember, that he told stories," I said.

"Just about drove your poor daddy crazy," Uncle Gray averred. "He couldn't figure out what the old man was up to, telling stories all the time. That was all he ever did. Might have been the only thing he knew how to do. But his tales preyed on your daddy's mind something fierce. I could never understand why."

"He might have been just the tiniest bit jealous," said Aunt Ora. "Joe Robert wasn't expert at telling stories."

"That's the truth!" Uncle Gray exclaimed. "When he tried to tell a windy, he'd get so tangled up, it was like he'd wandered into a laurel hell. He couldn't even tell the stories of his own pranks and antics. He tried to tell me how him and Johnson Gibbs put some banty eggs in a box of chocolate candy one time. I never did understand what all went on."

"Long time ago," Tod offered.

"Yes, that was long ago," Aunt Ora said. "So it really could not have been Uncle Zeno you spotted recently. I'm sure he's gone on to his great reward, though I never heard."

"Maybe not," said Uncle Gray. "Maybe he won't never die. That's what Joe Robert said about him one time. 'Uncle Zeno is immortal because he doesn't belong to this world. He lives in another world and only visits this one every once in a while to drive people insane.' That was his idea of Uncle Zeno."

"Gravesite," Bud said.

"That's right. Jess, would you like to walk over with Tod and Bud and inspect the burying ground we have here? We'll be glad to change anything about it you don't care for. We'd be extremely proud to welcome your folks here. They are precious to us," Aunt Ora said.

Uncle Gray let his chin droop to his chest for a moment; then he raised his head to look me squarely in the face. "Your daddy and mama did so much to help us out, I couldn't count the times. You'll find a lot of people who'll say that, but there's none more grateful than us." His voice crumbled just a little at the edges from the force of his emotion.

"All right," said Tod, and "All right," said Bud, and they rose and stood waiting expectantly.

I rose, too, and when the boys closed in on both sides of me, I felt oppressed, like a little honeymoon bungalow stranded between a couple of skyscrapers. Nevertheless, I was glad to step down into the yard and accompany them.

The Ireland farm was a spacious and well-kept spread of about three hundred acres. It boasted three large barns as well as a shed for two tractors and a good-sized henhouse. Corn and hay seemed to be the principal crops, with a small tobacco patch tucked into one corner and a happy, large produce garden laid out on the gentle slope below the house. There was one big pasture lot for horses and the rest was given over to sheep and a few milk cows.

The family graveyard was not far from the house and I was surprised to note that it wasn't fenced off. There were only eight graves here with modest markers, the older ones made of slate, and sheep grazed among them in peaceful unconcern.

When I mentioned the fact, Bud said, "Well, that's our way. That's how it's always been with us," and Tod added, "Seems more natural like this—like the old folks that used to be with us are more a part of the farm. Don't see no need to fence them off."

I admired the plan and told them so. In fact, I liked the

affable aspect of this place so much, I decided on the spot to choose it. I knew Mitzi would approve my choice; we couldn't have found a more idyllic setting if we'd painted it ourselves in pastoral watercolors.

"I need to ask a couple more favors of you gentlemen," I said. "If you'd be able to oblige me, my sister and I will be eternally grateful and we'll make it up to you any way we can. You have my solemn promise on that."

"Don't need promises," Tod said. "Don't need anything but to be asked. Mama and Papa are proud to help out, and they'll want us to do whatever you want. You just tell us what you've got in mind."

"Mitzi and I are having a big picnic Sunday afternoon over in Asheville," I said. "There'll be a good many folks there and some of them, probably quite a few, will be old friends of Uncle Gray and Aunt Ora. I want you to make sure your parents come. I know they'll have a good time."

"That ain't much of a favor to ask," Bud said. "It's more like you're doing us a favor. We'll come on over to Asheville after church. I thought you was going to ask for something hard. We'll bring Ned, too; he'd like to meet you."

"Sounds like fun to me," Tod said.

"I think the picnic will be fun. We're going to have music and fancy food and golden oratory and all sorts of things. Uncle Gray and Aunt Ora will have a good time. It's the second favor I'm going to ask that won't be much fun. It involves some hard physical labor and we'll be breaking the law."

"You ain't going to ask us to rob or murder, are you?" Bud inquired. "We wouldn't want to do nothing bad."

"If I was to get in trouble with the law, Mary Ann would take every inch of hide off of me," Tod declared.

"Nothing like that," I assured them. "This is just a little evasionary action."

"What do you mean?" Bud asked.

"Well, I'll tell you," I answered, and as we walked back to the farmhouse, I unfolded my mind to them.

Chapter Nine

INTO THE UNKNOWN!

*It takes a trillion yesterdays to produce
a single tomorrow.*
—Fugio

"Captain Kirkman!" my mother exclaimed. "I hope you are not seriously considering taking this rocket ship into the Quintessent Dimension!"

My father gave her one of his patented dazzling grins, boyish, charming, and yet informed with subtle authority. "First Mate Kirkman," he said calmly, "just stick to your navigational duties. This is something that has to be done. . . . You're not afraid now, are you, Cora?"

"Afraid?" Her blue eyes blazed with exasperation. "Of course I'm afraid. Ever since we left earth, I've been terrified.

I'll never understand how I let you talk us into this crazy stunt. Think of a man taking his wife and family—a nine-year-old boy and a four-year-old girl and a sixty-nine-year-old woman—into outer space in a rocket ship he built himself out in that dirty old workshop. It's absolutely insane.''

"I don't think it's insane. Jess doesn't think it's insane." He turned to pass me a merry wink. "You're not scared, are you, Jess?''

"No, sir." I knew he was only kidding about plowing into the Quintessent Dimension. He wouldn't do anything to endanger the *Isambard*.

He turned back to my mother. "And may I remind you, First Mate, that the only way to get to the moon is to leave the earth? It is not going to come to us, although I have long cogitated a theory about the origins of the moon as having been at first a part of our home planet. I mean, if you took the moon down from the sky and stuffed it into the Pacific Ocean, I believe that it would just about fit. Of course, you'd first have to drain the water out of the ocean, but didn't Dr. Sivanna have a theory—''

"Watch out!" she yelled, pointing at the great visiscreen that surrounded the interior bow of the vessel. "That comet's headed directly toward us!''

The captain's calm was unperturbed. "Pilot Kirkman," he said to me, "set starboard rudder vanes at full vent. Pronto.''

"Aye, aye, sir." I pressed the 4-8-12-4 series of the row of studs, the multicolored lights flashing swiftly as my hand passed over them.

"Monitor the visiscreen, Mate. What is our situation?''

"Disaster narrowly averted," the first mate reported. "Joe Robert, if you don't keep your mind on your business, this rocket ship is going to run into something out here and fly into a million pieces. Then where would we be?''

"Now, Cora," my father said. "I've told you a dozen times that the *Isambard* is not a rocket ship. Do you hear a roar from stern engines? Do you feel a vibration? No, Mate, this vessel works on the Kirkman drive, a device that taps into the intellectual capacities of past centuries. This means that it has a practically infinite energy source. I discovered that their mental forces do not disappear with the deaths of the great thinkers, but are stored in a stressed Riemannian sector of subspace. There they stand ready to be utilized like a fully charged battery waiting to be plugged into. In fact, that's what this subspace actually amounts to, an immense invisible battery whose energy I have learned how to harness."

"I don't understand how it works," I said. "It makes no sense to me at all."

"You'll understand when you get a little older. For now, just keep your eyes glued to that visiscreen."

"Aye, aye, sir," I said, thinking, No, I won't understand when I get older, because nobody will ever tell me; no one now alive will ever give me a hint.

My father relented a little; he must have observed the disappointed expression on my face. "Well, think about it, Jess. Two of the most important laws in physics are those of conservation of mass and conservation of energy. Isn't it logical that there must also be conservation of thought? Nature can't well afford to lose the mentalities of geniuses like Galileo and Dirac and Barbara McClintock and Eva Curie and Giordano Bruno and the others. When it happens that they must die, the voltage of those tremendous intellects is not going to be wasted. I only had to figure out where it was located in the space-time continuum and then to think of a way to make it accessible."

"How did you do all that?"

"With the concept of my floriloge. I'll explain that to you later. Right now, you only need to know that I was able to access another time stream. We are traveling through space to the moon, but we are also back on earth, enjoying a nice Sunday drive in the station wagon."

"How is that possible?"

"Well now, the technique is somewhat beyond your years. I'll tell you when you get a little older."

I knew I had to be satisfied with that. "Wow," I said. "That was really smart, how you figured all that out."

"Now if you could only figure out how to steer this thing," my mother said. "I'm positive you're going to jam us into a meteor or a planet or another rocket ship or something."

"Cora," my father said, "there is no danger to the *Isambard* whatsoever. Tell her, Jess, why we are perfectly safe."

"The visiscreen magnifies," I said. "Things outside are a lot farther off than they look."

"Tell her what would happen if a meteorite got within two hundred miles of us, Pilot Kirkman."

"Alarms would go off," I said, "and the force shields would come up to protect this craft from projectiles and meteorites and the disintegrator rays of space pirates."

"What am I supposed to do when an alarm goes off?" my mother asked.

"Your first duty is to check on Engineer Kirkman," my father said. He floated over to where Mitzi dangled happily upside down and sideways in her padded webbing. Of the four of us who were new to the project, Mitzi and my grandmother had accustomed themselves most readily to spaceflight. At four, Mitzi trusted everything my father did and would accompany him hand in hand into a raging volcano, if that had been one of his whims. My grandmother seemed to hold to the notion that the farther up we went into the sky, the closer we got to Jesus. I am not unalterably certain that's what she believed, but she was content to sit in the rocking chair my father had stanchioned to the wall, and now and again watch the stars slide by with the same expression of amused disbelief she exhibited when confronted with one of Uncle Luden's more flamboyant girlfriends.

"Are you really sure this . . . this rocket ship is safe?" my mother asked.

"I've thought of everything," replied Captain Kirkman. "Pilot Kirkman, program the *Isambard* for automatic transit. I'll conduct you and your mother and sister on a guided tour. It is important for you to understand and trust the ship as we go exploring. There must be no hesitation in your minds about my commands or the ship's ability to perform as needed. And let me say again, this is no rocket ship."

"Aye, aye, sir." I punched in autosequence, remembering the first time I'd heard my father iterate that last sentence. It had been only a few hours ago, but already it seemed like days.

Before leaving my pilot's seat, I checked the chronometer:
0718491630:
July 18, 1949, 4:30 P.M., earthtime.

He had told us to dress warmly, that he had a surprise waiting for us. Since it was a sunny Sunday in July, I figured we were headed to some windy mountaintop for a picnic. It could get chilly even in summer in Betsey's Gap or up on Wind Mountain. But when he had us bundled into the car and headed west toward Tipton on the old highway, I knew he had something else in mind.

He pulled the clankety Pontiac station wagon into the driveway of an antique clock shop. As we were getting out of the car, the shop door opened and out came a slim ash-blond lady dressed in a silver lamé jumpsuit. She saluted my father gaily, three fingers to the right eyebrow.

My father returned the salute. "Lieutenant Elden," he said, "I'd like to introduce my family." Mitzi had tumbled out of the car first and she ran toward this strangely garbed personage; then she stopped and gazed at her in awe and took her finger from her mouth and pointed it, shining wetly, at Mrs. Elden and didn't say a word.

My father introduced Mitzi first, his tone unnaturally solemn, and then the rest of us. The lieutenant nodded and beamed but shook hands only with my mother. "Everything okay?'' my father asked her. "Where is Royal today? I expected to see him for this special event."

"He's asleep," she replied. "The doctor has ordered him to get as much rest as possible. It's his heart, you know. Otherwise, we're all ready for inspection, Captain Kirkman."

"We won't be making a full inspection this morning," my father said. "I trust that you have kept the *Isambard* all safe and sound. We are going to take her out for a little spin. This is the first time the family has seen the vessel."

She smiled. "They're in for a treat, sir."

"Well, we may have some skeptics among us. Has there been any unusual activity, Lieutenant?"

"Not that I've seen, sir, and I've kept my eyes peeled."

"That's good. We'll go on down to the hangar, then."

As he led us around to the side of Times Past Antique Clocks and we descended the unsteady wooden steps, he offered an explanation none of us understood. "We've been a little concerned about espionage. If word got out about the *Isambard*, Preacher Canary and some of the other minions of the True Light Holiness Gospel Church might try to hinder the flight. But I'm sure Lieutenant Elden has kept a tight lid on things."

"What on earth are you talking about?" my mother demanded. She was carrying Mitzi in her arms; my little sister had found the unsteady stairs too daunting, but my grandmother came down spryly enough.

We marched around to a basement door, which he unlocked with a key from a jangling bunch that seemed as big as a basketball. "Come into my laboratory," he said. He entered before us and clicked on the dim overhead lights. "This has been my secret. Only Lieutenant Elden has known its location, and she has never ventured inside. Have a look around if you like, but don't touch anything."

At first, there seemed nothing extraordinary here, only the usual clutter you might find in anyone's garage or toolshed. My mother wrinkled her nose at the dust and set Mitzi down, warning her not to get all dirty and cobwebby.

"This is where it all took place," he said. "Someday this workshop will be marked as a historic site."

"Why?" my mother asked. "Because it is the nastiest workshop in the whole world?"

"No," he said patiently. "It's because the Kirkman alternating time drive was developed here, along with the other inventions necessary for the construction of the first multi-dimensional starship. I have named it the *Isambard* after that unstoppable genius Isambard Kingdom Brunel." He grinned an embarrassed apology. "I did think of naming it after you, Cora, but I wasn't sure you'd approve."

She snorted. "I don't see anything around here I'd want named after me."

"What's this?" I asked. I was standing by what seemed to be a blue porcelain cabinet of a type I'd never seen. It was about five feet tall by three feet wide and was set on small rubber tires. It was warm to the palm of my hand, and I could feel a steady throbbing inside. There was a black button on the otherwise-featureless front door and I reached over to touch it.

"No, not in here!" my father cried. "If you opened up the ship in here . . . well, I dread to think." He shook his head repeatedly. "What we need to do, Jess, is to roll it outside. I've measured it, so it ought to go through the door with no trouble. Getting all those dimensions into this little box—that was one of the most difficult problems."

He positioned me behind to push while he guided from the front. I thought I felt its throbbing quicken as we rolled it toward the door and wiggled it out into the grassy space behind the building. It presented a strange appearance out here among the natural things, the grass and trees and weeds and sky; it looked as if it belonged in a Technicolor movie or a comic-strip panel.

"Well, what do you think?" my father asked.

"About what?" I replied.

"The starship *Isambard*. This is it."

I considered. "It doesn't look like what I thought a starship would look like."

"That's because it's folded and put away—though I use those terms only for lack of better. Now we'll open her up." He looked around, counting our noses and seeing that we stood in safety. Then he walked over and pressed the black button and leapt back quickly.

The blue machine began to unfold—except that it didn't exactly seem to unfold. I felt I was watching the images in a mirror rise from the glass into three-dimensional shapes, then bounce back in again as they, in turn, were reflected; and then those new reflections also took solid forms. My description is not accurate, but it is the best I can do, because the transformation from blue cabinet to gossamer silver starship happened so quickly, I couldn't see it clearly. Even when it sat before us in the grass, there seemed to be a smoky blur all around it, a nearly transparent mist that blinked and twinkled with small sparks like fireflies lighting up a backyard at twilight.

"Now what do you think?" he asked.

"Wow," I said. "This is more like it."

"Cora?"

"Very clever, Joe Robert. But I hope you don't expect this thing to fly. It is too big and heavy to get an inch off the ground."

She was right about its size. It towered over us and stretched from one end of this field to the other. But it didn't look solid; it seemed a filigree of silver work enchased upon an envelope of softer material, opaque cellophane or maybe silk. I didn't see how it could fly and I didn't believe it could hold together in even a moderate hailstorm.

"It is actually a modest craft," my father said. "Not a ship, really. More like a yacht. It is fifty yards long and two stories tall. I could have made it a lot larger, you know. It wouldn't have cost any more or have taken up any more space in the workshop."

"How did you get it to fit in that little cabinet?" I asked.

"It wasn't exactly *in* there, Jess. The cabinet is an intradimensional portal; it can't actually contain anything. It only lets things come into our particular continuum."

"I don't understand."

"You'll understand when you—" Seeing my expression of bottomless disgust, he stopped and gave me a happy smile. "I'll be glad to explain it to you when we're out in space."

"Are we going out in space? When?"

"In just a few minutes."

"Who is going?"

"All of us."

"Mitzi, too?"

"We can hardly leave our chief engineer behind, can we?"

"Joe Robert, what on earth are you talking about?"

"Just an ordinary Sunday drive, Cora, except that we'll be going a little farther than we usually do."

"How far?" I asked.

"To the moon."

"The moon!" my mother exclaimed. She turned to my grandmother. "Mother, don't you think Joe Robert has taken complete leave of his senses? There's no way this . . . this rocket ship could go to the moon or anywhere else. It might blow up any second now and kill us all."

"Oh, I don't think so, Cora," my grandmother said. "Joe Robert was ever a one for science, you know. Except for that silly business about monkeys turning into people, he generally knows his facts."

This reply didn't satisfy my mother, but I could see she was somewhat mollified and was beginning to take an interest in the strange shape that sat so lightly in the grass. Like the blue cabinet, it throbbed steadily with a muffled but regular beat. She liked the design, too. This vehicle was not hard and aggressive-looking like a rocket; it was a more artistic object, inviting to the eye.

"I thought that when you decided to go to the moon, you'd build a rocket," I said.

"Oh phooey, darned old rockets," my father said. "All that smoke and noise. What would the neighbors say? And the danger of fire . . . We'll leave the rockets to the U.S. government. One of these days, they'll be building them by the score. But the Kirkman drive is clean and safe and silent—well, almost silent. We'll be making about as much noise as a hot-air balloon."

"Can we go inside?"

"Not yet," he said. "We're not properly outfitted yet. But if the ladies will go upstairs, Lieutenant Elden will get them into regulation uniform. I have yours, Jess, down here in the workshop."

"Uniforms?" my mother said. "You expect us to dress up in uniforms?"

"I'm anxious to know what you think. Lieutenant Elden helped me a little, but I mostly designed them myself."

"You designed some clothing? This I've got to see," my mother said.

"Just you three nip up the stairs and the lieutenant will outfit you in a jiffy," he said.

When they were gone, he took me back into his workshop and opened up an old battered steamer trunk. Inside was a box and inside that a neatly folded uniform. He took it out and presented it proudly. "Slip into this little number and let me know how it feels." He held it up for my inspection.

Oh, how I adored my uniform, my boots and trousers and tunic of space black, trimmed with silver piping. The high silver collar sported a glittering golden meteor. "This is great!" I said.

He smiled. "Well, I'm afraid it's not very original. I took it from the design for the old Galactic Patrol uniforms of 1937. But I think it holds up pretty well—and, besides, there's the sentimental value, you know."

"It looks super."

"Okay. You put it on now and come outside. We want to get this show on the road."

I changed as quickly as I could, chagrined that the dusty workshop contained no full-length mirror for me to preen in. But the suit was a neat fit and I knew I looked fine in it. Best of all, it made me feel important.

When I went back outside, my father was in uniform, too, standing in front of the entrance to the starship. "My uniform was already in my locker in the *Isambard*," he explained. "This is not really the first flight, Jess. Lieutenant Elden and I have taken her up four times to get the feel of her, to see if any kinks needed ironing out. But this will be her maiden voyage. So don't be disappointed. You're participating in a historic world event."

Now my mother and sister and grandmother came down the steps, accompanied by Lieutenant Elden. Mitzi looked silly, I thought, in her baby version of the Galactic Patrol outfit, but my mother looked as if she belonged in hers; it emphasized her accustomed air of command. My grandmother was dressed in an ankle-length clerical-looking robe with a discreet silver cross sewn over the heart.

"All right," my father said. "Let's see you fall in. Stand up straight. Shoulders back. Line up here beside our starship, Mitzi on one end, Annie Barbara on the other. That's it. No, Jess, don't slump your shoulders—military bearing at all times. Stand still, Mitzi; you look mighty sharp in your outfit." He ranged himself with us beside my grandmother. "All right, Lieutenant. Do you have your camera ready?"

"Aye, sir." She was holding our old Brownie box camera, looking down into the viewfinder, trying to get us centered. Her expression was one of serious determination.

"You may fire when ready, Gridley," my father said, and when she thumbed down the shutter latch, he added, "Someday this photograph will be of paramount historical importance."

"Yes," my mother said. "It will show a whole family of morons dressed up for Halloween in the month of July."

"Cora," he chided, "this day in July 1969 is going to be important not only for the Kirkman family but for all mankind, as well. Womankind, too."

"Womankind, too? Thanks a lot. But who is going to trust a creature who thinks it's already 1969? This may come as a shock, Joe Robert, but the year is actually 1949."

He was glowing like a lighthouse. "Indeed it is. It is 1949. But today and tomorrow are the two days in history when it is both 1949 and 1969 at the same time."

"You've lost your mind," she proclaimed gravely. "I suppose there wasn't a lot to lose in the first place, but now even that is gone."

"You'll see," he said. "Just wait till you get inside. You know, you look awfully cute in your spiffy new uniform. . . . But now, before we board the craft, I have to assign each of you your rating. I am the captain, of course, and—"

"Who said so?" my mother asked. "Who elected you leader of the world?"

"The *Isambard,* as I regret to inform you, is not a democracy. But if you feel capable of assuming command of this ship, why then, you are welcome to take my place."

"No, no," she said. "I don't think I could furnish anything like so entertaining a spectacle as you are capable of doing."

"Okay, then, we'll see how you function as first mate."

"What have you dreamed up as my duties?"

"Why, to see that my orders are carried out promptly and efficiently, of course. And to keep under control all undue griping and grousing that so direly corrode morale."

"That'll be the day."

He grinned that practiced innocent grin. "That'll be the day, *sir.*"

"*Sir,*" she repeated, but her inflection did not suggest subordination.

"And you, Jess, are our pilot," he said, "and Mitzi will carry out the duties of chief engineer. Annie Barbara, I was hoping you would serve as ship chaplain. I've stocked in a supply of

Bibles and hymnbooks and a few challenging theological volumes, along with a couple of essays by T. H. Huxley defending the ideas of Charles Darwin against some of the lesser religionists. What do you say?''

She smiled sweetly. ''Well, Joe Robert, as long as we have the Bible, we'll be all right.''

''Very well. So, Space Rangers—let's have a salute to the captain and a farewell salute to Lieutenant Elden and we'll board the craft.''

I thought my salute was pretty snappy and was ashamed of the slovenly, halfhearted way the rest of my family responded. Then he about-faced smartly and we all saluted Lieutenant Elden, three fingers to the brow. She returned the honor and then waved a gay farewell as my father entered the ship and we trooped in after him.

''We'll go directly to the bridge and I'll show you to your stations,'' he said. ''Once we're aloft and satisfactorily underway, I'll guide you around the ship. But first we want to make sure we're flying right.''

It was a much more spacious area than I'd imagined and my surprise must have shown on my face. My father patted my shoulder and said, ''That's right, Jess. One of the features of our vessel is that the interior is larger than the exterior. That will be true of all the intradimensional craft I design.''

He seated my mother at the navigator's table with its visiscreens, adding machines, and star manuals. On the bulkhead to her left was a large map of the moon. When she began to protest her ignorance, he said, ''Don't worry about a thing, First and Last Mate. Navigation will take care of itself.''

Then he assigned my grandmother to her rocking chair. This was an ordinary-looking chair, just like the ones on the porch of Times Past Antique Clocks, except that it was held up by a short steel post so that the rockers didn't touch the floor. It had a seat belt, too, and my father buckled her in. ''When we get into free fall out in space, this chair will be ratcheted up the wall on the track you see under your feet. That gives us a little more room here on the bridge. Your first duty is to pray for our safe liftoff. I will give you the signal when to begin. It has to be a silent prayer, though, because I'll be giving orders to the rest of the crew.''

"Very well. This is an impressive vessel, Joe Robert. You must have worked real hard.''

"Well, yes,'' he said. He was pleased, of course, but I could detect that he was a little put out because my grandmother hadn't responded in military fashion. But she would have formulated the special field theory of relativity before it would have occurred to her to say "Aye, aye, sir.''

Mitzi he lifted and snapped into a nest of padded webbing. There she dangled beside us like a mailbag hung out to be caught by a freight train's mail hook. She giggled and crowed; she liked hanging in the air.

Then he put his hand on my shoulder and guided me over to the pilot's deck chair. The console before me was a candy-store display case of inviting knobs, buttons, studs, levers, gauges, dials, and blinking lights. The moment I sat down, I wanted to push, pull, and spin every one of them.

"This looks complicated,'' I said.

"Nothing to it,'' he said. "Easy as breaking an egg.'' He showed me which buttons, which levers, which dials were to be fiddled with as he issued commands. "You can do it as long as you don't lose confidence. How does it feel, being the first interplanetary space pilot?''

"Great.'' I didn't say how close I was to throwing up from pure excitement.

"Very good.'' He stood in the center of the cabin in the glow of a baby spotlight that shone directly down on him and struck a dramatic pose, legs slightly apart, hands straight by his sides. He looked us over slowly, one by one, and nodded at last. Then: "QX for liftoff. Jess, ease the throttle forward and go to elevating sequence four-twelve-four-zero.''

"Aye, aye, sir.'' But of course I was too excited and I bounced the *Isambard* into the air like a pebble from a beanshooter.

Mitzi jingled in her harness like a wasp-stung mule.

"Whoa now. Slow down. We've got plenty of time. Run through the sequence again, but try to get some grace into it. Smooth, easy motions, that's what starship controls demand."

"Aye, sir." I let my hands drift easily over the console and could feel the ship respond gently, gaily, to my manipulations.

"Very good. Steady as she goes, now. We're making good speed already. Here—I'll give us the big visiscreen." He touched an unobtrusive switch on his silver belt and the cloudy material of the hull pulled back—or seemed to—and gave us the view from a great continuous screen that surrounded us on all sides. The sudden vista was so startling, I felt a brief moment of real fright, and I could tell my mother did, too, because she caught her breath so sharply.

My grandmother commenced her prayers, moving her lips silently.

"See if you recognize any landmarks," my father said.

At first, that was easy enough. To our right lay Asheville with its Art Deco towers and narrow streets, bottled into its plateau by Beaucatcher Mountain in the east. Tipton, smoky and tiny, lay to our left, and I thought I could make out the chimneys of the Challenger factory, though we were ascending so quickly, details blurred.

My father pointed out where Hardison County was crinkled into a thousand folds and ridges by the misty mountains. "Can you make out Downhill?" he asked. "It's that dark and dreary area right in front of our nose. Then over there you see the dim grayness of Vestibule. Beyond that is happy Upward with Brightening Hill as its crown. Do you see, Jess?"

I thought I glimpsed the topographies he spoke of, but we were making such tremendous speed, I couldn't be sure. We were traveling so fast, in fact, that the landscape was dropping away from us like an elevator descending so quickly, our feet left the floor. In just a minute, we could see the contours of the Atlantic coastline and then not even that, only a green landmass and a great blue ball of ocean.

Then we were in space, in free fall, and Mitzi stopped rattling in her webbing and my grandmother's rocking chair climbed, with a *cluck-cluck-clucking* sound, up the wall, and there she sat, like a strange oversized sconce. Yet she didn't show the least fear or even surprise. My father had explained to her what was going to happen and now it had happened just as he had said, and she accepted it.

"Whee!" said Mitzi.

"Cora, how are you feeling?" my father asked.

"Odd. Queer. Very strange. I don't know whether I like this or not. What do you call it?"

"Free fall," I explained. "That means we're out of the pull of earth's gravity. There's nothing to hold us down anymore."

"That's right, Jess." My father beamed at me.

"It's not as bad as I thought it would be," she said.

"How fast are we traveling?" I asked.

"That's a tough one to answer," my father said. "Since we inhabit more than one parallel time track at the same moment and are going at different speeds in each, there is no final solution to your problem. It would be meaningless to take an average of the speeds. On earth, we started off jogging along at thirty miles an hour in our station wagon. Of course, that was some years ago by earth calendar. In the *Isambard*, we achieve speeds up to and beyond the speed of light. On earth, time will pass faster for us than it does in our speedier vessel. To us, it will seem that only a few hours pass, but on earth, twenty years will go by. And as the *Isambard* dips in and out of a stochastic universe, we will travel backward in time from 1969 and end up in 1949, the day we started out."

"Oh, be quiet, Joe Robert. All this silly talk is giving me a headache." My mother rubbed her temples with her fingers to demonstrate the truth of her statement.

My father drifted out of his circle of light and went to float by her seat. He put his arm around her shoulders. "Let me look at these navigational charts a moment," he said. "It may be that we can save a little time by dipping in and out of the

Quintessent Dimension. It's never been tried before, and Lord knows what might be waiting for us in there, but I think it's worth a try."

"Captain Kirkman!" my mother exclaimed. "I hope you are not seriously considering taking this rocket ship into the Quintessent Dimension!"

My father grinned down at her to signal he had been teasing, but I could tell he was annoyed that she kept calling the *Isambard* a rocket ship. Their debate on this point was interrupted by the distant comet, which alarmed my mother. Then he instructed me to sequence the ship into autopilot so he could take us on a guided tour.

The ship was a larger and more complex structure than I ever could have imagined. He had told us the interior of the vessel was larger than the exterior, though he had not explained how that was possible. I was astounded at how large it actually was. There were many compartments and some of them attained to great size. When he opened the door to the room that housed the tennis court, my mother and I gasped and Mitzi swooped out onto the packed clay surface and began turning cartwheels that reached nearly to the ceiling, getting her spiffy uniform all dusty.

My grandmother was not with us. She had elected to stay on the bridge and study the book of Exodus.

"How can we play tennis in free fall?" I asked.

"It ought to be quite an interesting game," my father said. "I expect we'll have to be inventing new rules."

My mother only shook her head in mock disbelief, and she kept shaking it in that silly consternated way as we visited the other compartments. She repeated again and again that the whole thing was a ridiculous waste of time and money, yet it was apparent she was pleased with the greenhouse and its exotic orchids, with the hydroponic garden's jewel-like strawberries, and with the swimming pool that my father called a "natatorium." It wasn't a pool at all, but a big globe of water that floated in the air. I looked forward to swimming with my family in this oversized teardrop.

When we came to a door that was hidden behind a heavy velvet burgundy curtain, he said, "I think Jess and Mitzi will be highly pleased with this compartment." He winked at my mother as we entered a small but comfortable movie theater.

"Gosh," I said, "this is the real McCoy."

"The only thing missing is that there are no wads of chewing gum stuck to the seat bottoms," he said. "And I'm delighted to inform you, Jess, that this movie house only shows Westerns. Gene Autry, Roy Rogers, Johnny Mack Brown, Tim Holt. And serials—it runs a chapter of three different serials every week. *Brick Bradford, Batman,* and *The Purple Monster Strikes.*"

"No mushy love stuff?"

"No mushy love stuff," he replied gravely.

"Gosh."

"We'd better be getting back to the bridge," he said, "but I think we have time for a little ice cream. What would you say to that?"

We agreed that I scream, you scream, we all scream for ice cream, and he led us to the parlor compartment, sat us down at the little marble-topped tables with the black cast-iron legs, ducked behind the long marble counter, and dished up two strawberry sundaes and a banana split. He didn't partake himself but said he was proud of his skills and might take up soda jerking as a profession when he tired of space exploration.

We only peeked briefly into the bedchambers as we floated down the hall with its soft lighting and luxuriously padded walls, but we did have to make another lengthy stop. This was to inspect the armory. "We'll have an exhaustive review of this compartment later," he said. "We must all bone up on the different kinds of weapons we carry and the ways they are used. Each of us will have separate responsibilities in regard to the armory. Engineer Mitzi, for example, will be in charge of counting the number of weapons; she won't need to employ them yet, being excused from active frontline service. But the rest of us must learn.''

There was a wide array of them, polished and gleaming in their wall racks or laid out in display cases. There were ray pistols of all sizes and apertures, four small lightning-bolt cannons, and various types of projectile rifles; there were insulated boxes of ion grenades and explosive photon canisters, and one whole wall was given over to a selection of electronic swords.

My father noted how fiercely I itched to try them out, all of them at once and immediately. ''These are not toys, Jess,'' he warned. ''You're going to have to demonstrate to me that you can show a mature attitude in the way you handle yourself around these pieces. They are very dangerous indeed. One careless flick of a trigger stud would make a hole in the *Isambard* as large as a planetoid.''

''Yes, sir,'' I said, ''I'll be careful.'' But as I spoke, I was eyeing a sleek black ray pistol with omnidirectional focusing magnets and a phosphorous needle sight. My right hand yearned for this pistol the way a crossbow yearns for its arrow.

When we left the armory, my father gave me a significant look and locked the door with one of the keys of the monstrous ring of them he somehow wore unobtrusively. ''That's just to prevent any *accidental* mischief,'' he said. ''But come along. We'll go back to the bridge and head for our destination. Luna, here we come!''

As we drifted down the hallway, returning by a corridor different from the one we came through before, I spotted a couple of fairly large pictures on the wall. The images did not look to be attached to the wall, but floated in the air a few inches from it. ''What's this?'' I asked.

''Oh, these are merely two paintings I tossed off hastily to experiment with a kind of paint I invented. I call it refract oil because it interferes with light waves in such a way as to produce tri-di images.''

''Tri-di?''

"Three-dimensional," he explained. "You can see all the sides."

"What is this?" I was standing in front of a picture of a mysterious disk, dull white and gently ruffled over its surface. At first, I thought it was a huge chrysanthemum; then I thought maybe it was a crumpled bedsheet.

"It's a pie," he said.

"A pie?"

"It is a big old cream pie, though the filling is not exactly cream. Thirty inches in diameter and four inches thick at its deepest point. The dough contains no fewer than six eggs because the crust has to be tough and pliant enough to hold together during the pie's flight to its destination."

"Why in the world would you paint a picture of a pie?" my mother asked. "That is the most outlandish thing I ever heard of."

"It is to remind me of a little task I want to accomplish, a little something I have in mind concerning a bridge, a work of architectural genius of the first magnitude, destroyed by the barbarian forces of the most devilish form of contemporary commercial industrialism."

"Joe Robert," she said, "we have no idea what you're talking about."

"Just as well," he said. "That way, you won't get into trouble. Only remember it as the world's largest flying pie and that's all you'll ever need to know."

"What about this next one?" I asked.

"This is another project I have planned for the future," he told us, and it was plain to see that he took a lot of pride in this idea and was not going to be secretive about it. This painting was the same size as the pie painting but had much more detail and color. The pie was all in shades of white and beige, but this painting boasted a spectrum of different colors laid out in a fan shape. At the juncture of the spectrum, the narrow point of the fan, there stood a pylon or tower of some sort, dark, with splashes of yellow disposed along its height. The background was filled with different shades of green, dark and light, and looked like a meadow or perhaps a garden.

"Behold the Floriloge," my father intoned. "You are the first—besides myself, of course—to see my design for an important new method of keeping time. Literally, *keeping* time. I have been researching this little concept for quite a few years now and hope to begin the actual construction pretty soon."

"I can't make out what it is," my mother complained. "It's all jumbled-looking."

"Well, this is merely a quick oil sketch. When the real thing is finished, you'll see it very neatly laid out. Precisely laid out, in fact, for otherwise it won't work as it should."

"I still don't know what it is."

When I saw my father tug at his earlobe, I knew he was getting ready to talk at some length. My mother diagnosed the same gesture and added, "But you don't have to go on as long as *Compton's Encyclopedia*. Give us the *Reader's Digest* condensed version."

He was unflappable. "The trouble with all our modern methods of demarcating time is that they are artificial, geometrically derived, and embodied in flimsy mechanical contrivances. Not that I don't admire the skill and ingenuity of the clock makers, you understand. In fact, I think if I had another life to lead, I might like to be a clock maker; I have some choice new ideas along that line." He reached over and plucked Mitzi out of the air where she had been spinning like a pinwheel and held her to his broad chest. "But if I'd been a clock maker, we wouldn't be able to fly to the moon, would we?

"Anyhow, I have become convinced that time is an organic entity, a more flexible and unpredictable force than any of our modern gadgets can measure. Did you ever think how silly it is that we actually pretend to measure time by causing a dumb little pointer to complete the circuit of a circle? I tell you, Dr. Einstein got it right—and so did Shakespeare when he observed that time travels at diverse speeds with diverse persons. This stupid mechanical way of counting time has got the human race into big trouble. *Tick tick tick, bong bong bong.* Who can believe that those puny little gizmos have anything to do with *real* time?

"It is by bowing to those unreal coordinates, by taking orders from childish machines and regulating our lives by the interlocking of tiny gears that we have got out of whack in regard to the big plan. All of us need to have a more intimate relationship with the living and breathing cosmos, and to further that end I have been laboring on my Floriloge. I believe that if human beings begin to count time by means of this construction and others like it, we may be able to reestablish some sort of close and effective relationship with nature."

"How does it work?" I asked.

"You see this tall object here?" He pointed to the yellow-spotted tower at the apex of the fan shape. "Well, that is called the style, or gnomon, and it casts a shadow on these twelve colored areas below. Each of them stands for a different time of day."

"What is it made of?"

"It can be an artificial structure, but it is better if it is a tree of some sort. Best of all is a hollow oak tree. It supports a climbing golden rose of splendid beauty."

"And what are all these different-colored things that look like slices of pie?"

"They are roses. The whole thing is a big rose garden laid out in contiguous triangles. Each triangle is planted with a different breed and color. See, here you have your Martha Flandry rose, your Bess Lovett, your Mrs. Mawley and Mrs. Sinkins roses, your Marie Antoinette and your Annie Laurie. Twelve of them, all told, and they are for the twelve hours of the day, of course. In this way, nature itself is telling time for you with sunlight and shadow, color and perfume. The Floriloge induces the resonance of an essential harmony of human spirit with the regular processes of the cosmos. No more clicking and whirring, no more noises like a nation of asthmatic grasshoppers. Once these are established around the world, you'll see how folks slow down from the frenetic lives they lead and begin to enjoy the days as they pass. We will start to live in peaceful brotherhood with one another.''

''Joe Robert,'' my mother objected, ''all you've done is to reinvent the sundial. What's next? The wheel? Fire? The stone ax?''

''Well, yes,'' he admitted in a slightly sheepish tone, ''the Floriloge is adapted from the general idea of the sundial. But it is not some quaint mossy pedestal marked with a few Roman numerals and a scrap of sentimental Victorian verse. This is a serious idea; it is the primary concept that makes it possible to be aware of inhabiting several time streams at once. I intend for it to spread from the *Isambard* throughout all the world. Naturally, it still has flaws. For example, when we return to earth, we will have only confused memories, or none at all, of what happened to us on the way to the moon.

''But observe the gnomon in the painting. It is completely entwined with that superlative rose called Gold Mine. This gnomon is eighty feet tall and the rose beds are very large, though I forget their exact dimensions just now.''

''You said it had to be precise,'' my mother said. ''I don't see how it can be. What do you say when it's ten-thirty—that it's half past Bess Lovett? 'Good morning, Jess. You slept in late. It's already five rose petals to Mrs. Mawley.' This flowerbed notion is not going to work.''

''The planting has to be precise,'' he replied. ''But the computation of time will be freer, more relaxed, more humane than it is now. Those fictitious little units that drive us crazy will finally be erased from human consciousness. First, the nanoseconds will disappear; then milliseconds will go, then seconds and minutes and quarter hours and half hours. Finally, the concept of the hour will be wiped out and we will all saunter footloose and carefree through the daylight.''

''Speaking of daylight,'' she said, ''how are you going to tell time on the dark and cloudy days? How will you be telling time at night?''

His answer was imperturbability itself. "We won't. Those times will not be counted. Just think, Cora, how much longer each human life will be when the dark hours and the dreary nights are no longer counted."

She fell silent. I could tell that this point had escaped her and now that it was brought to her notice she was well-nigh overwhelmed by my father's brilliance and his deep concern for humanity.

Even so, I couldn't help bringing up a problem. "How about blind people, or people who are color-blind? How will they be able to tell the time?"

"Well, Jess, that's why we chose roses for our garden instead of orchard grass or seaweed. They can distinguish the time of day from the different perfumes of the different roses."

"But how will they know where the shadow falls?"

"By the differences in temperature between sunlight and shade. Blind people are much more sensitive to minor variations in temperature than sighted people are. Did you know that?"

"No, sir."

"Now you do—and that's a good thing. It is the duty of a Junior Space Ranger to learn one new thing every hour."

"All right, Joe Robert," my mother said. "Let's pretend it's early in the morning. Let's say it's breakfast time and this big sundial is right outside my kitchen window where I can see it. Now, for my breakfast on this particular morning, I want a three-minute egg. How do I determine when three minutes are up? By counting the number of Japanese beetles that come to visit the Martha Flandrys and calculating that twenty beetles equal three minutes?"

"You have not taken into account the greater purposes of my invention," he said. "After the Floriloge with its roses is firmly embedded in the consciousness and subconsciousness of mankind, our hearts and our minds will be serene. We will accept the world as it is, the universe as it is, gladly, in every aspect. You will not care, Cora, whether your egg has been cooked for three minutes, three hours, or three days. You will understand and accept the situation in present time. Yesterday, today, and tomorrow will be as one; 1949 and 1969 will occupy the same infinitesimal instant. All time will be present time. This will be the final triumph of Fugio."

"What is Fugio?" I asked.

He set Mitzi apart and she began to jump up to the ceiling, then to float down again by knocking headers against it like a soccer player advancing a ball. "Fugio is the name of my Floriloge," he explained. "It comes from the Latin and means 'I flee.' In the good old days, they used to put that word on sundials to remind folks that their days on earth were numbered. I mean it to signify that we have fled—we have escaped—the tyranny of mechanical time just the way the *Isambard* has escaped the tyranny of gravity. We no longer need to describe our mortal lives as 'our days on earth.' Just see how happy Mitzi is in free fall. With my Floriloge, all time will be in free fall."

"It is not going to work," my mother said. "There's no way in the world this flower clock can work."

"First Mate," he returned severely, "that is *oldthink*. On the good ship *Isambard*, we do not indulge in oldthink. When you say there is no way in the world the Floriloge can perform as designed, you seem to forget that we are no longer in the world but are about halfway on our journey to the moon. . . . Speaking of which—we'd better get back to the navigation cabin. The most dangerous part of our voyage is just ahead."

We left the paintings and went down the corridor. Mitzi was still playing with free fall, bouncing off both walls and the ceiling and floor like a racquetball. "Look what I can do!" she cried as she turned a triple somersault with a corkscrew flourish thrown in.

We went onto the bridge and looked into the large visiscreen.

"Uh-oh," my father said. "I was correct. We're running into some real problems."

"Where's Grandmother?" I asked. "She was sitting in the rocking chair up on the wall. Now it's empty."

My mother and I gazed at the deserted chair with its safety belt fastened over the empty seat. She turned to my father. "Joe Robert . . ."

He nodded sadly. "Yes, I know. Don't forget that we are traveling in time as well as in space. Pilot Jess, what does the chronometer say? Tell us in earthtime."

"The twenty-fourth of January, 1961, at eight A.M., sir."

"If you will recall, First Mate, we lost our chaplain in November of 1954 back on earth. Jess and I sat in the front room of the old brick house while you kept watch with her. These disappearances are inevitable to folks who travel through time. You have to remember things that haven't happened yet at the speed we are going. That's hard to do, and yet they actually have happened, only not on board the *Isambard*. Time is no longer stable. When the generation that Annie Barbara represented passed away, time became unfixed and untrustworthy. My invention of the Floriloge is an attempt to show us how to live in a time continuum we can no longer depend upon."

"No matter how long you talk, I will never understand," my mother said, and in her voice was a universe of sorrow larger than the one we were exploring in our spacecraft.

"It is very sad—but that is the way it is."

"All right," she said. "Just don't keep on explaining and explaining. I don't want to hear."

"Our duty now is to ourselves. We must protect ourselves and keep the *Isambard* intact. It looks like a Veilwarp has developed in front of us now, and I don't know whether our ship can pierce through it without breaking up."

"What is a Veilwarp?" I asked.

"Look ahead at the visiscreen. The moon is supposed to be showing dead ahead. But what do you see?"

"It looks like some sort of curtain," I said. "Or maybe like steam. I can see it moving inside itself, but I can't tell what it is."

"Do you see whether it contains any light or not?"

"It looks like there's a light behind it. Kind of dim, though."

"That's the moon," Captain Kirkman said, "and in order to reach it, we are going to have to travel through the Veilwarp, and that can be very dangerous indeed."

"All right," my mother said. "It's time to turn this rocket ship around and go home."

"We are home. We never left. We are still on earth, living out our lives in normal fashion. If we went back, we'd have to occupy the same space as our alternate-time selves, our other selves. The future is the only path we are able to take."

"I don't want to take it," she said. "I don't like the future. I never have liked it. There's never been anything in the future but loss and ugliness."

"Yes. That was true in the old world. But on the moon, the Kirkman family is going to build a new and better world. I have the plans all drawn up and laid out. I've been working on them for decades. We will found a new society on the principles of logic, fairness, and science. Our only obstacle is this Veilwarp. I don't like the looks of it."

"I see it," I said, "but I don't know what it is."

"It is a mysterious phenomenon," he told us, "but some scientists think it bears out that ancient suspicion of Aristotle's that space is not homogenous in every direction. This is one of the incompletely realized parts of the universe, a sector where the usual physical laws don't totally apply. It could be rough traveling and we need to find out if the moon is on the other side of it, so we'll know if it's worth taking the risk. It may be that the glimmer we see so dimly there is not the moon, but some property of the Veilwarp itself."

"How can we find out?"

He sighed and rubbed the side of his neck the way he did when faced with an unpleasant but necessary task. "I'll have to scout ahead and report back to you. We don't want to be blundering on without more and better information than we now have."

"So how will you do that? Do you have another spacecraft to travel in?" I pictured a compartment somewhere aboard with a mini *Isambard,* a lifeboat, stowed ready for use.

"I'm afraid not. And anyway, a scout ship would encounter the same problems we would run into. No, it's going to have to be a reconnaissance mission. There's no other method."

"But—"

"I will have to disengage my mind and send it soaring into space ahead of us and see what's inside the Veilwarp and what is beyond it."

"How—"

He bounded across the bridge to a wall locker and withdrew a weird chromium helmet with all sorts of dials and tubes and antennae. It looked like a combination football helmet and motorcycle exhaust, grafted onto the cooling unit from a Philco refrigerator.

"What's that?" I asked.

"This is a psychic observation projector. When I put this on, my mind can leave the confines of my body and of the starship and advance into space ahead of us. I will be able to report back to you by channeling my words through the ship's audio speakers. My body will remain here and must not be disturbed or my mind may become completely disengaged from it and never find its way back."

"It sounds dangerous," I said.

"It's not as dangerous as slipping the whole ship in and out of the Quintessent Dimension. That would endanger the lives of us all, though it is a sure way to avoid the Veilwarp. I think this is the better alternative."

"Oh, Joe Robert—" my mother began.

He grinned. "Yes, Cora, it's true. I was only teasing about entering the Quintessent Dimension when I mentioned it before. I really shouldn't kid around about the operation of the ship."

"But this projector or whatever—"

"Yes," he said again, "it offers some obvious perils. You can understand that. But I've never tried the mechanism before, and now that I have to—well, it's the best opportunity for testing that one could ever hope for."

"But it's so dangerous!"

"I'll be all right. But I will need your help, Pilot Jess. It is necessary for the *Isambard* to hang motionless in space while my mind is scouting ahead. It is your responsibility to maintain the gyros. Don't let us drift with the solar wind. And I must remain in a standing position, just where I am now, so that I don't move out of the isoatomic magnetic field. To orient myself in the vastness of space, I will need a portable visiscreen to look into. You'll find one in the larboard locker. Bring it over and place it in front of me, if you will."

"Aye, aye, sir." I acted as ordered, and by the time I'd got the small visiscreen in front of him and secured it with a magnetic tripod so that it wouldn't float about, he already had the psychic observation projector clamped to his head. At first, he looked strange with the gleaming and many-knobbed helmet covering his forehead and shading his eyes, but then I thought he looked the way he wanted to look, like a man with his eyes half-hooded to the present situation and his mind leaping forward into the unknown.

"All right," he said. "To your stations, Space Rangers. Mate Kirkman, secure the engineer in her harness. You be a good girl now, Mitzi, and don't disturb Daddy while he's trying to explore. Jess, take your seat at the pilot console and activate the Kirkman drive neutron battery; that is the energy source the projector will be transducing from."

"Aye, aye, sir."

He was busy with all sorts of buttons, rippling his fingers along his helmeted temples as if he were playing an accordion.

"First Mate, stand to the master visiscreen and make sure we keep sited along our star lines."

My surprise was boundless when she said, "Aye, aye, sir," but then she added in a warmly fond tone, "Joe Robert, please be careful. Please, hon."

His grin was crooked now. "QX, old darling . . . Jess, are you all set there at the console?"

"Yes, sir."

"Cora?"

"Yes."

"Mitzi?"

"Whee," she said. She had twisted her symmetrical shoulder web lines and was skinning-the-cat over and over.

"All right, then. Here we go."

He pressed a red button on the underside of his chin strap and nothing happened. He muttered a swearword that came through with sudden loud clarity over the audio speakers, and I was a little relieved my grandmother wasn't present to hear it, being now in a separate dimension of time. Then I pushed away again the thought of her disappearance.

He twiddled another dial, pushed the red button once more, and our navigation bridge was filled with a deep, steady hum, as of a hundred hives of bees. The sound was loud at first; then it subsided to a soft monotone that emphasized our silence rather than disturbing it.

We watched closely. Some twinges of pain or anxiety caused his mouth to tremble. He uttered a long-drawn sigh and then closed his lips tightly. His body stiffened. Yet little by little, it relaxed again, though it stood motionless in place.

It seemed a very long time before we heard his voice come over the speakers. His body did not move its lips; his voice must have been translated by electronic means directly from his thought processes. His words were the first real indication that his mind had departed his body and was voyaging out into space.

"Cold," said my father through the bridge speakers. "It is very cold and yet I cannot feel cold because I have no body with me to feel anything with. So it is merely the power of sensory knowledge I cannot shed. I believe that space is extremely cold, so I feel cold. Make sure the vocorder switch is on, Jess. Future scientists will want a record of my sensations as I travel."

"Aye, aye, sir," I said—but wasn't certain to whom, or to what, I was speaking. Nevertheless, I flipped the vocorder switch on the console.

"I am picking up speed at a tremendous rate. I cannot guess how fast I am traveling now. Must be near the speed of light. And yet the stars around me are not streaks of light. They are steady points. I don't know why, but this is an important observation.

"I am approaching the Veilwarp. Can't see into it very far. Can't say what it's made of. Seems only a muddle of space. I wonder if it is not the cross section of the space-time continuum of another universe that happens to be passing through our own and distressing the physics in its neighborhood.

". . . Just a moment. I'm getting lost now. Let me look into my visiscreen."

We watched him standing unmoving before the little gray screen and couldn't tell whether he was peering into it or not. He was as motionless as a pedestal. It was eerie to see him there and know that his mind was elsewhere, journeying in the infinite spaces that surrounded us outside the *Isambard,* our wonderful ship, which suddenly and for the first time seemed small to me, tiny and vulnerable and precious.

"Now I'm entering the Veilwarp. It is hot and cold at once. It is unbelievably dense. It is difficult. It is affecting the organs of my body. It is touching my heart with a hand of fire. It is squeezing the blood from my heart like the juice from a cluster of grapes. My lungs cannot expand. My eyesight is darkening. I will not be able to withstand much more of this."

The next sound was a wordless cry of agony.

All your systems are looking good going around the corner and we'll see you on the other side. Over.
Roger. Everything looks okay up here.
Roger, out.

L'Amor che move il sole e l'altre stelle
The Love that moves the sun and the other stars

My mother and I looked at each other and Mitzi floated quiet in her webbing. His body still had not moved, but his face had gone milk white and a fine sheen of perspiration covered his cheeks. She started to say something but managed to silence herself.

Now his voice sounded again through the speakers, strong and calm.

"I have passed beyond the Veilwarp. The moon is directly before me and I am hurtling toward it swiftly.

"I can see it clearly now and am beginning to make out some features. It is nothing like we have imagined, nothing like what the astronomers have described."

Roger. Reading you the same now. Could you repeat your burn-status report?
It was like—it was like perfect.

"It is not mineral at all, the moon. It is not a chunk of basalt and olivine. It is an organic entity. That much is obvious, but I can't tell what kind it is yet.

"I am coming closer and closer.

"The moon is different from what anyone has ever imagined. I don't know how to describe it to you. This is the most amazing and exciting adventure any man could ever have. Cora, Jess, Mitzi, I must tell you . . .

"Wait a minute. I really am getting very close now."

Eagle, *Houston. If you read, you're go for powered descent. Over.*

Mitzi was wide-eyed but silent. She stared, as my mother and I stared, almost not breathing, at the motionless figure of my father in front of his little visiscreen. Though his posture and expression had not changed, we could tell that he was concentrating with all his energies. In the dim light of the bridge, he almost seemed to glow.

Eagle, *you read* Columbia?

> And now I was enwrapped in living light
> > Whose own bright shining fashioned such a veil
> > That nothing around me could appear to sight.

"It is a rose," said his voice through the speakers. "The moon is an immense white rose. There are tiers and tiers of shining petals. It is almost blinding in its purity.

"It is inhabited. The rose hosts thousands and thousands of flying creatures that are evidently intelligent. They are winged creatures and . . .

"The light is unbearable. Not painful, but . . . And the sweetness is . . .

"I don't know if I can talk anymore."

My mother broke. "Joe Robert!" she cried. "Come back, hon. You've gone too far. You've gone way too far this time." She looked at me imploringly, but I had no idea what to do.

You are go for landing.
  Roger. Understand. Go for landing.

Three-personed Light, whose glowing where You are
    Delights all those who look upon You there,
    Guide us through the storm, O single Star!

My father collapsed as if dealt a blow by a hammer. His face
convulsed and his body flung itself into an anguished coil and
he tried to say our names, to say Cora, Mitzi, Annie Barbara,
Jess, Johnson Gibbs, but could only say "rose" before the
treachery of his heart closed the gates of his body and exiled
his spirit to the infinity it had always yearned after.

My mother cried out his name three times, four times, and
I tried to say it but could not speak as Mitzi screamed once and
then began to sob quietly and forever.

On the visiscreen before him, a small angular module that
looked like a tin wood heater fashioned into a cracker box
skimmed away at first but then righted itself and maneuvered
slowly and delicately as it set down upon the lunar surface.

Houston, said my father's almost brand-new 1968-model Zenith television set, that machine he had named his "visiscreen," *Tranquillity Base here.*

The Eagle *has landed.*

0720690417:32:

Thirty-two seconds past 4:17 A.M. eastern daylight time, July
20, 1969.

Chapter Ten

"PERHAPS YOU ARE WONDERING WHY I CALLED YOU ALL HERE TOGETHER—"

Thought is to time as . . .
—Fugio

"It's going to rain and spoil our picnic!"

"Maybe not, Jess," Debbye Crabtree told me, but she was only trying to soothe my apprehensions. The upper sky was covered with gray and now darker clouds had moved in beneath. No wind yet, but a rainstorm was inevitable. I could feel it in the air and the television forecast confirmed my impatient fears.

"Well, if it will only hold off a couple of hours, we'll be all right."

She glanced heavenward. "Oh, I think we've got that long,

at least. Here, help me with this case of Pepsi. If you keep busy, you'll stop fretting."

We lifted the box to the edge of the big barbecue hearth at the end of the long picnic shelter and she began stuffing the cans into a tub of crushed ice. From the other side of the hearth came squeaks, squawks, and screeches of sound as the New Briar Rose Ramblers tried to intimidate their tinny little sound system into doing its duty. I clapped my hands over my ears and made a face of mock agony.

Harley, the mandolin player, grinned. "Ain't electricity marvelous?" he said. "I could listen to feedback all day long; it just makes me want to get up and dance."

"You're getting hip now," I said. "That's the noise the teenagers like these days."

He shook his head sorrowfully. "I guess the Ramblers won't be doing many high school proms, if that's the way it is."

"You know," I said, "I'm not sure they even hold proms anymore."

Junior kept plucking his E string. "Harley don't call 'em proms," he said, giving me a broad wink. "He calls them cradle-robbing opportunities."

"They drop some fine lookers into the cradles these days," Harley replied. "Anyhow, my ma and grandma both got married before they were seventeen."

"I can tell your ma didn't have no experience raising younguns," Junior said. "Look at the way you turned out—can't even get that speaker to quit squealing."

"The last part of my correspondence course got lost in the mail," Harley complained. "Otherwise . . ." He made a last mysterious pass over the knobs and the feedback rose suddenly to a terrifying, ear-splitting wail. Then it smoothed out to a barely audible hum. Harley dusted his hands on his jeans and lifted his red straw cowboy hat from his forehead. All four of the Ramblers wore red straws, white shirts, and faded jeans. No fancy boots, though; just spit-shined street shoes. "There we go," he said, satisfied.

"Yeah," said Junior, "that ought to bring in all the hogs in three counties."

"I don't like to be playing for my own amusement." Harley took his mandolin from the seat of a folding chair and began tuning the strings two at a time.

"Now I hope you boys remember my special request," I said.

" 'Look Back All the Green Valley,' " said the quartet together, and the blind fiddler added softly, "Ain't likely we'd forget."

"Don't say that word in my presence," Harley commanded. "John, you know better than that."

Junior explained to me. "Last time out, Harley forgot the words to 'The Triplett Tragedy.' Now he don't allow anybody to say the word *forget*."

"I don't see *you* learning that song," Harley retorted. "It goes on for about half an hour and is as doleful as a year's worth of funeral services. I thought I did a fair job, considering."

"Fair, I don't think," Junior said. "You got the wrong woman murdered and the wrong man hung."

"Well, they shouldn't have been behaving that way in the first place."

"Just sing the words, Harley," said Dobber. "Let the preacher sort out the good uns from the bad uns."

" 'Look Back All the Green Valley,' " I intoned once more.

They nodded. I could see a wisecrack beginning to form on Harley's lips, but he suppressed it.

The picnic shelter was a long, homely shed located at the edge of Montrose Park, which was situated in a modest residential district. It was a popular place, Debbye had told me, for churches and volunteer fire departments and other civic organizations to hold fêtes. She was confident that most of the guests would already know where it was; no doubt some of them had carved their initials into the long plank tables, or the benches, when they came here as Boy Scouts or as Vacation

Bible School inmates. It had the feeling of having been used, casually but fondly, over busy decades.

I spotted Mitzi's car pulling into the parking lot at the top of the hill and walked halfway up to meet her. She scooted out and came quickly down, a little breathless, as always, but smiling cheerfully—as always. She was wearing new blue jeans and a white cotton blouse with a wide stiff collar turned up and looked as if she was ready for a photographer's magazine spread of a picnic. She gave me a quick hug and asked how things were going.

"Do you think it'll rain?" I said.

"Let's hope for the best," she replied, and I considered that if there were ever a sentence that characterized my sister's personality, that might be the one.

"Do you think folks will show up?" I took her arm on the slope and we stepped together over the little drainage ditch and came in under the shelter roof.

"I'm sure they will. In fact, I've already received a couple of phone calls."

"Who called?"

She told me, but the names were unfamiliar. I wondered if I would know many of the folks who turned up. Twenty years is a long time to be absent from a place, and if that place is what one still regards as home, twenty are as good as forty. I knew that I would feel a louring abashment if I failed to recognize someone who used to be close to our family. I felt a responsibility to recall, but it could not be an easy one to fulfill.

"Did you visit Mother this morning?"

"No," I said. "I'll stop by for a nice long visit on my way back to Greensboro tomorrow. I'll have some good news to tell her then. If I saw her today, she'd ask some embarrassing questions."

Mitzi gave me a quizzical look. "Are you sure you'll have good news? I only hope you've got this business figured out half as well as you think you have."

"Well, ma'am," I said, touching the brim of an imaginary Stetson, "I hope to settle your little difficulties up here in the purple hills of Carolina and ride off eastward into the sunset."

She started to reply, then caught sight of Debbye Crabtree in her message T-shirt and trotted over to gossip. As they chatted, Mitzi helped Debbye take foodstuffs from the big cardboard boxes. They seemed to be old friends, my sister and this New Age young lady, and they had probably spent a lot of telephone time discussing the details for the picnic.

I sat down and looked about me, worrying more than I had reason to. A couple of harmless black wasps nudged the yellow pine ceiling above me; cardinals and robins enlivened the surrounding oak grove with song and to-and-fro quick flights from laurel bush and viburnum. The table upon which I rested my elbow had scores of initials, hearts, and other insignia carved into its thick boards, and that would be true of the other tables, as well. There should be plenty of room to seat thirty or more, and if any younguns showed up, they could squat, stand, or wander while eating. That's what they would normally do, anyhow.

Harley called out to me. "Mr. Kirkman, Mr. Kirkman."

"What's this 'Mr.' stuff?" I asked. "My name is Jess."

He shook his head solemnly. "Not till after we get paid. Till then, it's Mr. all the way. How about coming up and testing the sound system? If you're gonna make a speech, you'd better try it out."

"All right." I crossed over and stepped up on the plywood riser the Ramblers had brought with them in the back of their dented Chevrolet pickup.

"Watch out your head and feet," he said as I dodged around the scramble of wiring. "Here—say something into the mike. Talk the way you usually do."

"All right." I accosted the old-fashioned steel-jacketed microphone and began:

> *"Ma prima avea ciascun la lingua stretta*
>   *Coi denti, verso lor duca per cenno,*
>   *Ed elli avea del cul fatto trombetta."*

"Whoa now!" Junior said. "Harley, you got the wiring all messed up again. I couldn't understand a word the man said."

"It didn't sound like that when I tried it," Harley complained. "What was that all about, Mr. Kirkman?"

"It's Italian poetry," I explained, "about an old devil who farted like a trumpet."

"I'll take your word for it. Of course, our microphone ain't used to a lot of salty speech. We do a family show—in the American language."

"It's really quite respectable," I told him. "Fellow's name was Dante, known as the greatest poet in the Italian language."

"They must be hard up for poetry," Junior said, "if the best they've got writes about farting."

"I think the sound system is okay," I said.

"Yeah, it's all right," Harley said. "The stink'll float off in a minute. But if they's any Eye-talians in the crowd, I hope you'll recall something different to recite."

"Don't worry," I said. "I've got it all thought out." I went over to the barbecue hearth and reached for my trusty black notebook and the precious manila folder from where I'd stashed them on a chimney ledge.

As I sat trying to cobble together my outline for the semiformal address I needed to deliver to our ancient friends and relatives and neighbors and acquaintances and friends of friends, they began to arrive. Into the parking lot above rolled sleek new Chevrolets, clumsy but honorable Fords, scarred veteran pickup trucks, and a couple of mud-crusted farm Jeeps. I watched as the folks made their slow and tentative way down the hill. It was not surprising that they were old, only that some were so very old—and the sight of all of them together was discomfiting. It was as if a race of beings forgotten by our scurry-hither contemporary age was disembarking from the galleon of past time upon the rugged shore of the present. How was I supposed to greet them? What tongue did they speak?

Many I did not recognize, but many I did—more than I had expected to distinguish, considering the changes that decades wreak upon face and figure. Here came Caney Graham and his wife and his daughter, now grown into a handsome young lady; here were the Reeveses, Ernest and Blanche, Ernestine and Ronnie; Ed and Rosalie Stansberry, with Eddie Junior; John and Nanette and Becky Caldwell and her brother John. Cousin Earlene Lewis came alone, invited by Mitzi for old times' sake; she possessed no family farm, but, as my sister said, "Every picnic ought to have at least one champion trout fisher." I thought I recognized in one wiry form that feistiest woman, Ginger Summerell, but she was on the arm of a gentleman who didn't look sufficiently cowed to be her spouse. If only I could recall the faces and the episodes they belonged to, this was the story of my youth unfolding and a larger tale, too, than that very small one: the chronicle of a period of mountain culture of rare and striking flavor.

For these reasons, I began to feel the first twinges of stage fright. Here were the men and women who had tousled my hair and addressed me as "little Jess" or "young Master Kirkman" when I knew them. They might be more irritated than amused when I rose to unfold my plans and open my father's mind to them.

Happily, Mitzi was present to lend aid and sage advice. She left off helping Debbye Crabtree with her tasks and came to the side of the shelter to greet our guests. She knew almost all of them, of course, and I saw how cleverly she learned those she did not know and how quickly she ingratiated herself. My sister, I thought, ought to run for the governor's office—or for President of the United States. Then I recalled that she shared our father's disdain for the majority of politicians. "Pierakers," he called them, employing a street term he had picked up at the farmer's market on Lexington Avenue in Asheville.

Some of the arrivals caught my eye and nodded when I looked up from writing in my notebook, but I could tell they were as uncertain about my identity as I was about theirs, and this realization reassured me a little, though not sufficiently for my bad nerves to settle. I was actually beginning to dread the office I had to perform.

It would be best, however, to let our guests engage with one another for a little while, and so they did, old friends spotting and helloing. Tentative identifications turned into swift embraces, but now and then an exchange of cool and distant nods indicated encounters something less than joyful. The women more readily than the men broke into volubility, talking weddings, funerals, and blood relationships close or tenuous. The men would shake hands gravely and say, "Been a long time, Hank." "Yup, shore has, Bill." "You're doing well, appears like." "Fair to middling is all I'll claim." "Well, been awful good to talk to you." "Yup, same here, Hank." Such discourse comprised their oral histories of two decades lost.

Here came the Irelands, five of them this time. Uncle Gray Ireland had put on a white shirt, blue tie, and gaily paraded red suspenders for the occasion, though he had donned no jacket. The sinewy Aunt Ora was in a dark blue nylon dress printed with small white flowers, and behind them came the lads with broad shoulders, Tod, Bud, and Ned. Ned was new to me but was such a match with his brothers, cropped sandy hair and forearms like shoulder hams, there was no mistaking him. I went over and chatted with the family, telling them how glad we were to see them, how much we appreciated their helpful friendship, and how deeply Mitzi and I were in their debt. I shook hands with the three brothers and murmured to Bud, "Now don't be late tonight."

Subtlety was not his long suit. "Don't worry about that, Jess," he boomed, and gave me so amicable a punch on the bicep, I knew I'd sustain a bruise as large as a saucer. "We'll be right on time."

"How's that?" said Uncle Gray. "What devilment are you boys up to?"

"It ain't nothing bad, Pa," Tod assured him. "Nothing for you to worry about."

"What's this all about, Ned?" he demanded.

Ned spoke in the same jovial thunder his brothers did. "To tell the truth, Pa, I ain't real sure. But it's nothing to fret about."

Their father turned to give me a shrewd look. "Jess, if you get my boys into trouble, you'll have to answer to me and Aunt Ora. I'm kind of easy, but she can be right stern sometimes."

"Your boys have told you there's nothing bad going on," I replied, "and from what I've observed, I don't think they're capable of lying to their dad."

He considered this thought carefully and then answered with a slow nod.

The band evidently had become satisfied with their electronic marvel of a sound system, for they had begun playing a soft slow waltz I didn't recognize. There were some chromatic passages that caused me to think it was an original instead of a traditional tune, and when the second chorus came around, I began humming with it as I scanned the crowd. Most of the people who were coming must have gathered by now, and I judged that there were thirty-five to forty of us, not counting the band and the Blue Luna caterers. The latter had done a sterling job already, I thought, because a large bowl of flowers, cosmos and daisies mostly, sat in the center of each of the three long tables. Debbye had understood instinctively the note Mitzi and I desired to strike. Or maybe those two had worked out the details in telephone conferences.

I searched among the faces for Mr. Hillyer, our other leading candidate for sainthood, but could not discover him. It wouldn't be easy for the old gentleman to drive out here to

Asheville, I thought, and that was just as well, if things fell out in the way I'd planned.

But my scheme demanded some show of nerve on my part and I felt it deserting me—or, actually, making itself known as mere nervousness. I was accustomed to teaching classes of young people about the same size as this crowd and to giving public poetry readings that sometimes drew an audience of as many as seven or eight befuddled listeners, but this occasion was a different situation. If I didn't soon begin, the task would only become more difficult, so I went over and took a place by the eight-inch-tall riser that served as bandstand and stood there till the New Briar Rose Ramblers finished out their charming waltz.

I'd had every intention of beginning with my well-rehearsed cornball line—"Perhaps you are wondering why I called you all here together"—but now that I stood exposed before this assembly, I could not bring myself to say it. The jest seemed too puny and remote to essay, and when I looked at the faces that looked back at me, faces lined with age and accustomed sorrows and secret joys and the long-endured dailiness of life, I knew that I owed these folks more than an obscure smart-ass remark. A joke would be in order, a good old familiar joke they all knew and could count on, but my thinly literary sally would be ineffectual, pointless.

So I only said "Hello" and "Thank you for coming this afternoon" and brought Mitzi up to stand beside me and say more or less the same things. She did so with a lot more aplomb than I could muster. She went on to introduce Debbye Crabtree, whose cutoffs were ordinary enough but whose T-shirt must have puzzled some of the oldsters with its aggressive query—WHAT SUCKS MOST? They couldn't know the back of the shirt replied HATE SUCKS, and probably would not have comprehended if they'd known. Debbye smiled prettily and said she hoped everyone enjoyed the food as much as she had enjoyed making it and to let her and Judy and Carlos ("Stand up, Judy and Carlos") know if there was anything they needed or wanted. Then Mitzi said, "Thank you, Debbye, and now I'll turn the microphone back over to brother Jess," calling me "Brother Jess" for the first time in my life within my earshot.

Then I introduced the Ramblers, omitting their last names because I was ignorant of two of those, and explained that they hailed from Hardison County, where all the best music comes from, and that they would be entertaining us this afternoon and would strike up a spirited musical interlude in just a moment or two, as soon as I could get a bit of business out of the way. "And let me tell you, folks, I've heard the Ramblers play, and it's something to look forward to."

Then I clenched my toes in my shoes, took a shaky deep breath, cleared my throat, and came out with it:

"Ladies and gentlemen, you have heard about the problem Mitzi and I have met with the burial arrangements for our mother and father. Because of some sort of mix-up, they cannot be buried side by side in Mountain View Cemetery, as they had counted on for many of the long years of their marriage. I don't see any use in passing out blame for the situation; what's done is done and the circumstances are not going to change. But my mother has her heart set on being buried next to her husband, so my sister and I had a discussion and decided we might try the good Christian charity of those who were close to our parents over the years. We thought we would ask those of you who have spaces for private family graveyards on your farms if we might lease some of that space from you in, I guess, perpetuity. We recognized that it was an enormous favor to ask, but you can see how we were at our wit's end. I mean, this is the kind of expedient that is born only of desperation, right?"

If I'd expected a reply to my rhetorical question, I would have been disappointed. But all the assembly, even the four or five teenagers scattered in the crowd, sat in expectant silence, like well-swept and dusted foyers waiting for someone to walk through their front doors. My hands shook so visibly that I stuffed them into the pockets of my trousers, where they immediately began to sweat.

"Well, it's a big favor, all right, a truly big favor. What we hadn't expected was the warmhearted response. Everyone who could do so made a generous offer to take our parents in. We were overwhelmed; we had not expected such kindness. I guess it shows how little we knew about our folks when we were young, and it certainly shows how magnanimous and loving their friends are and always have been. We received a large number of requests from families who wanted to do this favor for us. How many was it all told, Mitzi?"

"At least thirty-five," she said.

"Thirty-five requests to do us this huge favor. I'm sure I needn't say how honored you have made us feel. But it has also given us the problem of deciding who should be saddled with this . . . responsibility."

Having barely escaped the trap of saying *grave responsibility*, I made an elaborate ritual of clearing my throat and started again:

"So what we came up with was the notion of a public drawing. We thought this would be the fairest method. We don't want to hurt anyone's feelings and we want to make sure you all understand how much we appreciate your friendship and generosity. Now, does this method seem suitable to you? Does anyone have any objections?"

These queries were not rhetorical, as the other had been, and I had actually expected some response. I couldn't predict what it might be: laughter, anger, sorrow, irritation, astonishment—any of a thousand types and gradations of emotion. But, again, there was no response, except here and there a solemn judicious nod of the head.

I could hardly believe it. In order to find a way out of our dilemma, I'd tried to imagine what my father would have done if he had not been in this case so closely involved personally, though only as a silent partner. And it had come to me that he would have disposed of the problem by means of a lottery. More precisely, I thought that if it had been possible, he would have taken great delight in raffling off his own corpse, or in auctioning it, and at this moment I wished more than any- thing, harder almost than I'd wished ever before in my life, that it could be possible for him to stand beside me now in the darkening day, with the wind pouring cool through the rustic shelter, with his old friends before him and a bluegrass band at his back, and say, Now what offer do I hear bid on the splen- did corpus of Joe Robert Kirkman? It's in good shape, friends and neighbors; it is comely of face and figure, not marred or scarred in any important way, and in former times highly prized by tender members of the female species. It is true that just now at the present time this magnificent body is more than a little bit dead. But let me tell you, folks, there are those who knew him well who will say that Joe Robert never looked bet- ter in his whole career than he does at this very moment.

But my father wasn't standing beside me, except in spirit, and all I could think of to do was to ask once more if anyone had any objections to my procedure. When it seemed they didn't, I said, "Well, we'll go ahead with the drawing, then. You will find some little pads on the tables where you're seated and there should be some pencils or ballpoint pens there, too. If you-all will just write your first and last names on a piece of the notepaper and fold it up, we'll pass around a hat for you to drop it in. Is that clear? Does everybody understand what we're up to? Let me know if you don't."

But they found no difficulty in these instructions and moved to employ paper and pencil with all goodwill. The surprise I felt at the silent acquiescence was nigh boundless.

I turned to the band. "Looks like I'll need a hat," I said. "Can I borrow yours for a minute, Harley?"

"Better take John's. He's got the big head."

"I need my hat to keep the light out of my eyes. I can't see without my hat," John said.

"John," said Harley, "you can't see anyhow. You're blind."

"Well now," he replied, "that sure does explain a lot of things. Why didn't you tell me that a long time ago?" He lifted the big red straw hat from his head and passed it in the general direction of Harley, who passed it to me. I gave it to Mitzi, who delivered it to the farther table on my right.

"Now while the hat is being passed, we'll have some good old bluegrass music," I announced, and stepped down from the platform.

The New Briar Rose Ramblers attacked "Shady Grove" with such firepower, it might have been an enemy tank they were trying to destroy. Dobber drove the rhythm guitar at a daredevil but still steady pace and the others kept up with him effortlessly—or so it seemed. It was obvious that there was more in Harley's head than wisecracks; he made his mandolin—which I noted was a less-than-expensive model—as lyric as any mockingbird in a wild cherry, even at the fiery pace Dobber had set and which Junior backed on his banjo, grinning like an opossum surprised at the cider press.

But it was John, John, that fiddling man, who most thoroughly stole my heart away. After one clear statement of the tune, he set out to embroider it with flourishes surprising but inevitable, to decorate it from above and from below, always teasing and never punishing it, and the long lines he played kept looping and coiling, uncoiling and relooping in my mind like threads of silver.

To the microphone came then the bell-clear tenor, Harley:

"Shady Grove, Shady Grove,
  Shady Grove my darlin',
  I don't like no little fish,
  Gonna catch a big ole marlin."

"Aw, Harley," cried Junior, "them ain't the right words. Sing decent, why don't you?"

But it was too late for that. Harley had already stepped back

a little and started a challenge match with the fiddle, trading
choruses four at a time, then two, then only the one that
passed back and forth between them like a sizzling charge arc-
ing back and forth across electrodes.

That sort of brilliance couldn't last long, of course, but
"Shady Grove" didn't seem to sink to its close so much as it
zoomed out of sight beyond the clouds like an *Apollo* rocket
spearing into the unknown. Then the Ramblers looked at one
another like they'd done something completely unexpected,
like they were disembarking from a bus ride that had delivered
them to a place they'd never seen before and in a different
point of the compass from where their ticket indicated.

Harley made as if to wipe his forehead and asked of the
world at large, "Do you like pepper?"

Junior answered for us all: "Only when it's hot."

Here came Mitzi with the hatful of slips of paper. I took it from
her, got my notebook and cardboard folder with the manila
envelope inside, and mounted the little platform again. Harley
made room for me at the microphone.

"Did you ever hear a 'Shady Grove' with that kind of spirit?"
I asked. "How about a hand for the New Briar Rose Ramblers?"

Our guests managed only a smattering of hand claps. I
suspected that they were so puzzled and bemused by the procedure of choosing a Kirkman gravesite, they had only half-
heard the rendition that so impressed me.

To refresh my memory about the points I wanted to make,
I whipped open my good old black notebook to the place I'd
marked with a Holiday Inn matchbook. *"Dritto inizio* = real
beginning," I read—though, luckily, not aloud. *"Che fece a me
uscir di mente* = That it made me forget myself."

Obviously, I'd marked the wrong place in the notebook and
started turning rapidly through. In my haste and embarrassment, I turned one page so violently, it tore loose and fluttered

to the floor. Harley retrieved it and handed it to me after looking into it pretty thoroughly. "I do hope this ain't what you're
looking for," he said.

I saw that it was a passage from the *Paradiso* I had copied
out in order to ready myself to translate it, the episode where
Dante turns around, expecting to see Beatrice behind him, but
finds Saint Bernard instead and likens the unexpected emotional experience to a pilgrim's first visit to a holy shrine:

> *E quasi peregrin, che si ricrea*
> *Nel tempio del suo voto riguardando*
> *E spera già ridir com' ello stea . . .*

"Nope," I told Harley, "this is not it. I'm going to have to
wing it, looks like."

"Let her rip," he said. "If you start to mire down, we'll play
'Sally Goodin.' "

"Keep your fingers on the strings," I told him, and turned
to face my audience.

Another deep breath—then I said, "We'll have the drawing
of the name in just a few minutes, ladies and gentlemen, but
first there's a little something I found lately I'd like to share
with you. I had written out a few remarks to introduce this
document with"—I leaned over and took out the manila envelope and held it up for them to see—"but it looks like I've
misplaced what I wrote down. Such an occurrence is not unusual in my absentminded way of doing things.

"Anyhow, when I was going through my father's effects the
other day, I came across these pages marked 'Last Will and
Testament.' Now, this is in no sense a legal document, but just
some personal bequests he would have liked to make if he had
been able to; these are just some of his thoughts."

I brought out the envelope and carefully slipped out the fragile yellowed pages covered with that firm, precise handwriting.
"I won't read it all," I promised. "There are some opening parts
that are rather abstruse and later on there are some very pri-

vate passages. But I will share with you some parts I thought you might be interested in hearing.''

Looking up from the pages, I gazed about the shelter and discovered that I had captured the intense attention of everyone present, except for the very young. It was a gratifying moment and caused me to fear our friends might be disappointed. Perhaps I was making too much of these jottings.

''There is nothing here about money or land or houses or disposable property of any sort. Just bequests of a general nature.

''For example, he says, 'Item, I leave to the detractors, antagonists, and foes of my friend Virgil Campbell each and every one an astronomical telescope of a goodly focal length: You have set yourselves so far above the commonality of humankind, you may have lost sight of us poor sinners altogether: Peer down upon us through these lenses and find an ounce of sympathy in your hearts.

'' 'Item, to those who have enclosed their minds against the wonders of the universe and the plain scientific facts of the case, I bequeath a free ride on the good ship *Isambard*: Gaze into the visiscreen and be admiring: The cosmos is now your heritage and the heritage of your children's children.

'' 'Item, to sticky-fingered politicians, Gospel-thumpers, and confidence men, I bequeath my psychic observation projector: Clap this visionary helmet upon your heads and strain your minds forward to your lifetimes' endings: See how it feels to meet your Maker after all your years of sham and pretense.

'' 'Item, to fascists, Communists, socialists, capitalists, Republicans, Democrats, technocrats, plutocrats, oligarchs, and all other self-proclaimed monopolists of truth, I leave not the Phrygian cap of liberty, but the jester's cap and bells: Shake your heads to hear freedom ring.

'' 'Item, to bluenoses, hypocrites, high-horse riders, the self-applauding self-righteous, pulpit-mounters, and holier-than-thous, I leave the famous but long-lost recipe for the moonshine that Foley Hooper used to make: May it cheer your hearts and open your senses to the roses that bloom so invisibly everywhere.' "

Here I paused, not only because I needed to take a breath and reach for a sip of cola but because the Ramblers had seconded this latter bequest with cries of "Hear, hear!" and "Save me a sup of that mighty fine Foley shine." I turned and acknowledged them with a bow but hadn't the courage now to look up to see how my larger audience was reacting to the testament.

"Now the next few matters require a little explanation," I said. "My father bequeaths to the Board of Education in the town of Tipton a signed edition of the complete works of Charles Darwin. 'Is man descended from the monkeys?' he asks. Then he says: 'Not in the case of the Tipton school board, where such a descent has not yet occurred.'

"To the management of the Challenger Paper and Fiber Company, my father has bequeathed a three-week tour of the Gobi Desert, with only casks of the mill-polluted Pigeon River for their drinking water."

I'd figured on hearing a few hoots and hisses when I read that one, but only silence met my words. I amassed what nerve I could and risked a peek at my listeners. Many of them sat without expression, but others were smiling and nodding and murmuring to one another, and it occurred to me that they had probably heard these sentiments before. No doubt my father had regaled them at one time or another with this or another version of his mock will and testament. They were smiling because these pages reminded them of the golden days gone by. It was Joe Robert's own flavor of speech.

"Now," I said, "this next bequest goes to a couple of the old fellows we called 'Uncle' who stopped by our farm to spend some time with our family when I was a lad. To Uncle Gurton, my father has left a pack of hounds to track down and drive out the vermin in his overwhelming beard. To that strange man Uncle Zeno, who told stories that intrigued, irritated, and finally cooked my poor father's brains, he has left the thread of Ariadne. 'Maybe the old man can find his way out, with this thread aiding him, of the labyrinth of fable back to the world of reality,' he says here. I needn't tell you that this fixation of my father's was rife with perplexities and paradoxes. I'm quite sure I'll never understand it; it is just one more mystery of long-ago time. That is, unless"—here I leaned forward and grasped the mike stand near the top, trying to emphasize my words—"unless Uncle Zeno is still alive and wide-eyed among us. Ladies and gentlemen, I may have lost my mind, but I swear to the Almighty Power that I saw the fellow only five days ago in Mountain View Cemetery and he was *not* lying down. So I need to ask: Have any of you-all seen Uncle Zeno or heard anything about him lately?" I looked the crowd over, and the only reactions I could interpret were from Tod and Bud Ireland. They were both giving me that circular motion with the forefinger around the temple that indicated they thought I was about three stars short of a Big Dipper. "Well then, that settles it, I suppose. My wife and my sister have been telling me I've lost my marbles. It must be so.

"But, ladies and gentlemen, we all have our little quirks, manias, and miniature madnesses, and one of my father's peculiarities concerned a fellow named T. J. Wesson, who, when he still inhabited a mortal body upon this planet, was known in Tipton as the man whose irresponsible actions with a sluice gate of the water reservoir at the Challenger mill caused a flood that destroyed property belonging to a number of people, none of whom was angrier and sadder about it than my father. It was a little bridge the Wesson deluge carried away that meant all the world to Joe Robert and Cora Kirkman, so when I read in this 'Last Will and Testament' that my father bequeathed to T. J. Wesson a pie in the face, I was hardly surprised.

"But, my friends, I have to tell you this was no ordinary pie. It was no less than thirty inches in diameter and four inches thick at its deepest point and was made of a particularly unappetizing gluey custard. The dough for the crust was as tough as whet leather, containing no fewer than six whole eggs, and

I wouldn't be surprised if it was reinforced with cardboard or even sound oak planking. I will not distress your finer sensibilities by describing the composition of this custard, except to say that it contained a great deal of matter for which the digestive systems of many species of larger mammals had no further use.

"And this was to be the manner of its delivery:

"Mr. T. J. Wesson was to receive a telephone call requiring him to visit our house to discuss an urgent legal matter. So here he strolls, unsuspecting but, in my father's view, anything but innocent, dawdling along our front walk, armed with the knowledge that no matter what little point of law my father might wish to bring against him for his watery misdeeds, he was protected by the Challenger corporation's army of attorneys. Perhaps he is humming to himself on this fine spring day, or even whistling aloud, as he approaches our front door all unaware of his impending fate.

"But my father has been spying from the window, checking his stopwatch against the length of the front walk, which he has measured off many times with exquisite precision. When T. J. Wesson reaches a certain flagstone on his journey to our front door, my father leaps to the fireplace, sets off a charge of explosive he has placed in the flue, and up flies a nine-pound cannonball as if propelled through the barrel of a howitzer.

"This nine-pound cannonball emerges from the chimney top at just the right speed to drop onto the roof below, roll down along the side of the dormer, and fall into the gutter that runs along the porch eave. It travels down the gutter and the sound of its course fixes Mr. T. J. Wesson in his tracks. Then it drives through the hinged-flap gutter butt and hurtles downward to strike a trigger and set off a mechanism of four interlocking levers, the last of which flips this large and handsome pie, worthy of being painted in oils by a master artist, into the air. It turns over three swift times in its trajectory and then, full-face forward, it plops into the bland gray corporate but utterly astonished visage of T. J. Wesson.

"*SPLAT!*

"Oh, the joy that reigns in my father's heart! Oh, the sweet and total justice of the deed! Oh, the overwhelming savor of revenge that causes the eyes of Joe Robert Kirkman to roll back in his head and his mouth to salivate!

"*Splat.*

"Ladies and gentlemen, my father's life could have ended at this moment in a starburst of triumphant joy were it not for the fact that he had one last task he'd set himself—to travel to the moon, fulfilling not only the ardent desires of his heart but also the scorned yet finally vindicated visionary prophecy of his intellect.

"This accomplishment, too, was his, when all was said and done, and if there are those who would dispute my version of history, if there are those who would say that the orderous pie was never delivered into the smug countenance that so hugely deserved its benison and that my father never perfected the Kirkman alternating time drive to power his thistledown spaceship, the *Isambard,* into lunar orbit, why then, I say unto them, You have mistaken the nature of reality and made penurious this fleeting existence that it is our duty to enjoy and celebrate in all its splendors and miseries, in all its triumphs and anticlimaxes. What we imagine is what we are; what we desire is what we become. As Jesus told us in a different context, If we have so much as thought of the deed, then we have committed it.

"Everything has come true, ladies and gentlemen. Our lives are but poetry, after all, for see how the mighty have been humbled and brought low at last in the fullness of poetic justice and see how the moon has become an abode for humankind and look how the titanic thinkers of past time console us yet in our present perils.

"My father was mindful of these matters in his last days and, in his guise as the philosopher Fugio, left incomplete an idea that I have dared to finish out. Thought is to time, he might have said, as light is to energy."

I paused to collect myself, doubting if I had not lost my way entirely and could never get untangled. "Am I making any sense at all?" I asked the world at large.

Reply came from that plucky mandolin player when Harley struck a couple of notes and said, "Not yet, Mr. Kirkman, but if you keep on talking, maybe it'll rain."

"All right," I said. "In just a few minutes, we'll have the drawing of the name. Right now, why don't we enjoy some of the wonderful food from the Blue Luna Café and listen to the New Briar Rose Ramblers as they give us a special old-time favorite called 'Look Back All the Green Valley'? Are you ready, boys?"

"Ready as rabbits," declared Junior, but when they sounded their first notes, they were out of tune.

"Whoa back," said Harley. "Looks like my strings went slack while Mr. Kirkman gave us that powerful long message. Let's see if we can't get a little closer together."

They went through the process of touching strings and twisting tuning pegs. Finally, they were satisfied and settled into a slow minor throbbing in which I could hear the lorn spirit of Aunt Samantha Barefoot singing to the wind:

Now our days are dwindling down
The fresh green leaves have turned all brown.
Look back look back the Maytime days
Look back all the green valley.

Yet oh my darling think of me
When you are in that far countree
The wonders there so strange to see.
Look back all the green valley.

Look back look back the time will come
When you and I are past and gone.
Look back look back the Maytime days
Look back all the green valley.

I had thought that hearing it now might bring me to the verge of tears, but for all its full-hearted mournfulness, for all its lonesome elegiac keening, there was a dignity in it that held it steady to its starry truth. Aunt Sam's song brought the story to its close. If it remedied no sorrows of the world, if it could not console the time-abused heart or assuage all the distresses of the weary spirit, it brought them into the light and offered them an understanding to be found in nothing else but music, in the music that echoes beyond its own proper sound into that place where no sound is ever to be heard.

So I did not feel sad or downcast, but complete. Things have come round at last; all things will come round again—and the music and the words of the music will still be waiting to address them.

When the song ended and the fiddle fell silent, I rose from my chair with the blind man's hat in my hand. I proffered it to Harley, saying into the microphone, "Reach in there and pick us out a name, if you will, old son, and we'll know the name the Kirkmans will be grateful to all through the rest of our days and all the days beyond. Just pluck one out and hand it over and I'll read it out to the folks."

With awkward solemnity, the lean mandolin player extracted a folded slip and passed it. "Thank you, Harley." I opened it. *Paul Lunsford,* it read. "Well, it's Uncle Gray and Aunt Ora Ireland. That's wonderful, just wonderful." I tossed the guilty chit back in with the others and gave the hat a little shake for luck.

"So—that does it, ladies and gentlemen," I announced, and went on to reiterate our grateful thanks until I figured everyone was sick and tired of listening to them. Then I said, "Did I hear you boys mention 'Sally Goodin'?" and they grinned and started it up like popping off a long string of Christmas firecrackers with never a dud among them.

———

Debbye and Carlos dished me up a plate of food, including some of Blue Luna's vaunted free-range potato salad with organically grown aioli, and I mingled with the guests, introducing myself when I had to, but more often learning that when Miz Hawkins or Uncle Loper or Cousin Betty Sue had last seen me, I wasn't no bigger than a fice dog and twice as hard to keep quiet. Many recalled my father to me and everyone asked about my mother, "the sly Cora," as one or two named her. I understood that my father had spread his fanciful tales widely.

But I felt tired and was glad when folks began to drift off toward their homes. Mitzi and I stood watch at the edge of the shelter, not letting anyone leave without a farewell hug or a handshake. One or two of them gave me an amused or unamused glance as they stepped out under the darkened sky into the air that had grown cooler and now smelled dampish, as of moss and humus. They were still pondering my performance and wondering if I really was the complete fool I appeared to be.

After the last of the guests had left, I asked Mitzi if she wanted to go over to my motel room for a drink, but she had planned to help clean up the place a little and to go over the billing with Debbye. "All right," I said. "I'll call you next week from Greensboro." We hugged good-bye.

Time to pay the Ramblers. In the back of my black notebook, I found the envelope containing two one-hundred-dollar bills, added three twenties to them for good measure, and handed the package to Junior. "I'm trusting you to divide this up the right and just way," I said. "Not that I don't trust Harley, but it pays to be careful."

"I heard that!" Harley called from the back of the platform, where he was unplugging plugs and coiling up wires. "I want you to know I'm as honest as the day is long, Mr. Kirkman."

"Except that where Harley lives, the sun don't shine," Junior said.

"No, you got it wrong again, Junior," said John. "It's me that lives where the sun don't shine."

"Don't listen to him, Mr. Kirkman," Junior advised. "If you pay any attention to John about being blind, he gets mad at you for babying him. If you don't, he gets mad because you ain't paying attention."

"I figure I got a gripe or two coming," John said.

Dobber came over to shake hands. I was surprised at how soft his hands were, except for the fingertips, which were nubbled with calluses. "We thank you for calling on us, Mr. Kirkman. It was good to play for you."

"The pleasure was mine, believe me," I said. "And now you're supposed to call me Jess. I've paid Junior your money, so I have bought that privilege, I believe."

Harley came over to make his farewell. "No," he said. "Any man that actually does pay us to play is going to be called Mr. all his life."

"You boys have a fine band," I said. "It's good to know somebody's keeping Aunt Sam's songs and all the other good old good ones alive."

"Well, actually," Harley said, "it's the other way around. It's the songs that keep us alive—or keep the life worth living, anyhow."

In the motel room, I stretched out amid the litter on the bed and stared at the ceiling for a while. I was exhausted, drained by the day and the week and all the emotional energy that radiated within me so intensely, I felt that, like the sun, I must be giving off a corona.

Tired as I was, I didn't dare close my eyes. If I fell asleep, I would miss my next important appointment. I squirmed around to look at the bedside clock. It was already 6:30 and the boys and I were to meet at 8:00, so a nap was out of the question. Once asleep, I wouldn't wake till morning.

Scattered about me were the reminders of my various quests: my familiar black leather notebook and the folder that contained my father's defiantly nonlegal will and testament, a copy of Dante and a mess of scrawled pages of translation, notes, and mistranslation. Here were my father's notebooks, too, and several genetic charts that indicated he was trying to breed a new hybrid of rose to be called Sly Cora. But there were other jottings I didn't understand, as well as one whole red spiral-bound notebook full of symbols I couldn't interpret. There was a hard lump under my leg, as uncomfortable as a chunk of quartz, and I shifted around until I could dig out of my pants pocket that heavy ring of keys that had been my burden and my enlightenment since I received it from my sister a week ago come tomorrow. I held it in the air above me and jangled it.

Now it was time to call Susan and tell her I'd arrive in Greensboro tomorrow and was anxious to have some warmly personal commerce with her. We traded foolish endearments for a longish refreshing while and she asked more than twice what hour she was to expect my return.

"As soon as possible," I said. "First, I've got to call on my mother and reassure her that all is taken care of, that Cora and Joe Robert Kirkman will lie side by side in the grassy peacefulness she longs for."

"So everything is all set?" Susan asked.

"There's one final detail to take care of tonight. After that, we're all finished up."

"What kind of detail requires your attention at night?"

"Tsk-tsk. You're not getting jealous, are you? Is this the music a suspicious wife makes?"

"I'd be suspicious if I thought any other woman would put up with you, but I know better. No, I'm just curious, that's all."

"It's complicated," I said. "I'll tell you all about it when I get home. I've got a lot of things to tell, as a matter of fact. Do you know what I just this moment realized? I've been staring at something for a week without understanding what it means."

"What are you talking about?"

"This big heavy key ring that opened up my father's workshop—'' I hefted it, then jangled it close to the receiver so Susan could hear.

"Yes?"

"There are eleven other keys just like the one I used. There may well be eleven other workshops tucked here and there in Harwood, Buncombe, and Hardison counties."

"And what would that mean?"

"A hundred other projects of one sort or another. Eleven more secret lives made up of silly jokes, high-flown ideals, and impossible schemes. Eleven more rooms full of mysterious clues that could send me on eleven journeys. A whole eleven other Joe Robert Kirkmans in alternate universes. One for every hour of the day."

"But you *are* coming home tomorrow, aren't you?"

"Oh, yes, I can't give up my life to this kind of thing." I sighed and rubbed my forehead. "You know, I am the son who went searching for his father, just like the characters do in all those important well-received literary novels. But I didn't find a man. I found a boy."

"All right," said Susan. "But you knew that before you started out, didn't you?"

"Maybe. I don't know. Maybe." I reached across the bed to displace a cache of papers and retrieved a small green slightly mildewed book. "I've been thinking about the notation he put in the margin of the Shakespeare play, the one where I learned that he had read my poetry books. I've been thinking about using the passage he marked as a part of *Earthsleep*. It might tie up pretty neatly the four-elements theme I've been working with."

"What passage are you talking about?"

"*Twelfth Night,* act two, scene three." I read the lines to her, taking care to pronounce them slowly into the mouthpiece. Shakespeare, I figured, was not designed for telephone communication.

"How will you be able to use that part?"

"I'm not sure yet. Maybe I could add it at the end as a tail-piece."

"As what?"

"As a tailpiece."

"Tailpiece." She giggled. "Nice word that is."

"It's a technical term." I found myself smiling through my exhaustion. "I'll be home tomorrow and explain it to you," I promised. "With diagrams and demonstrations. I think you'll find it entertaining."

"Sexy talk," said Susan, "but I don't know if I entirely believe you. It's probably nothing but poetry."

"What else is there?" I asked, burning to know.

THE

MOON

GONE AWAY

"I don't see nothing, not a blessed thing."

There was another flicker of lightning that revealed the speaker as Ned. Now that I knew his voice, I thought I could sort the others out.

"I believe Jess is seeing things not there. He's getting spooked."

That would be Tod, I thought, and replied, "No. I saw him. Plain as day."

"Well, he ain't there now," said Bud. He played the flashlight beam that way again. "Who do you think it was?"

"Uncle Zeno," I said.

"Can't be Uncle Zeno. He'd be older than the hill we're digging into. He'd be older than rocks."

"Maybe he really is immortal," I said. "That's what my father thought. Maybe that's how he knew the story."

Ned jumped down into the hole and said, "Ouch."

"What's wrong?" Tod asked.

"I hit a rock or something," Ned said.

"What story are you talking about?" Bud asked.

"The story of the world," I said. "The story of you and me. All the stories that ever were or will be."

"It ain't a rock," Ned said, "but I can't tell what it is."

"Nothing wrong with stories," Bud said. "Stories can't hurt you."

"Dig around it a little," Tod said. "Maybe we've found the casket."

"Uncle Zeno's stories used up the world," I said. *"When he told a story about you, you were trapped inside of it and couldn't get out."*

"That don't make good sense," Bud said.

"Wouldn't we hit the liner first?" Ned asked. *"They make them durn things out of concrete. I have not been looking forward to prizing the liner open."*

"I guess not," I said, *"but that's the way it was, anyhow."*

"Piece of a plank is what," Ned said, *"with the corner of it sticking straight up."*

"What would he be doing out here in the cemetery this time of night?" Bud asked.

"He goes everywhere at all times," I said, then asked, *"What kind of wood?"*

"Now how in the name of Chrysler could I tell that in the dark?" Ned was aggrieved.

"Chrysler?" I asked.

"Ned don't take the Lord's name in vain," Bud explained.

"And this is a fitten place not to," Tod said.

The first raindrops fell, warm, large as silver dollars. I could smell the grass freshen and the dirt come alive.

"My father was buried in a plain pine coffin," I said. *"He would hear of nothing else."*

"But we'd hit the liner first," Ned complained. *"All I'm finding is wood, mostly rotted away."*

"There'd have to be a liner," Bud said. *"Concrete. That's the law."*

"We've done and left the law behind two hours ago," Tod said gloomily.

"Whoa now," Ned said.

"What is it?" one of us asked.

"Piece of bone," Ned said.

"You sure?"

"I think. Yep, piece of bone. Here it is. A bone of some kind."

There was a pause in the rain, but it was going to come hard in just a minute.

"Better let me dig from here on," I said. *"If there's trouble about the bones, I'll take all the blame."*

"It's an awful little bone," Ned said. *"Here, give me a hand."*

We struggled to haul him out and the rain started again, small drops this time, and stinging.

I lowered myself carefully and asked for the little garden spade. *"This is going to be slow slogging,"* I said.

"Just be easy," somebody said, and somebody else handed me the spade, handle-first.

"What's that?" Bud asked.

"What's what?"

"Shine the light over that way. I thought I heard something."

"It's raining," Tod said. *"They ain't nobody out in the rain in the cemetery in the dark midnight but four complete and total fools."*

"Shine the light down here," I said. *"I need to see these bones. Who's got a pocketknife?"*

"I'll toss it down where I'm pointing the beam," Ned said.

My hands were wet and slick with mud, so it was hard to get the knife open. Then I started scratching the soil away tediously, feeling the rain on my back and the storm and the darkness and the planet earth all around my body.

"This is not my father," I said. *"I don't know what this is."*

"Dig a little more," Ned said. *"Dig over there where the head is supposed to be."* He moved the light to the corner of the hole.

I dug up the skull. It was small and long and wicked, with a grin full of sharp teeth.

"It's an animal," I said. *"I don't know what it is."* I rose from my knees and handed the bones up.

Ned directed the light on it. *"Possum,"* he said. *"Who'd be burying a possum in the graveyard?"*

"Lord a mercy, Ned," said Bud. *"This ain't no possum. It's way too big. Don't you know what this is?"*

"Devil possum, maybe."

"Fox," Bud said. *"This here is a fox's skull."*

"Fox?" asked Tod.

"Fox."

"I guess we'll have to dig deeper, then."

"No," I said. "Give me a lift out of here."

"Don't you want to find the coffin?" Bud asked. He pulled me out with one hand and I was glad to be standing on the grass. "Let me dig for a while to spell you."

"No use in it," I said. "He's not there. It was the fox and that's all."

"How do you know?"

"I just know."

Because I wasn't going to say, That's him; *my father was the fox, even though it was the living, breathing truth, obvious as fire.*

"What's that?" Ned said. "There's somebody sitting over there on that gravestone."

But when he struck the beam that way, there was no one. Yet we all thought that someone had been seated there and only a moment ago had stood up and walked away into the rain.

SIR TOBY: A false conclusion; I hate it as an unfilled can. To be up after midnight and to go to bed then, is early; so that to go to bed after midnight is to go to bed betimes. Does not our life consist of the four elements?

SIR ANDREW: Faith, so they say; but I think it rather consists of eating and drinking.

SIR TOBY: Thou art a scholar; let us therefore eat and drink. Marian, I say! a stoup of wine!

—*Twelfth Night*